THE CACKLE OF CTHULHU

Books Edited by Alex Shvartsman

The Cackle of Cthulhu

The Unidentified Funny Objects Series
Unidentified Funny Objects:
An Anthology of Science Fiction & Fantasy Humor
Unidentified Funny Objects 2
Unidentified Funny Objects 3
Unidentified Funny Objects 4
Unidentified Funny Objects 5
Unidentified Funny Objects 6

Dark Expanse: Surviving the Collapse
Coffee: 14 Caffeinated Tales of the Fantastic
Funny Science Fiction
Funny Fantasy
Fantasy Horror
Humanity 2.0

Books by Alex Shvartsman

Explaining Cthulhu to Grandma and Other Stories
H. G. Wells, Secret Agent

THE CACKLE OF CTHULHU

Edited by
Alex Shvartsman

THE CACKLE OF CTHULHU

This is a work of fiction. All the characters and events portrayed in this book are fictional, and any resemblance to real people or incidents is purely coincidental.

Foreword © 2018 by Alex Shvartsman; "The Shunned Trailer" © 2000, 2018 by Esther Friesner. First published in *Asimov's Science Fiction*, February 2000; "The Captain in Yellow" © 2018 by David Vaughan; "My Little Old One™" © 2018 by Jody Lynn Nye; "Tales of a Fourth Grade Shoggoth" © 2015, 2018 by Kevin Wetmore. First published in *Mothership Zeta*, October 2015; "Friday Night at Brazee's" © 2018 by Mike Resnick; "To Whatever" © 2014, 2018 by Shaenon K. Garrity. First appeared in *The Drabblecast*, August 2014; "The Doom that Came to Providence" © 2018 by Brian Trent; "Explaining Cthulhu to Grandma" © 2013, 2018 by Alex Shvartsman. First appeared in *Orson Scott Card's Intergalactic Medicine Show*, April 2013; "The Call of the Pancake Factory" © 2013, 2018 by Ken Liu. First appeared in *The Drabblecast*, August 2013; "The Innsmouth of the South" © 2016, 2018 by Rachael K. Jones. First appeared in *The Drabblecast*, December 2016; "WWRD" © 2018 by Yvonne Navarro; "In the Employee Manual of Madness" © 2018 by G. Scott Huggins; "Shoggoth's Old Peculiar" © 2004, 2018 Neil Gaiman. Reprinted with permission; "H.P. and Me" © 2018 by Gini Koch; "The Greatest Leader" © 2018 by Aidan Doyle; "But Someone's Got to Do It" © 2016, 2018 by Konstantine Paradias. First appeared in *Eldritch Review*, March 2016; "The Call of the Uncopyrighted Intellectual Property" © 2018 by Amanda Helms; "Cthulhu, P.I." © 2018 by Laura Resnick; "A Stiff Bargain" © 2012, 2018 by Matt Mikalatos. First appeared in *Unidentified Funny Objects 2*, October 2013; "The Shadow Over My Dorm Room" © 2018 by Laura Pearlman; "The Tingling Madness" © 2018 by Lucy A. Snyder; "The Girl Who Loved Cthulhu" © 2018 by Nick Mamatas.

Copyright © 2018 by Alex Shvartsman

A Baen Books Original

Baen Publishing Enterprises
P.O. Box 1403
Riverdale, NY 10471
www.baen.com

ISBN: 978-1-4814-8300-1

Cover art by Dave Seeley

First Baen printing, January 2018

Distributed by Simon & Schuster
1230 Avenue of the Americas
New York, NY 10020

Library of Congress Cataloging-in-Publication Data: TK

Printed in the United States of America

10 9 8 7 6 5 4 3 2 1

Contents

THE CACKLE OF CTHULHU

Foreword

By Alex Shvartsman

THE LOVECRAFTIAN Mythos has a lot going for it. Its mythology is truly original: perhaps the only major pantheon of gods and monsters introduced in the twentieth century that can't be easily traced back to some combination of folklore, classic works of fiction, and religious texts that predate it. Howard Phillips Lovecraft and his contemporaries created a shared universe that has inspired generations of writers to build upon it and create dark, moody, atmospheric fiction that combines his pulpy brand of existential nihilism with modern writing techniques.

Not me though.

Crazy cultists? Batrachian denizens of New England? Giant, snoozing octopi? I find those things *hilarious*. I'd argue that, overall, the Mythos is as rich a source of hilarity as it is of cosmic dread. And I'm not alone. Writers have been poking fun at the Mythos for decades. There's the excellent *Scream for Jeeves* by Peter H. Cannon, several short stories by Neil Gaiman (one of which is included in this book), The Laundry Files series of comic horror novels by Charlie Stross, not to mention a plethora of cartoons, internet memes and funny T-shirts.

I reached out to some of the funniest writers in the business to see if they wanted to thumb their noses at Cthulhu with me, and they took to the project with the manic glee of half-crazed cultists. Their tales will take you on a whirlwind tour of well-trodden Innsmouth, on a visit to the sunny shores of Florida and California, and for a peek into the dreary, inhospitable locales of Hell and North Korea. You will find Cthulhu in a wading pool, at a weekly poker game, moonlighting as a private eye, or inhabiting the plastic body of a love-dispensing Elvis doll. Even Lovecraft himself hasn't escaped the sharp pen of our authors, appearing as a character in a couple of the stories.

There are sure to be some readers who do not appreciate my sentiment. They may dislike some of the swipes at Lovecraft's prejudices and his adverb-laden prose, jokes often written by the "sort of people" he might've crossed the street to avoid. "How dare you poke fun at one of the cornerstones of horror literature?!" those readers might shout as they prepare to toss this book across the room. To those readers I have two things to say:

First, print books are heavy and throwing your e-reader might damage it irrevocably.

Second, the sincerest form of flattery isn't imitation. It's satire.

On an episode of *The Big Bang Theory*, guest star Stephen Hawking laments, "I have never won a Nobel Prize." He adds, "It's fine. I've been on *The Simpsons*." There's a reason Hawking appeared on both of those sitcoms: he's important enough to have become a pop culture phenomenon. The same is true of H. P. Lovecraft and his oeuvre. Whatever the man's flaws, he's *important*. Important enough to have been a character in works by Ray Bradbury and Alan Moore, and in TV shows like *Supernatural*. Important enough to have influenced not only the horror genre but pop culture in general, in ways very few writers—nay, individuals—ever have.

It is with the acknowledgment of this importance and respect for his accomplishments that we mercilessly lampoon Mr. Lovecraft and his Mythos within these pages.

Happy reading,

Alex Shvartsman

The Shunned Trailer

By Esther Friesner

WHEN SPRINGTIME lays its impertinent hand upon the stony bosom of New England, it is deemed no extraordinary thing for a young man of my years and education to venture forth in search of certain genial entertainments such as may only be procured in sunnier climes than the cobbled streets of Cambridge. Alluring though the houris of sweet Radcliffe may be when snow is drifted deep over Harvard Square, when the Charles River is a ribbon of gray between icy banks, and when a man is willing to date a moose if there is an outside chance that he may get lucky, it is an indisputable law of nature that the local ladies lose their former powers to charm once the thaw sets in. Accordingly I had determined to spend my vernal academic hiatus from the hallowed halls of Harvard in pursuit of the Three B's, namely Brew, the Left One, and the Right One.

I set out upon my pilgrimage of grace with some trepidation. Alas, my finances were not of the most robust, which situation precluded my engaging an aeroplane flight to the enchanted dream-city of unknown Daytona Beach. Like some latter-day goliard, it was my misguided intention to make so long a journey by presuming upon the kindness of strangers and, in an extremity, upon the reliability of shank's mare.

My expedition into alien lands at first seemed blessed by my guardian gods, for I was able to engage the attentions of a carload of

5

young ladies passing through Cambridge on their way south from the red-litten towers of Bennington. It was truly unfortunate that our jolly fellowship came to an abrupt and distasteful end when the maiden who owned our common conveyance discovered me paying my compliments to one of her comelier companions. Being of an excitable nature, she was unwilling to overlook our lack of a chaperone, despite the fact that it is virtually impossible to engage a trustworthy *duenna* at three in the morning when one is more or less completely naked.

Thus it was that I found myself engaging alternate transportation somewhere south of our nation's capital. My luck seemed to have departed with my first ride, for the second car to offer me a lift was full of Vassar girls.

I came back to my senses on an isolated stretch of dirt road well below the Mason-Dixon Line. Apart from a vague sense of having been thoroughly exploited in any number of ingenious ways, and the presence of a gaudy tattoo on my left shoulder which referred to Stephen Hawking as (I blush) the "Mac Daddy," I had no recollection of my ordeal. In and of itself this was a mercy, save only for the fact that I likewise had no notion of where, precisely, I was nor of in which direction I must now set out in order to find my way back to a more traveled road.

As I stood thus lost and bewildered under the moon's indifferent Cyclopean eye, the heavens grumbled their displeasure and it began to rain like an upperclassman pissing on a flat rock. Now my need was both clear and immediate: I must find shelter from the storm. As I staggered along the dirt road, which was rapidly becoming a muddy slough beneath my Nikes, I thought I spied a light in the distance. Hastening toward it, I soon became half-blinded by the rain, which had intensified in both rapidity and vigor. Ere long I could see nothing before me but that one encouraging blur of light, and when ultimately I reached the door which it illuminated, I took no notice of my surroundings but only pounded upon the portal with my last strength.

The door swung open under my unrelenting blows and I toppled into what I thought was a safe haven. Ah, how little I knew then the nameless horrors that awaited me! And yet I must in honesty confess that even had some admonishing angel with a fiery sword appeared to forewarn me of how I then stood in peril, body and soul, I was so grateful to have come in out of the rain that in all likelihood I would have replied to that winged messenger, "Bite me."

No sooner was I under shelter (and ere I was able to take in my surroundings) than the full physical impact of my late hardships manifested itself. My limbs were seized with a mighty trembling, my body was racked by chills and fever, and through my delirium I heard myself declaiming a rather saucy sestina about Voltaire and a well-disposed Merino. I had just arrived at the third iteration of "*Vive les moutons et la France!*" when overtaken by benevolent oblivion.

I awoke to the smell of mildew, stale beer, and deep fat frying. My burning eyes opened to behold a dwarfish, gray-skinned creature which hunched over a miniature gas range, its keg-like bulk swathed in a purple-flowered housedress. It clutched a plastic spatula in one paw, and with this it traced arcane symbols in an unknown alphabet within the depths of a black cast iron skillet. Somewhere a recording of Jeff Foxworthy routines was playing at top volume. So this was Hell.

As I lay there, amid sheets as damp as the hands of drowned men or importunate Vassar girls, furtively observing the creature at the stove, I was ignorant that other eyes were at the same time observing me. I was made aware of this only when a voice behind me unexpectedly exclaimed, "Look there, Ma! He's woke!"

At this, the spatula-wielding thing turned its head slowly toward me. Ah, pitying heavens! What manner of countenance now met my eyes! It was a face that might be termed human only as a courtesy. The skin thereof was, as I have already remarked, of so drab a cast as must be classified as gray. The few tufts of wiry hair atop the broad, flat head were of no perceptible color at all. The bulging eyes and wide, almost lipless mouth, were batrachian features whose like I had never seen outside of my elementary biology dissection lab. Indeed, as the creature approached me, I imagined that it was preceded by the aroma of formaldehyde, although I quickly realized that this was merely the smell of breakfast.

"So he is," the creature said, and when it spoke I presumed from the timbre of its voice that it was a female. She smiled, a grimace which set my stomach to quaking like a blancmange. In fear for my powers of peristalsis, I sought to revive my intestinal fortitude by diverting my eyes from that uncanny visage and fixing them upon some pleasanter sight.

Fat chance. Above my head a low, curved, poorly lit ceiling stretched off into ill-omened shadows, suggesting a dwelling shaped according to no sane architectural principles but rather based on the Hostess Twinkie™. It was narrow to the point of inducing claustrophobia in snails, yet these tight confines had not deterred its inhabitants from packing every available inch of wall, shelf, and countertop with the wretched idols of Kitsch, demon-god of yard sales. To my left I beheld a calendar illustrated with a photo of a pig wearing lingerie. To my right loomed a row of syrupy-eyed children, pastel-colored figurines adorned with idiot simpers and odious observations like: "A Friend Returns Your Car Keys But Holds Your Heart." Nor might I evade the horror by staring directly overhead, for someone had affixed to the ceiling a Mylar imitation of a mirror framed by the words *If You Ain't Smiling Yet, It's Not My Fault.*

"Dear God!" I exclaimed. "I'm in a trailer!"

"Whoa, can't hide nothin' from you, college boy," Ma said dryly. She brought the sizzling skillet almost under my nose. "Hungry?"

"Ah . . . maybe?" I replied, pulling the sheets up to my chin. I was fully in my senses now, after having had them frightened out of me, and had just become cognizant of the certitude that I had been sleeping *au naturel*. In a moment of painful epiphany, I knew that what I passionately desired more than anything else in this world—even beyond certain private fantasies I had long entertained concerning the Spice Girls and a large tub of chocolate frosting—was to get my pants back on and myself the hell out of there.

My distress must have painted itself plain to see upon my face, for the creature snickered in a dreadfully *knowing* manner, and even went so far as to make a playful feint at the nether hem of my enshrouding bed linens with her spatula.

"'Sall right, honeybug, they's just dryin' out some. Yer jeans, that is. Won't know about them sheets until later if you get my drift and I think you do, heh, heh, heh, *chuggerumpf!*"

"Aw, now, *Ma*—!" The same voice which earlier had declared my waking state now sounded again in my ear. The thin mattress beside me sagged as a second being, marginally nearer the human form than Ma, plopped himself down beside me on the bed. "Don't you mind her none. She always gets kinda brassy to guests when it's our turn to host the sabbat prayer meet."

"Sabbath prayer meeting?" I echoed, or thought I did. The minor difference in our exchange eluded me, although later on its dreadful significance did not. Of course by *then* it was too late. It always is.

"*Brassy*, am I?" Ma's tone hit somewhere between a first alto and a blender full of cockatiels. She boxed her offspring's ear smartly and snapped, "That how I learned you manners? You keep a civil tongue in your head, boy, or I swear I'll—!"

"Shoot, Ma, where else *would* I keep it?" he replied, and with that an unimaginable stretch of flabby blue-black flesh shot out of his mouth and flew the length of the trailer, returning with terrible alacrity and a copy of *TV Guide* stuck to the tip. "Thee?" he concluded as he wrestled with the tongue-tying periodical.

The sight of this unmanning spectacle at first stunned me, then caused me to break into a nonstop stream of mindless chatter, alternately thanking mother and son for their philanthropy and begging them to give me back my clothing that I might no more abuse their hospitality. The monstrous pair was visibly baffled.

It finally devolved upon the son to address me, when he could get a word in edgewise. "Friend," he said, "I can tell you're a little put off by what I just done, but I can't help it; it's my nature. Not the sort of thing you're used to, what with your big city ways and your canned eggnog and your edible underwear and all of them other high-tone delights of civilization. Well, Ma and me, we're just simple, Elder Godsfearing country folk. Our ways ain't your ways, but we don't mean you no personal harm. Less you'd happen to be a virgin—?" His voice trailed off on a hopeful note, which it was my duty to squelch at once. He was crestfallen, but continued. "Too bad, too bad. Anyhow, I'm assuming that you're mostly upset by our looks. That right?"

"Well, you *do* look a bit—" I groped for a way to speak accurately without insulting the folk who had literally taken me in out of the rain "—batrachian." It was a good word to use, for the odds were excellent that these people had never heard it and, rather than taking umbrage, would mistake it for a compliment.

To my shock and chagrin, I was half wrong. The son slapped his meaty thigh and looked extraordinarily pleased. "That's *it*! That's just *it*, brother! You have gone and hit the nail smack dab on the head. What we are, see, is New Liturgy Batrachians, the only spawn of Great Cthulhu who have preserved His teachings and commands and assorted hideous gibberings in the *truly proper and orthodox manner.*"

"Not like them sinners up north in Innsmouth and Arkham," Ma put in scornfully. "Hoity-toity little shitepokes, ever' last one of 'em, think they're so all-fired great 'cause they got them Dagon churches with store-bought roofs on 'em and a coupla stuck-up high priests that snuck their sorry froggy butts through Yale Divinity. Hunh! Why, they're no more fit to greet the rise of sunken R'lyeh from the depths than a pig to sing Kenny G's greatest hits."

With those words, the full horror of my situation struck me: Cthulhu! Innsmouth! Arkham! Sunken R'lyeh! Names, alas, whose sinister meaning was not unknown to me. When I was a boy at home and a day student at St. Dimmesdale's Prep there had been one among my schoolmates whose pale complexion, grim mien, and demon-haunted eyes had provoked my curiosity. His name was Randolph Akeley, a boarding student who seldom spoke of his family, nor of much else save the occasional froward Latin declension. Intrigued by his reclusiveness, I resolved to learn more of him. One day I stole into his room, on the pretext of borrowing a condom, and nosed about. He came in and caught me studying a large, expensively framed photograph of a smiling angler displaying a fish almost as large as he was himself.

"Nice catch," I remarked, trying to put a bold face on things.

"That's what my sister said when she married him," Randolph replied in his flat, affectless voice.

"I meant the fish," I said.

"So did I. Was there anything else you wanted?"

I stammered out my contrived excuse for calling upon him and he detained me only a moment while he located the item I had requested. I was deeply startled to discover that a person of Akeley's unsociable temperament had such a thing to hand, yet there it was. It was of an unfamiliar make with nothing upon the wrapper save the image of a black goat in one of those red-circle-and-sideways-slash symbols. Later on, when again my inquisitive nature got the better of me and I opened it, to my horror I perceived it to be *a condom of alien and unknown geometry!*

That was enough to put paid to any further fascination young Randolph Akeley might have held for me. We never exchanged another civil word, although shortly thereafter I received in the post a crudely printed pamphlet entitled *Cthulhu Awareness for the Non-Inbred Seeker*. In this manner did I learn of the Elder Gods, of Nyarlathotep, of Azathoth, of Yog-Sothoth and Shub-Niggurath and a dozen others whose names alone seemed to be the product of a demented mind with a bad lisp. Within the pages of that hellish tract did I read of how they had been banished for a time from the sight of man, likewise of the arcane and unspeakable worship still done to these deities from beyond the stars, worship by depraved, half-mad cultists whose ultimate goals were to bring about the Elder Gods' return from well-merited exile and to reestablish their vile reign over all the earth!

I returned the pamphlet to Akeley privately, in politic silence, although I did feel constrained to give him a dollar when he thrust his *Save the Shoggoths* collection can under my nose. At the time it seemed a cheap price to pay for my escape.

What price would such flight be now?

My hosts, mother and son, were somewhat troubled by the silence whither my apprehensive recollections had deposited me. Ma shook her head and sadly said, "Y'know, if'n I had a nickel for every time I heard people like you go on all smarmy-like about how looks don't *really* matter and it's what a body's like on the *inside* what counts, I'd be able to buy me a decent Sunday-go-to-orgy dress and then some. But talk's cheap, even for a bigot like you."

"I am *not* a bigot! I'm a Harvard man!"

"*Ha!* If you was any more fulla shit, your eyes'd be brown. You ready to swear you're not carrying 'bout half a hunnerd prejudicial thoughts 'gin Butchie and me just because we happen to look like frogs and worship the Elder Gods and—?"

"Bu-Bu-Butchie?" I repeated idiotically. It did not sound like a name proper to a potential purveyor of human sacrifice.

It was the first time I had ever seen someone with gray skin blush. "'S'not my real name," he said sullenly.

"Which is—?"

Butchie swallowed hard: "Kermit." The corners of his mouth turned down, which placed them somewhere in the vicinity of his knees.

In the ensuing awkward silence, Ma left the trailer briefly, returning with my clothes. They smelled of sunshine, fresh air, and Tide.

(Though, for all I knew, it was a malign and fantastic Tide that once had swirled about the spires of Great Cthulhu's blasphemous abode in sunken R'lyeh and—oh, the hell with it, it was plain Tide laundry detergent, probably bought on sale at Wal-Mart.)

"They're startin' to arrive," Ma said as she tossed my apparel onto the bed. "Cousin Ephraim's just now pullin' in with that old family rattletrap of his, and the car don't look too good either. Now, city-boy, I don't mind you talkin' down to me under my own roof, but I'm tellin' you right now I won't have you doin' the same to my blood kin, nor my friends and neighbors, so if you can't get down off your high night-gaunt and act mannerly, you can just hit the road right now. Otherwise you're more'n welcome to stay, and maybe we can scare you up a ride to the bus depot after. Like Butchie says, we're hostin' the sabbat here today and I wouldn't mind an extra pair of hands to help me get the food on the table."

"I'd be more than happy to oblige," I said. "It's the least I can do to thank you for taking me in last night." What evil angel possessed me to give such a reply, so glibly? It must have sprung from some lingering ghost of shame for my indefensible bias against Ma and Butchie, a prejudice based solely on their looks, their creed, their economic and social standing, and their abuse of the Budweiser logo as an interior decorating motif. No sooner were the words out of my mouth than I repented them, but there could be no going back. No stronger bond exists upon this earth than the word of a Harvard man, I don't care *what* that self-styled Camilla-Mistress-of-Pain person over on Brattle Street claims.

Ma was more than pleased. "Well, that's *mighty* pink of you, city-boy, *mighty* pink. Me and Butchie'll give you some privacy so's you can get decent, and then you just come on out and join the fun." With that they left the trailer.

I dressed with alacrity. I was not in any hurry to become a part of the "fun," as Ma termed it, but reasoned that the sooner I discharged my obligations, the sooner I might be on my way with a clear conscience. Fully clothed at last, I flung wide the trailer door and stepped into a nightmare.

I also stepped into something else. I regret to say that this accident caused me to curse loudly enough to draw Ma's attention.

"Gods *damn* it, Billy-Joe Tindalos, you pick *up* after them hounds o' yours!" she bellowed, shying an empty bottle at the head of a snot-nosed abomination from beyond the stars or under the porch or somewhere.

As I scraped the muck from my shoes, I looked around. The space before the trailer teemed with all manner of weird beings, some of the same amphibian appearance as Ma and Butchie, others whose hair had a disquieting tendency to hiss, and still others whose skin bore the leprous cast of a fish's belly. To these, one and all, Ma extended the hand of kinship and greeted them with a cheerful, "*Iä, Iä*, y'all! Grab a cold one and kick back, we'll start the nameless rites and obscene gibberin' soon's the band tunes up some."

Something tapped me moistly on the shoulder. I turned to face a pair of Ma's guests, beings of such abhorrent and alarming appearance as to make even Jerry Springer think twice before booking them. The male was clad in a grease-stained sweatshirt, the sleeves cut off, the front limned with faded runes proclaiming it stolen from the Miskatonic Co-Ed Naked Chug-a-Lug Team. His mate sported a similar garment, its message to the world simply *I'm With Eldritch*.

"Yo, city-boy," the male said, his breath a musky compendium of all things foul and loathsome, with just a hint of Cheez Doodles. "You seen our kid?"

"I'm sorry, I'm a stranger here," I replied. "I wouldn't know the little fellow if I tripped over him."

The female snickered. "Oh, if you done that you'd *know* him all right! Right before he sucked your brains out through your eye-holes."

"*I heard that*, Selma Jean!" Ma's words boomed out as her formidable presence manifested among us. "What d'you think yer doin', tryin' to run off this nice young man when he's said he'll help me set out the noon meal? Maybe you don't *want* to eat my prize-winning barbecue after sabbat?"

"*Your* barbecue?" The male licked his lips, a gesture which likewise wetted down all of his face and part of his lady's. (Fortunately this was a sight for which Butchie's earlier display of lingual excess had prepared me.) "Man, your barbecue kicks *cloaca*. Let's get this show on the road, 'cause once we hit that last 'Cthulhu f'thagn,' I'm beatin' feet for the table." He grabbed Selma Jean and dragged her away.

"Services be startin' real soon now," Ma informed me. "I got to go, but meanwhile why don't you see to the spread? All the stuff what's s'posed to go out on the tables's in them coolers under the tree."

There was only one tree she could mean, a titanic, gnarled, lichen-shrouded botanical anathema that only a deeply kinky druid could love. The trailer which had been my haven the previous night was—as I now saw—but one of many which nestled, like scabrous mushrooms, among its far-flung roots. In its distant shade reposed a number of picnic tables, a pyramid of beer kegs, and the prophesied coolers.

As I approached the tree it was my misfortunate necessity to pass between several of the other trailers, a gauntlet of visceral terror. Innumerable lawn flamingos, their plastic beaks twisted into leers of unholy malice, followed my progress with glittering, evil eyes. The incessant *creak-creak-creak* of spinning pinwheel sunflowers thrust their droning paean to iniquity through my throbbing skull. The one ray of hope that fleetingly lightened my way—the sight of a welcomely prosaic statuette of the kind commonly referred to as Our Lady of the Upended Bathtub—was instantly extinguished when I noticed that the supposed Madonna had more tentacles than conventional iconography generally allows.

I was in a cold sweat and breathing heavily by the time I reached the coolers, but I soon stiffened my backbone and set to work. As I relieved the coolers of their contents, I was only half aware of the muted sounds of Ma's kinfolk raising their voices in worship. The glubberings and whinings, the shrieks and ululations, the bad guitar riffs and worse banjo solos, all united in one quasi-musical discord that would probably go platinum in a heartbeat if anyone from ASCAP showed up in these parts with a tape recorder.

"Purty sound, ain't it, city-boy?"

I looked up from my labors and saw yet another of Ma's relations perched atop the table beside me. She was a young female of certain healthy thoracic dimensions which permitted me to overlook the fact that she had a mouth that even Mick Jagger would have to kiss in installments. The thin fabric of her top (one which announced *My Parents Howled on the Frozen Plateau of Leng and All I Got Was This Lousy T-shirt*) was stretched to the point where merely watching her breathe was a religious experience.

"H-how do you do?" I rasped.

"Jus' fine, less'n Daddy catches me," she replied with a grin that covered two zip codes. "Name's Beulah May Waite. Uglier'n a shaved dog's ass, ain't it? I like my nickname better."

"Which is—?" I asked, leaving a cooler still half-full of gelatin salads to look after itself.

"Can't Hardly." My comprehension registered as a beautiful scarlet flush, which only encouraged her to straighten her shoulders in a way designed to bring down empires. "Tsk-tsk, city-boy. Maybe you better reel in that tongue o' yours before someone mistakes you for one o' the family and hauls your butt back to services. They's compulsory, y'know."

"In that case, why aren't *you* over there?" I countered, scrambling to recover some miniscule portion of my self-possession.

"'Cause Daddy thinks I'm doin' homework." She waved a familiar black-and-yellow booklet at me. I never knew that Cliff's Notes published a study guide to the *Necronomicon*. I was about to ask my bosomy batrachian babe where she'd purchased such an item, as a clever prelude to less academic discourse, but it was not to be. My suave moves perished unmade, my cleverly seductive chit-chat never left my lips. A dire air of cryptic menace fell over the trailer park, an atmosphere redolent with such ominous significance that I found myself immobilized like one who has stumbled upon the site of ancient and unhallowed sacrifice, or has studied for the wrong subject during finals week.

"Yog have mercy!" Beulah May cried, wringing her hands.

"What is it?" I was at her side, ready to defend her fair person against any peril. "What's wrong?"

"There! Look there!" She pointed to the north and moaned with fear.

Well might she moan! For now I too saw, against a morning sky gone suddenly dark, the unmistakable funnel shape of an onrushing twister in search of its natural prey, the trailer park.

The gravity of our situation had a peculiar effect on me. Rather than run away screaming in mindless panic, I felt instead washed by a great calm. Solemnly I said, "Ms. Waite, we must warn the others."

"Oh, it's no good, not a lick of good at all!" she keened, clutching her hair. "They's all deep into the rites by now; they won't quit in mid-*Iä* for no one or nothin'!"

"That remains to be seen," I replied and, taking her firmly by the hand, we sought out the place where Ma and the rest were calling upon the Elder Gods.

They were conducting their services in an open space behind my hosts' trailer. The same innate curiosity which in former days had made me snoop in Randolph Akeley's room now manifested itself as an unhealthy desire to view the infernal shrine to which they paid their cacophonous homage. After all, I reasoned, with the twister fast bearing down upon us, this Stygian fane might soon be literally gone with the wind. Fast in the toils of my own overweening nosiness, I winkled my way into the crush, Beulah May in tow, for a better look.

I winkled my way out again double time and stared at my companion. "That's a wading pool in there," I stated.

"Uh-huh," she said.

"Your extended family is standing there, three deep, chanting barbaric hymns to a child's wading pool."

"Sometimes they do an up-tempo number, too," she offered.

"They are standing around a child's wading pool—a child's *Power Rangers* wading pool, might I add—with a folding lawn chair set up in the middle of it."

"Well, they can't just plunk the idol of Great Cthulhu straight in the *water*. That wouldn't be respectful. If you already got a shrine and an idol and a *salaried* preacherman like we do, you gotta have an altar, too. *Anyone* knows that." She spoke disdainfully, like every religious Insider who has ever relished telling an Outsider that he is ignorant, ineffectual, and inferior, a smug state of mind which allowed her to forget our imminent danger.

I did not care to be condescended to by the likes of Beulah May Waite. "Your *shrine* is a *Power Rangers* wading pool, your *altar* is a folding lawn chair, your *idol* is a stack of Mrs. Paul's frozen fish sticks boxes, and your *preacherman*—salaried or not—has just placed a paper party hat on top of the whole soggy mess."

"I should hope so; it's Great Cthulhu's *birthday*. But I guess you didn't know that *either*, huh, city-boy?" Ms. Waite had fallen out of temper with my reportage of the obvious, and apparently impatience brought out a viciously mean streak in the girl for she then sneered: "I guess they just never taught you anything about that up at *Yale*."

"*YALE*?!"

That did it. That was the straw up with which my proud Harvard-educated camel's back would not put. Her effrontery had no excuse: I was wearing a crimson and white shirt proud with the name of fair Harvard. She could not hope but know; the insult was deliberate, and one that I would not brook even from a woman of twice Ms. Waite's endowments.

Anger kindled in my belly. Deep within my entrails I felt the old powers churn. My eyes burned with the rage of a thousand demons. Minor lightnings crackled from my fingertips and potent words of austere and fearsome condemnation roared from my mouth. The worshippers around the wading pool broke off their mesmeric chant, although the banjo player wouldn't take the hint. I blasted him to strings, splinters, and moist froggy smithereens with a minor side-spell and inwardly thanked God that I had opted to major in something more practical than English.

The amphibian congregation scattered before me in terror, hopping into their waiting vehicles and speeding off at a furious rate. Beulah May vaulted onto the back of a Harley, straddling the bitch seat behind a jacket-wearing member of the Yuggoth's Angels. I laughed triumphantly to watch her flee my just and awesome wrath.

Silly me: I'd forgotten all about the tornado.

It had not forgotten about me, though. I heard its approaching roar and felt the first lashings of its captive winds at my back. I fell to my knees then and there and raised my voice in prayer. "O Lord," I began, my eyes tightly closed against earthly distractions. "Lord, I implore Thee, save me. And if that's not possible, then at least don't let me have to watch a cow go flying past before I die. If I've got to go, let me do it without suffering the indignity of any stupid movie clichés first, please. Amen."

Hey, I liked that scene with the flying cow!

My eyes shot open. "Who's there?" I demanded, though I had to shout my challenge down the throat of the screaming wind.

Me, said the wading pool. And with no more prologue than that, the tentacled countenance, leathern wings, and squamous bulk of Great Cthulhu erupted from the waters. He was wearing the paper party hat and looked like a squid on a toot.

Thus is it written in ancient tomes of forbidden lore: *Verily the Elder Gods do not fart around.* (This sounds better in Latin.) With a single stroke of his gargantuan paw, Great Cthulhu swept the tornado from the sky. A grateful hush fell upon the heavens and the earth. I tried to stammer my thanks as well, but the strain of the moment would not let me do other than raise my voice in a reedy rendition of "Happy Birthday to You."

The Elder God stopped me before I got to the end of the "How old are you now?" verse. Perhaps he was sensitive about such matters.

Look, don't mention it, all right? he said. *I was summoned anyway, I might as well answer a prayer or two as long as I'm in the neighborhood.*

"But I wasn't praying to *you*," I felt bound to point out.

Hey, Coke or Pepsi, Mickey D's or Burger King, paper or plastic, who gives a shoggoth's ass? His bat-like wings rose and fell in an affable shrug. *Besides, if you weren't praying to me now, you will be some day.*

"I . . . don't really think that I'm going to—"

Sure you will! My demurral did not seem to affect his good humor at all. *Because it's guaranteed; you won't have a choice. Baby, it's comeback time!*

"This comeback, it's not going to be *too* soon, is it?" The thought of my dear Mummy's reaction if I didn't get married in the Episcopal church scared me worse than Great Cthulhu ever could.

Sooner than you think, college boy. I haven't been wasting all my time dreaming the aeons away in sunken R'lyeh. Damn sharks keep swimming up my nose every few centuries, for one thing. I figure that since I can't get any decent REM sleep anyhow, I might as well get off my thumb, bring about the return of the Elder Gods, overrun the globe, reward our followers, destroy our enemies, and yada, yada, yada.

"Is that why they were invoking you here?" I asked, unable to repress a shiver. "To begin the conquest of Earth?"

The fearsome being gave me a disbelieving look. *On my* birthday?!

In a more amicable tone he confided, *Listen, college boy, these are nice folks out here, so nice that I don't have the heart to tell 'em how all their rites and sabbats and pep rallies and frozen ichor socials won't do dick to bring back the good times. Oh, that sort of thing was all right once, but it'll take more than faith to float sunken R'lyeh. If you really want to* accomplish *something these days, you've gotta have the chops, the tech, the brains. And to get that, it's not what* you *know, it's who* you *know: Network, network, network!*

He slapped one paw into the palm of the other to emphasize his words.

Which is exactly what I've been doing. No more seeking out the debauched mongrel races of the world, no more scattering my spawn like there's no tomorrow, no more breeding with cannibal South Sea islanders and barbarian savages in the cold wastes and people from Massachusetts, nuh-uh. Besides, who knows where they've been? No sir, nowadays I've got some really scary guys on my side, and I didn't even have to say "Of course I'll respect you in the morning" to get them!

"Who are they?" I demanded. "What manner of men would be so degenerate, so corrupt, so possessed of an unfeeling lust for pure, ultimate, uncontested power and worldly dominion that they would betray their fellow human beings and serve *you*?"

The horrendous creature from between the nighted gulfs of space winked at me and flicked his party hat to a more rakish angle with the tip of one bloodstained claw. *Tell you what, sport, I'm gonna leave you a clue.*

Something dropped from his paw. It splashed into the water at his feet, creating a plume of fetid smoke and a violent burbling on impact. Ere the last seething hiss died away, he was gone.

I stood for a time recovering my composure. Then, with rapidly beating heart I steeled myself to face the smoldering token which the awful Elder God had left in his wake. By inches I sidled closer to the edge of the deceptively peaceful wading pool and with a manful effort gazed down at what reposed beneath the softly lapping waters.

Ah, the accursed thing! Even now, even here, safe once more within fair Harvard's ivy-swathed incubation pouch, the memory thereof fills me with a griping nausea and a terror whose claws are set into the uttermost depths of my soul. That thing, that damned "clue" which the departing Elder God had left me was no ordinary object, but a warning to all mankind, an omen which wordlessly spoke of our predestined doom, a harbinger of the inevitable extinguishment of all things kind and warm and good and human in the earth, in our lives, and in our very hearts. For you see, it was—it was—

It was the class ring of a graduate of M.I.T.!

The Captain in Yellow

By David Vaughan

April 29, 2317

Day one as a crew member on the Brotherhood's flagship! My shuttle from New Innsmouth station met the *Carcosa* in orbit around Yuggoth. You hear a lot of stories, but until you see her up close you can't possibly understand. She's a mountain in space. Four nacelles sweep back from her hull like enormous, glistening metal tentacles. I wiped away a tear of joy as I boarded her.

Before you ask: No, I haven't met Captain Hastur yet. Obviously, my dream assignment is to the bridge crew, but it's a long way to the top. The first officer greeted me in the shuttle bay, though. Commander Nyarlathotep lives up to his reputation. Tall, swarthy, handsome, with a jet-black beard and slicked-back hair. I stared, slack-jawed, as he pinned a Yellow Sign comm badge to the chest of my jumpsuit.

"Gorgonzola?" he asked.

I blinked. "Excuse me, sir?"

"Gorgonzola? Brie?" He gestured to a spread of crackers and fancy cheeses laid out for the new arrivals. I shook my head. He led me to an elevator.

The commander simply oozes confidence. The rest of the crew practically worships him. He turned every head as he escorted me through the halls to my quarters. Nobody paid me any notice, but I suppose ensigns come and go on a starship like this.

I'm sharing a room with a Deep One named Ensign Y'hoo-nthleth. He's green and scaly with big, bulging eyes and constantly palpitating gills. He wears a kind of fishbowl on his head, filled with saltwater or something. The computer translated his croaks for me. Seems polite enough. We'll probably be best friends in a week.

Big day in Engineering tomorrow. Start of my meteoric rise. Good night!

Little after 0200 hours now. Couldn't sleep. Kept hearing a gravelly voice whisper "fhtagn" over and over. Probably just my imagination.

Y'hoo-nthleth snores a lot.

April 30

Engineering is . . . not what I expected.

I mean, I graduated with honors from Miskatonic Academy. I know my way around a starship's engine room. Shining trapezohedrons warp space-time to traverse the black seas of infinity, Brotherhood engineers program the silver keys of the light beam envelopes, etc., etc. But the *Carcosa* is different.

The entire engineering deck is a vast, empty room. At its center is a podium holding a single, arcane text. Chief Engineer Chandraputra, a blind man from the blue caverns of Tsath, sits on a chair next to the podium. A metal visor strapped around his face somehow allows him to read the old book day and night. He mutters so quietly that I can't make out what he's saying, but apparently he's reciting spells that magically propel the *Carcosa* across the universe. They call this system a "book drive."

A few other crew members sat on folding chairs around the room. I approached a young woman named Lt. Whateley. She picked at a platter of cheese and crackers (maybe the same cheese and crackers as yesterday?) and read something in her lap.

"Do we cast spells, too?" I asked her.

She frowned at me.

"What? Oh, no. This is a magazine." She waved it. "We just take turns giving the chief his eye drops, or changing his bedpan. Speaking of which, new guy . . ."

I spent the evening washing my hands in my quarters. Y'hoo sat on his bed and watched me the whole time with his creepy, unblinking eyes. Weirdo.

Kind of a rough start, Journal. But I'm staying positive!

May 5

This is a nightmare.

I haven't slept in days. "Fhtagn fhtagn fhtagn." I asked Ensign Mason what it means, and do you know what he said?

"It's R'lyehian for 'dream.'"

Are you kidding me? How the hell am I supposed to sleep with someone whispering "dream" all night long? And who's whispering anyway?

Not Y'hoo, that's for sure. He spends every night snoring like an angry walrus. We had a big argument after I covered his fishbowl with pillows.

Meanwhile, I use my advanced degree and considerable skills to warm a seat cushion and watch a blind man read. This dead-end job will never earn me a promotion to the bridge crew.

Oh, fantastic. Here comes Whateley. She's going to tell me to stop writing in my journal and shove some gruel down the chief's gullet. Tomorrow I'm asking the commander to transfer me to Astronomics.

May 7

The *Carcosa*'s science officer is literally a brain in a jar.

Fine, it's not a jar. More like a big metal cylinder, but same difference. Apparently, Science Officer West was on the *Hetty* when it was captured by the Mi-Go during the Elder Wars. The bug bastards experimented on West for months. By the time he was rescued, the S.O. was nothing but gray matter in a box. Instead of giving him an honorable discharge, though, the Brotherhood stuck some wires in his cylinder and put him back to work.

Not surprisingly, the S.O. is an ornery S.O.B. I can't believe this, but I miss Engineering. At least the chief didn't yell at me while I wet his eyeballs. The S.O. barks orders at me all day long. Via text messages, of course. Fortunately he can't see the faces I make at his stupid jar.

At least, I don't think he can see me . . . Oh, shit . . .

May 20

You might think that these jumpsuits are waterproof. Having stood hip-deep in a swamp for the past two hours, let me assure you, they are not. Also, I'm pretty certain that something is crawling around in my pants.

Sorry, Journal. Let me catch you up.

After the S.O. fired me, Commander Nyarlathotep re-assigned me to Security. I'm a grunt now, further away from the bridge than ever.

Two days ago, the *Carcosa* received a distress call from the Nug-Soths of planet Yaddith. The "book drive" zapped us across the void in an instant. I winced when I saw the planet through the porthole in my quarters. Yaddith is a disgusting ball of mud in space, orbiting five red suns and surrounded by five black moons. I felt sorry for the poor losers who had to set foot on that hellhole.

That's when my comm badge beeped.

"Danforth!" growled the security chief, Lt. Graah. He's a satyr from Leng, but more bull than goat. "Report to teleportation. You're on the away team to Yaddith."

The chief engineer can move an entire spaceship across light-years in the blink of a blind eye, but we still have to teleport from ship to surface. Go figure. And the *Carcosa*'s 'porters are notoriously unpredictable. When we appeared on Yaddith in a sparkle of green energy, Ensign Lake's arm was impaled on one of Lt. Graah's horns. After a lot of screaming and crying on Lake's part, the lieutenant managed to tear himself free.

It gets worse. Sub-Lieutenant Warren didn't even make it. There's nothing left of her but a few scraps of her red uniform jacket and two eyeballs in a mound of flesh. When I close my eyes, I see hers staring at me.

This swamp is so cold. Can't stop shivering.

We've been marching across this soggy bog planet for hours. Y'hoo would be right at home. Why'd I get stuck with this duty while he's in our warm, dry room, doing whatever it is that he does? Jerk.

We haven't found a sign of the Nug-Soths who sent the distress call. Maybe they left. Who could blame them?

For the love of . . . What is Lake screaming about now? "Dolls?" "Holes?" He probably stepped in some—

Bloody hell! DHOLES!! They're everywhere. Tell my mother I—

May 21

I'm alive, Journal. Barely.

Dholes are even more horrible than the training videos led me to believe. Gigantic, slimy worm-monsters, sure. But the teeth. Nobody said anything about the teeth.

It's impossible to run in a swamp. All you can do is slog through the muck while huge, white worms explode from underneath and devour your mates. Oh, the chewing . . .

Every time one of them ate another crewman, I thought, "You're next, Danforth. This is where you die."

I didn't, though. Thanks to Lt. Graah. Just when the brackish water around me began to bubble, Graah shoved me out of the way. A dhole burst up between us. Graah grappled the monster with both arms and wrapped his hairy goat-legs around its gooey body. He dug his fingers into the dhole's hide and somehow steered it away from me, toward the other monsters. The last thing I saw of him before he vanished in a tangle of writhing, viscous tubes was the mad grin on his face.

I think he enjoyed it.

The dholes took the rest of the away team. I'm the only one left. Alone, wet and frozen, stranded on a dirty, dank planet under a blood-red sky. It's only a matter of time before the monsters return. I'm waiting for death.

"Fhtagn," whispers the voice in my ear. "Dream."

If I could just close my eyes for a few minutes. Sleep.

This wasn't what the brochures promised. "Join the Brotherhood! See the Universe! Follow the Yellow Sign!" I expected fun and adventure and a steady day job, eventually a position on the bridge, a chance to prove myself. Instead . . .

For crying out loud, the Yellow Sign! I totally forgot about my comm badge. Hang on, Journal. Hang on.

Everything's turning green and shimmery. Oh no, not the telepo—

May 30

Doctor Morgan says that the teleporter accident could have been much worse. My bandages should come off in another four to six weeks. She was able to remove my leg from my shoulder and reattach it in the right place, but there's nothing she can do about my pinky toe.

Y'hoo came to visit me in sickbay. He's been assigned to the bridge as Captain Hastur's new chief of security.

My right eye won't stop twitching.

June 27

My third session with Counselor Shirefield went as badly as the first two. She's a K'n-yan telepath, which basically means that she can read me like Chief Chandraputra reads an open book.

"Have you always harbored such resentment toward the Deep Ones?" she asked.

I fed her a line about the anguish I felt as a child when my pet goldfish died, but she didn't buy it. What was I supposed to do, bad-mouth a member of the bridge crew? That was practically insubordination. The Brotherhood would keelhaul me.

Besides, I wasn't really jealous of Y'hoo. Not anymore. I don't want to work on the bridge or meet the captain.

I just want to go home.

We sat there in silence for a while, Counselor Shirefield in her high-backed chair, I on my back on the couch. It was comfier than the bed in my quarters and I started to doze.

Finally, she said, "Tell me about your dreams."

"Fhtagn!" I blurted.

She raised an eyebrow and began writing on her notepad.

I might be in trouble.

July 3

She didn't have me committed, but she didn't send me home, either. Instead she transferred me to Interstellar Communications. At this rate I'll work at every duty post before my probationary period is over.

Commander Nyarlathotep personally escorted me to my new station. He continues to take an interest in me for some reason.

InComm is located in the bowels of the *Carcosa* in a sad room lit by dim, flickering fluorescent lights. Communications officers sit at long tables, hunched over computers like old crones, sagging under the weight of their oversized headphones.

"You'll be on our R'lyehian desk," the commander told me.

"What am I listening for?" I asked, sliding into a seat next to another miserable sap.

The commander grinned. "The call."

July 4

There isn't much time, Journal.

I heard it before lunch. At first, I thought my headphones were broken. All I picked up was static. That changed to buzzing, then a low hum, and eventually a whisper so soft that I couldn't make it out.

I pressed the cans against my ears.

"Fhtagn," said the voice in an otherworldly timbre. Then, as I transcribed the words, it yelled, "Ph'nglui mglw'nafh Cthulhu R'lyeh wgah'nagl fhtagn!"

My head hit the desk. The InComm room disappeared. I floated in the darkness of space. Asteroids tumbled past me, trailing globules of strange new colors, almost impossible to describe: the color of old paper to a sightless swami; the color of a jar to a brain with no eyes; the color of a dhole's digestive juices seen from the inside.

A space rock exploded and revealed Him in His terrible glory.

Mighty Cthulhu swam among the stars. His tentacles pinwheeled as he drifted nearer to me. I trembled beneath his shadow. Our eyes met.

"Gorgonzola?" asked Cthulhu. His feelers undulated as he chuckled.

My supervisor shook me awake. Apparently I was laughing uncontrollably in my sleep, but I don't remember that at all. I looked down at the cord dangling from my ear. My headphones had never been plugged in to anything.

Commander Nyarlathotep was alerted. I stood at attention as he approached me. *This is it,* I thought. *He finally shoves me out an airlock.*

But when he read what I'd transcribed, he put an arm around my shoulder and walked me to the exit. "Congratulations, Danforth. You're being reassigned. You'll never guess where . . ."

I'm writing this in the bathroom, Journal. The commander agreed to a pit stop on the way to the bridge, but I can't hide forever. Smells like limburger in here. Or yellow . . . Yellow what? Other colors, without names. It's hard to gather my thoughts. They're slipping away like eyeballs through melted flesh.

Nyarlathotep is knocking on the stall door. My time is almost up. Captain Hastur is waiting.

UBS *Carcosa* Helmsman's Log: Space Date 97XQ-441@5-L'Z

Lt. Danforth here, reporting another magnificent Brotherhood day!

All hail He Who Must Not Be Named! The Captain in Yellow sits atop his throne of bones at the center of the bridge. From behind a pallid, tattered mask he gives the word: go forth and serve great Cthulhu!

Powerful Nyarlathotep sits on the captain's right, and the immortal psychic of K'n-yan on his left. Their counsel is wicked and wise. Hoo hoo!

A disembodied brain, forever entombed in a steel coffin, towers over the operations console next to mine. He processes the data of different dimensions.

Our security chief, my dear friend Y'hoo-nthleth, paces the bridge, ever vigilant against threats to the ship. "CROAK!"

Chief engineer! Ready the book drive! Give the gift of reading! New or gently used arcane texts accepted!

And I, the humble helmsman? My eyes have been opened and at last I dream. Cthulhu taught me to swim. Lost *Carcosa*! Seek out old life, old civilizations! Abbith, Kythanil, Chavignol, Neufchatel, Shonhi, Roquefort and Xoth, Wensleydale and Vhoorl!

Let us explore strange, old worlds.

My Little Old One™

By Jody Lynn Nye

AT THE LOW HISSING NOISE, Regina Gutierrez looked up blearily from her smartphone. An ebony-clad figure loomed over her. She jumped, suppressing a scream. He—she assumed the towering figure was a he—was draped in a long, black, trailing cloak with the hood pulled down so far that she couldn't see a face inside it.

"Pardon me for mentioning it," the faceless one murmured, "but did you know your child is creating . . . mayhem?"

Regina sprang to her feet. Quentin! The ExCelO Ultimate baby stroller at her knee was empty. Her wonderful, precious toddler was missing! Where was little Quentin? She scanned the grounds of McLaughlin Park, peering between thickly leafed trees and under the wooden seats of the benches. She hoped he hadn't wandered toward the bay. He was so attracted to deep water.

Her heart pounded in panic as she ran around, trying to find him. Other mothers, sitting with their well-behaved children, glanced up at her from their own smartphones with an air of annoyance at the disruption. She gave them each a faint, guilty half-smile.

A frantic shriek arose from the area of the playground behind the stand of bushes. Regina scrambled toward the noise.

As she had feared, Quentin stood over a smaller girl, his fist wound in her long blonde hair. The girl cried and struggled, which only served to make Quentin determined to hold on. The other mother hovered

29

over the two of them, reluctant to touch someone else's child, even though her own little darling suffered the consequences. Regina swooped in.

"No!" she said, grabbing up Quentin and untangling his fat little fingers from the strands of gold. She smoothed his dark curls, trying to calm him down so he would listen. "Do not invade someone's space without their permission!" She turned a rueful gaze toward the other mother, now enfolding her own sobbing chick. "I'm so sorry. I . . . We're going now."

She retreated hastily. Quentin kicked his little feet against her khaki-clad thighs as she hauled him back toward the park bench. Those miniature Adidas sneakers hurt, but she didn't want to scold him for what had, after all, been her choices. She had bought the shoes, and she had been the one who decided to take him to the park. And, she admitted reluctantly, the one who had taken her eyes off him.

The hooded figure now sat silently on the bench beside the stroller. She sat down too, holding tight, because Quentin wanted to return to his . . . well, mayhem really was a good word for it.

"I'm so sorry," she said to the stranger. "I am just so exhausted. He hasn't slept through the night since he was born."

The cloaked figure recoiled as if in awe. "The . . . Sleepless One?"

"We call him that," Regina said, with a bitter laugh, straightening the collar of her patterned Lacroix jacket. "I wish it wasn't true. Sometimes I question whether I actually gave birth to him, or if the nurses switched our baby for a little monster . . . ."

She pressed her lips together, realizing that she had just unloaded onto a total stranger. God only knew what kind of face he was making under that massive hood.

"I'm sorry," she said again. "I shouldn't say that." She leaned forward to put a hand on the enveloping sleeve. The arm inside it felt as if it were mere bones. "We love Quentin; really, we do. But if we could get him to sleep, our lives would be a lot easier. It's an issue every single night. He just won't do anything we want him to. I know he's close to hitting the Terrible Twos. Kids that age just aren't human. We'd do anything to get him to settle down."

"You would do . . . anything?"

Regina widened her eyes in alarm.

"Well, almost anything. We won't change his diet. We feed him organic whole foods, full of all the nutrients that a growing child needs."

The harsh whisper seemed to resonate inside her head. "No change in diet is necessary. No. You need the aid of the Sleeper of R'lyeh. Have you ever heard of My Little Old One™?"

Regina could distinctly hear the trademark symbol. "Why, no. What is it?"

The cloaked one reached into the Stygian folds of his cape. From it, he produced a figure about a foot high, but so hideously shaped that Regina could hardly look at it. From sidelong glances, she gathered that it was faintly humanoid, but with scaly green skin, a head like an octopus, and skimpy little wings on its back. The gnarled, bloated body was naked, the eyes stared with unveiled malice, but the really ugly part was where the mouth ought to be, a mass of tentacles sprouted beneath the eyes. The whole thing shone with an unearthly gleam.

"This is Cthulhu™. Give it to him. It will help him to find his way."

Regina felt like gagging.

"This is for kids? It's slimy, not fuzzy."

The figure shook its head. "I think you will soon find that it will not matter."

Quentin struggled and kicked on Regina's lap. To her surprise, he was reaching for the horrible toy. She fended off his grasp, and he started screaming in fury. Regina blanched. Everyone was going to hear him! She had no choice but to take the hideous green object. Even touching its rubbery, slick surface made her shudder.

Quentin snatched it from her and folded it into his arms, making a harsh, grunting noise. How she wished he would learn to use his words!

"Are you sure that this will help?" she asked the dark, hooded stranger.

"I promise you he will become . . . obedient. That will be twenty-nine ninety-five." From the sleeve came an arcane but familiar shining device. "I take credit cards."

Bedtime was always a struggle. At dinnertime, Quentin had thrown his food all over the kitchen. Just when Regina and her husband Justin had cleaned up the baby, and the quarry-tiled floor and tasteful, gray-toned walls, Quentin produced a hidden handful of pureed kale and ground it into their beloved Shiraz carpet. He kicked as much of the water out of his BabyClean bathtub as he could, flailed his round little legs as she and Justin diapered him, and writhed so he wouldn't have to be put into his violet, organic flannel sleeper with the cute teddy bears embroidered all over it. But when Regina put the Cthulhu™ doll into the high-sided crib, Quentin fought to get in with it.

"He never does that," Justin said, his dark eyes wide with astonishment. He settled his small son on his back in the crib, careful not to touch the ugly toy, then tiptoed out of the room.

Counting it as a small victory, Regina read a brand-new bedtime story from a stack of colorful little books that had been delivered just that afternoon. She had rehearsed the text, although Quentin never seemed to pay attention to the subjects of her nightly reading, or her attempt to portray all the characters in the books with humorous voices and sounds, only the duration. He wanted the attention to go on as long as possible, as though tallying some form of tribute. Just in case, Regina pronounced every word clearly, and made the words at once entertaining and soothing.

When she reached the last page, he glared at her as always, but not with the usual malice in his deep-set, dark eyes. No screaming!

Taking a deep breath, Regina started to tuck him in. He clutched the My Little Old One™ toy to him and actually let her fold the organic cotton coverlet around him. She backed away from the crib, staring but ecstatic.

"Good night, Mommy-and-Daddy's darling," she called. "We love you."

Quentin snorted. She turned out the lights and crept out of the room.

"So soon?" Justin asked in an undertone, as she went into the living room, where he sat with the lights turned down low in case they disturbed the baby. The trendy architect they had hired on recommendations from Berkeley's hottest interior design blog had assured them that Quentin couldn't see them from his room, but the child always seemed to know if any light brighter than ten watts was on anywhere in the house.

"It's a miracle," Regina said, setting herself down carefully on the

Eero Saarinen couch, so as not to make any additional noise that her precious baby might hear. "I had five new books ready, but he didn't seem to care about anything but that disgusting toy."

"Wonderful toy," her husband corrected her.

Regina shook her head. "There's something about it that makes me feel . . . well, uneasy."

"Me, too," Justin said, firmly. "But I am not looking a gift monster in the mouth. Especially if we can get a couple of hours of uninterrupted sleep, please God."

A tremendous crack of thunder shook the house. Both of them looked up at the ceiling, then out the window in dismay at the calamitous downpour suddenly flooding their manicured garden and custom-made sandbox. The solar lights dotting their yard looked like evil topaz eyes.

"Was rain predicted for tonight?" Regina asked.

Justin shrugged. "I don't care. I'm so tired it hurts."

"Your turn for the two a.m. wakeup," she said, as she trailed behind him toward their bedroom.

Regina and her best friend Martine slid into the only table open at the baby-friendly coffee shop on the main shopping street of their upscale Berkeley suburb. Regina glanced with regret at the other coffee spot across the street with Swedish designed furniture and soft music, her favorite morning hangout PQ, pre-Quentin, but it did not allow children, and, the managers were keen to point out, particularly hers. At the moment, her little darling was play-talking with his sinister-looking toy in his usual pre-verbal babble. She was grateful that it kept him from attacking Polly, Martine's sweet little girl, as he usually did. The smaller toddler seemed puzzled, staring at Cthulhu™ with open curiosity.

"You look wonderful," Martine said. Regina bristled. That was Bay-speak for "Have you had some work done?"

"Quentin slept through the night," Regina said, in a hushed whisper, as if to say it aloud would jinx it. "The whole night! When I woke up at four to check on him, he was still sound asleep. He didn't start crying until six!"

"That's amazing," Martine said, genuinely impressed. They had met in Lamaze class and bonded over shared numerous grievances of child-rearing. "Polly still wakes up with night terrors at least five times. We have to have quiet time together again and again, and it's ruining my complexion. What did you do?"

"My Little Old One™," Regina said, feeling her cheeks burn at having to say the name aloud. It did sound pretty stupid. "His new favorite toy." She pointed at the green excrescence in her precious child's arms. "That."

Martine's sculpted eyebrows rose into her lowlighted brunette hairline. "That horrible thing? Why in heaven would you give him a thing like that?"

Regina explained where it had come from. Martine stared open-mouthed in horror.

"Oh, honey, please! How do you know that weird stranger wasn't trying to recruit you for something? You've heard all those stories about death cults popping up all over the country. A long, black, flowing robe?"

Regina shrugged. "At the time, I wouldn't have noticed if he was wearing a spacesuit. But he was right! It works. Something about that . . . nauseating, scaly monstrosity . . . makes Quentin happy."

"Well, he's a boy," Martine said, straightening her back. "Delicate children like Polly wouldn't touch something that hideous."

At that moment, Polly took her finger out of her mouth and reached out toward Cthulhu™. The tiny pink tip merely brushed one of the bent wings on the scaly back, and Quentin shrieked loud enough to make everyone in the crowded shop turn to look at them. Polly was undeterred. With her little brow furrowed, she tried to pull the green toy away from Quentin, first with one hand, then with both. Quentin, much larger and stronger, actually had to fight to break her grip. At last, he succeeded, and yanked the toy out of her reach. Polly began to cry.

"Oh, my God," Martine said, in horror.

At that moment, a blinding bolt of lightning pierced the distant sky. A sudden torrent of rain streamed down in the street outside the coffee shop, making the joggers and cyclists in the street dash for cover. Regina shook her head.

"I didn't think rain was predicted for today. Did you?"

Regina couldn't say that Quentin was a changed baby, now that he had Cthulhu™, but it was easier to do other things than monitor him constantly to make sure he wasn't committing . . . mayhem. Instead, it looked as though he and Cthulhu™ had their own little cabal, huddled in a corner, watching her and Justin with malevolent glares. In a way, it was a nice change.

It didn't mean that he wasn't still a challenge at every step. They managed to get him bathed and changed for bed, but when Justin offered him his sippy cup for one last drink, Quentin shook it so violently that the cap came off, spilling water all over the three of them and Cthulhu™. The baby looked accusingly at the wet toy and turned a furious gaze at his parents.

Justin sighed and hoisted the struggling toddler out of the crib.

"You go get some clean PJs and a sheet, honey. I'll clean him up."

Regina retreated, feeling a small measure of satisfaction. They shared parenting duties down the middle as they had agreed to do even before marriage. Stuffing the wet onesie in the hamper, Regina went for clean pajamas and a fresh cup, one with a better seal. With cuddles and coos that would have soothed any normal baby, they tucked Quentin into his dry bed and tiptoed silently out.

Justin took a bottle of pinot noir out of the wine fridge and presented the label toward Regina.

"We deserve this," he said. She nodded avidly. She could almost taste the dry fruitiness on her tongue. But just as he reached for a couple of tall wine glasses, shrieking and wailing broke out from the direction of the nursery. Regina glanced down at the baby monitor on the counter. She frowned.

"Did you leave My Little Old One™ next to the camera?" she asked. The ugly homunculus seemed to fill the entire room except for a corner of the screen in which the crib was visible.

"No," Justin said. His expression changed to one of horror. "Oh, my God, it's moving!"

It did look as if the horrible toy had grown to fifteen feet tall and was oozing toward their child, all its extremities reaching for him. She ignored the sounds of the approaching thunder as Quentin screamed and bounced up and down on his mattress, clinging to the bars of his crib. He shook them like a condemned prisoner in fear for his life. Her heart pounding, Regina knew she should run to him, but she stood frozen, watching. The massive-seeming form of Cthulhu™ lifted one of its mouth-tentacles, and touched Quentin in the center of his forehead. The baby fell backwards onto the mattress, silent and still.

Regina grabbed her ten-inch Sabatier cooking knife out of the teakwood block on the counter, and Justin snatched up a tennis racket. They rushed into the room. Quentin lay flat on his back. Regina put the knife down and picked him up, searching for wounds or burns. His forehead was unmarked, and he wasn't hurt, just deeply asleep. She joggled him in her arms, unwilling to put him down.

"Where's the monster?" Justin asked, casting around. Cthulhu™ sat on the top of the dresser, looking malevolent and disgusting, but still only a foot tall.

"We're dreaming," Regina said, her heart pounding so much it made her voice shake. "We're just hallucinating. He's fine. I don't know what we saw. Maybe one of the neighbors' routers is cross-glitching with the baby-cam when they're trying to download a horror movie. He's fine."

Still limp and dreaming, Quentin didn't wake or protest as they tucked him in again. Regina put the awful little toy down beside him. Quentin hugged it to him without ever waking up.

The next day at the coffee shop, Regina studied Martine. Her friend's usually perfect makeup was a little askew, and the middle button of her Anne Fontaine blouse was undone. She was concerned.

"Anything on your mind?" Regina asked, kindly. That was Bay-speak for "you look terrible."

Her friend shook her head. "Polly was up and down all night. The thunder kept waking her up. She cried and cried. I was on a Skype-chat with my sister. She has a son a couple of months older than Polly. He doesn't sleep either. I don't know what to do." Her mouth twisting as though she had taken a bite of something bitter, she met Regina's gaze. "Do you think you can introduce me to the guy who sold you My Little Old One™?"

No one answered the phone number on the electronic receipt, so Regina and Martine went back to the park. She had never seen the cloaked stranger in the park before the day she had bought Cthulhu™ for Quentin, and hadn't seen him since, but the moment the two women pushed their strollers into the nature preserve, the figure glided out of the thick trees overlooking the inlet.

"You have need of my services?" he hissed.

Martine gulped at the appearance of the sinister stranger, but she swallowed her fear. Regina held her arm tightly for support.

"I'll try anything to get my baby to sleep overnight," Martine said.

"*Anything?*" the hooded figure asked, his rattling voice rising to a higher note. Martine twisted her lips in disgust.

"Do you have to talk like a bad movie?"

"I apologize," the figure said, dropping to a sinister whisper. "It is . . . force of habit."

"It's a miracle," Martine said the next day, as they huddled over their lattes. "I can hardly stand to touch the damned thing, but Polly loves it. She feeds Cthulhu™ and insisted that I bathe it with her."

"Quentin, too," Regina agreed. "He talks to it all the time. And he listens to it. You know, I thought he was too young for play-acting. All the baby-raising books say so."

"Do you think it's really talking?" Martine asked, watching the two toddlers side by side in their strollers.

"It certainly doesn't sound like it," Regina said. The two babies, each with their own Cthulhu™, chattered at each other. Whatever rivalry or disagreements they usually had, they'd found a bond in the horrible little dolls.

"*Ph'nglui mglw'nafh Cthulhu R'lyeh wgah'nagl fhtagn,*" Quentin said, leaning his head against his horrible toy.

"*Ph'nglui mglw'nafh Cthulhu R'lyeh wgah'nagl fhtagn,*" Polly said, shyly, combing her Cthulhu™'s tentacles with her fingers. Quentin let out a bark of laughter. Polly ducked her head and giggled.

Regina stared. "I don't believe it; he's being nice to her."

"I know!" Martine said, shaking her head in wonder.

Normally, Quentin would try to take both of the toys. But Polly was defending herself now, too. When another girl in a nearby stroller tried to take her Cthulhu™, Polly screamed multisyllabic abuse at her just the way Quentin usually did. Martine was embarrassed but Regina tried to make her feel better.

"She's asserting herself," she said. "And Polly is more verbal than Quentin is. He's still talking gibberish. I wish that he could speak as well as she does."

"Well, they're learning from each other," Martine said, mollified.

"And you're not going to believe this," Regina said, "but Quentin slept through six a.m. today."

"So did Polly!"

"Excuse me," an African-American woman with a squirming toddler in her lap said. The little girl's curly hair was tied in puffs bound with pink bows. She was trying to tear one of the ribbons off. The mother looked as exhausted as Regina had been a week ago. "Did you say your children are sleeping through past six in the morning? What's your secret?"

Martine nudged Regina in the ribs.

"As a matter of fact," she said, "it'll only cost you twenty-nine ninety-five."

Before long, most of the mothers in the coffee shop had bought their small children My Little Old Ones™. As abhorrent as the toys were, they worked. The small boy with big dark eyes who shrieked when anyone looked at him huddled contentedly over a long, skinny Nyarlathotep™, and the bruising three-year-old with curly red hair stopped pushing other children around when he got his very own Azhorra-Tha™. For the first time, Regina and Martine could carry on a conversation over their coffee without shouting to be heard over crying babies.

"You should get a commission," Martine said, toasting her with her pumpkin caramel macchiato.

Regina shook her head. "I'm just grateful something worked."

Quentin's temperament didn't exactly improve over the following weeks, but he became more predictable, and a hair more social. In fact, she thought that Quentin's intelligence was being stimulated by the interaction with the creature. Whenever they saw another mother with one of My Little Old Ones™ in the park or the coffee shop, he would grunt at them, and they would exchange the spate of baby talk that he and Polly shared.

"*Ph'nglui mglw'nafh Cthulhu R'lyeh wgah'nagl fhtagn,*" he called, holding up Cthulhu™. The other child shouted the phrase back at him. Both children wore smug smiles, as if they shared a deep secret.

"Don't you think it's weird that they all know the same noises?" Martine asked, rocking Polly. She was careful not to touch either her Cthulhu™ or the Shoggoth™ that Polly had cried for when she saw another child's maggot-like toy.

"Polly's very quick," Regina said. "She heard it from Quentin, and they both like the sound of it. Modeling is important to small children. Polly probably said it to them, and they retained it. Children are like sponges."

"I can't pronounce it, can you?"

"No," Regina said, with a sigh. "I just wish he would learn to talk. We've been working with him with all the word books and phonics lessons from the internet, and all the parenting websites, but nothing is getting through yet. We've even tried pretending that Cthulhu™ was saying the words, but he didn't seem interested."

"Count your blessings. He's playing normally. I'd even say he has leadership potential."

That, Regina could not deny. As Quentin got bigger and stronger and more mobile, he seemed to lead a pack of toddlers that followed him through McLaughlin Park like his acolytes. If Regina happened to lose sight of him for a moment, she knew she would find him sitting in the center of a group in the park. Instead of tearing up the flowers or terrorizing passing dogs or senior citizens, the children seemed intent on Quentin and their horrible toys. Regina almost fancied that it looked like a coven or a cabal. They chanted their weird words over and over to one another. If it had been a group of adults, or even older children, she'd have thought they were plotting something . . . sinister. Regina wanted to ask the cloaked man about it, but she never saw him again.

Quentin only showed some of his old attitude when parents dared to interrupt the strange conclave of children to take their own little ones out of the circle. Regina apologized for his savage snarls, but at least he wasn't hitting anyone anymore. She was grateful that he was finally showing signs of socialization, however weird the impetus that had spurred it.

As the sun started to dip behind the tops of the trees and the air began to cool, she gathered her toddler up and bundled him into the Audi. The Cthulhu™ doll in the crook of his arm seemed to peer up at her with its weird, red eyes. *It isn't real*, she told herself, uneasily putting the car into gear. *It's just a toy.*

She took Quentin home. While Justin broiled salmon for their dinner, she pureed some kohlrabi with a little fresh ginger and spinach for Quentin. The toddler rejected it, spitting out the mouthful of green glop. He fed Cthulhu™ some Cheerios instead. Suddenly, he looked up at his parents, his mouth moving. His face was intent in a way that they had never seen before.

"Look, honey," Regina said, excitedly. "He's trying to talk!"

They dropped to their knees beside the high chair, doing their best to encourage him.

"Come on, baby," she said.

"Say Dada, Quentin," Justin urged him, enunciating the syllables carefully. "Da da."

"D...d..." Quentin struggled with the syllable, then a malevolent gleam came to his eyes that almost perfectly reflected the evil face of My Little Old One™. "D... dethtruction."

Both adults rocked back on their heels.

Regina looked at Justin and shrugged. "At least he's sleeping through the night."

Tales of a Fourth Grade Shoggoth

By Kevin Wetmore

(by beloved children's author H.P. Lovecraft,
the author of *Are You There, Azathoth? It's Me, Margaret.*
as transcribed from the handwritten original
by Kevin Wetmore)

I WON C'THULHU at Harley Warren's birthday party. Everyone else got a goldfish, and at first I felt bad that I didn't get one, but I guessed the correct number of pseudopods on the thing in the basement (it was seventeen!) and so Mrs. Warren announced, "Randall Pickman Whateley came closest to the actual number of pseudopods and so he wins the grand prize," and then handed me a small glass bowl with a tiny castle inside with strange non-Euclidean geometry. Inside the castle I could see two eyes and some tentacles.

"It's an evil baby octopus!" she cooed. All the other guys in my fourth-grade class were jealous, and looked at their goldfish like it was no longer anything special. For a moment I knew what it was like to be one of the cool kids in school. But I knew it wasn't going to last. My little brother would probably do something to ruin it.

My little brother's name is Wilbur Ezekiel Whateley IV, but only my mother calls him that and only when she's mad at him. Everybody else just calls him Fhtagn because it's easier to pronounce, especially for him. Everybody knows my father, Old "Wizard" Whateley. He's really well-known in town and everybody either likes him or is afraid of him. Sometimes I think he's disappointed that I'm his son. I liked it when it was just me, my mom, and my dad, but then they had to give me a little brother.

My mom is crazy. I know everybody thinks their mom is crazy, but mine really is. Sometimes she stares off into space and sometimes she shrieks a lot or looks at Fhtagn and starts to giggle and weep at the same time. Like when he brings home half a dog carcass and just leaves it in the front hall. I mean she always tells us to clean up after ourselves and she's always talking about keeping the house neat, but sometimes Fhtagn just leaves carcasses around and it drives her crazy.

At a neighborhood Walpurgisnacht party a few years back, while the bonfire was being lit, I heard a neighbor tell another neighbor that my mom was actually my father's daughter, but that is crazy. Why would she be my mom if she was also his kid and why would my father want to marry his daughter and why would she want to marry her dad? I knew it didn't make any sense. Still, last year in third grade they told us we had to make a family tree, but when I went home and asked my mom, she just locked me in the basement for a week and I heard her crying a lot. So like I said, my mom is crazy.

I don't think my mom is disappointed in me like my father is, but she also spends a lot more time taking care of Fhtagn than she does with me. I mean, I know he's only two and it's not that I need my mom to take care of me. I'm already ten, and although I'm not as tall or big as Fhtagn, I'm not a baby like he is. I can't help that I'm afraid of swimming. I just don't like it. I must be the only kid in Innsmouth who doesn't like the water. Every year, my father rows us out to Devil's Reef and pushes us in the water and every year I scream until my mother says, "Oh, Wilbur, can't you see he's not ready yet?" and pulls me out. Last year, for the first time, he pushed Fhtagn in. Fhtagn, of course, just floundered around in circles for a minute and then moved his pseudopods so that he dove deep and then began moving toward the land, singing and giggling the whole way. I hated him. My father was so proud. "Look at him," he said to my mom. "Fhtagn is already swimming like a Marsh!" And he rowed furiously to keep up with my stupid brother.

Having a little brother is one of the most stupid, annoying, horrific, eldritch things that can happen to a kid. Fhtagn is always ruining my life. But now I won something. I named the evil baby octopus C'thulhu and brought him home. I didn't want to show him to my parents, who can be funny about pets, or to Fhtagn, who tries to eat them, so I hid the bowl under my cloak when I came in through the back door.

"Randy, is that you?" my mother called.

"Yeah," I yelled.

"How was the party?"

"Okay, I guess. We played some games—I really liked 'Pin the Tail on the Dimensional Shambler'; they're not as scary in the game as the pictures daddy has—and we buried this one kid, and ate cake."

"Well I hope you haven't spoiled your dinner. There's something on the stove that smells of offal and fish and your father wants us to eat it before sundown."

"Okay, I'm just going to get washed up," I yelled, moving down the hall to get to my room before she could ask more questions or say she wanted to see me.

I ran up the stairs to my room and slammed the door. I looked around. "Fhtagn, you better not be in here!" Sometimes he's invisible, although at six feet tall and with three trunk-like legs it is hard for him to hide. He just goes invisible, then you run into him and he giggles. He thinks it's the funniest thing. I hate him.

I took the bowl out from under my cloak and showed C'thulhu my room. "This is where you live now," I told him. "Here is my bed, and my desk, and my grimoire, and here is my poster of John Dee, and this was my great-grandfather's skin, and here is my collection of bottle caps. You're going to live here," I announced, and I put him on top of my dresser, next to the skull.

Then the door flew open, despite the fact that I had closed and locked it, and Fhtagn came into my room. He can't say my name right but just calls me Tekeli-li, which doesn't even sound like my real name.

"Tekeli-li okay?" he gurgled. He was standing there in his three-legged footy pajamas, holding on to his favorite stuffed nightgaunt. My grandma gave it to him and it's a good thing it didn't have a face because he chews in his sleep and the thing was already missing an ear and my mom has had to sew the neck closed several times from when he really gets going with the chewing.

"Get out of my room, Fhtagn, or I'll tell mom," I warned him. He was already leaving a pool of slime in the doorway that I was going to have to clean up. My mom says that because Fhtagn is special we have to take care of him, but I don't know why I should have to clean it up when he leaves a trail of loathsome slime in my room. It's not fair!

"What Tekeli-li got?" Fhtagn asked, pointing a hand-like tentacle at the bowl on the dresser.

"Nothing, Fhtagn! Go away!" I yelled, putting myself between C'thulhu and Fhtagn.

"Fhtagn play?"

"NO, Fhtagn! MOOOOMMMM, FHTAGN'S IN MY ROOOOM!" I sang over his shoulder, down the stairs.

"You boys play nice!" Then she began to giggle quietly and I heard a thumping noise. Usually that noise means she is banging her head on the wall or floor. When she does that, I know she isn't coming. Fhtagn knows it, too.

"Fhtagn play with Tekeli-li and bowl?"

"No, Fhtagn. Let's go to your room and play 'Black Goat of the Woods with a Thousand Young and Indians.'" He loved that game. He liked pretending he was an Indian.

"Okay, Tekeli-li!" We ran to his room and immediately I began the chant and waving my arms like they were tentacles. Fhtagn picked up his headdress and bow and arrow and began stalking me. We then jumped up and down on the pile of rags he slept on until our father came in.

"If'n ya caynt keep quiet whilst I'm reading, I'll sacrifice ya both, next new moon!" he said sternly. He can be angry when he gets home from work. Or when he's reading. Or talking to our mother. Or talking to anyone. Or any other time. We know he probably won't sacrifice us, but when he tells us to be quiet, we are very quiet.

The next day I went to school and when I came home, my bedroom door had been smashed open again and there was slime everywhere. I was gonna kill Fhtagn until I looked at my dresser and saw the bowl was empty. And a bite had been taken out of one of the drawers as well.

"Dagonit, Fhtagn," I screamed, so angry I didn't care that I might get in trouble for swearing. "Did you eat C'thulhu?"

Mother came tentatively up the stairs. "Now, Randy, stop yelling. What's wrong?"

"Fhtagn ate C'thulhu! And one of my drawers. I think he might have gotten some of my socks. But C'thulhu was mine! Why did he have to eat my pet?"

"He ate your what?" I forgot she didn't know about the baby evil octopus.

"I won a stupid baby evil octopus at Harley Warren's birthday party and it was in my room and it was mine and stupid Fhtagn came in here and ate it while I was at school!" I promised myself I wouldn't cry, but I could feel the hot tears forming. I wanted to be a big boy but I was so tired of Fhtagn ruining my life and eating my stuff.

"Now, Randy, don't call your brother stupid."

"He *is* stupid, and selfish, and I hate him!"

"Don't say that!" She looked around nervously. "Your brother might hear you."

She didn't have to say because he might be invisible in the room with us just then.

"Good. I hope he does. He should know he is stupid and selfish and I hate him."

"Son," she said, "I know you are unhappy with your brother right now but you do not hate him. He's your brother and he is special and we need to give him some extra kindness because he is so special."

"I'm so tired of being told how special Fhtagn is. Nobody else has to put up with a six-foot-tall little brother who destroys all his stuff and eats his pets. I liked it better when it was just you, dad, and me. Why did you have to have him?"

She got that look in her eye again and started to giggle. "Well, Randy, sometimes you don't plan to have . . . sometimes someone chants the wrong thing while inside you . . . and when the doctor tells you about the pseudopods on the sonogram and then you feel it kicking inside you . . . and we love your brother, he is so special . . . Excuse me, please, I need to check dinner."

And with that she walked out of my room and down the stairs and a minute later I heard the banging again. It sounded like the living room floor.

I cleaned up the slime and threw away the bowl. Just as well, I thought. The strange non-Euclidean geometry of the castle in the fishbowl had given me nightmares last night, and had also made it difficult to find the door when I had to go to the bathroom. Still, Fhtagn had no right!

I saw him later in his room as I walked by on my way to dinner. "Tekeli-li mad?"

"I'm not talking to you, Fhtagn," I told him and kept walking. I could hear him twittering and crying for much of the night, but it served him right.

The next day, I was at school and during recess we were all outside playing. I'm not great at kickball, but they let me play and I usually get to kick the ball once. Then some kid started screaming, followed by more.

I saw the kids starting to run and then I realized why. A dimensional shambler had manifested on the playground. It had picked up one of the Marsh girls, Emily I think, and was draining her blood. You could tell because even though it was kinda invisible her blood was flowing through what looked like air as she dangled ten feet up. Everyone else was screaming and running, but a dimensional shambler was not as scary as my dad when he was really angry.

My dad had gotten me this book for Candlemas last year, *My First Unaussprechlichen Kulten*. The pictures were really disturbing and gave me nightmares, and my father was disappointed in me again, but I remembered some of the spells from it.

The dimensional shambler dropped the now-desiccated remains of Emily Marsh and began lumbering toward a group of second graders pushing their way back into the school. I ran and jumped in front of it. Making strange gestures in the air, I said the Zoan Chant. The dimensional shambler shrieked, and vanished. The second graders kept screaming and it took Mr. Alhazred, the principal, ten full minutes to restore order.

"Mr. Whateley, you are responsible for this?" he said, looking down his nose at me.

"No sir. A dimensional shambler manifested in an invisible form on the playground. I banished it, sir."

"Be that as it may, Mr. Whateley, we still have to call your parents."

I waited patiently for an hour on the bench outside Mr. Alhazred's office for my mother to show up. The door finally opened and my father strode in.

I knew I was in the deepest trouble I had ever been in. My dad didn't even look at me. He just walked straight into Mr. Alhazred's office and shut the door. I could hear their voices through the door, low and dangerous. Finally, my dad emerged and, without looking at me, said, "C'mon."

We got in the car and I waited for him to start yelling at me and threatening me with death, sacrifice, or being grounded. Instead, he said quietly, "Mr. Alhazred sez there was a dimensional shambler on the playground and you got ridda it."

"Yes, sir." Not knowing his mood, I dared not say any more than that.

"How'n ya do that?"

"I did a Zoan Chant like in the book you got me."

Dad's head snapped to look at me closely, as if he were seeing me for the first time. "Zoan Chant canna banish nothin'!"

"No, sir. But dimensional shamblers don't just show up. So I figured this one was sent by someone. And a Zoan Chant would send the malevolent beast back to the caster that summoned it."

He smiled at that. "Yeah! A Zoan Chant would send that beast straight on to the one what called it! Whoever sent the fearsome brute afta the young'uns would be drained dry as a matchstick. How'd ya think to do that, lad?"

"Well . . . it was in the book you gave me for Candlemas last year. And I've watched you do the Zoan Chant sometimes, like when you figured out Dr. Muñoz was trying to curse you, and you made him rapidly decompose. So I figured somebody was trying to kill kids with the dimensional shambler and if I sent it back to the one who summoned it, it would drain him and maybe kill his family."

My father slammed on the brakes, then pulled to the side of the road and gave me the biggest hug he's ever given me. "My son is a Whateley after all! I'd given up hope on ya, boy! But you can cast spells and get terrible revenge on folks what try'n harm ya! You're like your old man, after all! This calls for celebration. We gotta eat dinner out!"

"Will we go home and get mom and Fhtagn?" I asked.

"Nope. Yer mother has locked herself in her room agin, bangin' her head on the floor. Tonight is just about the Whateley wizards, right?"

And he took me out to eat at the Crab Shack. He let me get anything I wanted off the grown-up menu. When we got home, he told my mother what I had done and she smiled at me in between screams.

Even Fhtagn was proud of me. "Tekeli-li a wizard, just like daddy!" and hugged me with all his pseudopods. "Tekeli-li the best big brother ever!"

That night, when I went to bed, I didn't mind having a little brother, or an angry father. Because I knew that, like them, I was a Whateley, and I had power. I was going to start tomorrow by bringing little C'thulhu back from the dead. And someday, when I was big, I was going to make them all pay. Fifth grade was going to be great!

Friday Night at Brazee's

By Mike Resnick

WE MEET AT Johnny Brazee's house every Friday for poker: me, Mac (I think his real name is MacTavish, but everyone calls him Mac), Willie the Shyster (who's a legitimate lawyer, but it's what we call him), and Alec Copperberg (who changed his name from Silverberg after he took a beating in the futures market).

We'd been meeting and playing for about half a dozen years, the five of us. We used to change venues every week, until Johnny bought a house with a paneled den a couple of years ago, and now we all show up there every Friday at eight in the p.m. and don't break up until after midnight.

Except that on the night in question the clock hits eight, or it would if it was that kind of clock, and we realize that Alec isn't there. He hadn't called anyone, and no one could ever remember him being late before, so we figured he'd blown a tire or got stuck in traffic, and we decided what the hell, the world wouldn't come to an end if we waited fifteen or twenty minutes for him to show up, especially after Willie suggested that we could play the average hand in five minutes, and we could fine him an ante for every hand he made us miss.

Well, eight-fifteen rolls around, and so does eight-thirty, and Mac says that we could either play poker with just four of us, or he could turn on Johnny's TV and we could all watch re-runs of *Gilligan's Island*, and by an instant and unanimous voice vote—well, scream vote, actually—we decide to start dealing the cards.

The game was going pretty well, which is to say I was thirty bucks ahead, when I noticed an odor coming from the kitchen. I pulled out my handkerchief, realized it was the one with the image of Bettie Page on it, put it away, and grabbed a Kleenex instead.

I noticed that Mac and Willie were also holding handkerchiefs to their noses, and suddenly we all turned to Johnny Brazee.

"I think you have a dead skunk in your kitchen," said Mac.

"Or at least a lovelorn one," added Willie. "Though it's hard to imagine that lady skunks find *that* attractive."

"I've got nothing in my kitchen except my stove and my fridge and . . ." Johnny stopped to think. "And my sink."

"I hate to correct my honorable host," said the Shyster in his best courtroom manner, "but inanimate objects do not smell like that."

"Unless they were animate prior to losing a battle with a Mack truck ten hours ago," added Mac.

Johnny sniffed the air a couple of times and frowned. "Who would imagine that a piece of Florida Flossie's cheesecake could smell that bad?"

"Not me," I said.

"And it certainly can't walk!" added Willie, staring at the kitchen door.

We all turned and looked, and there was something kind of large, and sort of green, and oozing slime over a few dozen tentacles, each of which could choke a horse or perhaps strangle him, and it didn't smell any better as it left the kitchen and began kind of sliding toward us.

"I am Cthulhu!" it intoned.

"I'm Mac, and he's Willie, and"—Mac pointed to me—"he's Milton, and he's"—he tripled his volume—"our host Johnny Brazee."

"Where is he?" demanded Cthulhu.

"Right there," we all said, pointing to Johnny.

"No, you fools!" Suddenly his voice became even more ominous. "I have come for Alec Copperberg, he who possessed the knowledge and the foolishness to invoke the powers of Yog-Sothoth to reverse his losses in the commodities market."

"You just missed him," said Willie in his best courtroom manner. "He was heading north when last we saw him. You can still catch up with him if you hurry. I don't think he has more than a five-minute start on you."

"Silence, fool!" growled Cthulhu. "Lie to me once more and I will defenestrate you. I guarantee you will not enjoy it."

"Defenestrate?" repeated Willie, pulling out his tablet. "Can you spell that, please?"

Cthulhu stared at him coldly. "Do I look like I majored in spelling?"

"I think maybe we'll both be a lot happier if I don't tell you what you look like," said Willie uneasily.

"All right," said Cthulhu. "Where is Alec Copperberg?"

"We don't know," said Johnny.

"Do not lie to me, mortal!" growled Cthulhu. "There are five chairs at the table, and I only see four of you."

"I know," said Johnny.

"What does this mean?" demanded Cthulhu.

"It means that your eyes, all eight or ten of them, are working," said Johnny. "There are only four of us here. Alec has obviously been delayed."

"Let me consider . . ." said Cthulhu, lowering what passed for its massive head in thought. Finally it looked up. "If I destroy the house and all in it, he will take one look and go the other way. Therefore I will stay here and wait for him." He glared at each of us in turn. "Unless there are any objections?"

"I left all my objections in my other suit," said Mac.

"I only object when my clients pay me to," added Willie.

It turned to me. "And you—the ugly one?"

"I object to being the ugly one," I said. "On the other hand, I got no objection at all with you waiting for Alec to show up."

"Then it is settled," said Cthulhu.

"What the hell," said Johnny. "As long as you're here, you might as well grab a chair and sit in on a few hands until Alec gets here."

The creature seemed to consider the suggestion for a moment, then shrugged, which caused some noxious little critters and foul-smelling slime to fly off its body.

"Why not?" it said at last, oozing most of itself onto the empty chair.

"You got money?" said Mac. "It costs money to play."

"You want dollars, pounds, francs, lira, marks, shillings, yen, or rubles?" asked Cthulhu.

"You carry all that with you?" I asked, surprised.

"I started out this morning just with lira," answered the monster. It sighed heavily. "It's been a long day, even for me."

"Two dollars to ante," said Mac.

"Two dollars to Auntie Who, and for what?" asked Cthulhu, looking around.

"Two dollars to play each hand," answered Mac.

Cthulhu reached into what looked like a body cavity along its left side and withdrew a pair of slime-covered dollar bills.

"Okay," continued Mac, trying not to inhale through his nose. "I think we'll start with draw."

"Pen or pencil?" asked Cthulhu.

"Don't understand me so fast," replied Mac. "The name of the game is draw poker." He spent about three minutes laying out the rules, then waited for the rest of us to ante up and dealt out five hands.

"Jacks or better to open," said Johnny.

"Are aces better than jacks?" asked Cthulhu, looking at its cards.

"I'm out," said Mac.

"Me too," said Johnny.

"That makes three of us," said Willie.

I looked at my hand again: a pair of sixes, a pair of nines, and a jack.

"I'll open for ten bucks," I said.

"Now you match it, raise it, or drop out," explained Mac.

"I don't have any bucks," replied Cthulhu. "What country are they the currency of?"

"It's another name for dollars," said Mac.

"Okay," said Cthulhu, tossing in a ten-spot. "Now what?"

"Now you keep as many cards as you want, hand the rest to the dealer face-down, and he'll give you replacement cards."

Cthulhu stared at its hand, and turned in three cards. Johnny immediately gave it three more.

"And you?" said Johnny, turning to me.

"One card," I said, handing in my jack.

He dealt me a single card. I picked it up with my two pair, fanned the hand slowly until I could peek at the new card—and it was a nine.

"Up to you," said Mac, looking at me.

"I'll bid twenty," I said.

Cthulhu matched my double-sawbuck with one of its own.

"Let's see what you've got," I said.

It showed us three aces, plus a queen and a seven.

"Gotcha beat," I said, laying out my full house and grabbing the pot.

"Ready for another?" asked Mac.

"Definitely," responded Cthulhu. "This is fascinating!"

It lost again, but then it won two in a row, and finally we were able to tell where its mouth was, because its smile displayed four rows of ugly green teeth.

"I *like* this game!" enthused Cthulhu. "The only problem is that it's over so fast."

"You want something slower, something that'll lengthen the tension?" asked Mac.

"Tension is what makes the world go round," answered Cthulhu. "Well, tension and bloodlust and torture and pillage and—"

"Let me explain seven-card stud to you," said Mac, who like the rest of us didn't really want to hear Cthulhu's want list of things that made its world go round.

The explanation took him a couple of minutes, and then I dealt, and we all looked at our two down cards, and bet on the first face card, and then each of the next three. I dealt the final down card, looked at my hand, and Willie and Cthulhu had me beat on the table, so I folded.

Willie stared at his hand for a long moment, and then shoved a ten and a five into the pot.

Cthulhu seemed to be concentrating on its own hand when Willie yelled "Cut that out!"

"Cut what out?" asked Johnny, puzzled.

"He's peeking into my hand!" snarled Willie.

"What are you talking about?" I said. "He's sitting across the goddamned table from you."

Willie made a quick grabbing motion. "What about *this*?" he demanded.

We all looked at the mildly spherical object he held in his hand.

"What is it?" asked Johnny.

"Just follow the muscle or nerve or whatever the hell it is," growled Willie. "You'll figure it out."

There *was* something attached to the object, and it circled the table until it stopped at Cthulhu's chair and slid into an opening in its head.

"It's his eye!" exclaimed Mac.

Willie glared at the creature. "Didn't anyone ever tell you that it's immoral to cheat?"

"Certainly not," answered Cthulhu. "Otherwise I would have cheated from the start."

"If you want to play with us, you won't cheat again."

"Never?" asked Cthulhu.

"Never," said Willie. "I want your promise on that."

Cthulhu raised an appendage. "Honor bright and greenie to the sky." It shoved a twenty into the pot. "Raise you five."

"I'll see you," said Willie, pushing another five into the pot. "What have you got?"

"Three Nyarlathoteps."

"Those are kings," said Mac.

"They are far greater than kings," replied Cthulhu.

"In poker, Nyarlathoteps are kings," said Willie.

Now that it had been explained in terms Cthulhu understood, it nodded its head in agreement. "And what have you got?"

"A queen-high straight," answered Willie.

"That's an Azathoth-high straight," Cthulhu corrected him.

"Either way, it beats three of a kind," said Willie pugnaciously.

I nodded my agreement. "Those are the rules," I told Cthulhu.

"Fair enough," said Cthulhu. "Though 'fair' is not usually in my lexicon." It paused, kind of frowning, or at least folding the skin about four or five of its eyes. "Is anyone getting thirsty?"

"We haven't even been playing for half an hour yet," said Johnny.

"So sue me," said Cthulhu. "I'm an Elder God. We get thirsty a little sooner than most."

"So what'll it be?" asked Johnny, getting to his feet and heading off to the kitchen. "Beer, or beer?"

Everyone chuckled except Cthulhu. "Beer, please," it said. Then it looked around the table. "Isn't anyone joining me?"

"I'll have some beer," agreed Mac.

"What about you?" it asked me.

"I've had enough beer already," I answered.

"Then perhaps you'd like *my* favorite drink," said Cthulhu, reaching into some other dimension and withdrawing an ornate silver goblet filled with some kind of liquid with a layer of green slime on top of it. It handed it to me, and I took a sip.

"Well?" asked Cthulhu.

"Kind of . . . I dunno," I said. "Strong. And maybe a bit salty. And . . . I don't know . . . something else. What do you call this stuff?"

"Shoggoth blood, with just a pinch of the Midnight Worm of Ikaalinen." It lowered its voice confidentially. "It's the Midnight Worm that does it."

It lifted its beer bottle, poured the entire contents into an orifice that was roughly in the center of its face, then emitted a satisfied purr.

"May I have another, please?"

"Sure thing," said Johnny, popping into the kitchen and coming back with another bottle.

"You like?" asked Mac, indicating the beer bottle after Cthulhu had taken about five seconds to drain it.

"Wonderful stuff!" exclaimed Cthulhu. "This has been a truly delightful evening. A great new game, the excitement of gambling, the noxious taste of an alcoholic beverage. By Azathoth's blaspheming whiskers, I even almost like you guys. I haven't enjoyed myself so much in 14,303 years, give or take a month."

"And what did you enjoy so much back then?" asked Mac before we could shut him up.

"It would take eighty-three hours and sixteen minutes to relate it to you, since that is how long Nuada of the Silver Hand survived." Cthulhu paused, smiling at the pleasant memory. "Of course, now he is known as Nuada of the Crooked Toe, since that is all that is left of him." It shook its head. "But in truth, this shapes up to be an even more enjoyable experience, though of lesser duration."

Just then the front door opened, and in walked Alec Copperberg.

"Hi, guys," he said. "Sorry I'm late, but someone trashed my car and my apartment, and—"

"*Alec Copperberg*," intoned Cthulhu, getting to its feet—well, to most of them, anyway, "*prepare to meet your fate!*"

"Oh, shit!" muttered Alec. "I'm outta here." He turned and raced out the door. "South America, here I come!"

"It could take me a few hours to catch him," said Cthulhu, rising and walking to the door. "But keep my chair warm. I'll be back as soon as I send what little remains of him to the forbidden city of R'lyeh."

"Well, you do what you have to do," said Johnny. "But some of us have to get up for work in the morning, so the game breaks up around midnight and they all go home for another week."

"You won't stay?" said Cthulhu, with a tremor in its voice. "Even if I ask you politely?"

"We can't," said Willie. "I've got to be in court at eight o'clock tomorrow morning."

"And my office opens at nine," I added.

"And I was enjoying myself for the first time in more than ten millennia," said Cthulhu bitterly.

"There's an alternative," said Willie, who was always the quickest on his mental feet.

"Oh?" said Cthulhu hopefully.

"I think it's safe to say that Alec's never coming back," continued Willie. "That means we've got a permanently empty place at the table. Let some other nameless fiend from the pits of hell—how'd you put it—defenestrate him and pull up a chair."

"You mean it?" said Cthulhu, its voice as innocent and hopeful as a child's.

"Why would I lie to an Elder God?" said Willie. "Just please bring a strong deodorant next time, and go easy on the slime. Johnny's gonna have to have the carpet cleaned."

"Bring me another beer!" bellowed Cthulhu happily as it sat back down at the table. "Now whose deal was it?"

And that is how our Friday night poker club got its newest member.

To Whatever

By Shaenon K. Garrity

TO WHATEVER lives in the walls—

Please stop taking my half & half.

Let's get this out of the way: I know you're there. Don't think I'm unaware of the scrabbling sounds, the walls creaking from your bulk, the way my razor in the morning is never exactly where I left it the night before. Richard always said it was the building settling—as if a building, however old, could take apples out of the fruit crisper—but he was as wrong about that as he was about a lot of things beyond the scope of this note. And since he moved out I feel you've gotten bolder.

I'm not trying to tell you what to do. About living in the walls, I mean. I don't own the building. But when I come into this kitchen to pour my morning cup of Ethiopian roast and the carton of half & half in the fridge is empty—well, that ruins my whole day. It's no good with milk. I need half & half.

Who returns an empty carton to the fridge? Do you know that's rude? That's very rude in our society.

Anyway, that's all. And I'd feel better if you stopped messing with my razor.

The tenant in 3B

To whatever—

You didn't have to do that. Really, I just wanted to not be left with an empty carton when I need some half & half in the morning. But this morning I come down and in my fridge is a brand-new carton. So thanks for that.

Tell you what. You need something, my fridge is open to you. I'm guessing you get hungry. You sound pretty big. My only demand is that you not leave me with empties. I've got my needs too, you know? And, you know, maybe you can do a little shopping once in a while. Or whatever it is you do.

Ethan

To the tenant in the walls—

I'm so sorry about Tuesday. When I called the landlord about a funky smell in the apartment, I honestly thought it was the sink trap backing up again. It never occurred to me that it might be you.

You've been coming around more at night, haven't you? Are you here during the day while I'm at work? What do you do? Never mind, I know you won't answer. You never answer when I talk to the darkened living room, even when I can see the shadow in the corner that isn't shaped like my chair. I just find things in the morning: polished stones and iron tools (sculptures? utensils? is there a use for the knobs, the spikes?) on the coffee table, fresh apples in the crisper.

And on Tuesday the super found clumps of hair and scales under the sink. I told him it was a friend's dog. He gave me the no-pets lecture but I don't think he believed me. He left in a hurry.

I hope I haven't compromised your safety. You must be worried about the same thing, because every night since Tuesday has been quiet here. I understand. Probably you have other apartments. Other buildings? Or is this your only home?

No, forget the questions. I just wanted to let you know, if you happen to pass through and find this note, that the super has not been back and I will not call the landlord again. I have, however, purchased family-size bottles of several shampoos and conditioners which you will find in the closet outside the bathroom along with the towels, and if I happen to hear the shower running in the middle of the night I will not get up to investigate.

I'm sorry, but the smell was starting to cling.

Sorry again,

Ethan

To wall guy—

You may have noticed that today I rearranged the living room. The loveseat is now behind the sofa. The small lamp table is next to the loveseat, with just enough room for a bowl of apples, a gallon of milk, and several beers.

The Golden Globes are tomorrow evening. I was going to watch them with someone but there was a cancellation. Never mind the details. So I will be watching alone, on the sofa, with my own beers. If anyone sits behind me I won't turn around.

The red-carpet coverage starts at seven.

Ethan

Hey there—

"Amazing Race" again tonight? You bring the beers. Or whatever it is you bring—you know, in the green bottles. The salty undertaste takes getting used to, but it's got to be at least 7.0, so no complaints. I'll be home at the usual hour unless something comes up at the library, but I don't expect any trouble once the senior book club meeting clears out.

I'll be ordering a pizza. Don't panic when the doorbell rings. Last week when the Thai delivery arrived there was a sudden stench like a skunk exploding in the kitchen, and afterward I found symbols scrawled in damp charcoal all over the walls. The *param pak* and pineapple fried rice I left on the lamp table disappeared while my back was turned, though, so presumably you don't have anything against Thai. You just get shy around people, huh?

Anyway, anchovies on your half. I know how you like it.

Be not quite seeing you,

Ethan

Hi—

Just a heads-up: tomorrow I'm getting drinks with the new guy in 4C. No high hopes, just being a friendly neighbor. His name's Willem, so you know. Grad student in physics or something like that. Cute accent. I helped him carry boxes of books up the stairs, and you know how I like a fellow reader.

So, basically, I have to take a rain check on Parcheesi night. Maybe Thursday?

Later,
Ethan

hey—

sorry fr coming in late. early. whatev. hope didnt wake u up. leftovrr risotto in frigde. plz clean up slime trail in case company.

good to get out of apt. sometimes right? funnnn!

E

Hey roomie—

Willem says he's been having vivid nightmares about a five-dimensional city where cats with clown faces pursue him through Klein-bottle alleys, nipping at his legs. He showed me the little bite marks all over his calves. I only bring it up because it sounds suspiciously like those places that sometimes appear during the commercials when we're watching TV. You remember last week when I had Hulu on, and it switched away in the middle of a Geico ad? Five-dimensional cat-man city. I assumed that was you changing the channel. It was, wasn't it?

Well, I'm cool with having it on our TV, but the dreams are freaking Willem out. I don't know how it is where you're from, but around here we don't change the channel in people's heads.

Oh, and have you seen that crystal spiral you gave me a while back? The blue one. It's perfect for unclogging the washing machine downstairs.

Your roomie,
Ethan

Roomie—

Look, I apologized for missing dinner. I didn't know you were making spaghetti and trapezoidal prisms—I'm not very good at reading those runes that only appear in the bathroom mirror, you know. They're backwards, and also runes.

Yes, all right, I did promise to be home for dinner, and then I didn't, and that's on me. I'm sorry. I'll make it up to you.

But it's unfair of you to take it out on Willem. Last night he woke up screaming and babbling about the city again. I tried telling him to ignore the man-face cats and get to that green mandala neighborhood that's always hovering over the iron bridge, because it looks like it has nice bars, but he just stared at me. Now he's in a mood and I don't think he's even noticed the mark branded on his back yet. There'll be hell to pay when he sees that.

It's immature of you, is all. He doesn't need this. He's got to defend his thesis next month. And his car broke down. He's under a lot of pressure, is what I'm saying, without getting teleported into bad neighborhoods.

Ethan

Excuse me—

It's none of your business how I know what Willem screams in the dead of night. That's not the point.

It's not.

Your roommate

Milk

Cereal (Life or Grape-Nuts, no sugary stuff and no gray flakes in a pouch)

Half & half

Bananas

Frozen peas/baby lima beans

Beer

Gelatinous ovoid things

I'll be out for a couple of days, and you never clean so the least you can do is pick up some groceries while I'm gone.

Hi—

DO NOT PANIC.

Slight problem you may need be aware of. Now that the medication is keeping Willem's night terrors manageable and we found a hairdresser who is a wizard at covering the recent white streak in his hair, he's had space to think. Now he's asking questions. The scientific mind, I guess. He keeps demanding to know how I knew about the mandala and the bridge. I told him I saw them on TV, which is true, but he isn't satisfied.

He's been poking around the building, drilling into walls. I don't know how long he's been at this. Possibly longer than I thought.

Again, DO NOT PANIC. DO NOT RELEASE THE FACE CATS OR SEND HIS MIND TO THE RED ALLEY. That is not cool, and anyway it'll just raise his curiosity even more. I'll try to get him focused on something else. The medication helps with that, and once the bites heal he won't be reminded so often.

I'll be home tonight. You want Thai? Let's order Thai and talk. Or I'll talk, and you'll hover in my blind spot, watching, your eyes reflecting like torches off those odd green bottles. Just like old times.

DON'T PANIC—

Ethan

Oops—

He found the brand on his back. It's been spreading. Gotta smooth this over. Not coming home tonight.

Dear Roomie—

I know this isn't going to be your favorite idea, but I've got to come out and say it. Would it be so bad if you showed yourself? Or at least let the neighbors sort of know you exist? What would the actual fallout be?

It's just that Willem thinks he's going insane, especially since you left whatever it was you left behind the toilet in his bathroom, and I feel terrible about it. I hate the lying and the sneaking around. He's a great guy if you give him a chance. He can be overbearing, I guess, but that's part of his charm. And, again, he's already stressed out from his thesis.

I'm not saying we should all have dinner together. Or maybe I am saying that. I don't know. I want to make this work, for all three of us, and the current status quo is not healthy. The dishonesty is getting toxic, you know?

Please get back to me. Lately your runes have been cryptic.

Your friend (?),

Ethan

Dear Roomie—

I've made a terrible mistake.

Let me back up.

No, never mind. I'm no good at long explanations. I may as well start with this morning after Willem ran out the door, late for a semiotics class. It always seemed a little weird that he took so many humanities courses for a physics student, Gnosticism and linguistic anthropology and stuff about Joseph Campbell. But, you know, to each his own.

I thought it made him multi-dimensional.

After he left I noticed he'd left his laptop behind, which he never did, and it was on, which it never was. So I went to turn it off, definitely not trying to invade his privacy or anything like that, you know me, just doing a favor. And that was how I saw his thesis.

He chose this building over two years ago, turns out. It's mentioned in some 16th-century manuscripts and identified on old maps, and there was a poem by a minor Romantic who died of madness and consumption—"*Étude de la Désolation*," I think was the title—but maybe you already know all that. It's probably old news in the Elder City St'betnet.

Anyway, it looks like Willem's been studying this for a while. Studying our home. I can't say I understood his thesis paper—it mashes the quantum gravity research I thought was his main field with a bunch of alternate-universe models, Egyptian-Berber mythology, syntactic theory, complicated math, and stuff I think he got out of old sci-fi paperbacks, to be honest. The best I could make out was that he discovered some kind of gate and came here to study it. He was expecting the noises and smells and the dreams. He just wasn't as prepared for them as he thought he'd be.

He wrote about you.

I should wrap this up. There's only one page left in our "We've Got a Latte to Do Today!" magnetic refrigerator notepad.

So. I told him I read his thesis. It turned into a scene. I'm embarrassed to say it escalated to me going full-on Oscar Moment and demanding to know if our entire relationship was just part of his research.

He said, "Once I realized you'd been touched by They Who Walk Between, what else could I do? The department has been demanding hard evidence."

He said, "You understand. I'll be defending my thesis in less than a month."

And that's that.

I'll get a new notepad tomorrow.

Your trusting idiot,
Ethan

Dear Whoever,
Did you always suspect there was something up with him? Did you catch him skulking around collecting his precious data?
Or did you just not like him?
I liked him.
I passed him in the lobby this morning. He didn't say hello, but he looked fine. Like he was fresh off a good night's sleep and a plate of French toast.
I'm surprised you didn't send him to the city. I know you promised not to do that anymore, but this whole situation has got to have you on edge. Good work resisting the temptation. It would have been petty.
But I have to admit, I was tempted to ask.
Your roommate,
Ethan

Dear Whoever,
Please stop by tonight. I haven't seen you in days—okay, I've never *seen*-seen you, but you know what I mean—and we need to talk. Willem's been avoiding me in the halls. That's fine with me, but I get the impression he's up to something. Probably just me being paranoid. It's just me being paranoid, right?
What will we do if he publishes this thesis?
Will you have to go?
Leave me some kind of message. Burn runes into the kitchen floor or scrawl on the walls in bile. I don't know what to do.
Yours,
Ethan

Dear Whoever,
Where are you?
Yours,
Ethan

Dear Ethan—
As I seem lately blocked from your cellular-phone and social-

media accounts, perhaps the antique practice of the note slipped under the door will prove a more efficacious means of contact. I confess, in honesty, to feel peculiarly comfortable expressing myself in the epistolary mode, to the point that I quite prefer it to common speech. Possibly my queer and curious course of obscure study, combined with my extended stay at this legend-haunted pile known to more mundane thinkers as Perelman Apartments, has intensified this natural tendency to the point of eccentricity. This, I leave you to judge.

My purpose in contacting you is not, as you may fear or hope, to reopen our prior relationship. I think that well behind us. I must instead address your disturbing reaction to your discovery—and our subsequent less-than-fruitful discussion—of my thesis paper. To be brief—"Be brief, Willem!" I hear you, and any nameless reader who may by chance come across this correspondence in some future tome of scholarly letters of note, beg—you should seek help of a psychiatric nature.

Whether you believe it, my feelings toward you remain those of friendship—of friendly concern—of avuncular well-wishing—of regard. Knowing firsthand the grotesque magnetic pull of this place and its more squamous inhabitants, I fear for your psyche. Over the course of mere weeks I began to feel these uncanny effects, as well you know—and you, Ethan, have resided far longer than I. Nor is your mind as strong as mine, as honed by long study in the hard sciences to withstand affronts to Euclidean logic and to comprehend even the sublime. More than comprehend, but capture, dissect, and expose it to the disinfecting light of science! . . . I digress.

There is no question in my mind that you have been in communion with one of They Who Walk Between. How deep this communion, and how long it has been allowed to continue unabated, I do not know. But from my research I know the power of the Walkers and the clutching effect the presence of such entities may have on the ordinary, unschooled human brain. I believe, in short, that you are not yourself, that you have developed an abnormal fascination—an attachment to something uncanny, something beyond your understanding.

You are in danger, Ethan. The *particular* attachment to which I refer may not be an issue at present, but if you persist in inhabiting this forsaken temple to the unearthly, allowing its unreal geometry to remold the very shape of your mind, you will only fall further from the normal capacity for human relationships. I tell you this only as a friend.

Leave this place. Find a therapist.
Best wishes,
Willem

Willem—
Christ, you're an asshole.
—Ethan

Dear Ethan—
Your reaction only proves my suspicions correct. What I wrote, I wrote strictly out of respect for our former relationship and what lingering tender concern I might harbor toward your well-being. That you chose to respond so irrationally tells me I can do no more, not that I had any intention of continuing our correspondence.

Just as well. My thesis is almost complete; I present on Friday. And, as intimated in my previous missive, the particular entity that has of late polluted your spirit and your apartment is no longer, for you, an issue. Feel free to do as you please.

Farewell,
Willem
P.S. I learned some weeks ago, with the aid of the dread grimoire *Tore von Schatten,* my copy of which was reportedly unearthed at Salem, how to block the dream-paths of the Elder City. The method has quite cleared my mind and guarded my sleep. I may be willing to loan you photocopies if you find yourself troubled by similar afflictions from another of They Who Walk—as you doubtless will be if you stay here—but only if you apologize first.

WILLEM
WHERE THE HELL IS HE YOU BASTARD
ANSWER YOUR DAMN PHONE

WILLEM—
I AM NOT SHITTING AROUND HERE.

Willem—
Please get back to me. I'm begging you.
You have him. I know you have him. Whatever you're planning to

do with him, don't. He's so shy. He just wants to be left alone, watch some TV, have his coffee in the morning the way he likes it. Half & half, no sugar, stirred with a wand of yellow bone. Little things.

Tell me what you want in return. Anything. Just talk to me.

Promise you won't hurt him.

Ethan

Dear Mr. Lanigan,

Sorry to bother you, but for once I'm not writing about the missing recycling bin or fixing the sconces in the lobby.

There seems to have been a break-in or something at 4C. I only glanced in, but it's a real mess: books and papers everywhere, furniture overturned, burn marks. No idea how much was stolen. Maybe it was teenagers messing around. We get goth kids trying to talk their way into the building sometimes. Apparently they think this is some kind of mystical site? I don't know anything about that stuff, I'm just a librarian.

One weird thing: there's a big cage or crate in the apartment. From my glimpse of the thing it looked like it was broken open and empty. I certainly hope the tenant in 4C wasn't keeping some kind of big dog in there. I'm very aware of the building's no-pets policy. I read all your notes about those cats people keep spotting.

Anyway, the tenant hasn't been back—I think his name was Willem, we talked a few times—so please contact the police. Or whatever the procedure is for this situation. As a resident, I'm concerned for my safety.

Your loyal tenant,

Ethan (in 3B)

Dear You,

Let's hope this teaches both of us the importance of communication. I should have been more open about Willem and the red flags he was sending up, yes. And you really needed to be clearer about a lot of things. Don't sulk (I can picture your spines rising as you read this), you know it's true.

If you'd let me know how to open the gates to the Elder City and walk the paths Between, just the basics for emergency situations, I could have gotten you away from that asshole so much sooner. For

God's sake, he almost managed to exhibit you to his stupid thesis committee. He almost had proof.

Good thing for both of us, not to mention the structure of reality, that he's such a blowhard. He may think his skin-bound, written-in-blood edition of *Tore von Schatten* is oh so special, and okay, it's probably a very impressive piece of incunabula. But it's hardly the only copy. I tracked down a grimy 1970s paperback translation through interlibrary loan and learned exactly the same damn incantations he did, and then some.

Thanks to the illustrations, I realized the thing I've been using as a salad tong is in fact the Key of Tssil, which helped open a lot of paths. Thanks for giving me that. You really could have let me know what it was for, though. This is exactly what I'm talking about.

Anyway, I didn't leave Willem in the Red Alley. That seemed excessive. I put him in that tower with the orbs. I figure by the time we let him out, he won't be in any state to come off as a reliable witness.

Trust me, no one on the earthly plane is ever going to find his thesis.

You'll notice I've rearranged the living room again. The loveseat is front and center, just enough room for two. I'm making spaghetti, and there's a bottle of pinot noir breathing on the coffee table.

Sit down. We'll see what's on TV.

Yours,

Ethan

The Doom that Came to Providence

By Brian Trent

"LOOK HERE, Howard," the man in the pinstripe suit spoke through wreaths of smoke. "Do you mind if I call you Howie? I like that better. Good. Look Howie, I don't know if you're a prophet or if you just got lucky. But I knew I had to find you."

The tall, unnervingly pale, cadaverous man blinked. "How *did* you find me?"

"You can find anyone in Providence. Especially now, since most of the people were washed away. The population is low enough that a blind census taker could finish his headcount by dinnertime and still have time to screw his wife. You married, Howie?"

The tall, pale man seemed to grow a shade grayer, offended by the metaphor and the question. "No," he said.

"Just as well. So where were we?" The man in the suit—Luigi Argenta, known as "Loud Lou" or "Large Lou" or even "Loud and Large Lou" to friends and enemies alike, took another puff of his cigar. "So I had my boys out in boats, paddling up and down the flooded streets, searching for you. Started worrying that maybe you had been killed when that . . . um . . . that big monster rose up from the ocean. What was it called?"

"Great Cthulhu."

The man's nostrils flared. "Right, Cthulhu. Are you calling him great because you think he is, or because that's part of his name? I knew this dame once, her name was Daisy. *She* was pretty great."

The cadaverous man—Howard Phillips Lovecraft, now known as Howie to a man who might be friend or enemy—patted his sweaty forehead with a handkerchief. "*I* certainly don't think that monster is great! So many have died!"

"Yeah, I guess that's true. If you were a disciple of this Cthulhu fella, worshipping and what not, you'd be rolling in dough, am I right? You wouldn't look . . ." He squinted at his guest. "Like you look. No offense, Howie, but you look like the next man to be called in the Grim Reaper's waiting room." He slapped his fat tummy. His goons, all in handsome suits and narrow-brimmed fedoras worn slightly askew, chuckled.

Lovecraft blinked a long, slow, languid blink. "Why did you kidnap me?"

"I'm coming to that. Though I'd rather you admitted it was a rescue, see? You were stranded on the roof of that hideous mansion on Angell Street when my boys found you."

"That's my childhood home. I wanted to die there."

"I brought you here to make you rich, see?"

Lovecraft had known fear throughout his life. Like a hydra of many forms, fear had been the relentless tormentor. Fear of the cold, of the sea, of sex, of loud sounds and bright colors, of tight spaces and immense crowds. He'd known only two respites from these crippling phobias: the stories he occasionally sold to magazines, and the comforting sanctuary offered by his childhood home.

Now, he realized that his experience with fear had been the mildest of prologues. For days after the oceans rose and the ships on Providence's coast were sent smashing into the seaside warehouses, Lovecraft had been plunged into a raw, animal panic. He couldn't think. Could barely breathe. Even the rooms of his house seemed constricting, and so he had climbed onto the shingled rooftop, gasping for air, as the streets below became watery canals and people screamed and monsters flew overhead. Flames rising from the horizon, howling beasts scampering along the narrow alleyways, mountains that seemed to move in the distance, and a dewy, omnipresent fog that cloyed to the skin and never went away.

The arrival of these scary men in their boats, his abduction into their keeping and into this rotting old hotel, merely added another dimension to his abject horror.

"It's all just as you predicted!" Luigi Argenta was saying. "You were right about everything! Fucking incredible. I try not to read, you know, but two years ago we were shaking down this pharmacy and it was taking a while, so I picked up a magazine from the racks. Started reading. Didn't mean to." He shrugged in a somewhat apologetic fashion. "The story was a chiller about these old, forgotten monsters who were sleeping, but who one day would wake up. *You* were the author of that story!" He pointed, delighted.

Lovecraft made no expression.

"Only that was in '33, two years before all this started! So last month, when everything went to hell, I called my boys in and I said . . . Jimmy, what did I say?"

The fleshy hulk named Jimmy nodded. "You said, 'This Lovecraft guy is a goddam prophet.'"

The mobster slapped the desk. "That's *exactly* what I said! Jimmy's got an elephant memory! I said, 'This Lovecraft guy is a goddam prophet.' And a prophet can turn a profit, see?"

"The Old Ones are here to destroy us and drive us mad," Lovecraft said in a hollow, broken voice. "You can't make a profit off that."

"Everyone in power has needs. Man or woman, human or . . . thing. And where there's needs, there's a potential market."

"But . . ."

"Let's talk about this Cthulhu guy. What does he want?"

"How should I know?" the writer cried.

"You wrote it."

"Cthulhu wants . . . nothing. Everything."

Luigi looked at Jimmy. "This is going to be tougher than getting Nick to spill where his wife hid those jewels. Let me try this: How many factions are there? I'll help you out: One of them is Cthulhu." His cigar was burnt down to a nub and he flicked it away, plucking a fresh one from his suit jacket and placing it like a withered sausage on the desk. "Who else?"

"Well, there's Yog-Sothoth. And Nyarlathotep."

"Sounds like an A-rab."

"He's the messenger for Azathoth, the blind idiot god gibbering at the center of all creation."

"Excellent!"

Lovecraft scowled. "It isn't excellent. If Azathoth were to awaken, if the tuneless flutes were to cease . . ."

The mobster held up three fingers. "Keep going. I'm thinking there are more factions, each one opposed to the other."

"Well, there's the Mi-Go. And the Old Ones. And the shoggoths. And the Great Race of Yith . . ."

Luigi ticked off more fingers. He was grinning.

Lovecraft's mouth felt dry, and it was a mark of his exhaustion that in this den of mobsters, in this city of monsters, all he wanted to do now was curl up into a ball and sleep. "There's others, but those are the chief factions, as you put it."

"Terrific stuff, Howie. We couldn't manipulate the market if there's only one slimy son-of-a-bitch in charge. But this is great!"

Lovecraft adjusted the tie he always wore, a nervous habit. "These things occurred to me in dreams. I'm a writer, not an augur."

"Is that like a prophet"?

"Yes."

"Then why not say 'prophet?' Jesus, you writers are difficult people!" Luigi stuck his new cigar between his teeth and lit it. The room was now steeped in a smoky miasma; the windows were sealed tight, nailed shut and covered with planks of wood in case *something else* was watching them.

The mobster slid a sheet of paper over to Lovecraft. "So here's the deal, Howie. You write down the players and what they want. Does Cthulhu have it in for the Mi-Go? Do the shoggoths want to overthrow the Old Ones? Do you see? Everyone wants something."

Lovecraft stood shakily, finding courage born out of despair. "I won't help you with this insane plan! Human civilization has been overthrown! Our great cities cast down into awful barbarism! This is a time for grief and mobilization! Our tanks and planes need to strike back!"

The mobster raised an eyebrow. "Nah. They tried that. We heard a broadcast from the president a week ago, right before he started screaming about the color out of space, whatever the hell that means. Seems that one of those old gods has laid claim to the air and is swatting down our flyboys."

Lovecraft shivered where he stood, like a very tall tree in the wind.

"But let's talk about you, Howie. You help me, I help you. What do you want? What gets your parts moving? Is it dames? My boys have rounded up the few survivors in New England. There's some lookers. I'll get you all the dames you want."

Lovecraft turned gray.

Luigi raised an eyebrow. "Let's be frank, Howie. I'm sensing you're not into dames. What is it? Men? Boys?"

Lovecraft turned green. "God, no!"

"I'm afraid I'm running out of options. You gotta give me something here."

"I want human civilization to rise again! I want cities and markets and books! I want crowds. Never thought I'd say it! I want crowds!"

"There, that wasn't so bad. Cities, markets, books."

Jimmy the bodyguard interjected, "Crowds, boss."

The mobster nodded and rubbed his chin. "Yeah. Crowds might be tough." But he paced through the room, the cigar glowing and exuding smoke. "You give me a month, Howie, and I'll figure out how to give you what you want. I've got some deals to strike. You want some tea? You look like a tea guy. When I come by tomorrow, I'll bring some just for you, partner." He struck out his large hand.

Lovecraft blinked at the proffered hand.

Dealing with a mobster? Had the world really come to this?

He shook the hand at last. It was cool, dry, smelled faintly of old cologne.

A moment later, Loud Lou departed with his goons, leaving Lovecraft in a hotel room of peeling yellow wallpaper and greasy brass furnishings.

Lovecraft lay down on the bed, closed his eyes, but didn't sleep. He wondered what the sunless morning would bring.

The morning was indeed sunless, and terribly cold, and it saw Lovecraft clutching to the back of a small motor boat that roared down the flooded streets of Providence's Federal Hill district. Scampering hunchbacked creatures turned faceless visages to them as the boat sped past like a rocket riding a plume of white foam.

There were five boats, actually, and Lovecraft sat in the flagship while Luigi stood proudly at the bow like some parody of Washington crossing the Delaware. The sea level had risen so much that old rooftops were like islands. The water was slimy and viscous, more like oil, and debris bobbed in grim patches.

"There it is!" the mob boss boomed, pointing to a stone steeple jutting up from the water. There was a trapezohedronal window of stained glass on level with the water-line. Lovecraft gasped as he realized they were hurtling straight at it.

"What are you doing?" he cried.

The mob boss held onto his fedora. "Ever crash a party, Howie?"

"Well, the Kalem Club has these literary discussion gatherings that you *could* construe as parties and . . . ahh!"

Their boat blasted through the stained glass, showering their shoulders and hat-brims with multicolored pieces. Lovecraft ducked between his knees, thinking: *I'm among madness! Everywhere I look, everyone I meet.*

Amazingly, Luigi hadn't flinched from his upright, revolutionary posture, even as the tinkling glass fell around him. One by one, the boats killed their engines and glided into the half-sunken church.

Lovecraft brushed off the crumbled glass and considered the building's interior. He had passed by this place on his many strolls. An old stone church of uncertain denomination, dusty windows. He had even pressed to the glass on occasion, trying to see inside and catching only sight of moldy pews. Now, the church interior held a black lake. Robed men and women walked about on the rafters (which now acted as piers.) A gnarled, knobby old man—presumably the high priest— stood at a wooden altar, arms raised to a hideous idol suspended by ropes of flesh above.

This grim congregation was in the middle of a booming chant, when they heard the noise and saw the lanterns from the approaching boats.

"Hey there!" Luigi cried. "I'd say good morning, but truth be told I don't know what the hell time it is anymore! The one clock I found had four goddam hands spinning in all sorts of directions."

The high priest gaped at him, eyes filled with astonishment and fury. "What is the meaning of this?" the man squawked.

"Looking for the high priest, a hybrid deep spawn fish-guy named Splut." Luigi squinted. "My guess is that would be you."

"Seize him!" the priest cried, extending a flabby finger. Cultists scrambled toward them from the rafters like aggressive spiders.

"Seize *this*," the mobster said, and he handed a ragged scrap of parchment to Lovecraft, who sighed and began reading aloud:

"*Grel'yifi*
Pnguit-hai
Fintushushushushu
Yik!"

The cultists hissed and fell backward; one lost his purchase on the rafters and dropped into the water, where he floundered and splashed in panic. Lovecraft, for his part, kept reading, repelling the overhead attackers as if they were vampires confronted with garlic fumes.

"Enough!" Splut, the high priest, cried.

"Oh, you don't *like* the Testament of his holiness Yog-Sothoth?" Luigi adjusted his tie, making a show of surveying the damp church. "This is a rather nice Esoteric Temple to Dagon. Would be a shame if anything *happened* to it . . ."

He snapped his fingers, and Lovecraft broke off his recitation.

"Listen up, Splut," the mobster said. "Yog-Sothoth has had his many eyes set on this place for a long time. It won't take much convincing to bring him through, you see what I'm sayin'?"

"This is consecrated ground to Dagon!" Splut insisted.

"Oh?" the mobster raised an eyebrow. "Hey Jimmy, do you see any scaly monster around here?"

"No, boss."

"How about you, Howie?"

"No," Lovecraft muttered, shivering in the boat.

"Looks like he don't got your back no more, Splut. That means you deal with us, or Yog-man will be breaking down your door . . . only he don't *need* to use the door."

"You will be sacrificed! Your blasphemy shall—"

"Howie!"

Lovecraft began to read again.

The priest covered his ears and howled in agony. "No, please! I beg you, no!"

Again, Luigi snapped his fingers. The air smelled of ozone and had a heavy, greasy quality that hadn't been there before. "See Splut, my wisehead here could easily summon the Yog-man. Have him step across his . . . um . . ." Luigi looked to Lovecraft.

Lovecraft sighed. "The black seas of infinity."

"Yeah, right." The mobster stooped over the side of his small boat, seized the splashing parishioner, and hauled him aboard. "Or you could pay up. I'll take two of your parishioners, and one of those nifty Dagonic amulets, and then you won't have to see me no more until next month when Jimmy comes around. And I *know* you'll treat him with the proper respect next time . . ."

When there was no sun to mark the passages of day, life melted into one continuous dreary grayscape. Chronically sleep-deprived, Lovecraft couldn't even guess at the progression of time—only a wild, desperate hope kept him going, burning as brightly as the sunrises of his memory. The hope that civilization was merely licking its wounds somewhere, and that he might be the one to usher it out of darkness with all its glorious rules, regulations, and routines. He fiercely clung to that hope, despite how it seemed that every time he blinked he would find himself in a new place, contemplating a new horror.

The latest horror was the plate of seafood he was being offered by Luigi.

They were in the dining hall of the seedy, waterlogged hotel. The room had been off-limits, as a bloated, blistery thing had claimed it as a lair, but that was a while ago—several hundred blinks ago, at any rate—and the creature had since been banished by Lovecraft's reading of the Pnakotic Manuscripts.

"Eat up, Howie!" Luigi said. "That's fresh tilapia. Just like *mamma* used to make."

"I don't like Italian food." He scowled. "Or Italians, for that matter."

"Don't be sore. Things are working out great! We got monsters that want human souls. Monsters that want human flesh. We even got monsters who want human women: Yog-Sothoth wants a willing human female partner. In my book, that makes him more human than you, Howie."

Lovecraft pushed his food away and glanced toward the nearest window, as if escape might be found there. "I don't understand how you did this," the writer said.

The mobster shrugged and lit his cigar. "Couldn't do it without you. Look, my family came from a shit-town outside Naples. Not too far, actually, from another shit-town outside Naples that got itself covered in volcanic soot long ago. You see my point?"

"No."

"Bad things happen. Some die, some suffer, some profit. I've been putting out feelers . . . no, not the monstrous type. Been talking to people. Finding ruins and secret temples, all water-logged and hidden but now floating to the surface, out in the open. With your expertise and my leadership, we're going to be rolling in salad!"

Lovecraft looked at his shoes. "We should be . . . organizing. Compiling resources and intelligence to use in the war against these things! Not trying to turn a profit!"

Luigi's eyes grew wide. "*Succeeding* in turning a profit!" He had begun to sweat despite the cool air, and he loosened his tie.

"But people don't want this! Humanity wants civilization again . . . the paperwork, the ordinances and laws and guidelines to defy chaos! What do *you* expect to do in a ruined world?"

The man stood and steered Howie closer to the window. He pointed to a hilltop that, surrounded by glittering canals, looked like an island. "Gonna build myself a palace right there. Or a tower. What do you think of towers, Howie? A big tower with ten thousand steps, going up and up and up . . ."

Luigi trailed off, and for a long time, said nothing.

Lovecraft dislodged himself from the man's grip. "I don't suppose you could find a cat for me?"

"A cat!" the mobster whirled to him in delight. "Oh, I know lots of—"

"Not that kind."

"Oh." The man sounded disappointed. "Look Howie, we already negotiated your pay. You didn't say nothing about cats before." His eyes trailed back to the hilltop. "But maybe I could find you a cat, if I built those stairs, Howie. Those endless stairs going up and up and up to the black vault of the sky . . ."

Lovecraft gaped. "Um . . . there's blood coming out of your eyes!"

Luigi barely seemed to notice. "Get some sleep. Tomorrow we got more stops to make."

The sagging old factory bent sorrowfully toward the sea, its bricks awash in dreadful violet-hued fungus, and Lovecraft remembered that once upon a time he had actually applied for a job here. He climbed the zig-zagging steps to the foreman's office, letting Luigi's boys barge in ahead of him. Wearily, he followed after the din and ruckus had died away.

Inside, Lovecraft stared around the office. The mobster and his goons fanned out in the narrow workspace. Filing cabinets, desks with circular stains, and stacks of papers were the expected sights, though these were now covered by that furry, garish mold.

And there was an Old One. That was a new feature to the office, too.

The creature resembled a rotund stalk of celery, if you ignored the presence of tentacles atop its cone. It had been watering stacks of fungi, feeding them old shipping manifests, when Luigi and his retinue burst in.

Luigi circled the trilling creature. "Yy-kshurla! You weren't *going* anywhere, were you? I mean, if you were planning on taking a vacation, you would have settled your debts first, right?"

The Old One stammered in a series of agitated clicks.

"I mean, by the look of things—and I could be wrong here—it *looks* like you're trying to skip town." He indicated the triangular slabs of basalt that had been piled outside the office window landing. "If I were to open your luggage, I'd bet I'd find your very best fungus, and scrolls, and your finest membrane-cloth. That suggests to me that you were planning on a discreet exit."

The Old One warbled and droned in protest. With one of its tentacles, it pointed to the packed luggage in panic and began making some excuse.

"Jimmy, what did I say last month to Yy-kshurla about him trying to leave town?"

"You said, 'Leave town and I'll give you a glimpse of eternity,' boss."

"That's *exactly* what I said." He snapped his fingers at Howie, and then said to the creature, "Yy-kshurla, take a look in the corner there."

The Old One rotated around and shrieked—a piercing sound that shattered the nearest window.

Lovecraft barely had time to avert his own eyes and return the conjuring talisman back in his pocket. The corner of the office was bubbling and frothing, like yellow river scum that accumulates at the wrong fork in a stream. He had a fleeting impression of gelatinous geometries stacked atop each other, and several gibbering mouths. The air began to burn around Lovecraft's eyes.

The Old One began to rock back and forth, crying out something that sounded like "Tekilili! Tekilili!" And the dematerializing shoggoth began to parody this demented sound.

"Tekilili! Tekilili! Tekilili!"

The mobster put his arm around the Old One. "Next time," he said affably, "I'll have you look for *five* seconds, and then we'll see if you can put your sanity back together again." He turned to the door. "Take care, Yy-kshurla. I'll send Jimmy next week to collect what you owe: seventeen fungus buds, and some of your Yithian scrolls."

The Old One gibbered and rocked in the corner.

The rest of the week was a shuttling of living nightmares. Lovecraft found no escape even in his dreams, which were a great emptiness, as if his imagination had disgorged its contents into the real world and was now a deserted cupboard.

Maybe my imagination was never mine, he thought as he rose from his bed on what he wanted to think of as Saturday morning. *Maybe my mind was always empty, making me ideally suited to receive, not invent, the vibrations of the coming cataclysm.*

He shuffled out into the communal kitchen. Luigi was there, reading a paper, a cup of steaming black coffee set before him. A delicate teacup in a saucer was set out for Lovecraft.

"I thought you tried not to read," Lovecraft muttered, settling into a tall-backed chair.

The mobster shrugged. "You got me started on it." He folded up the pages and tossed them into a corner. "Sleep well?"

"No." Lovecraft stirred his tea and glanced to the hotel windows. His heart lifted at the sight of humans hurrying along the neighboring rooftops. Searching for food, or hiding from monstrous pursuers, trying to survive in this ruined world. A grim chapter in civilization, Lovecraft mused, but there had been grim chapters before, hadn't there? Bubonic plagues and terrible wars and dark ages. People always found a way of bringing back the municipalities and institutions that they cherished! Civilization with all its glorious, wonderful, enthralling features would arise again like the fabled phoenix and . . .

His fantasy broke off, as he noticed Luigi staring intently at him.

"What?" the writer asked.

Luigi gave an embarrassed smile. "I was just thinking about your skin. It's real nice."

Lovecraft slid his chair away from the table. "Now listen here . . ."

"You got it wrong. I ain't complimenting you in a sexual way. I was just thinking." The embarrassed smile rose again. "Was thinking of . . ."

"Of what?"

"Of . . . um . . . peeling your skin off your face. Sorry." Luigi rose from the table and headed for the doorway. "Come on, Howie, we got monsters to peel around. I mean, push around."

It was a wholly indescribable parade of mutants and monsters, minotaurs and madmen, visits to old asylums and sunken abbeys, shipyards that had washed up to the highest hills of Providence, and steeples which had sunk to the lowest pits. It was, Lovecraft thought, a demented fever dream of what he'd always imagined foreign port cities might resemble . . . except he had never seen foreign port cities and didn't like foreigners.

And yet, as the weeks passed, Lovecraft saw people huddling behind cracked windows and glimpsed them on foraging runs. He even once heard laughter—not wild, insane cackling but normal mirth, the kind that binds people in the most dire of times. Human beings, the seedlings of civilization which had yet escaped the madness in the way that tree buds may fly aloft of a forest fire to take root on safer, fertile ground.

The more he thought of it, the more anxious he was to do his part to bring back that liberation.

It was difficult to tell when a month's time had lapsed, but Lovecraft found that Luigi seemed to increasingly have a sense for it.

"Luigi!" he called out, walking across the pier outside their commandeered hotel. Again, he glimpsed people going about the business of survival—paddling down the watery canals, casting nets for food, darting quickly from building to building like rats in the walls.

Luigi stood on the pier. He had discarded his pinstripe suit and now was clad in some fleshy, meaty robe that seemed to have hair growing from its sleeves. He didn't turn around as Lovecraft approached from behind. Instead, the mobster stood admiring a tall, needle-like construction-in-progress, built on a hilltop, aiming at the sky.

"One month has passed, hasn't it, since I agreed to help you?" Lovecraft stared at the man's back, steeling himself for refusal or threats. "I wish to be paid now."

The mobster turned. Lovecraft cried out and recoiled so that he almost tumbled backwards into the black water.

"What happened to your eyes?!"

Luigi Argenta frowned, as if the writer had made a bizarre query. "What? Oh, those. I didn't really need them anymore, Howie." He pointed to the grotesque minaret that seemed to jab the purple-bellied heavens. "I can see better this way. I'm building the ten thousand steps!"

"I'm happy for you." Lovecraft sighed. "Where is Jimmy?"

Again, the confused frown. "Who? Oh, right! Well, Jimmy was great and all, but . . . um . . . I started realizing how nice his skin was . . . so . . ."

Lovecraft tensed, his gangly legs trembling. "Pay me what you owe me."

The eyeless monster who had once been a mobster (and even then had been considered a bit of a monster) stared sightlessly at the tower-in-progress.

"Did you hear me?"

"Course I hear you. It's not like I tore my ears off . . ." he hesitated. "Though that's not a bad idea, now that you mention it."

"I didn't mention it. Pay me, and our business is concluded!"

Luigi slung his arm around Lovecraft's shoulder and steered him toward a large, sea-facing structure. "Oh, do I ever have a surprise for *you*, Howie. Have I told you how much I just adore your skin?"

Lovecraft expected to find many things on the other side of the building's door. Hideous beings from other dimensions. Mutated human cannibals. Cultists gathered around a bonfire of sacrificial victims.

Instead, the door opened onto an open courtyard hemmed in by other buildings. An insular, protected garden spot, filled with . . .

Lovecraft blinked.

A market occupied the center of this community, complete with vendor stalls, display racks, and kiosks. It was a shabby-looking arrangement, built of driftwood and what might well have been the bones of some unknown beast, but it was a market, nonetheless!

And there were books! Lovecraft almost wept, rushing to the ancient bookshelves which appeared to have been ripped out of a library wall. He saw bundles of newspapers, leather-bound tomes, cheap paperbacks, and lurid magazine covers. Books! How long had it been since he'd enjoyed the simple pleasure of reading a book?

"Cities, markets, books," Luigi said, nodding in satisfaction. "That's what you asked for, right?"

His fleshy robe quivered and said, "And crowds, boss."

"Right! Crowds." Luigi brought his fingers to his mouth and whistled.

From the buildings, a trickle of humanity began to appear. Men and women, children and teenagers, wizened veterans of a lost age and bright-eyed innocents.

Lovecraft cried, "A crowd!"

Luigi nodded his eyeless head. "I always keep to the terms of my business deals. You got yourself your own little city now, Howie. A city, market, books, and crowds."

There were almost forty people, hardly a crowd by old world standards, but the old world was gone now and forty people was the most Lovecraft had seen in a long while. He found himself grinning.

"Welcome!" he said, almost singing the word. "Welcome to civilization again!"

"Take care, Howie," the mobster said, walking off.

The writer almost shoved the man away, and he bolted the door as the mobster departed. Then he turned to the crowd and clapped his hands together in delight. "Civilization! Even as a tiny flicker in a shattered hearth, we will rebuild the old world we all cherished so much! Gather 'round, everyone! We are delivered from madness!"

The first town meeting of what became known as Howardtown was held on the very next day. January first, Mayor Lovecraft said, though in truth no one could really confirm that it was January at all. But Mayor Lovecraft's first mayoral act was to start a new calendar: January 1 of the New Age.

"We shall all work again!" Lovecraft told the gathering. "We can create time-cards to keep track of everyone's hours; anything over forty hours will be considered overtime, which will have to be approved by the labor board." He smiled. "And taxes will be collected every April; I strongly advise you visit the tax office, which we will establish later today."

"Taxes?" someone in the crowd muttered.

"Yes, of course! We have many projects to undertake, if we wish civilization to rise again. Now, I'll need some bankers, and accountants, of course. And a robust working class to grow food and manufacture the things our little town will require. I have already taken the liberty of typing up employment forms."

"Employment forms?" a woman asked. "You mean, we can't just . . . work?"

Lovecraft admonished her. "We are recreating civilization! Civilization requires order! You all must register with our new census bureau! Just fill in your name and occupational skills. And your ethnicity... that's *very* important for me to know. And I strongly suggest you select a formal political party for when elections kick in next year."

The people of the crowd looked about, giving sidelong glances at each other.

Somewhere far away, a lonesome keening of some terrible creature split the night.

Lovecraft clapped his hands. "Civilization! We all want it back, yes?"

By morning, Howardtown was deserted, except for the tall, unnervingly pale mayor, sitting at his desk outside and filling out paperwork for anyone who might choose to return.

In these latter days of the world, it is said that on certain nights the voice of the mad mayor can be heard crying out town ordinances, or reading the minutes of Howardtown's empty departments, and reminding anyone who dares to listen that taxes must be filed with the correct forms by mid-April.

Explaining Cthulhu to Grandma

By Alex Shvartsman

I JUST MADE THE DEAL of the year and I couldn't wait to tell Grandma.

As soon as the customer left, I locked the front door, flipped the cardboard sign to Closed, and headed into the back. Clutching my latest acquisition to my blouse, I entered the packed stockroom, dodged around the bronze naval cannon, nearly caught the hem of my skirt on a rusty suit of armor, and made my way through a plethora of other items too large or too heavy to be stored on the shelves. Most of this stuff has been here since before I was born, and will likely remain in the same place long after my hypothetical future children take over the shop. You never know when the right buyer might come along, and the family is in it for the long haul.

Grandma Heide was in our office, sitting at the desk. She had moved the keyboard out of the way to make room for the game of solitaire she was playing with a thirteenth-century Egyptian tarot deck. She barely glanced up when I walked in.

"You do know you could play this *on* the computer, right Grandma?"

She set down a card in one of the columns after a few seconds' thought. "Can your newfangled gadget fake the feel of shuffling a dog-eared deck of cards? Simulate the pleasure of placing one in just the right spot to make a perfect play? I didn't think so." She looked at me over her glasses. "The old ways are almost always best."

"Yes, well, I'm not here to argue about that again. Guess what I just picked up on pawn."

I stepped closer and placed a pocket dimension in front of Grandma. It looked like a pyramid-shaped snow globe the height of a soda can. It was filled with ocean water. In the center floated a being of scales and tentacles and shapes so unnatural that staring straight at it caused a headache. When not stored outside of our space-time continuum, it was the size of a cruise liner and must have weighed as much as a small mountain, which is what made pocket dimensions so darn handy.

Grandma picked up the pyramid, pushed the glasses up her nose and peered inside.

"What is this?" she asked.

"Cthulhu," I said, smug with satisfaction.

"*Gesundheit*," said Grandma. I couldn't tell for certain if she was kidding or not. Probably not.

"I didn't sneeze," I said. "Its name is Cthulhu. It is an ancient god of anxiety and horror, dead but dreaming."

Grandma didn't appear impressed. "What does it do? Besides dream." She turned the pocket dimension slowly to examine its contents.

"Do? It's a symbol for the unknowable fathoms of the universe which dwarf humanity's importance. Besides, it's a god. How long has it been since we had one of *those* in the shop?"

"1982," she said immediately. "The government of Argentina pawned a few of the Guaraní nature gods to help fund the Falklands conflict. Little good it did them."

I didn't remember this, but I was still in diapers in 1982.

"Pre-Columbian godlings barely count. This," I pointed at the pyramid, "is the real deal."

Grandma finished inspecting the god and placed the pocket dimension on top of the computer, next to a mug filled with ballpoint pens. She turned her attention back to me.

"And what did you pay out for this rare and unique item?"

I told her.

Grandma pursed her lips and stared me down. Ever since I broke the wing off the stuffed phoenix when I was a little girl, it had been the withering expression Grandma Heide reserved for when I screwed up especially badly.

"Whoever pawned it will have taken the money and run," she declared. "They won't be back. Enjoy it for the next month, and let's hope some fool gets as excited about this overgrown octopus as you did. If not, then maybe we can sell it off by the pound to the sushi chains."

"You never have any faith in the deals I make." I crossed my arms. "I'm not a little girl anymore, and I spent my entire life around the shop. When will you begin to trust my judgment? I say we got a bargain and I'll prove it."

"This shop is full of the mistakes of overeager youth, Sylvia." She pointed toward the stock room, brimming with stuff. "I made my fair share when I was your age. The pawn shop business is simple. Stick to quality common items that are easy to move, and pick them up cheap. The sooner you accept that, the sooner you'll be ready to take over the family enterprise." Then she drew the next card from her deck, indicating that the conversation was over.

When your family is in the business of running the oldest pawn shop in the world, there are big shoes to fill. I wondered if Grandma had similar trouble when she became old enough to work at the shop, back before Gran-Gran Hannelore had retired.

Under the terms of the pawn, the customer had thirty days to come back and claim his item. That gave me plenty of time to line up potential buyers. There were a number of leads for me to pursue, but I started with the obvious.

I unlocked the front door, flipped the sign to Open, powered up my laptop, and logged on to Craigslist.

It didn't take a month. The first interested party showed up within days.

"I'm Keldmo, the Grand Prophet of the Deep Ones," announced the enormously fat man. He was wearing some sort of a toga or bathrobe getup, probably because no one made pants in his size. "I understand that you've recently come into possession of the great Cthulhu?"

"We did. Or we will, if the previous owner doesn't pay back the loan in three weeks' time. How much are you prepared to pay?"

"Is the undying gratitude of thousands of worshippers not enough?"

"Not nearly."

"I don't have a lot of money." Keldmo wiped the sweat off his ample chins with a handkerchief. "The congregation hasn't been quite as devout in recent years. The collection plate brings barely enough to keep food on the table."

I bit back the obvious retort. Besides, Keldmo wouldn't have appreciated the barb. If he ever had a sense of humor, he probably ate it a long time ago.

"Having the actual Cthulhu to display at services, I'm sure that would turn things around," he said. "Reinvigorate the worshippers, help with the recruitment drive, that sort of thing."

"You aren't planning to wake it up and unleash it upon the world, are you?"

"Heavens, no," said Keldmo. "A living god can be dangerous and unpredictable. What if it has different ideas and plans for its followers than I do? No, it's best to let sleeping horrors lie."

"Good," I said. "Now, what are you willing to pay, really?"

Keldmo made his offer. It was significantly less than the amount I had invested, but it was a start. I told the cult leader that I'd be in touch and sent him on his merry way.

A week later a group of beings from a parallel universe showed up. They looked a lot like the alien grays on TV, if alien grays had fins and gills. I stared, perhaps beyond the point of politeness. Visitors from a parallel universe were a rare sight indeed, even in an establishment such as ours.

"We seek the services of your underwater god," said the leader of the group.

"What kind of services?" I just had to know.

"We are aquatic beings," said the leader, whom I mentally dubbed Nemo. "Our waters have recently become infested with sea serpents. Being that we are pacifists, we can't handle this calamity on our own. But it is well known that the Deep Ones are the ocean's natural predators. We wish to awaken Cthulhu and release it into the wild, so it can eat all the sea serpents."

I had my reservations about this plan, and about what Cthulhu might do to Nemo's people once it ran out of sea serpents. But at least they weren't planning to awaken Cthulhu in *this* universe. That was a big plus.

"How much can you pay?"

The aliens huddled.

"In addition to being pacifists," said Nemo, "we're also a moneyless society. We don't mine, or fish, or produce artwork. We live in harmony with nature and eat algae. I'm afraid we possess nothing you would find of value. However," he added brightly, "we don't want to buy your god. We only want to borrow it. We'll be happy to return it to you, in perfect condition, after it feeds."

I frowned. The idea of getting Cthulhu back, awake and nourished, wasn't appealing.

"You'd be helping to save an entire civilization," said Nemo. "Surely the concept of compassion exists in this universe?"

I felt bad for the naïve pacifists, but I was also fairly certain that I wouldn't be doing them any favors by unleashing Cthulhu on a society that couldn't even cope with a few sea serpents. Also, I was running a business, not an Interdimensional Wetlands Conservation Society.

I told Nemo that I'd think about it, and ushered him and his friends out of the shop.

"No one is going to give you any money," Grandma called out from the stock room once the door closed behind them. "But I'm sure you can find plenty of folks who'd be willing to take it off your hands for free."

I gritted my teeth and went back to sorting and labeling the rack of love potions. Thanks to that song we were perpetually sold out of Number Nine. Despite the fact that, from what I heard, it tasted like troll vomit.

Nearly two weeks had passed and I was beginning to worry, when another interested party arrived. This time it was a tall, lean man who wore a mantle decorated with a lion's mane draped over his shoulder. He seemed unperturbed by the balmy August weather outside. His broad chest was adorned with several rows of teeth hanging on strings from around his neck. I could've sworn a few of the teeth were human, but I'm no dentist. A long sword dangled off his belt.

"I'm Sir Barnabas, the Grand Knight of the Order of Saint George," he announced, more loudly than was absolutely necessary.

"Welcome," said Grandma. Sir Barnabas' bulging muscles and deep baritone summoned her from the back as if by magic. "I'm Heide. And that's my granddaughter Sylvia. She's single."

"Madame." Sir Barnabas bent down to kiss Grandma's hand. "My lady," he gallantly bowed to me next. I could swear that I heard Grandma swoon.

"On behalf of the Order of Saint George, I seek the monster Cthulhu that is said to be in your possession. Will you aid me in my quest?"

"Is your quest dedicated to any Lady?" asked Grandma.

"What do you want it for?" I asked before Grandma could get up to any of her matchmaking.

"We're the Order of Saint George," said Barnabas. "Isn't it obvious?"

"Humor me."

"We hunt and slay dragons."

"Dragons are extinct," said Grandma.

"You're welcome!" said Barnabas. "We shall hunt this Cthulhu and kill it, too. It will be glorious. Songs will be composed about—"

"Cthulhu isn't a dragon," I interrupted.

"Strictly speaking, you're right," said Barnabas. "But it's got scales and wings, and it's a vile beast. That's as close as we can hope for, these days."

"I see." The idea of a bunch of knights trying to defeat an elder god by poking spears at it was amusing, but only until I remembered that I shared the same planet with them. And that those spears would probably make Cthulhu mad. Madder. "What is your order prepared to pay for the privilege?"

"The Knights of St. George take a vow of poverty. But your assistance in this quest shall be immortalized in the annals of our order. That's better than mere money."

Grandma frowned. "Poverty is the stupidest vow a knight could take. However is one supposed to come up with a proper dowry then?"

For an excruciating fifteen minutes, Sir Barnabas kept trying to convince us to hand over Cthulhu to him, gratis. I promised to consider it, just to get him out the door.

"Told you no one will pay money for this thing," Grandma said, checking out the knight's posterior as he walked down the street.

She was wrong.

★ ★ ★

Two days before Cthulhu officially became the property of the shop, the next and final potential customer had arrived. He was a nondescript middle-aged man of medium height wearing a dark blue suit, the sort of person you would never look at twice in a crowd. The only distinguishing characteristic about him was an aluminum attaché case, which he plunked onto the counter in front of me.

"I'd like one Cthulhu, please," he said as he opened the case. It was full of money.

Grandma appeared out of nowhere again. The only thing capable of summoning her faster than a set of perfect pecs was a briefcase full of cash.

"It's a deal," she said. "But you'll have to come back on Wednesday. The original owner has until then to claim his property. Rules and regulations, you understand."

"I'm from the government, ma'am. I assure you that you won't get into any trouble for handing over the creature a few days early."

"What do you want with it?" I didn't trust the government. Who does? "Is it the whole 'why settle for a lesser evil' thing? But the elections aren't for another two years."

"Very funny," he said, but his tone and eyes did not agree. "My department is charged with destroying dangerous items and beings, before they get the chance to break free and bite everyone in the ass. Your operation is always on our radar." He turned to Grandma. "You should make things easy for yourself and take the money. I could've just as easily classified Cthulhu as a weapon of mass destruction and confiscated it with no compensation for you at all."

Grandma stood up straighter and glared at the government agent, fire in her eyes. "No. You couldn't have. This is an ancient place of power, and there are wards and protections layered upon it by a hundred generations of my ancestors. It is much too tough a nut for the likes of you to crack.

"Go." Grandma pointed at the front door. "I don't appreciate being threatened in my own establishment. Come back in two days' time and we will *think* about accepting your offer."

Without another word, he went.

On Wednesday, Grandma and I were awakened well before business hours by loud noises coming from the street. Both of us got dressed and came down to the shop to investigate. Outside, there was pandemonium.

Hundreds of the Deep Ones' worshippers faced off against an equally impressive force of soldiers who had a pair of helicopters and a tank. In the middle of the street, a dozen knights stood shoulder to shoulder and sneered at anyone who came too close. And all around, small clusters of gray-skinned, gilled aliens milled about, getting underfoot of everyone else.

"This is madness," I said. "They're going to begin killing each other any minute now."

"I knew this Cthulhu was nothing but trouble," said Grandma. "I've half a mind to let them fight it out." But I knew she didn't mean it.

We were perfectly safe inside. The shop is protected by a collection of charms, spells, and enchantments laboriously assembled by the family over the centuries. An intruder would have an easier time getting into Buckingham Palace or the White House.

But that didn't stop them from brawling with each other in the street. And, Grandma's offhand comment aside, we couldn't let that happen.

"I know you like to do things the traditional way," I told Grandma, "but I'm responsible for causing this mess, and I have to set things straight. This situation calls for a forward-thinking, unorthodox approach. Will you please trust me to handle it?"

Grandma hesitated for only the briefest of moments, then smiled at me and nodded. I unlocked the shop's front door and stepped outside.

A few minutes later, I had gathered the leaders of each group inside the shop. Keldmo, Sir Barnabas, Nemo, and the agent whose name—unsurprisingly—turned out to be Smith scowled at each other. The tension was so thick you probably couldn't cut it with Sir Barnabas' sword.

"I can resolve the issue at hand to everyone's satisfaction," I said. The four of them paid close attention.

"Sir Barnabas, meet the interdimensional alien. His world is suffering from a terrible sea serpent infestation."

"Oh?" The knight was practically salivating at the thought of hunting sea serpents.

"Would you agree that sea serpents are phylogenetically much closer to dragons than a dead elder god?"

"Most assuredly, my lady," said Sir Barnabas.

"Will you undertake the noble quest of hunting them down and, in exchange, abandon any future claim on stalking the Cthulhu?"

"Gladly, my lady." He pumped an oversized fist on the breast plate over his heart.

I addressed Nemo: "And will you accept the help of the knights and give up on the foolish idea of releasing an even more dangerous predator into your ecosystem?"

"They seem bloodthirsty enough," said Nemo, "and yet honorable. It appears to be a great solution."

The two left the shop to break the news to their people. They were already discussing logistics, munitions, and the songs to be composed in the knights' honor.

"Well, that was the easy part." I turned my attention to the remaining parties.

"I won't let a dangerous creature fall into the hands of a cult," said Smith.

"I won't let them murder my god," said Keldmo.

"You can't stop me. I have the entire military at my disposal."

"My disciples are everywhere. If you dare to harm a single tentacle on our god's head, they will exact a bloody revenge. My people are willing to kill and die for me." Keldmo sighed. "Well some of them, anyway."

"No dying. No killing. I already told you, I have a solution. Wait here," I dashed for the stock room.

I returned with a large silver plate under my arm.

"Keldmo, you told me that you don't want to wake up Cthulhu, you just need an impression of him to rally your followers."

Keldmo looked at me, waiting to see where this was going, but made no protest.

"This is an enchanted plate, part of a matching set. It will display an exact replica of whatever item is placed on the other plate, for as long as it remains there." I tapped the side of the plate gently and the pyramid pocket dimension appeared on it. I offered the plate to Keldmo, who grabbed for it greedily. "You can see it, touch it, and verify that it's safe and sound on the other plate, which is at the back of our shop. Just don't remove the replica from the plate's surface or you'll break the spell."

"As for you," I turned to Smith, "killing Cthulhu isn't an option. You don't need the trouble with Keldmo's followers, and I seriously doubt you could kill it anyway. So instead, I will offer our shop's services to store it for you permanently." Smith looked dubious, but I pressed on. "There are few locations in the entire world more secure than our shop. You know this, or you would have come in guns blazing, trying to take Cthulhu by force. No one will get at it here, and anyone who might want to try will believe that Keldmo's people have it anyway. Keldmo will make sure of that, won't he?"

Keldmo nodded, with a huge grin on his meaty face. Smith thought about this and finally nodded, too.

"We will, of course, require payment for our services. That bag of money will cover rent for the first hundred years. Our descendants can renegotiate after that."

Smith mulled this over a while longer, but he could find no obvious flaw in my plan.

Several hours later the contracts were drawn up (in triplicate—that's how the government rolls) and signed, and everyone finally left. The briefcase full of money sat in the office next to the silver plate housing Cthulhu. Smith wanted the case back, but Grandma got peevish at the last moment and insisted we keep it as part of the deal. She must've been still punishing Smith for his bullying earlier.

"Did you like how I managed to make everyone happy and sell a silver plate for a giant wad of money in the process?" I did good, and deserved a chance to brag. "And we even get to keep Cthulhu. Governments and cults come and go, and who knows what it will be worth a few generations down the line? And are you convinced I'm ready to take over the shop now?"

"Not yet," said Grandma. "If only you didn't pick up this beastie in the first place, we could've avoided all this nonsense altogether."

I frowned, but didn't argue. Expecting too much and complaining regardless of outcome is the prerogative of family.

"Not yet," Grandma said again, "but you're getting closer."

I came over and hugged her. She pursed her lips, but in her eyes I caught a hint of a smile.

The Call of the Pancake Factory

By Ken Liu

THE BAR IS PLENTY KITSCHY: goofy statues made from coconuts everywhere and strings of shell beads hanging from the ceiling. I smile when I see a coconut sporting a pair of mouse ears made from scallop shells.

Tourists from all over the world are sitting around, ordering drinks non-stop because the sun is so hot at this time in Indonesia that you'll wilt if you go outside and also because the drinks are so watered down. But that's all right with me. I'm here to blend in, not to get drunk.

"You look like an American!" A middle-aged man sits down on the stool next to mine. He's ruddy-faced, balding, and so friendly that it makes the New Yorker in me recoil. "I'm Steve. It's nice to see another American out here in the Banda Sea."

"Likewise," I say, and ignore his extended hand. I scan around the bar one more time to be sure I don't see anyone who looks like they could be after me. I see a couple of Taiwanese guys by the door, but they look too happy to be working for Boss Gou.

"I didn't catch your name?"

I try to keep the irritation out of my voice. "I didn't tell you my name, and I'm not going to."

He stares at me, the smile on his face frozen. But he's drunk enough that, despite the chilly reception he's getting from me, he decides to ask more questions rather than slink away. "You a gangster or something?"

He's so wide of the mark that he's almost hitting Boss Gou. Yeah, some of you may know Gou as the Taiwanese mogul who owns all these theme parks all over Asia, but I bet not many of you know he runs a few casinos out of Macao as well. He's got hired goons running around chasing down people who—*allegedly*, I emphasize—stole from him.

Since Steve doesn't seem to scare easily, I decide that I need to appear kooky enough to drive him away so he'll leave me alone. "I'm a spy," I whisper conspiratorially. Well, the technical term is Competitive Research Analyst, but close enough. Sometimes the truth is just strange enough that people will think you're nuts.

"Oh, like with the CIA?"

"No, I'm with the—" I pause. I don't want to give the name of my employer outright—they do have a reputation to uphold. I can't use too obvious a code name either, like, say, "Mus musculus." But then the fact that he mentioned the Pickle Factory inspires me. Countless parents have appeased their children on Sunday mornings by making pancakes in the iconic shape involving one big and two little circles. "—Pancake Factory," I finish.

"I had no idea restaurants needed spies."

"Oh, you'd be surprised." In truth, few people know how competitive the Pancake Factory's business is. Boss Gou, our direct competitor in Hong Kong, is cutthroat. A month after the "Journey to the West Adventure" opened in our theme park, his theme park opened the "Monkey King Rebels Against Heaven" attraction, which did everything ours did, only better. Somehow he had gotten our plans ahead of time and worked out how to beat it. It was a disaster for gate receipts. "It's like any business. You have to stay informed about what your competitors are doing: new dishes, ambience, trade dress, service model, and so on."

"So you're here to research authentic Indonesian cuisine, is that it?"

This guy is like a leech that you can't shake. I mumble at him, distracted because I need to stay alert and look around to see if Boss Gou has tracked me all the way from Taipei to Indonesia. You see, I managed to get ahold of his plans for the next water park, and he's not happy. I can't just get on a plane back to Florida because the plans are in the form of a gel-filled model. Devious, that Boss Gou. So we're playing, *ahem*, cat-and-mouse around his backyard until I can get the model replicated in some TSA-approved material.

"Listen, if it's authentic, traditional Pacific Island cooking culture you're after, you might want to go check out this island twenty miles or so east from here. They've got a New Age commune-thing going on there with a guru and stone ovens and all sort of . . ."

I'm only listening with half of an ear. Now, it could be that I'm just paranoid, but I could have sworn I've seen the same Jeep passing by the bar twice in the last hour. And that yacht in the bay . . . why do I get the feeling that I'd seen it in Tamsui Harbor?

". . . You should take the offer to tour their island. They ask you about your dreams and there are bonfires and roast pig and crazy dances in the middle of the night and ancient tribal liquor. You'll get a kick out of it."

"Where can I find this guide?" I ask. The Jeep just went by a third time, and I duck down, hoping whoever's inside can't see into the dim interior of the bar. A trip to some obscure island so I can hide with a New Age cult sounds like just the way to shake off Boss Gou. Besides, I can do some research for our Pacific-themed attractions.

I and five others are whisked to the island by speedboat. Our guide, Otto, is a man of indeterminate age whose bronzed and heavily tattooed skin makes a nice contrast with his white shirt and dress pants.

I try to make conversation as we skim over the waves glimmering in the afternoon sun. "How long have you been with the . . . um . . ."

"Cult?" he says, a smile on his face. "You can say what you think."

"I was going to say community."

"I prefer school of philosophy, myself. I joined about twenty years ago, and now some would say I'm the leader of my fellow philosophers. Before that, I was a wanderer like you, blinded by pursuit of the meaningless."

If the guru himself has to be out recruiting, they aren't doing so well in the revenue department. "What drew you to this school of philosophy?"

"An acceptance of the permanent state of ignorance of our species and the ultimate futility of seeking knowledge."

"That"—I struggle to find a diplomatic way to phrase this—"does not sound very attractive. I like knowing things."

"Do you?" He appraises me with some care. "You are a scientist then?"

"Not exactly, but I know a little bit about lots of things, and a lot about a few things."

"Just the kind of men our arrogant modern world is so good at producing," he says. "You and I are members of one species on one planet that is no different from billions of others in a galaxy that is itself but one of a trillion galaxies in the universe. What can we possibly know?"

This is standard touchy-feely, airy-fairy nonsense. Next I imagine he'll spew some poetry about the known unknowns and the unknown unknowns. But I play along. "We know much more than our ancestors, and the speed of discovery is exponentially increasing."

"So optimistic," he says. "Imagine, if you will, a colony of ants. They explore the land around them, the grass and the flowers, the dead beetles and dropped crumbs. They formulate theories to explain their environment: why there's a region where the giant rose bushes are laid out in rows; how much of the landscape is dominated by one species of grass all about the same height; what causes water to sprinkle down from great geysers in the ground at certain times during the day. They believe, with time, they can explain everything they see."

Another well-worn fable, but the breeze across the sea is pleasant, and it would be rude to excuse myself now from this conversation. "I'm guessing we're the ants."

"They believe they're gaining knowledge and understanding until the day they're crushed into pulp at the foot of a child, a being who has never paid attention to them until that day, and whose parents are responsible for all the features of the backyard world they have sought in vain to explain. The ants were never even part of their plans save for extermination. The gods care as little about us as we about the ants, and that is why all our efforts at understanding are useless."

"So what should the ant in your fable do, if not to pursue useless knowledge?"

"Beg for mercy," he says. "And pray that the Great Ones hear."

★ ★ ★

The unpleasant speech from Otto aside, members of the cult—or "school of philosophy"—certainly know how to throw a party, especially considering that they have no electricity or modern conveniences to work with, as far as I can see.

There was a very touristy and inauthentic Pacific luau to welcome us for the evening. They claimed that the roasted pig had been cooking underground all day, but I had seen two men carrying the pig out of the gigantic stone edifice set a little back from the beach to the burying spot as we disembarked. The pig tasted fine, even if it was probably cooked on a gas grill in an industrial kitchen. Otto was a loquacious and engaging host, urging everyone to drink and eat and made no mention of his gloomy beliefs. I used my cellphone to take a few photos of the festivities, noticing that I got no reception here.

And now there's a big ring-shaped bonfire on the beach, and as we visitors sip our drinks—not watered down this time, for sure—the cast members—oops, wrong lingo, I mean our hosts—are dancing around the fire, enacting a ritual that I'm sure some anthropologist would point out is a theatrical, incongruous admixture of dozens of real cultures. I don't judge. The Pancake Factory does the same thing.

In the middle of the ring of fire is a stone platform on top of which is an idol. If I squint hard enough it seems to be a lizard with wings whose head sprouts tentacles—again, probably cobbled together from the mythology of several real cultures.

They whoop and shout, stripping off their clothes in their ecstasy. The other visitors sitting around the fire look mesmerized, or, perhaps more accurately, dazed. I noticed after my first drink that there was a medicinal aftertaste and have been careful since. Who knows what kind of hallucinogens they've mixed in to help set the mood?

The language they're using in their chants is incomprehensible and nothing like what I've heard before. I wouldn't be surprised if it's also made up. Considering the rough conditions on this remote island, their dedication to creating a complete experience for their guests rivals the Pancake Factory's.

What I can't figure out, of course, is the money angle. Otto has not charged any of us for this little Pacific-themed cruise or even made us sign pledges to attend some proselytizing session, the way time-share salesmen connected with the Pancake Factory would. Maybe they rely on having members join and give to the cult all their worldly possessions, but that's a highly uncertain revenue model. Maybe I should talk to Otto and give him some advice.

Still, whatever I have drunk is having an effect. The dancers seem to be floating in the air as they gyrate, and the rhythmic chants with their heavy beat is making me rather drowsy. The idol in the center of the ring of fire seems to be coming alive in the flickering light of the flames and shifting shadows.

I stand up and sway, my footing uncertain, and Otto is at my side instantly.

"Ready to sleep?" he asks.

I nod.

He brings me to the entrance of the great edifice whose walls seem formed from giant blocks of stone, all sharp angles and flat surfaces. The effect is one of prehistoric antiquity. I seriously doubt this is real either, as the seams and joints seem too neat and clean, reminding me of some of the Pancake Factory's re-creations.

He brings me through a few twisting tunnels lit only by torchlight, and the lingering effect of the drink is such that it seems sometimes we're moving *up* a downward slope and sometimes we're walking with our feet on the ceilings. Begrudgingly, I admit that if this is all part of their presentation, it's very well-conceived.

Finally, he brings me to a windowless room lit with oil lamps, and points me at a bed in the corner. I crawl into it and fall asleep almost immediately, hearing only a whispered wish for "sweet dreams."

My sleep is filled with bizarre images and nightmarish visions. Great, lumbering *things* as big as skyscrapers fall out of the sky. They look like giant versions of the idols I had seen, complete with tiny wings—useless for flight—and writhing tentacles around their heads. I suppose I've been thinking about how to revamp our horror-themed attractions too much lately.

I wake up, my body covered in a sheen of sweat. I feel completely sober, and I don't know how many hours have passed.

"You have one of the most attuned minds I've ever seen," says Otto from the darkness.

I almost jump out of the bed. The creepy man is standing in the shadow by the door.

"Have you been here all this time?" I demand. "Watching me sleep?"

"You can hear him, can't you? The call of Dread Cthulhu?"

Something is speaking in my mind all right: thunderous, immense, the syllables and sounds strange and impossible for me to imitate. I gather that the noises Otto is making with his mouth are meant to imitate this alien sound in my mind, the unpronounceable name of his deity.

I don't know how he's doing this but I have a guess. Back at the Pancake Factory, we experimented with ultrasonic speakers that beam sounds to a specific point so that only the person at that point can hear it. It's great for haunted mansion type of rides since it sounds like the voice is speaking from inside your head. We never got the kinks worked out to put it into production, but apparently Uncle Otto here has got it working on his island. Most impressive.

"They come from the stars, you know," says Otto, his tone full of reverence. "Uncountable eons ago, they came to our world and ruled it when our ancestors were barely conscious. Then they fell into a deep slumber in cities beneath the sea. But they continued to dream, and in dreams they communicate with those of us who are attuned to them. We worship them because one day, when the stars are aligned again, they'll awaken from their deep sleep and rule over us again, and the world shall be cleansed in a wild apocalypse of flames and ecstasy—"

"Okay, okay, I get it," I interrupt him. The purple prose was getting on my nerves. I like theatre, but this was a bit too much. "We are the ants, and this Cthulhu is the little boy in your fable. And you want me to start praying to him, before he decides to squish me."

He's taken aback by my lack of awe. But once you know how the sausage is made, the magic ceases to hold you—a professional hazard. I sometimes wish I could enjoy our rides as much as the guests. "Strictly speaking," Otto says, "Cthulhu is more like one of the parents of the child in my fable. But you *do* hear him?"

"Oh, loud and clear. This is a very good job. I like how you've got the electricity to power all these speakers but you don't reveal it with any electric lights. I do think the use of the drugs is effective but a bit dangerous—what if I had an allergic reaction? Personally, I think some flashing lights judiciously used can really add to the experience. Maybe even some animatronics."

"This isn't some kind of theme park ride!"

"Sure it isn't," I say. "Look, I'm on your side here. I like what you've done. Just trying to help you make the presentation a bit crisper. I know what I'm talking about and I'm not even charging you at my consulting rate."

He frowns at me and shakes his head. "You must come and see for yourself."

Once more we go through dark, twisty tunnels lit only by flickering torches. I'm impressed by the craftsmanship and attention to detail. I run my fingers over some of the cracks between the stone slabs: there's even moss, actual, living moss! Considering how small a staff he's working with here, this is nothing short of a Stonehenge- or Easter Island-level of achievement.

Though I'm now no longer drugged—or at least I don't think I am—in sections of the tunnels I still feel as though I'm walking uphill when the tunnel seems to be slanting downward, and the rivulets of water along channels in the floor are flowing *upward*. The effect is extremely realistic. Hidden pumps? Hydraulics that tilt sections of the floor as we move over them? I make a mental note to try to dig the secret out of Otto. Whether or not he knows it, he's really a genius for theme park design, and maybe there's a way I can recruit him for the Pancake Factory.

Finally, we arrive at a cavern the size of a stadium whose walls are ringed with torches. In the middle is a giant, bottomless pool.

"Prepare to have your illusions shattered, mortal," he says, and begins to chant:

Ph'nglui mglw'nafh Cthulhu R'lyeh wgah'nagl fhtagn.

On cue, the water in the pool begins to churn.

"Amazing," I say. "Again though, I think you've overdone the lighting here. I understand the desire to rely only on non-electric light for ambience, but I think a few spotlights hidden behind some rocks can really add to the visual experience. Sometimes, authenticity is enhanced with—"

I'm interrupted by the most amazing animatronic creation I've ever seen rising out of the water. There's no word to describe it: immense, gigantic, cyclopean, monolithic. Oh, it's a monster!

The head rises out of the pool until it's towering over us like a four-story building. Tentacles as thick as me and twenty, thirty feet long writhe about the cave-like maw. Cascades of water slough off the head, leaving behind slime and seaweed. The stench of fishy rot fills the whole cave.

And the monster begins to roar.

I'm utterly entranced, my mouth agape. This is without a doubt the finest animatronics display I've ever seen. Nothing back home in Florida can even touch it. The full sensory experience is complete. As the head waves about and the monster's body hits the edge of the pool, the entire floor of the cave shakes.

The monster begins to turn its head in our direction.

"I thought you said it's asleep," I say.

"It is," says Otto. "But as it dreams, it sometimes rises to the surface to observe this world, a god opening an eye for a moment before sinking back into his slumber."

I'm about to heap more praise on Otto for his artistry when the monster's head stops moving, and the eyes suddenly snap open: ancient, otherworldly, completely alien.

And in that moment, a great pressure impinges on my skull and I fall down, unconscious.

I wake up again to the concerned face of Otto flickering in the torchlight.

"How long was I out?" I groan.

"About fifteen minutes."

"It seemed much longer." I sit up. Behind the shadowy figure of Otto, the immense form of Cthulhu is bobbing up and down in the water. His eyes are closed for the moment.

"Did you dream-converse with him?"

"Yes," I say. My mouth feels dry, like I've woken up after falling asleep on a transcontinental flight. "It is indeed as you say. We're insignificant ants digging about in the backyard of Dread Cthulhu."

Otto beams. "And now you understand the futility of seeking knowledge."

"Absolutely."

"And the utter hopelessness of the human condition before cosmic horror."

"Indubitably so."

"And the acceptance of our insignificance at the space and time scale of our god Cthulhu."

"It is exactly as you say. In the long run, we're all dead."

"And you're now prepared to pray and beg for mercy, and dedicate your life to the preparation of his eventual awakening when the stars are aligned."

"Eh, that's a bit too much planning for me."

I begin to chant, doing my best to imitate Otto:

Ph'nglui mglw'nafh Cthulhu R'lyeh wgah'nagl fhtagn.

And in one swift motion, Cthulhu lashes out with his tentacles and snatches up Otto. Before he even has time to scream, Cthulhu stuffs him down his maw, and Otto is no more.

You see, during those fifteen minutes I was out, Cthulhu and I did indeed have a "dream-conversation," as Otto would say. It's not so much conversing in words as showing each other pictures—a skill I'm very good at, as the Pancake Factory is a big believer in not using words where pictures will do, considering we have visitors from across the globe. They don't call us "imagineers" for nothing.

The topics that Otto was so interested in didn't take very long. I mean, once I accepted that Cthulhu was real, none of the rest of it was worth arguing.

But, and here's the but: I'm a guy focused on the here and now. I don't really care if in a hundred generations, after the stars have aligned or whatever, Cthulhu enslaves my unknown descendants. I don't even worry about global warming, and you want me to think *that* far ahead?

I quickly explained to Cthulhu what I did. I'm not sure the concept of the Pancake Factory made much sense to him, but the idea of millions, billions even, craving images of him and paying tribute to see him did appeal. I explained how we managed to make children the world over worship and demand to be taken to visit idols of *rodents*, and he was suitably impressed. Like all gods, Cthulhu likes worshippers, having lots and lots of worshippers. I've no idea why. Maybe he thinks they'll make his eventual reign more pleasant.

But the point is: ants don't always have to beg; they can sometimes bargain.

I promised to make him at least as dreaded and feared by men and women and children the world over as the iconic rodent is beloved— provided that he listen to me and do what I say.

Cthulhu convulses and spits out a few bones. They clatter at my feet. Sometimes, to create the most authentic experience, you have to rely on the real.

"Okay, we can't do that once we get to the coast of Florida," I say. "You have to promise not to actually eat any visitors. Only pretend."

Cthulhu grumbles, and the whole cave shakes again.

Boss Gou and his goons no longer seem such a big deal, not when I have this with me.

Cthulhu World has a memorable ring to it, I think. I already have some ideas about how to set up the main attraction—a pirate ship, an abandoned island, lots of cast members dancing about a bonfire, possibly a musical. But I really need to work out the merchandizing possibilities.

The Innsmouth of the South

By Rachael K. Jones

AT R'LYEH FUNLAND, you never entered the tower unless summoned. That's because our boss, Mr. Whateley (no relation to *those* Whateleys—you know the ones), only called people up for one of three things: to chew you out, scapegoat you, or fire you. So when he called for La'vonne over the loudspeakers, I knew nothing good would come of it.

I kept one eye on the tower from my concessions booth, *The Innsmouth Look*, where I served up fried calamari, sashimi, and other assorted not-so-authentic Savannah, Georgia delicacies. Of all the attractions in the park, the tower was the biggest eyesore, the sort of thing imagined by people who vaguely knew the word "Lovecraftian" but had never actually bothered to read anything by the man. The tower had a certain gothic sensibility, sure: all soaring spires and flying buttresses and period-appropriate arches over the windows. But the park's designers had also slapped on fake blood, skulls, and some tacky plastic bats on strings, like the kind you find in a low-budget Halloween prop shop. It completely ruined the effect.

La'vonne shambled back from her meeting with the boss, still wearing her shoggoth suit, minus the hood, which made it look like the monster was devouring her feet-first. A dad trailing twin girls stopped her for a picture, but she threw him a look so withering he scooted along toward the *Mountain of Madness*, our most unstable roller coaster (it had a batwing inversion after its second drop, and a low center of gravity, which gave riders whiplash).

I let La'vonne into the little kitchen where we battered and fried the calamari for the Cthulhu Cthombo. She wet some paper towels in the sink, mopped up the worst of her running mascara, and began picking at the eyeballs that hid the shoggoth suit's zippers. "C'mon, Karl. Help a girl out?"

"God, La'vonne. What happened?" I worked the flimsy zippers gently so they wouldn't jump their tracks. La'vonne was far less gentle. A fabric eyeball ripped and fluttered to the floor. She kicked the torn bits underneath the counter.

"Mr. Whateley happened, that's what. He fired me. I asked to trade shifts with Mikki this Saturday for my graduation. Just a couple hours so my daughter can see me walk across the stage. That's important. She needs to know we put education first in our house, even without her dad around. *Especially* without her dad."

"He fired you for *that*?" La'vonne worked harder than anyone I knew. After her husband died in Iraq, she began attending design classes at SCAD. She wanted to do costume design for movies someday. She'd even designed some of our costumes—the shoggoths and the Mi-Go and a few of the cultists.

"The real kicker? I put in for the time off months ago," La'vonne continued. "The bastard damn well knows I wanted it. *He knows.* But the new schedule went up, and guess who's been assigned head priestess at the 8:00 p.m. Esoteric Order of Dagon Parade?" She ripped the last zipper open and the shoggoth pooled on the floor around her ankles. She beat lint from the T-shirt and shorts she wore underneath. "Ugh. This crap is all through my weave now."

I hunted for bits of shoggoth lint clinging between her braids. "So there wasn't anyone to cover for you?"

"No. That's the thing. I'd already worked it out with Mikki. She'd be priestess on Saturday, and I'd take Asenath Waite on the Miskatonic U tours on Sunday. We're the same size, so we could costume-swap, no problem. But Mr. Whateley said nobody would find me *believable* as Asenath." La'vonne rolled her eyes. "You know. Because he can cast white people as offensive Native American stereotypes, but nobody can buy a black Asenath for one afternoon."

"You *told* him that?" I whistled. "Damn, girl. You've got more balls than I do."

"See where it got me." La'vonne wiped her eyes. "Should've kept my mouth shut a little longer. Can't afford to be out of work."

"Hey, you're graduating. You'll land something a whole lot better with your new degree."

It was almost 2:00 p.m., and I hadn't served up any calamari in over an hour. The display plate had acquired a moving coat of flies. "Tell you what. First shift's ending soon. Let's round up the crew and knock off a little early. We should celebrate."

La'vonne gave me the barest hint of a smile, which made me feel all warm and tickly. Truth be told, I had a small crush on La'vonne that liked to flare up whenever she kicked tentacles and eyeballs into the sludge beneath a kitchen counter. "Sure. I'd like that."

I thought they grossly oversold R'lyeh Funland. *The Innsmouth of the South*, Mr. Whateley called it, except he pronounced Inns*mouth* so it rhymed with *South*, and wouldn't let anyone correct him. Not that the average tourist knew or cared. They only came because it was cheaper than a ghost tour for a family of six in downtown Savannah, and you didn't have to pay for parking, and you could get a bumper sticker that said *R'lyeh, Y'all*, even if most of them didn't get the joke.

We collected Patricia and Talon from Miskatonic U, and La'vonne's best friend Mikki from the Nameless City. On the way out the gaping tentacled demon-mouthed entrance, we passed Reverend Pete waving a Bible and shouting himself hoarse at the patrons in the ticket line.

Reverend Pete wasn't really on staff. He hailed from the local Independent Bible Church. He'd been protesting the park on grounds of Satanic influence since the day it opened. Mr. Whateley thought he added to the ambience, and besides we didn't have to pay him anything, so he let the reverend stay. Boss even let us walk out a complimentary water to him when the days got midsummer-hot, that sticky miserable Southern heat that made you want to die just so they'd bury you beneath a nice cool slab of marble.

I waved at Reverend Pete. "Howdy, reverend. How goes the sermonizing?"

Reverend Pete's eyebrows bore down like thunderheads. "*Through his policy also he shall cause craft to prosper in his hand,*" he shouted, flushing redder as he gained steam, "*and he shall magnify himself in his heart, and by peace shall destroy many.*"

"Yeah, sure," I said. "Look, reverend. We're knocking off a little early to have a beer with La'vonne. It's her last day. You want to come with?"

"*No drunkard shall inherit the kingdom of God,*" the reverend said archly.

"I'm bringing lemonade," said Mikki. "I don't mind sharing. It'd be nice to have another teetotaler in the mix." She was three months pregnant and had given up beer.

It must've been tiring business, being Reverend Pete. A whole theme park full of demons to condemn, but we were just regular people in costumes scraping by under a terrible boss. Hard to hate someone who offered you lemonade. But Reverend Pete was just taking orders himself in his own way, so we didn't mind when he quietly tagged along.

We met at our favorite drinking spot by the Savannah River, where you could dangle your legs over the dock and toss back a six-pack of Terrapin Reclaimed Rye. We shared around a pound of chocolate pralines from the confectionary on River Street. Mikki split canned Minute Maid with the Reverend while La'vonne regaled us with a reenactment of her firing.

Everyone had a Mr. Whateley horror story. Mikki had gotten relegated to playing a Mi-Go when she told him she was pregnant ("Nobody wants to see fat girls," he'd said). Patricia had just been promoted to assistant manager, only to find she was now Mr. Whateley's favorite scapegoat to corporate. Mr. Whateley had asked Talon to pose for some promotional photos, which Talon later found slapped across Mr. Whateley's online dating profiles. Even Reverend Pete had opinions on the Man of Iniquity prowling uncostumed amongst the lambs, or such. I'm not sure I followed his complaint, but it sounded pretty bad, even by Pete standards.

La'vonne just shook her head and opened another beer. "That park's too damn big. Nobody knows the half of what goes on there. How about you, Karl?"

I had Mr. Whateley stories for days, but none of them captured my secret resentment, the injury he'd inflicted upon my soul.

"I used to like Lovecraft," I admitted. "He was my favorite author. I've read the *Collected Works* cover to cover at least five times. I own every issue of *Weird Tales* with a Lovecraft story in it, the vintage ones from the 1930s. I got a tattoo of the Yellow Sign on my palm when I graduated high school. I had a Lovecraft-themed birthday party when I was thirteen, and lost all my friends over it because their parents thought I was a Satanist. And you know what? I didn't care, because the Mythos was awesome. Yes, Lovecraft had serious racism issues, and his expansive purple prose was surpassed only by his fear of miscegenation. But ultimately, the Mythos was bigger than the sum of its parts. I didn't need friends who couldn't understand that.

"I have a degree in mechanical engineering, you know. I should be *designing* those rides. With the market so bad, I took the job at R'lyeh Funland, figuring it's the closest I'll ever come to actually living in the Mythos. Hoped I'd be first in line when the engineering team at corporate had an opening. But that's all over now."

It was probably the beer, but tears stung my eyes, and the wind dragged them out sideways.

"Someone should teach him a lesson," said Mikki. "Put the fear of God into him."

"Fear of the Elder Gods, maybe." Patricia squinted out over the river. "We could put out the word online for people to show up dressed as cultists. Parade around like they work there. Mr. Whateley won't know who he can legally yell at. Maybe he'll screw up, get sued."

"There's thirty gallons of visceral ooze in the Yuggoth zone left over from Halloween," said Talon. "It wouldn't be hard to pump it into the ventilation system of his tower. It'll come down in strings from the air vents."

"Pfft. Y'all are such amateurs." La'vonne opened her satchel and pulled out a high-end *Necronomicon* from the gift shop, latex faces screaming from its imitation human skin cover. "Let's just skip the middleman and summon Cthulhu like good ol' R'lyeh Funland staffers."

She flipped open the *Necronomicon* and began to read. "*Pun-gluey muggle-nuff Cthulhu Real-yeah wagga-naggle fuh-thoggin!*" Her Savannah drawl sapped all the terror out of it. It was terrible, and we all laughed our asses off.

"You're cute when you fhtagn," I teased.

"But that's what it looks like," said La'vonne. "*You* try and do better." But before she could pass me the book, Reverend Pete bore down all angry-like and snatched it from her hands. He looked *pissed*.

At first I thought we'd offended him on account of his religious beliefs, which made me feel bad, since I'd invited him. The last thing I wanted was to make him uncomfortable. I thought he was going to chuck the *Necronomicon* into the Savannah River, but instead he flipped it open and trailed a finger down the page.

"That ain't no way to read an invocation. I'll show you how you do it proper." Then he thundered out a cultist's chant that put the rest of us to shame: "*Ph'nglui mglw'nafh Cthulhu R'lyeh wgah'nagl fhtagn.*" I guess all that time in the pulpit really did build talent.

"Wow," I said, because what else could you say? There was some scattered clapping.

"Wow, man. Have a beer," said Talon.

"Thanks." Reverend Pete accepted the beer, but set it down untasted. He probably didn't have many friends and was therefore more susceptible to the forces of peer pressure.

Thunder growled in the distance. "Looks like rain," said Mikki.

"I'd better scoot," said La'vonne.

We all scattered before the rain got worse. Out over the river, I thought I saw hissing steam and bubbles. A wood duck *plished* into the water and didn't resurface. I pulled up my hood and walked to the bus stop, letting the thunderstorm pour over me. The raindrops felt unclean. They left a slick, oily feeling on my skin, a rank fishy odor that wouldn't wash out even with a hot shower.

I was ten minutes late to work the next morning. Mr. Whateley hunched over the kitchen counter in my booth, picking tiny white worms from sashimi with a pair of tweezers. He was a pale, curdled-looking fellow with greasy black hair, like Benedict Cumberbatch left in the sun too long.

"You're late." He stacked the dewormed tuna slices on the cutting board.

"Sorry. Power went out in last night's storm, and it reset my alarm." I opened the freezer to get the frozen calamari, but nasty octopus water sloshed out, wetting my shoes.

"I don't want to hear your dumb excuses. Even a nerd like *you* should be capable of arriving to work on time." He shoved the tweezers into my hands, half a worm speared on the tip. "I don't have time for this fiddly stuff. It's your job. Get your act in order, Karl, or you're out."

I didn't dare point out the danger of serving warm, wormy sashimi to the customers, never mind the calamari unthawing all night in the broken fridge. I tried another tactic. "Can you have someone run out for more fish later? This won't get us through the lunch rush."

Mr. Whateley curdled a little more. Every time he had to do his job instead of pawning it off on someone else, he got a little more acidic. "I'll send out the janitor."

Instead, a new staffer turned up, a man with the best Innsmouth fish-person costume I'd ever seen. Green scales peeked out from beneath his black hood. He'd even thought to apply latex gills to his neck, although I only caught flashes when he turned his head. He had huge, unsettling eyes that never seemed to blink enough, and a voice like church bells tolling in the distance.

"The master sent me to assist you," he said.

"Cool. I'm Karl. What's your name?"

"Wilbur," said the new guy. His eyelids blinked sideways, closing corner to corner instead of top to bottom. I'd never seen that particular special effect before, but it didn't surprise me too much. We always had a few hires that got into character and stayed there.

"Nice job on the eyes," I said.

"Thanks."

"We're still waiting on the delivery. Can you clean up the counter while I work the fryer?"

He took the plate of worm bits and scraped them into his mouth, licking the platter clean.

"Gonna give you the runs later," I told him. Doubt tugged at my mind. I recalled Patricia's drunken revenge-plan. "Hey, did Mr. Whateley hire you, or did . . . I mean, was there something posted online?"

Wilbur just smiled at me, blinked sideways, and straightened the soy sauce packets up front.

At least he was good with the customers. Mr. Whateley must've hired a bunch of people after his firings the other day, or else Patricia had carried through with her threat to recruit Craigslist randos. I ran into a lot of unfamiliar sorts who'd been let loose without a proper orientation. Over at the Non-Euclidean Nightmare Plane (a hall of mirrors with some gelatinous animatronic fungi suspended from the ceiling), the lights had broken so you just got a few flickers in the center of the maze. And some greenhorn was stalking tourists, scratching at the walls and panting until they ran out raving.

There was more of the same all over the park. Too many shoggoths. Too many cultists. Everyone terrorizing the tourists willy-nilly until they thinned out, and it was just employees milling around, not exactly pulling their own weight when it came to puke cleanup.

After lunch, I caught Wilbur in the kitchen chewing on La'vonne's discarded shoggoth suit, which had soaked up a bunch of octopus water because I'd forgotten she'd stashed it on the floor.

"What the hell, man?"

Wilbur stopped gnawing on the fake eyeball and blinked sideways with those too-wide eyes. "It tastes like one of the others," he said.

"What's that supposed to mean?" I yanked the suit away from him. An eyeball caught and tore on his pointy teeth. "This doesn't belong to you."

"*Sssssss.*" Wilbur licked his lips. "The master awaits the gathering of the faithful before it bestows the final reward."

"Look, I love this place as much as anyone, but you've got to knock that off when you're in employee areas or nobody will take you seriously," I told him. The torn Velcro shoggoth eyeballs stuck to my sleeves.

Outside the booth, the loudspeakers crackled, announcing the midday Esoteric Order of Dagon Parade. Wilbur's eyes widened until it looked like they might roll out. "We have been summoned. To the tower!" He flung open the door and charged toward Mr. Whateley's office.

I raced after him, suppressing laughter. "Wait! That's just the parade. It happens twice a day."

But everything had gone all wrong outside.

Huge crowds of people streamed toward the tower, all wearing the cheap monogrammed cultist bathrobes the gift shop sold. I couldn't tell the staffers from the tourists anymore. It looked like the midday parade, another Dagon sacrifice, except I didn't see any high priestess leading the *iä! iä!* chorus. Above the tower, thunderheads gathered and swirled, heavy and violet. Flecks of rain pattered into the dirt. The droplets held their shape like Jell-O. I nudged one with my boot. It quivered and hissed against the rubber, burning a hole in the toe. Acid.

No way *that* was special effects.

I pushed and shoved a path through the ecstatic, chanting cultists. The crowd thinned as we approached the tower. That's when I spotted La'vonne standing on the landing beneath the flying buttresses and fake bats, shouting at Mr. Whateley.

"I want my fucking paycheck," said La'vonne. "You don't get to just fire me without paying me for hours worked."

"I can, if I fire you for cause." Mr. Whateley seemed oblivious to the crowd around him. His default mode for handling any crisis at the park was just ignoring stuff until it got so bad he had to notice, and the swirling vortex overhead was still a few shades short of apocalyptic.

"What cause could you possibly have? I've been a model employee for two years now. You should return all the costumes I made, too. Nobody paid me for those. You don't own them."

"Just try to prove it. Take my property and the police will be at your door. Who do you think they'll believe anyway?" He spun on his foot and tried to slam the faux-stone office door, but La'vonne wedged her foot in.

"I'm warning you," she said.

Thunder boomed again. As one, all the cultists began chanting. I didn't recognize the words. It wasn't the famous Cthulhu chant we always did, but something inhuman, produced deep in the throat with not enough vowels and too many apostrophes for comfort. It made my skin crawl.

The whirling thunderheads coalesced to a point like the pupil of a great eye. The aperture split open, drawing back, unveiling a dark that was darker than any earthly twilight. No, this was darkness that destroyed all hope, the dark that dwelled beyond the gates of time and space. Something awful slithered from that darkness, something long and white and covered in ichorous slime. It crawled around and around the tower, knocking down the fake bats, cutting into the cheap plastic facade with thousands of hook-tipped legs. Huge tusk-like teeth, serrated on all sides, stuck out from what must have been its head.

"*Master!*" the cultists chanted. "*Master! Master!*"

I searched through all the Lovecraft stories I could remember, trying to identify this thing. Yhashtur, worm-god of the Lords of Thule, rival of Nyarlathotep? Crom Cruach? Idh-yaa, Bride of Cthulhu? Rlim Shaikorth, the White Worm? Lovecraft sure loved his worm-gods. It didn't matter, because the horror had slithered between La'vonne and Mr. Whateley. She fell backward, scrambled on her hands to my side. To my surprise, I realized the others had joined us too: Patricia, Mikki, Talon, and even Reverend Pete, who wasn't wearing a wristband and therefore was technically trespassing.

"It knows we summoned it," whispered Pete. "We spake the words. Blood calls to blood." In the right time and place, Pete would've made an excellent cultist. He had the proper skill set.

Talon wiped sweat from his forehead with his fedora brim. "What's the rule about these situations? You serve Cthulhu, and your reward is he eats you first?"

"Pretty sure that's not Cthulhu," said Mikki.

La'vonne jerked her chin at me. "Karl's the expert."

Everyone expected me to do something. Even the cultists, who had a whole evil god to ogle. It sucked being a hero of a Lovecraft story, because your only options were to get eaten or go mad, and I liked my body and brain intact, thankyouverymuch. The real fun of Lovecraft was gawking at those poor saps, and feeling relieved it wasn't you.

So I decided to take a page out of Mr. Whateley's book. I shifted the blame. "Y'all, it seems what we've got on our hands is a job interview. New management. Follow my lead."

I approached the two creatures oozing from the tower. One was a pale, gibbering blight upon nature, monstrously indifferent to all human suffering it caused. The other was an Elder God.

"O Great One! We are but humble servants, unworthy of your attention. We summoned you, O Great One, at the behest of our master, who stands there at the foot of his dark tower!" I pointed a finger at Mr. Whateley. It would've been more dramatic without the shoggoth eyeballs Velcroed to my arm.

But the great Worm wasn't buying what I was selling, because it unfurled its proboscis and spat more sizzling gelatinous acid, which melted some of the plastic bats littering the ground around the tower.

That might've begun my descent into madness or excruciating death, had it not been for Reverend Pete. I'd never seen the man so full of fight. Hellfire danced in his eyes and his Bible looked twice as big—wait, no. It was just a gift shop *Necronomicon*.

"Woe!" he thundered, his voice bouncing and echoing off all the park's cheap facades. "Woe to the false shepherd that destroys and scatters the sheep of the pasture! Wherefore his way shall be unto him as slippery ways in the darkness: he shall be driven on, and fall therein." He threw the *Necronomicon* toward the tower. It whistled right under the creature's slithering bulk and flopped open at Mr. Whateley's feet. "Behold, the Man of Iniquity standeth in his crumbling kingdom."

All those pretty "shalls" and "woes" succeeded where I'd failed. Even monstrous worm-creatures know that mad doomsday prophets always tell the truth. It twitched its big head around to look at Mr. Whateley, who was trying to slam the door shut again. The creature tore the door off its hinges with one hooked leg.

"I'm not in charge of them. I don't even know them," said Mr. Whateley. But he was the one standing in the dark tower, so it was like blaming your farts on the dog when you only had a Roomba.

The nightmarish worm bestowed upon him the ultimate reward, and devoured him. It was every inch as gruesome as you can imagine. Through the monster's translucent skin, you could see bits of Mr. Whateley traveling through its digestive tract piece by piece, ahead of the rest of Mr. Whateley, who gawked and screamed, watching his own progression. It looked a little like roller coaster carts climbing up and up the tower.

When it had finished its meal, the worm crawled right into the managerial tower, pulling the broken door closed behind it. The swirling storm crackled out and disbursed. The sun even came out. I'm pretty sure I saw a rainbow.

At that point it seemed safe to clock out and head home for the night. So we did.

When your boss dies from *Necronomicon*-related causes at a Lovecraft theme park, it's hard to decide whether you should return to clean out your locker in the morning, or just sleep in and update your resume. I guess my dedication to all things Lovecraftian won out, because I drove back to the park just a couple hours late for my shift.

The ticket line ran out the doors and down the sidewalk. I'd never seen so many patrons. Reverend Pete worked the line with a shiny new gold-edged Bible and his very best doomsday voice. I'd never seen him so happy. He could finally rail against an actual demonic creature, and he wasn't about to waste the opportunity.

"What happened to the monster?" I asked Pete.

He nodded toward the tower. The Worm had cocooned it in thick gray webbing. Bits of the stuff fluttered all over the park and stuck to everything, smelling of mildew and old graves. "Got ourselves a real live Blasphemy Beast, right there. I read all about it in Revelations. *And he causeth all, both small and great, rich and poor, free and bond, to receive a mark in their right hand, or in their foreheads*, just like the Good Book says."

"No, Pete, we already had the hand stamps *before*," I told him, but nothing I said was going to kill his joy today.

Mikki and Patricia cordoned off the entrance to the tower, but left space for tourists who wanted a good photo op.

"I guess the Worm is in charge now," said Patricia. "It won't leave the tower. It's been quiet ever since it ate Mr. Whateley."

"Looks like a cocoon. Elder Gods can sleep for a long, long time, you know," I said. "Whole lifetimes."

Even though the new management was a nightmare creature which hailed from an unknown terror-realm, it brought a lot of positive changes to the park, enough so corporate never made a fuss about Mr. Whateley's absence, especially since they didn't have to pay it. Its cultist retinue made staffing issues a problem of the past. Those of us who cared about paychecks got raises. La'vonne played Asenath Waite while she applied to costuming jobs, and now she's out in Los Angeles doing zombies for next summer's blockbuster hit. I miss her, but she's invited me to visit when I can. Patricia ranked highest on the managerial ladder, so she assumed most of Mr. Whateley's responsibilities, like making the schedule and payroll, although not his office. Mikki quit the park altogether after her baby was born and took a gig doing ghost tours. They paid better, and you could collect tips from drunk tourists.

As for me, I've handed off *The Innsmouth Look* to Talon and so I can take over ride design. I want to build a coaster called *The Lurking Fear* around the Worm's tower. It's going to be red carts in a clear structure climbing up and rushing down and inverting at the doorstep, so your stomach falls into your shoes when you just glimpse something pulsing and slithering inside the gray webbed cocoon.

Only I know better than to get too close. After all, at R'lyeh Funland, you never enter the tower—unless summoned.

WWRD

By Yvonne Navarro

THE DOLL started talking to Lenore the first day her little brother gave it to her as a birthday present. It was a typical Brian gift, something he thought was rockingly cool and so he bought it with zero thought that the recipient might not agree. With almost thirteen years' difference in their ages, there wasn't a whole lot in common between the two of them, but with this gift he had, somehow, nailed it.

Let's face it, the doll was ridiculous. Still, you had to give it up for someone who created a squishy, winged Cthulhu doll holding an eyeball-topped baton, then shoved the thing into a sparkly white suit with a cape and stuck an Elvis pompadour on its head. The red plastic eyes and eight green face tentacles just made it that much better.

Although being currently boyfriend-challenged sucked in a lot of ways, it also had its upside: a full dinner at the parents' house—her mom cooked like she was the love child of Bobby Flay and Giada De Laurentiis—and an evening of cake, games, and goofiness with them and Brian. It sounded all kinds of sixties family drippy and maybe it was, but Lenore liked spending time with the family. She loved her job as an interior designer and her career was moving forward at a steady pace that required a lot of hours. Her last boyfriend had stretched her free time to the maximum, even if a lot of that time had been waiting at home or various restaurants while he was late in picking her up. Right now she was free and easy, stuffed with mom's gourmet cooking and an oversized wedge of homemade red velvet birthday cake, looking forward to a glass or three of her favorite wine to cap off the day marking the start of the twenty-sixth year of her life.

Arms loaded with birthday loot, Lenore got the door to her apartment unlocked and made it over to the small kitchen table before everything slid loose. Most of it stayed on the table, except for a couple of cards and the doll, which landed face down on the "no-stain" laminate flooring the landlord had installed a couple of months previous. A foot or so to the left of its head was a blob of dull purple, a spill courtesy of a guy she'd dated for three whole weeks before kicking him to the curb with his various empty liquor bottles. The stain was vaguely South America-shaped and not nearly as easy to get rid of as he had been.

She sorted through the items and headed to the fridge with the containers of leftovers—another perk of visiting her parental units. Lenore shoved the food inside then shut the door and went to grab her favorite wine glass.

"Would you get my face off the floor, please?"

Lenore jerked and almost lost her grip on the wine glass. Thank God she'd always had good reflexes; she caught it with two fingers and slid it back onto the safety of the counter. "Who said that?"

The voice came again, slightly muffled and on the scratchy side. "Me. Down here. The part about my face being on the floor, remember?"

She stretched her neck but didn't move closer. She could just see that crazy Cthulhu doll about a foot away from the table leg. The white tip—presumably a claw—of one wing had twisted over the other and was jutting above its satin-covered butt. The toes of its feet, covered in faux white leather, were turned inward and looked kind of pitiful.

"Dolls don't talk." Her throat felt dry and closed, but once she got the words out, she felt better.

"I'm not a doll. I'm a stuffed entity. A very *powerful* entity, and I don't like being so close to that red spot on the floor. It makes me uncomfortable."

Lenore frowned. She was surprised, yes, but she wasn't all that afraid. "You don't look very powerful."

"If your nose was smashed into the floor you wouldn't look powerful either."

She took a cautious step forward, angling around the side of the table. "So—"

"Lenore, *please.* Up off the floor, okay?"

Her mouth fell open. "How do you know my name?"

"You know what? I'm not talking anymore until you do what I told you."

It took an hour and two glasses of wine for Lenore to convince herself she'd imagined the whole thing. By then she had everything put away and had changed into her favorite pajamas, a ratty flannel top and bottom decorated with a pattern of faded, smiling mice. On the way to the refrigerator for her lucky third glass of vino, she bent and scooped the Cthulhu doll off the floor without hesitating.

"*About time.*"

Her empty wine glass bobbled in her suddenly nerveless fingers, but she managed to hold on. Her other hand snapped forward and flung the doll across the room, where it landed on its side on the couch. She exhaled through her clenched teeth, making a noise that was forced and loud and a lot like the half moans, half hisses that came out of her during her pathetic attempts at working out.

"That was uncalled for," Elvis Cthulhu said.

"Stop it," she said. "I am not hearing this."

"You're not crazy," it said.

Frozen in her kitchen area, all Lenore could do was stare across the ten or twelve feet that separated her from that talking . . . *thing.*

The scratchy voice came again. "Look, I think we got off on the wrong foot. Let's start over, shall we? My name is R'lyeh. R-apostrophe-l-y-e-h. I'm named after a city that you probably never heard of. It's too hard to pronounce in the language of the Old Ones, so just use the Americanized version. Sounds like *Riley.*"

Lenore wanted to respond, she really did. Unfortunately her lips felt like they'd turned into dead fish.

"This is the part where you say 'nice to meet you,'" the doll—R'lyeh—prompted. When she still didn't respond, it sighed. "Okay, even if you don't want to say anything, would you please sit me upright? I hate being tipped onto my side almost as much as I hated the face plant."

"For a doll that can talk, you can't do a whole lot, can you?" Lenore

body is here, of course, but that's it. I'm totally making up this entire conversation."

"I am not ugly!"

"Shut. Up."

For once, R'lyeh obeyed. Or was it her own mind finally doing what she wanted? At this point, Lenore couldn't tell.

She finished cleaning up the wine spill, then tried to decide if she should go for a replacement third round. Why not? There was just enough left in the bottle to go back to the half-full amount that society thought was so respectable. This time she clicked off the light in the kitchen and went to the living room, settling on the flowered rocking-recliner that was positioned at an angle to the couch. From here she could sip her wine and keep her eye on that Cthulhu doll. Not that it was going to move or anything, but you never knew. She'd figured out the voice was in her own head, yes, but there was still a little part of her that suspected one of the thing's plastic red eyes—the pupils were vertical, like a goat's—would suddenly wink at her.

Rocking and drinking made Lenore feel like someone's grandmother, or at least a hip version of one. Was this how she was going to be in thirty or forty years? Sure, she was still young, but the doll voice had been right—her relationship record sucked rocks. Not that she *needed* a man to make her life perfect, but she kind of *wanted* one. Good nookie notwithstanding, she liked company and affection, and she liked giving affection. She just always picked the wrong guy.

"W-W-R-D," the doll said suddenly.

She groaned and knocked back the rest of the wine in her glass. Not again. "What would R'lyeh do?"

If a stuffed doll could make a chortling sound, this one did. "Exactly! That's why I'm here, you know. To provide you with guidance."

She was afraid to ask, but she did anyway. "How so?"

"So you've already established that I'm you, right?"

Lenore's forehead drew in. "Uh . . ."

"I'm your own voice in your head," R'lyeh said patiently. "Right?" When she didn't answer, he continued. "But everything has a purpose, and mine is to help you make those hard decisions, the ones you keep mucking up on your own. Well, one hard decision in particular."

She rubbed her eyes. "Which is?"

"Companionship," R'lyeh said without hesitation. "I shall assist you in finding the man of your dreams."

"Seriously?" Lenore couldn't help rolling her eyes, although her head was starting to throb and the movement just made it worse. "Will you please just not talk anymore?"

"Not this time," R'lyeh said.

She scowled at the doll but, thank God, it didn't move. "So what now?" She couldn't believe it. As much as she didn't want to, she was still talking to a doll.

"We're going out."

"I can't believe I'm doing this," Lenore said. Her voice was more of a mumble, too low to be heard by the people around her. She was standing at the edge of a darkly polished bar in a neighborhood place called The Wendigo. It was small and very crowded and not particularly well lit, although at least it smelled good. Still, that could have been attributed to the girl hurrying past with a large tray of wings and burgers. As she did with all joints like this, Lenore looked at the floor only if she had to—you never knew what the heck was going on down there—and kept one hand firmly on her purse. It would have been just another Thursday night except that cradled in her other arm was R'lyeh the Cthulhu doll. As far as she was concerned, it was the first sign that the kernel of madness taking root in her head was starting to grow into the real world. In one way she was desperately trying to hide it; in another, it had to be obvious from the sideways looks and smirks directed her way that she was off her flipping gourd.

Well, she couldn't just come in and stand here without doing something bar-like. She got the bartender's attention but they didn't have white zinfandel; she settled for a glass of rosé, wincing at the dry taste of the wine.

"Hey, what's up with the dorky-looking toy?"

Lenore turned and ended up face to face with a guy who matched her height. He had light brown hair and a pimple next to his nose. She had an up-close view of it because apparently he had zero notion of personal space. "What?"

"The doll," he said. She thought there was an edge of impatience in his voice. "Why are you carrying that thing around?"

She stepped back, feeling the round edge of the bar bump into her spine. "I like it," was the only answer she could come up with. "It's like a . . . security blanket." His eyes—he was close enough that she could see they were pale blue—widened, so maybe that hadn't been a good response. Best to try and change the subject. "My name is Lenore."

"I'm George." He leaned even closer; now she could smell his cologne. Something overpowering and familiar, in a daily, crowded-train sort of way. "My friends call me Georgie."

Lenore edged sideways, trying to get back into breathable air range. "Really."

George grinned at her, showing teeth that were even and white. Well, except for his canines, which were just a bit longer than they should have been. "Yeah. You know that old nursery rhyme, right? *Georgie Porgie, puddin' and pie.*"

Suddenly R'lyeh's voice floated into her mind, a barely discernible whisper amid the noise in the bar. "Kissed the girls and made them cry."

Lenore blinked. "What?" she asked out loud.

Oops.

"What *what*?" George asked. He was still grinning as he glanced from her face to the doll, then back. "Is that thing talking to you?" Before she could think of a response, there he was again, all up into her space. "Come on, baby. I'm dying to know the story behind Elvis here. Is it kinky? I love that stuff."

Lenore looked at him in horror. "What—*no!*"

She was pretty sure her expression was one of total disgust, but apparently George was not put off in the least. Now he was so close she could smell his cologne *and* his breath—onion rings and ketchup, gross; one more micro-inch and their arms would be skin to skin. "I have an Elvis tattoo that looks like your doll, but it's in a sensitive area so I can't show you here. You want to go somewhere?"

"Not with you," she blurted before she could stop herself. "Or anyone remotely related to you." Where had *that* come from? She'd never talked to anyone like that in her life.

George's eyebrows raised so high they almost met his hairline. "Whoa. You don't want to, just say no. No need to insult my family."

Lenore stared after him as he spun and pushed his way through the crowd, then she jumped when R'lyeh spoke again. "You wouldn't have liked him anyway. He was a biter."

"A . . . what?" she asked, trying not to move her mouth.

"A biter. You know, a person who likes to bite when they—"

"Thanks," she interrupted. So far no one was noticing her as she talked to the Cthulhu doll. "I think I got it."

"It's all about those canine teeth."

Lenore ignored R'lyeh and checked out the crowd. She hated to view people in terms of stereotypes—and Georgie Porgie had certainly rattled *that* notion—but across the room was a guy who was clearly a lawyer in a world all about himself: chiseled features that were a little too handsome, a precise, stylish haircut that probably cost more than the blouse Lenore was wearing, sharp eyes that missed nothing— even as he talked to one person, they scanned the room like a wolf looking for that tasty rabbit. He was with a couple of friends who complimented him perfectly, yin to yang, while they all talked up three women so exquisite they could have stepped out of the pages of a Paris magazine. Lenore was glad for the distance between herself and them, the bodies that would shield her from sinking into a puddle of mere mortalness should they get too close.

"How about him?" R'lyeh asked when her gaze paused thoughtfully on a broad-shouldered man-boy working his way through the crowd. He stopped to say something to a couple at a table, giving Lenore the chance to inventory him. Even covered by a blue denim jacket and a plaid flannel shirt—how very all-American—it was obvious he had a nice build. A cowboy hat sat on his head like it had grown there, no awkwardness even in this city bar, and his jeans had a looseness that bespoke of comfortable wear. He smiled and reached out a big hand to shake with the guy at a table, then glanced in Lenore's direction. Their eyes locked for a second then his head turned back to the couple.

"Hmmm," she murmured to herself. Maybe she should pursue this. Idly she wondered what Cowboy Bob would think of her Cthulhu doll, then had a sudden, bizarre image in her head: R'lyeh lassoed to the longhorn hood ornament of a Cadillac with Texas license plates, a highway blurring past at an insane speed, a man's deep, slightly manic laughter.

"Well?" the doll asked impatiently.

"No," she said.

"Why not? Maybe he'll take you for a ride."

It was a snide little comment but it hit close enough to the vision that it made her want to retaliate. "More likely he'll take *you*," she snapped.

R'lyeh said nothing but she felt a twinge of something . . . surprise? Hurt? "Sorry," she said under her breath, feeling childish. "I just got a weird feeling about him, that's all."

"There's a lot of weird going around right now," he replied in a quiet voice.

True that, but it was vaguely comforting to hear him acknowledge it.

"You need someone more like me," the doll said.

"What?"

"Like me. You know, considerate but not smothering. Stylish but not . . ."

"Weird?"

"I was going to say flamboyant."

"Okay, you are so far off base—"

"Maybe that was the wrong word," R'lyeh said hastily. "Dull?"

"Stylish but not dull," Lenore repeated thoughtfully. "Okay, I can go with that."

"Someone who looks like me, right?"

She glanced down at the doll. "I can do without the tentacles. Just saying."

"I was thinking Elvis."

"Not really me," she said. "I can also live without poufy hair."

"You don't have to get personal!"

"Don't get all defensive on me," Lenore said. She realized the words had come out louder than she'd intended, but when she looked at the people closest to her they hadn't noticed.

"It's part of my style. You said you liked that."

She started to point out that he was twisting her words when someone lightly bumped her shoulder from behind.

"That's an interesting thing to bring into a bar."

Again? But to be honest, she probably should expect it. Keeping her glass in hand, Lenore sighed inwardly and turned toward the voice. The speaker was a tall guy with short, dark hair. She wouldn't consider him drop-dead handsome, but that was actually a plus. His clothes were Modern American Yuppie—a Ralph Lauren polo shirt and

Levi's—but he was wearing some kind of strange little earring. "It was a, uh, gift," she said. "From my little brother."

He grinned. "Special occasion?"

"My birthday," she said reluctantly. It occurred to her that he must think she was pretty sad to go pub crawling the night of her birthday. Crazy was more like it, because she'd taken a doll with her. She started to lie and say she still had it because she hadn't been home, then changed her mind. Instead she held up the toy and jiggled it. "He's my birthday mascot. See?"

The guy laughed. "Well, happy birthday. My name's—" Whatever he said was lost as something happened on the television over the bar that made a cheer go up from a group of people next to them. "What's yours?"

"Lenore." Another cheer, and this time her companion cheered with them, everyone in the bar shouting and raising their glasses. She glanced at the television and saw a baseball game coming to a close. It was too loud to hear the announcer but the words scrolling across the bottom said "Cubs win the World Series for the first time since 1908!" A hundred and eight years was a long time, and she couldn't help smiling along with everybody, then toasting with the folks around her.

The guy with the dark hair bent close to her, trying to be heard. His eyes could have been dark blue or brown, but she just couldn't tell in the low light. One thing she could finally get a good look at, however, was that earring. It was a tiny red, white and blue Cubs logo. "Listen." He almost had to shout. "I have to go. My dad's from Chicago and he's a huge baseball fan. I promised him I'd come and help him celebrate if the Cubs won."

She nodded, forcing a smile. Damn, they'd barely had a chance to talk.

He took out his wallet and pulled a business card from it, then made a handwriting gesture in the air at a passing server, who handed him a pen. "Your number?" His expression was hopeful as he offered her the pen with the card. The knot of disappointment faded and she juggled her purse, the doll, and finally just set the nasty glass of overly dry wine on the bar and pushed it away. She wrote down her number and handed the card back to him, liking the way he smiled as he took it.

Too late she realized she should have turned the card over and read it. She took a deep breath. "So I don't get embarrassed when you call," she said—and yes, she noticed that the word she'd used was *when*, not *if*—"let me admit right now that it's so noisy in here I didn't catch your name when you told me."

"It's Riley," he said. "Riley Arkham." He reached forward and gave her hand a brief squeeze, then headed out the door.

Lenore stared after him. "You've got to be kidding." She said the words aloud, but thankfully everyone around her was still yelling about the game.

"My work here is done," a familiar voice said.

She glanced down at the doll squeezed between her ribs and her arm, waiting to see if it said anything else. But it didn't, of course, because it was just a doll.

An Elvis Cthulhu doll.

Named R'lyeh.

In the Employee Manual of Madness

By G. Scott Huggins

Initiation:

Iä!

The High Chef and Priest of the Innsmouth Dominüs thanks you for your service in arising from the welcoming arms of The Deep and returning to land to increase the Feeding and Following of our Dread Lord, the Great Cthulhu, as an employee of Dominüs Pizza.

Alternatively, Human Cultists, you have been permitted to learn the Great Mysteries of the Deep. Fail not in this charge on peril of your Initiation.

More alternatively, Slave chattel, you are doomed to a life of servitude until such time as your shattered minds and withered bodies shall be sacrificed to feed the Majesty of the Outer Dark.

In all cases, read and memorize this Employee Manual and Code of Conduct, and sign it in your own blood. Slaves' True Names will be registered on their Bills of Possession, but will be entered in the Shift Schedule and referred to at all times as "Chuck."

Codes signed in ichor are evidence of either a successful assault upon a superior being or advancement in the Cult of the Deep and in either case, the Elder Management will consider the employee for a salaried position.

Shift Schedule:

Shift Schedules will be determined at each new moon by invoking the Will of Cthulhu Who Lies Dreaming, or at the random whim of the High Chef and Priest, whoever is the most evil. All employees are expected to call in daily to determine which shift is being followed.

Unexcused Absences: Unexcused Absences from work shall be punishable by Death (see Excused Absences)

Excused Absences: Excused absence policy varies with the Excusing Event and the Employee Class, as detailed below.

Religious Holidays: Deep Ones will be excused from their shift to respond to the Call of Cthulhu no more than once per lunar year when the moon is waxing gibbous. For Human Cultists, working the Shift is their most important religious obligation, and Chuck has been cut off from the "mercy" of its false and feeble gods and can expect no redemption, so will work its Shift in either case.

Illness: The servants of the Great Cthulhu do not get "ill" except by His explicit Will, and are therefore expected to work their Shifts.

Death (of another): The Deep Ones know That Is Not Dead Which Can Eternal Lie, Cultists are severing their ties with Humanity, and Chuck is beneath contempt. All are expected to work their Shifts.

Death (yours): Dead Employees will be expected to work their shifts as the Will of Great Cthulhu permits, their souls bound into their glabrous and decaying flesh until such time as they are released or reclassified by Human Resources (see below).

Employee Appearance Standards:

Deep Ones are expected to maintain the appearance of humanity at all times on shift. Extra eyes, fingers and tentacles should be concealed beneath clothing. Deep Ones are reminded that humans blink frequently. Human Cultists are expected to wear a tattoo binding their souls to the worship of the Dreamer Cult at all times. Said tattoo must be concealed beneath clothing such that it can be easily revealed to Elder Management on demand. Tattoos are expected to be tastefully placed and not near any human erogenous zones, which Elder Management, frankly, finds disgusting. Chuck is expected to wear its uniform, whether on shift or not, until its desecrated clothing merges with its festering flesh.

Orders:

Dominüs Employees are expected to obey all orders without exception on pain of painful and excruciating death for a first offense. Subsequent offenses will be more severely punished.

Food Orders:

Step 1: Greeting Clients

Human clients should be greeted in as surly a manner as possible, unless they reveal by sigil or cant that they are Cultists of the Deep, in which case, serve them as Deep Ones except with the Lesser Genuflection. Deep Ones receive the Greater Genuflection and a 20% discount at all times.

IMPORTANT: Any human identifying itself as a Health Inspector should be immediately referred to Elder Management where its body will be processed into Sothothage as painfully as possible, and its shriveled soul be left naked and sent to the Great Old Ones. If at any point the creature is found to lack a soul, please offer it Employment Package RLYH-1 if it retains sufficient faculties to perform its duties.

Step 2: Pickup or Delivery

Clients should be asked whether they wish their order for Pickup or Delivery if the option exists. Refer to Order Table 1:

ORDER TABLE 1:

Client Level	Carry-Out	Delivery
Human	Reluctantly	Laugh Sneeringly
Cultists	Yes	Full Charge
Deep Ones	Yes	Reduced Charge
Elder Things of Yuggoth	Yes (see note below)	Full Charge
Great Old Ones	NO!	FREE: Special Drivers ONLY! (see below)

NOTE: **UNDER NO CIRCUMSTANCES MAY ELDER THINGS SEND SHOGGOTHS**

G. Scott Huggins

TO PICK UP ORDERS.

Step 3: Taking the Order

Pizzas can be ordered with the following toppings: Cthulhumari, Húmburger, Sothothage, and Ghost Mushrooms. Any clients ordering pizza with double Ghost Mushrooms should be gently dissuaded. If they cannot be dissuaded, a driver should be sent to collect their remains and clean up the mess before the end of the shift.

Sides (Onion Things, Fringe Fries, and Fried Cthulhumari) will be prepared fresh daily (see Food Prep below).

Desserts (Frozen Yog-Urt-Sothoth and the Float-With-A-Thousand-Young) will be taken from the Cold Air Room upon demand. NOTE: These items cannot be ordered for Delivery due to the risk that upon melting they will flow around and consume the driver. The only exception is Special Drivers (see below)

Step 4: Payment

Until the dark and glorious Day of the Arising of Great Cthulhu from the Deep, we still accept payment in USD from humans of all sorts. Make sure to note whether you are taking cash or credit and enter it in the till. Deep Ones may pay in pearls and other treasure from the sea. Elder Things may tender Ckthark of Yuggoth. Do not under any circumstances attempt to collect payment from a Great Old One. These orders are entered in the till under "Sacrifice."

Morning Inspection:

Employees:

Managers are responsible for the inspection of all employees and food prior to opening. Employees not meeting the Standards of Appearance will be Reprimanded. Employees suffering from Death (or Chuck, regardless of whether or not it is dead) who can no longer meet the Standards of Appearance should be removed from the Shift Schedule immediately and Reclassified (see below).

Equipment:

Ovens and Fryers will be turned on in the morning. Fryers will be filled to a depth of six inches with ichor or fat.

Toppings:

Toppings will be inspected by the Manager. Any toppings suspected of being spoiled will be fed to Chuck. If Chuck shows adverse reactions (dizziness, vomiting, death, madness) it (the Chuck) will be Reclassified immediately (see Human Resources below). Then mix the toppings with fresher toppings so that no one notices. Toppings cost money, and are under no circumstances to be thrown out.

Sides:

Sides will be inspected and prepped at the beginning of each shift. Raw Onion Things, Cthulhumari and Fringe Fries should be the Color Out of Space. Discard any that does not meet this standard. Chuck will test a sample of the Cthulhumari in a Fryer. If Chuck starts screaming because the Cthulhumari is writhing into eldritch sigils too terrible for its feeble human mind to comprehend, it (the Cthulhumari) should be placed on the line for serving. Otherwise, discard as desecrated.

IMPORTANT: Onion Things are NOT Cthulhumari. Employees who cannot tell the difference between quivering roots and quivering tentacles should be Reprimanded with Extreme Prejudice.

Dough:

Dough should be flabby, pale, and quivering slightly. Discard any quiescent dough.

Goat-with-a-Thousand-Young Cheese:

Cheese should show grayish-green mold at all times. Unhealthy (white or pink) cheese should be fed Ground Chuck for one day, and be discarded if it does not return to health.

Sothoth:

IMPORTANT: Pizza Sothoth NEVER goes bad. If you receive complaints about black Sothoth from Deep Ones assure them that it is a blessing of the Great Old Ones. If they continue to complain, or if humans complain, give them a refund if there are any witnesses. Otherwise, lure them into the back where they may be sacrificed for blasphemy. *Be VERY CAREFUL about the witnesses—Elder Mgmt.*

Preparation (Prep):

IMPORTANT: These are not full recipes. For full recipes, refer to the copy of the *Necronomnomnomnicon* possessed by Elder Management.

Pizza: Managers will ensure that the Ritual of Pizza-making is clearly posted and followed. All pizzas will be prepared with a minimum of 1/4 cup of Sothoth and 1/3 cup of Goat-with-a-Thousand-Young Cheese.

Sides: Fried Cthulhumari and Onion Things will be dipped in Yog-Urt-Sothoth and rolled in bread crumbs fresh daily.

Drivers:

Drivers are required to keep meticulous track of their time, but managers and drivers both are expected to lie about it continuously to make the store look better, and all parties to this lie may be Terminated at whim. Drivers will be paid a gas allowance of $1.50 per delivery. Drivers are expected to keep their vehicles looking neat. Kelp and seaweed are to be removed after any delivery to Deep Ones. Drivers must on no account use the hypergeometry of the rear parking lot to cut corners off their time, unless delivering to Yuggoth, R'lyeh, the Dreamlands, or the Plateau of Leng.

Special Drivers: Deliveries to the Great Old Ones should be carried by Chuck, who will be told that it can earn its freedom by making a delivery. It will use the Dominüs company vehicle for this. Remains (if any) in the car when they return should be hosed out thoroughly. If a regular driver's car must be used for this purpose, the driver will be paid a cleaning allowance at the end of Shift. Special Drivers will be Reclassified (see below) but *their remains must not be used as toppings.* They are now consecrated to the Great Old One whom they fed. Any other use of their bodies is blasphemy and cause for Termination.

Human Resources:

Reclassification: In the event that a Human Cultist or Slave displeases Elder Management to the point that its services are no longer required, it will be Reclassified. Cultists must be Excommunicated and then Terminated. Slaves' Bills of Possession must be burnt with the appropriate rituals. Their True Names must then be inscribed in the *Necronomnomnomnicon*. They are thenceforth available for use as Ground Chuck, which may be rendered at will into Húmburger and Fryer fat.

Termination: The bodies of the Terminated are to be stored in the Cold Air Room and rendered into Sothothage.

Questions and Complaints:

All questions that cannot be answered by Elder Management should be addressed by invoking the Dread Nyarlathotep via the Threnody of Azathoth chanted over a stone altar upon which is sacrificed a pint of human blood. All such communication is recorded, and may be used against you at any time.

Shoggoth's Old Peculiar

By Neil Gaiman

BENJAMIN LASSITER was coming to the unavoidable conclusion that the woman who had written *A Walking Tour of the British Coastline*, the book he was carrying in his backpack, had never been on a walking tour of any kind, and would probably not recognise the British coastline if it were to dance through her bedroom at the head of a marching band, singing "I'm the British Coastline" in a loud and cheerful voice while accompanying itself on the kazoo.

He had been following her advice for five days now and had little to show for it, except blisters and a backache. *All British seaside resorts contain a number of bed-and-breakfast establishments, who will be only too delighted to put you up in the "off-season"* was one such piece of advice. Ben had crossed it out and written in the margin beside it: *All British seaside resorts contain a handful of bed-and-breakfast establishments, the owners of which take off to Spain or Provence or somewhere on the last day of September, locking the doors behind them as they go.*

He had added a number of other marginal notes, too. Such as *Do not repeat not under any circumstances order fried eggs again in any roadside cafe* and *What is it with the fish-and-chips thing?* and *No they are not.* That last was written beside a paragraph which claimed that, if there was one thing that the inhabitants of scenic villages on the British coastline were pleased to see, it was a young American tourist on a walking tour.

For five hellish days, Ben had walked from village to village, had drunk sweet tea and instant coffee in cafeterias and cafes and stared out at grey rocky vistas and at the slate-coloured sea, shivered under his two thick sweaters, got wet, and failed to see any of the sights that were promised.

Sitting in the bus shelter in which he had unrolled his sleeping bag one night, he had begun to translate key descriptive words: *charming* he decided, meant *nondescript*; *scenic* meant *ugly but with a nice view if the rain ever lets up*; *delightful* probably meant. *We've never been here and don't know anyone who has.* He had also come to the conclusion that the more exotic the name of the village, the duller the village.

Thus it was that Ben Lassiter came, on the fifth day, somewhere north of Bootle, to the village of Innsmouth, which was rated neither *charming*, *scenic* nor *delightful* in his guidebook. There were no descriptions of the rusting pier, nor the mounds of rotting lobster pots upon the pebbly beach.

On the seafront were three bed-and-breakfasts next to each other: Sea View, Mon Repose and Shub Niggurath, each with a neon VACANCIES sign turned off in the window of the front parlour, each with a CLOSED FOR THE SEASON notice thumbtacked to the front door.

There were no cafes open on the seafront. The lone fish-and-chip shop had a CLOSED sign up. Ben waited outside for it to open as the grey afternoon light faded into dusk. Finally a small, slightly frog-faced woman came down the road, and she unlocked the door of the shop. Ben asked her when they would be open for business, and she looked at him, puzzled, and said, "It's Monday, dear. We're never open on Monday." Then she went into the fish-and-chip shop and locked the door behind her, leaving Ben cold and hungry on her doorstep.

Ben had been raised in a dry town in northern Texas: the only water was in backyard swimming pools, and the only way to travel was in an air-conditioned pickup truck. So the idea of walking, by the sea, in a country where they spoke English of a sort, had appealed to him. Ben's hometown was double dry: it prided itself on having banned alcohol thirty years before the rest of America leapt onto the

Prohibition bandwagon, and on never having got off again; thus all Ben knew of pubs was that they were sinful places, like bars, only with cuter names. The author of *A Walking Tour of the British Coastline* had, however, suggested that pubs were good places to go to find local colour and local information, that one should always "stand one's round," and that some of them sold food.

The Innsmouth pub was called *The Book of Dead Names* and the sign over the door informed Ben that the proprietor was one A. Al-Hazred, licensed to sell wines and spirits. Ben wondered if this meant that they would serve Indian food, which he had eaten on his arrival in Bootle and rather enjoyed. He paused at the signs directing him to the *Public Bar* or the *Saloon Bar*, wondering if British Public Bars were private like their Public Schools, and eventually, because it sounded more like something you would find in a Western, going into the Saloon Bar.

The Saloon Bar was almost empty. It smelled like last week's spilled beer and the day-before-yesterday's cigarette smoke. Behind the bar was a plump woman with bottle-blonde hair. Sitting in one corner were a couple of gentlemen wearing long grey raincoats and scarves. They were playing dominoes and sipping dark brown foam-topped beerish drinks from dimpled glass tankards.

Ben walked over to the bar. "Do you sell food here?"

The barmaid scratched the side of her nose for a moment, then admitted, grudgingly, that she could probably do him a ploughman's.

Ben had no idea what this meant and found himself, for the hundredth time, wishing that *A Walking Tour of the British Coastline* had an American-English phrase book in the back. "Is that food?" he asked.

She nodded.

"Okay. I'll have one of those."

"And to drink?"

"Coke, please."

"We haven't got any Coke."

"Pepsi, then."

"No Pepsi."

"Well, what do you have? Sprite? 7UP? Gatorade?"

She looked blanker than previously. Then she said, "I think there's a bottle or two of cherryade in the back."

"That'll be fine."

"It'll be five pounds and twenty pence, and I'll bring you over your ploughman's when it's ready."

Ben decided as he sat at a small and slightly sticky wooden table, drinking something *fizzy* that both looked and tasted a bright chemical red, that a ploughman's was probably a steak of some kind. He reached this conclusion, coloured, he knew, by wishful thinking, from imagining rustic, possibly even bucolic, ploughmen leading their plump oxen through fresh-ploughed fields at sunset and because he could, by then, with equanimity and only a little help from others, have eaten an entire ox.

"Here you go. Ploughman's," said the barmaid, putting a plate down in front of him.

That a ploughman's turned out to be a rectangular slab of sharp-tasting cheese, a lettuce leaf, an undersized tomato with a thumb-print in it, a mound of something wet and brown that tasted like sour jam, and a small, hard, stale roll, came as a sad disappointment to Ben, who had already decided that the British treated food as some kind of punishment. He chewed the cheese and the lettuce leaf, and cursed every ploughman in England for choosing to dine upon such swill.

The gentlemen in grey raincoats, who had been sitting in the corner, finished their game of dominoes, picked up their drinks, and came and sat beside Ben. "What you drinking?" one of them asked, curiously.

"It's called cherryade," he told them. "It tastes like something from a chemical factory."

"Interesting you should say that," said the shorter of the two. "Interesting you should say that. Because I had a friend worked in a chemical factory and he *never drank cherryade*." He paused dramatically and then took a sip of his brown drink. Ben waited for him to go on, but that appeared to be that; the conversation had stopped.

In an effort to appear polite, Ben asked, in his turn, "So, what are *you* guys drinking?"

The taller of the two strangers, who had been looking lugubrious, brightened up. "Why, that's exceedingly kind of you. Pint of Shoggoth's Old Peculiar for me, please."

"And for me, too," said his friend. "I could murder a Shoggoth's. 'Ere, I bet that would make a good advertising slogan. 'I could murder a Shoggoth's.' I should write to them and suggest it. I bet they'd be very glad of me suggestin' it."

Ben went over to the barmaid, planning to ask her for two pints of Shoggoth's Old Peculiar and a glass of water for himself, only to find she had already poured three pints of the dark beer. *Well*, he thought, *might as well be hung for a sheep as a lamb*, and he was certain it couldn't be worse than the cherryade. He took a sip. The beer had the kind of flavour which, he suspected, advertisers would describe as *full-bodied*, although if pressed they would have to admit that the body in question had been that of a goat.

He paid the barmaid and manoeuvered his way back to his new friends.

"So. What you doin' in Innsmouth?" asked the taller of the two. "I suppose you're one of our American cousins, come to see the most famous of English villages."

"They named the one in America after this one, you know," said the smaller one.

"Is there an Innsmouth in the States?" asked Ben.

"I should say so," said the smaller man. "He wrote about it all the time. Him whose name we don't mention."

"I'm sorry?" said Ben.

The little man looked over his shoulder, then he hissed, very loudly, "H. P. Lovecraft!"

"I told you not to mention that name," said his friend, and he took a sip of the dark brown beer. "H. P. Lovecraft. H. P. bloody Lovecraft. H. bloody P. bloody Love bloody craft." He stopped to take a breath. "What did he know. Eh? I mean, what did he bloody know?"

Ben sipped his beer. The name was vaguely familiar; he remembered it from rummaging through the pile of old-style vinyl LPs in the back of his father's garage. "Weren't they a rock group?"

"Wasn't talkin' about any rock group. I mean the writer."

Ben shrugged. "I've never heard of him," he admitted. "I really mostly only read Westerns. And technical manuals."

The little man nudged his neighbour. "Here. Wilf. You hear that? He's never heard of him."

"Well. There's no harm in that. *I* used to read that Zane Grey," said the taller.

"Yes. Well. That's nothing to be proud of. This bloke—what did you say your name was?"

"Ben. Ben Lassiter. And you are . . . ?"

The little man smiled; he looked awfully like a frog, thought Ben. "I'm Seth," he said. And my friend here is called Wilf."

"Charmed," said Wilf.

"Hi," said Ben.

"Frankly," said the little man, "I agree with you."

"You do?" said Ben, perplexed.

The little man nodded. "Yer. H. P. Lovecraft. I don't know what the fuss is about. He couldn't bloody write." He slurped his stout, then licked the foam from his lips with a long and flexible tongue. "I mean, for starters, you look at them words he used. *Eldritch*. You know what *eldritch* means?"

Ben shook his head. He seemed to be discussing literature with two strangers in an English pub while drinking beer. He wondered for a moment if he had become someone else, while he wasn't looking. The beer tasted less bad, the farther down the glass he went, and was beginning to erase the lingering aftertaste of the cherryade.

"*Eldritch*. Means weird. Peculiar. Bloody odd. That's what it means. I looked it up. In a dictionary. And *gibbous*?"

Ben shook his head again.

"*Gibbous* means the moon was nearly full. And what about that one he was always calling us, eh? Thing. Wossname. Starts with a b. Tip of me tongue . . ."

"Bastards?" suggested Wilf.

"Nah. Thing. You know. *Batrachian*. That's it. Means looked like frogs."

"Hang on," said Wilf. "I thought they was, like, a kind of camel."

Seth shook his head vigorously. "S'definitely frogs. Not camels. Frogs."

Wilf slurped his Shoggoth's. Ben sipped his, carefully, without pleasure.

"So?" said Ben.

"They've got two humps," interjected Wilf, the tall one.

"Frogs?" asked Ben.

"Nah. Batrachians. Whereas your average dromedary camel, he's only got one. It's for the long journey through the desert. That's what they eat."

"Frogs?" asked Ben.

"Camel humps." Wilf fixed Ben with one bulging yellow eye. "You listen to me, matey-me-lad. After you've been out in some trackless desert for three or four weeks, a plate of roasted camel hump starts looking particularly tasty."

Seth looked scornful. "You've never eaten a camel hump."

"I might have done," said Wilf.

"Yes, but you haven't. You've never even been in a desert."

"Well, let's say, just supposing I'd been on a pilgrimage to the Tomb of Nyarlathotep . . ."

"The black king of the ancients who shall come in the night from the east and you shall not know him, you mean?"

"Of course that's who I mean."

"Just checking."

"Stupid question, if you ask me."

"You could of meant someone else with the same name."

"Well, it's not exactly a common name, is it? Nyarlathotep. There's not exactly going to be two of them, are there? 'Hello, my name's Nyarlathotep, what a coincidence meeting you here, funny them bein' two of us,' I don't exactly think so. Anyway, so I'm trudging through them trackless wastes, thinking to myself, I could murder a camel hump . . ."

"But you haven't, have you? You've never been out of Innsmouth harbour."

"Well . . . No."

"There." Seth looked at Ben triumphantly. Then he leaned over and whispered into Ben's ear, "He gets like this when he gets a few drinks into him, I'm afraid."

"I heard that," said Wilf.

"Good," said Seth. "Anyway. H. P. Lovecraft. He'd write one of his bloody sentences. Ahem. 'The gibbous moon hung low over the eldritch and batrachian inhabitants of squamous Dulwich.' What does he mean, eh? *What does he mean?* I'll tell you what he bloody means. What he bloody means is that the moon was nearly full, and everybody what lived in Dulwich was bloody peculiar frogs. That's what he means."

"What about the other thing you said?" asked Wilf.

"What?"

"*Squamous.* Wossat mean, then?"

Seth shrugged. "Haven't a clue," he admitted. "But he used it an awful lot."

There was another pause.

"I'm a student," said Ben. "Gonna be a metallurgist." Somehow he had managed to finish the whole of his first pint of Shoggoth's Old Peculiar, which was, he realised, pleasantly shocked, his first alcoholic beverage. "What do you guys do?"

"We," said Wilf, "are acolytes."

"Of Great Cthulhu," said Seth proudly.

"Yeah?" said Ben. "And what exactly does that involve?"

"My shout," said Wilf. "Hang on." Wilf went over to the barmaid and came back with three more pints. "Well," he said, "what it involves is, technically speaking, not a lot right now. The acolytin' is not really what you might call laborious employment in the middle of its busy season. That is, of course, because of his bein' asleep. Well, not exactly *asleep*. More like, if you want to put a finer point on it, *dead*."

"'In his house at Sunken R'lyeh dead Cthulhu lies dreaming,'" interjected Seth. "Or, as the poet has it, 'That is not dead what can eternal lie—'"

"'But in Strange Aeons—'" chanted Wilf.

"—and by *Strange* he means *bloody peculiar*—"

"Exactly. We are not talking your normal Aeons here at all."

"'But in Strange Aeons even Death can die.'"

Ben was mildly surprised to find that he seemed to be drinking another full-bodied pint of Shoggoth's Old Peculiar. Somehow the taste of rank goat was less offensive on the second pint. He was also delighted to notice that he was no longer hungry, that his blistered feet had stopped hurting, and that his companions were charming, intelligent men whose names he was having difficulty in keeping apart. He did not have enough experience with alcohol to know that this was one of the symptoms of being on your second pint of Shoggoth's Old Peculiar.

"So right now," said Seth, or possibly Wilf, "the business is a bit light. Mostly consisting of waiting."

"And praying," said Wilf, if he wasn't Seth.

"And praying. But pretty soon now, that's all going to change."

"Yeah?" asked Ben. "How's that?"

"Well," confided the taller one. "Any day now, Great Cthulhu (currently impermanently deceased), who is our boss, will wake up in his undersea living-sort-of quarters."

"And then," said the shorter one, "he will stretch and yawn and get dressed—"

"Probably go to the toilet, I wouldn't be at all surprised."

"Maybe read the papers."

"—And having done all that, he will come out of the ocean depths and consume the world utterly."

Ben found this unspeakably funny. "Like a ploughman's," he said.

"Exactly. Exactly. Well put, the young American gentleman. Great Cthulhu will gobble the world up like a ploughman's lunch, leaving but only the lump of Branston pickle on the side of the plate."

"That's the brown stuff?" asked Ben. They assured him that it was, and he went up to the bar and brought them back another three pints of Shoggoth's Old Peculiar.

He could not remember much of the conversation that followed. He remembered finishing his pint, and his new friends inviting him on a walking tour of the village, pointing out the various sights to him. "That's where we rent our videos, and that big building next door is the Nameless Temple of Unspeakable Gods and on Saturday mornings there's jumble sale in the crypt . . ."

He explained to them his theory of the walking tour book and told them, emotionally, that Innsmouth was both *scenic* and *charming*. He told them that they were the best friends he had ever had and that Innsmouth was *delightful*.

The moon was nearly full, and in the pale moonlight both of his new friends did look remarkably like huge frogs. Or possibly camels.

The three of them walked to the end of the rusted pier, and Seth and/or Wilf pointed out to Ben the ruins of Sunken R'lyeh in the bay, visible in the moonlight, beneath the sea, and Ben was overcome by what he kept explaining was a sudden and unforeseen attack of seasickness and was violently and unendingly sick over the metal railings into the black sea below . . . After that it all got a bit odd.

Ben Lassiter awoke on the cold hillside with his head pounding and a bad taste in his mouth. His head was resting on his backpack. There was rocky moorland on each side of him, and no sign of a road, and no sign of any village, scenic, charming, delightful, or even picturesque.

He stumbled and limped almost a mile to the nearest road and walked along it until he reached a petrol station.

They told him that there was no village anywhere locally named Innsmouth. No village with a pub called *The Book of Dead Names*. He told them about two men, named Wilf and Seth, and a friend of theirs, called Strange Ian, who was fast asleep somewhere, if he wasn't dead, under the sea. They told him that they didn't think much of American hippies who wandered about the countryside taking drugs, and that he'd probably feel better after a nice cup of tea and a tuna and cucumber sandwich, but that if he was dead set on wandering the country taking drugs, young Ernie who worked the afternoon shift would be all too happy to sell him a nice little bag of homegrown cannabis, if he could come back after lunch.

Ben pulled out his *A Walking Tour of the British Coastline* book and tried to find Innsmouth in it to prove to them that he had not dreamed it, but he was unable to locate the page it had been on—if ever it had been there at all. Most of one page, however, had been ripped out, roughly, about halfway through the book.

And then Ben telephoned a taxi, which took him to Bootle railway station, where he caught a train, which took him to Manchester, where he got on an aeroplane, which took him to Chicago, where he changed planes and flew to Dallas, where he got another plane going north, and he rented a car and went home.

He found the knowledge that he was over 600 miles away from the ocean very comforting; although, later in life, he moved to Nebraska to increase the distance from the sea: there were things he had seen, or thought he had seen, beneath the old pier that night that he would never be able to get out of his head. There were things that lurked beneath grey raincoats that man was not meant to know. *Squamous.* He did not need to look it up. He knew. They were *squamous*.

A couple of weeks after his return home Ben posted his annotated copy of *A Walking Tour of the British Coastline* to the author, care of her publisher, with an extensive letter containing a number of helpful suggestions for future editions. He also asked the author if she would send him a copy of the page that had been ripped from his guidebook, to set his mind at rest; but he was secretly relieved, as the days turned into months, and the months turned into years and then into decades, that she never replied.

H.P. and Me

By Gini Koch

"NOW CHILDREN," Professor Lovecraft said, as he handed out small cans of Savior Spray to the class, "as we prepare for our first field trip, I must remind you that where we're going is quite dangerous."

"We're all officers in Necropolis Enforcement," Amanda Darling pointed out politely. She was a vampire and my best friend and tended to be quite earnest and dedicated. "We're used to danger."

"And we're also all adult beings," her younger brother, Maurice, added. "Who have been undead longer than you, professor, no insult intended."

Insult or not, considering that the professor was a brand-new undead and everyone in this class had died at least a hundred years prior to 1937, this was an understatement. However, what looked like another Great War was brewing, and though none of us were allowed to take active part, evil of this level on the human plane meant the Prince was doing his best to create havoc on all the Planes of Existence. Meaning we of Necropolis Enforcement needed to be ready. For anything. Hence, here we were, in Lovecraft's first class at Necropolis University.

"Oh, none taken, young man," Lovecraft replied cheerily. "Pointing out the known only helps us to spot the unknown."

"Uh huh. And we're already prepared, so to speak." Maurice flicked his cape dramatically to show a variety of weapons tucked into sleek pockets. He really enjoyed being a vampire, being gay, and being snarky. Most of us tried not to antagonize the professors—Maurice made it an art form.

"True enough," Professor Lovecraft said merrily. "So you children must realize that the danger is extreme if I'm warning all of you brave beings of such."

I was beginning to wonder if I'd blown it by taking Lovecraft's Gods and Monsters for Beginners class this semester. P.T. Barnum had been offering How to Fool Anyone at Any Time again, and I loved Barnum's classes. But, in order to move up in the ranks, a being needed to cover all the bases and the Gods and Monsters were pretty much the be-all end-all of why we were doing this in the first place.

But I did have a question. "Why the Savior Spray, professor?"

Maurice wasn't wrong—we were all carrying weapons that could immobilize if not dust pretty much any undead being in existence. And we ourselves were weapons. Of course, so were those we were fighting.

Lovecraft smiled at me. "Because, Victoria, one never knows what one will find when venturing into the Depths."

This quieted the class. "Excuse me?" Maurice asked finally. "I think I misheard you. Where did you say we were going?"

"Into the Depths. First level only, though," Lovecraft said, still merrily.

"Our field trip is taking us into Hell?" I managed to ask that without my voice squeaking. I was proud. Werewolves weren't supposed to sound like Pomeranians.

"Indeed!" Lovecraft rubbed his hands together. "Let's get going and meet your first official Old One."

In addition to having undied recently, Lovecraft being a new professor at the university meant that his class was supposed to be fun and easy.

I kept reminding myself of this as he led us toward a convergence point that would allow us to enter the Depths of Hell, busily exclaiming and pointing things out like any other newbie. They usually weren't teaching classes when this happened, of course. Or heading to the Depths as if it was nothing.

"I always knew places like this existed," he said happily as we left the university grounds and headed for our destination, wherever that might be.

There are points in the world where the occult pull is particularly strong due to all the various factors like ley lines and weather and more merging together. Where the forces are so strong that an entity forms that shouldn't be able to exist in reality. What's created has been given many names, almost all of them wrong.

What's created exists in its own plane of reality and all the others at the same time, formed by everything and nothing, something not born that can never die. What my kind call an Undead City.

Necropolis was the largest Undead City in the world. Basically, if you could make it as an undead here, the rest of the Planes of Existence were your crustacean of choice.

"I'm so pleased to have been recruited," Lovecraft added. In a way that sort of begged for a response.

"Yes," I said since no one else seemed ready to throw him a bone. "We all know of your work while you were limited to the human plane."

"How flattering." Lovecraft seemed genuinely pleased.

"Suck up," Maurice muttered under his breath.

"Ah, professor," I said quickly, hoping he hadn't heard Maurice, "I know you had options. May I ask why you chose to become a zombie for your unlife?"

He chuckled. "Oh, it seemed fitting, all things considered. Why did you choose to become a werewolf?"

"I didn't really have a choice. It was get bitten or die horrifically." It was far more complicated than that, but now wasn't the time to share details with Lovecraft or the class. "But I like being a werewolf."

"I'm all for being a vampire," Amanda said, choosing the sucking up course of action. The rest of the class decided to show some enthusiasm and chimed in that they were also keen on their undead unlifeforms. Even Maurice deigned to share that being a vampire was all that and an extra-large bag of blood.

We reached an alleyway in the Red-Light District. Some beings enjoyed lurking in alleyways and Necropolis did its best to provide. Only this alleyway was different from the last time I'd seen it—there was a small golden glow at the end.

Samuel and Sarah, who were both ghosts, did a fast fly-around to see if we were alone. "No one but us," Samuel said when they were done.

Sarah shivered. It took a lot to make a ghost shiver, and I knew she wasn't faking it. "I don't like it here. There's something off about this place." She nodded toward the glow. "That shouldn't be here."

"You mean *we* shouldn't be here," Hansel's middle head said, while his other heads looked around nervously. "I think this is against Enforcement rules."

"I'm sure it will be fine," his sister Gretel said in the half-snarl, half-purr that was daemon cat speech. "The professor wouldn't put us into harm's way."

Lovecraft looked over his shoulder at her. "Why, of course I would. However will you learn what to do if you're not put into the situation? Preparedness is key, young lady."

"Ah, books, studying, tests," Maurice ticked off quickly. "Safe simulations."

Lovecraft waved his hand. "Oh, that's for average students. I've seen your records. You're all quite impressive."

"You do realize it's the first week of classes," Maurice said.

"I do. I also realize that each one of you is set to move up to real authority in Necropolis Enforcement in the very near term. And as such, it's my duty to ensure that you're all prepared."

"Prepared for what?" Amanda asked.

"Anything and everything," Lovecraft replied with a smile that might have been kindly and might not. Then he shoved against the wall where the convergence point was sitting. And we got to see just what we were heading for.

All the undead can see into at least two planes of existence, and most can see into more. Vampires and liches can see almost as many planes as a god. Werewolves aren't quite as powerful magically, so we have limits. Which was okay with me. I had enough fun keeping Necropolis separated from the human plane on a regular basis. Besides, I never found not being able to look into one of the levels of Hell without trying to be a hardship. I didn't care for Hell and never wanted to go there. And yet, apparently, I was about to visit. Lucky me. Lucky all of us.

Convergence points tended to be small, usually about the size of a quarter. They were points where time and space and the various planes of existence all met. They were part of the space-time continuum and tended to shift—a convergence point might stay in one place for a week, a month, maybe even a year, but rarely that long. Some disappeared within minutes. Convergence points also glowed golden—when people were dying and thought they were going into the light, there was a convergence point in or on them somewhere. If they came back, it was because they'd been moved to a positive plane. If they didn't, the chances that they'd been moved into the Depths were, sadly, high.

As we stared, the convergence point grew. And grew. It was easily six feet long, three feet wide, and two feet high. Which was anything but normal.

"It's a doorway," Eustace, the altar-demon said. "A doorway to the Depths."

"It is that," Lovecraft agreed. "And we're going through it. Now, everyone stay together and stay close." And with that, he stepped through. One moment here, the next glowing golden, and the next gone.

We all looked at each other. "I don't want to go through," Henry said slowly, which was how golems did everything. "At all. Ever. I may be a golem, but the heat from even the first level of Hell is going to bake my insides."

The rest of the class agreed that this was the last trip we ever wanted to take and thankfully no one inquired as to what things Henry, or any other golem, had on the inside. Until such time as it was necessary, we were all cherishing our ignorance on that subject.

The base of my tail started to tingle. "What if the professor isn't safe in there?" I asked the others. "I mean, he seems so green, and I don't mean his skin color. He hasn't been a zombie long enough to discolor. But what if he's overstepped and doesn't realize it?"

"Then I think we say it's been nice knowing him and we ask if we still get credit for taking this insane class," Maurice replied. It was clear the rest of the class agreed with him.

"The Count, also known as the head of enforcement, also known as our boss, doesn't want the Prince to get him," I felt compelled to point out. "He wants the professor's expertise to be used for the Gods and Monsters."

Amanda gave me a supportive smile. Everyone else seemed to be backing Maurice because werewolf hearing is the best around and I definitely heard the words "suck up" being muttered under a variety of undead breaths.

I ignored them and considered our options. If I really wanted to be the best officer in Necropolis Enforcement that I could be, I had to be brave. You never left your partner "in there" alone. And while Lovecraft wasn't anyone's partner, he was one of us, his soul dedicated to the Gods and Monsters in the war against the Prince of Darkness.

I pulled the special gun I carried at the small of my back. It had spelled projectiles in it that could at least slow down if not destroy some if not all of the Prince's minions, and I had a feeling I'd need all the extra firepower I possessed. I still had the can of Savior Spray in my other hand. Ready for anything.

Taking a deep breath, I shifted from human form into werewolf. Thankfully, wiser minds had created suits that allowed those of us who shifted to do so without having to be naked or, in the case of those of us with fur, looking like we were wearing stupid coats.

All werewolves had three forms—human, wolf, and werewolf. We were the least attractive in werewolf form, but by far the most effective at fighting, and that included being able to hold and manipulate things in our paws. And I had a feeling I was about to fight.

"If I'm not back with the professor in ten minutes, call the Count." With that, I stepped through the convergence point.

I exited into what looked like a waiting room, though one without any windows and only one door opposite from me, also with no window. There were chairs around the walls, but no one was sitting in them. No one was in the room at all.

The room looked boringly benign and, at first glance, so did the door. However, the longer I looked at it, the more it appeared to be moving, as if the door was actually made of rubber and things were pushing against it. Things that didn't look normal in any way. Things that definitely looked Depths-like.

Checked behind me. No sign of the convergence point. My tail drooped—I was trapped here, wherever here was.

Gave myself a good doggy shake. So I was trapped in here. So what? I was a junior officer in Necropolis Enforcement and a Werewolf with Honors. I might not be Best in Show but I wasn't going to come in last, ever.

I sniffed deeply. Werewolves had better senses of smell than any other canines, and every being knew that canines had the best sniffers in the business. This room didn't smell pleasant—it had an antiseptic tang mixed with Urban Back Alley. Actively chose not to consider if it smelled of various types of urine because various beings had wet themselves in terror. It also had a faint smell of Lovecraft. His scent was definitely on the door in front of me.

As I stepped toward the creepy door, what looked like a fist made of claws shoved at me through it. I heard sounds behind me and spun around, to see Amanda and Maurice. Amanda appeared to be dragging Maurice with her, but still, they were both here.

"We're not letting you do whatever it is you're doing alone," she said firmly.

"I was willing, but being the youngest means I get dragged everywhere," Maurice shared. "Hansel and Gretel wanted to come through, too, but we told them to wait, in case we needed rescuing." He looked around the room. "Which we apparently will."

"How will they know we need them?" I asked.

"I'm hoping keen animal senses," Maurice said. "Since my wrist communicator seems to be nonfunctional."

I'd forgotten about the communicator, which I'd have berated myself for, only Maurice was right—they weren't working. "I think we just go through the door and see what's waiting for us."

Amanda nodded. "Yes." It looked like she was going to say more, but while her mouth was open, no sounds came out. Her eyes were wide and staring over my right shoulder.

I spun around again to see that the door had opened. And what was coming through wasn't pleasant. It was also something I'd never seen before.

Something that was all eyes and claws and smelled like what I presumed the inside of a golem did—burning pottery mixed with over-fried calves' liver—walked in. Well, that was using the term loosely. Clawed in was probably more appropriate. It was the size of a puma, if a puma was round instead of normally animal-shaped.

"Eeep," was Maurice's contribution. I couldn't blame him.

The vamps flipped their wings out while my claws and fangs grew. Seeing Claw Face here meant that my hindbrain took over and ensured I was ready for action.

Claw Face seemed as shocked to see us as we were to see it. "Eeep!" it replied. Somehow. I saw no mouth or other orifices, but, truth be told, I wasn't looking that hard for them.

"Do we kill it?" Amanda whispered.

Claw Face spun around and clawed off at a run, down what appeared to be a large corridor made of flames, eeping all the way. And I ran after it, flames or no flames.

Some of this was because I had no idea if we should kill, contain, or ignore Claw Face—this was my first time in the Depths. But mostly I ran because all canines liked to chase things, things trying to get away from us especially. Things making prey sounds in particular. And I was too revved up to resist the instinct.

Luckily, the flames didn't touch me. They also didn't smell of burning wood, burning dung, burning vampire wings, burning fur, or much at all, really. And I felt no heat from them, either. Nor did Hellfire have a lot of scent and it didn't give off a lot of heat. It just dusted you, fast. Lovecraft's scent was here, too, though it was faint.

I wasn't on all fours, but werewolves are fast and I trained a lot for speed and endurance. I caught up to Claw Face quickly. Which meant it was time to determine if I shot it, sprayed it, bit it, or let it alone.

Self-preservation said that biting all those claws could be very painful. My mouth shared that biting all those eyes would be squishy and gross while my stomach shared that it would definitely toss whatever was in it if I chose to be that level of aggressively enthusiastic. Enforcement training said that a being running away from you was possibly a suspect and possibly an innocent bystander, and the wise officer determined which before using lethal force. Instinct said that Claw Face was in the Depths and I should kill it and let the Gods and Monsters sort it out.

Amanda landed in front of Claw Face, who now had nowhere to go. It eeped again and sank in on itself.

"I think it's more scared of us than we are of it," Amanda said, sounding far more confident than she looked.

I sniffed. Claw Face was definitely giving off a fear scent. I heaved a sigh and holstered my special gun. "Necropolis Enforcement. Identify yourself and explain why you ran from us."

"Ah," Maurice said from behind me, "Vicster, I don't think it ran from *us*."

I spun around yet again to see that Maurice was most likely right. "Amanda," I said as calmly as possible, while I pulled my special gun right out again. "I have a suggestion that's more like an order."

"Yes?" Her voice was shaking.

"Pick up Claw Face and keep on running away from this flame monster or whatever it is we see before us that's approaching aggressively."

Maurice shoved past me. "Already handled! You cover the rear, Officer in Charge Victoria! Amanda, go, go, go!"

I knew without looking or asking that the vamps were again airborne. Though I wasn't sure that they could outfly what I was going to insist until advised otherwise was a very large and angry flame monster barreling toward us. At least I assumed a being that was easily eight feet tall and resembled Henry on a really bad clay day, only made out of fire, was a flame monster. Was practically certain I couldn't outrun it because, sadly, it wasn't a golem—no golem could move as fast as this thing.

I fired one round into the flame monster. It gave no reaction other than to roar at me. It sounded as hot as it looked, meaning if it touched me I'd probably dust quickly. Holstered my gun yet again, so I could have it away from my paws if I had to run, since I was fastest in wolf form. And being repetitive had its own naïve charm. Then I took the Savior Spray and used it in the prescribed manner—up, down, right, left.

This burned a cross-shaped hole in the flame monster. Which apparently only made it madder and faster somehow. I decided that listening to the Bard's advice about discretion being the better part of valor was my best go-to move. Tossed the Savior Spray into my jaws as I went to full wolf form and raced off after Maurice, Amanda, and our either prisoner or protected victim.

"What is that thing?" Amanda shouted. "And what's the thing Maurice is carrying?"

"Denizens of Hell," Maurice shouted. "One of which we're protecting."

"I was talking to Victoria!"

"She's got a spray can in her mouth, Amanda. Do you seriously think she can reply? Or that she even knows? This is the class that's supposed to teach us all about these 'new friends.'"

Claw Face eeped in a way that sounded hurt.

"Sorry, you seem fine," Maurice said to Claw Face in a rather kindly, albeit out-of-breath, tone. "I promise to only allow whatever that thing is after us to dust you if it's a choice between you or me."

"You'd let it dust me or Victoria?" Amanda sounded furious. Still scared, but furious.

"Yes! Because you and Vicki *forced* me to take this heinous course instead of Professor Mulan's Dragon Discovery class where you get to *pet* a *tame baby dragon*. So if whatever that is gets you, so be it!"

"This is the class that will let us move up in Enforcement!"

"This is the class that's going to dust us in the first week and I have not yet slept with every icon from history so I am too young to dust!"

Maurice was in the lead, so he reached the end of this corridor first, though he and Amanda kept up the sibling squabbling the entire way. I wondered if all the bickering was making the flame monster slow down, because it sure made me want to. However, a quick look over my shoulder shared that my tail was in danger of becoming far less long and luxurious. I sped up toward the lesser of the two evils.

The corridor didn't end but turned sharply to the left. Maurice flung himself and Claw Face around the corner. And instantly we heard shrieking. The moment Amanda and I rounded the corner we came to a screeching halt because the walls and ceiling of this part of the hallway seemed to be made of sharp, shiny spikes. One of which had gone through Maurice's cape. He was dangling on a side spike, halfway up to the ceiling.

"Gods and Monsters preserve us," Amanda said, sounding horrified. "M-Maurice?"

He glared at her. "It caught the fabric, not me. Thank the Gods and Monsters."

"What happened to Claw Face?" Amanda asked.

Maurice was holding nothing other than fetid air. "I have no idea. I tripped and somehow ended up hanging here like a Christmas ornament. But here's a thought—let's not care and let's figure out how to get out of this literal Hellhole. As fast as possible, if not sooner."

I shifted back to human form and spat the can of Savior Spray into my hand. "As the officer in charge I agree with Maurice. In no small part because this place smells like we just entered a dragon's dung heap. And by the way, dragons are noble but dangerous creatures who we need to learn to respect and repel, not pet. And for someone who showed off his weapons collection less than an hour ago, you wouldn't know that you remembered how to use any of them. Or how to avoid being speared by obvious spikes."

"They weren't here when I first rounded that corner."

Which meant Maurice had triggered something. I looked around for other potential triggers and in doing so I spotted Claw Face—it was about midway down this section of the hallway, hooked on a spike, struggling like things without limbs do when they're pinned.

Claw Face heard us, sort of turned toward the sounds, and eeped. In a manner that indicated Claw Face was in trouble and glad its good friend had come to save it.

"Yes, yes," Maurice said testily. "We're coming. Just as soon as someone gets me down."

"What now?" Amanda asked as she helped her brother. I was busy checking behind us to see if the flame monster was going to round the corner. Thankfully, we appeared flame-monster-free in this section. Lucky us.

"We save Maurice's new friend. I think one of its claws is caught on a spike."

I stepped forward. As I did so, a row of spikes raised up from the floor behind us, blocking us from the flame-monster section of the hallway. Nice to know Maurice wasn't the only one failing to retain anything from Professor Fawcett's Deadly Traps and How to Spot Them class.

We all yelped and I accidentally squirted some of the Savior Spray as we were jumping away. Not in the approved manner, either. The spikes sizzled where the Savior Spray hit them.

"Ah, the floor spikes appear to be hot." Tried the Savior Spray in the approved manner. The spikes continued to sizzle, but not melt. And another row started to rise up. We stepped forward.

"Fantastic," Maurice said. "I can't wait to dust in this way. Amanda, remember that it doesn't always have to be a wooden spike through the heart."

"It's nice to know you care," she said. "Suddenly."

"I do. You make an excellent shield."

"Why did I save you and make you an undead?" she asked.

"You had a flash of genius." As he said this, a third row rose. No one had to mention that we needed to get going.

We moved as fast as we could, which wasn't as fast as we'd have liked, since the spikes on the ceiling started to lower, while the spikes on the walls went in and out, and rows of spikes kept on coming up from the floor. We were at a trot, dodging and ducking, by the time we reached Claw Face. Maurice grabbed it, tossed it carefully over his shoulder, and we kept going.

The ceiling spikes pulled all the way up suddenly. We took our opportunity and ran for it. There was a door in the distance which looked totally normal. Risked a look over my shoulder—the floor spikes were still coming up. Faster than they had been. "Hurry up!"

Maurice was in the lead and he flung the door open. Fortunately, we all had fast reflexes and Amanda and I both grabbed him and leaped back as a wall of spikes that was on the other side of this doorway fell forward. It missed Maurice by a hair's breadth, though the door we'd opened was totally unscathed. Go figure.

"Those fun denizens of the Depths," Maurice said shakily as the dust settled. "What will they think of next?"

"I shudder to find out," Amanda replied.

I looked ahead. Saw nothing. I looked behind. The spikes were coming down from the ceiling again and the ones in the floor were almost to us. "We're not going to wait long to discover whatever it is because we need to get out of here, right now."

"That's why you're in charge and, now, in the lead," Maurice said as he patted Claw Face, which was eeping in quiet terror.

We scrambled over the fallen wall of concrete and steel just before the spikes in the floor smashed up into it. They didn't go through, but they did shove the wall of spikes back up into position, presumably all the better to fall onto someone else. I actively chose not to think about what would have happened to us if we hadn't been fast enough, because dusting in this way was not only horrible and probably painful, but it was embarrassing, too.

The room we were in was dark. "Waiting room again," Amanda whispered. "Or maybe another section of hallway."

"Only far darker," Maurice pointed out.

"Thank you, Officer Obvious. We would never have realized we could barely see without your keen insights." I sniffed. "This area doesn't smell."

"You'd think you'd be happy about that, not complaining," Maurice said.

"It smells of nothing. It smells *like* nothing. I can't even smell the two of you. Or Claw Face." Or Lovecraft. Which boded. What if he hadn't managed to avoid the wall of spikes?

"Can I say that's not good, or will that earn me another snide remark?"

"Three guesses, the first two don't count."

"I see another door," Amanda said. As she stepped toward it I stopped her. "Is that another convergence point?" There was something glowing golden behind her.

"Looks like it," she said. "I wonder how it got here—I haven't seen it since we left the weird waiting room."

"It wasn't here when we got in here, wherever here actually is, because, as Officer Obvious shared, it was dark and we'd have seen it."

"I'm ignoring Vic now, but I think it's following you, Amanda. I'm not sure if that's a good thing, a bad thing, or a terrifying thing, by the way."

"If it gets us out of the Depths, it's a good thing," Amanda said firmly.

"Should we test it?" Maurice asked.

"Sure. Put your hand through it. I would, but as the officer in charge, I'm delegating that duty."

Maurice shot me a very nasty look. "No thank you. We'll assume it's working as advertised."

"What advertisement are we speaking about?" Amanda asked. "I've never heard of a convergence point that follows someone as if it was a terrier."

We stepped toward the door. It moved away from us. We stepped forward again and the door moved again. "Try running at it," I suggested. We did. The door moved away from us faster.

"This seems futile," Maurice said. "Did the convergence point follow you, Amanda, or is it still stationary or, as our luck goes, gone already?"

Amanda's mouth opened then closed. She pointed behind us. Looked over my shoulder to see that the wall of spikes was up, spikes side-turned toward us, and it was moving. Toward us, naturally.

"Ah, does that door now have feet?"

"Yes," Amanda said, voice shaking.

"What look like weird bird feet, if that bird was gigantic and really enjoyed using its claws," Maurice added.

Pulled my gun and fired several rounds into the wall of spikes. On the plus side, they hit. On the negative side, as with the flame monster, the wall of spikes didn't seem fazed and it sure didn't stop coming. Seriously asked myself why I bothered to carry the gun at all. And, naturally, the convergence point was now behind the wall of spikes.

"It's time to *go*." I turned toward the door that didn't want to stay still and started to run, the others right on my tail. The faster we ran, the faster the door moved. But we couldn't stop because the wall of spikes was still coming for us.

"It's changing," Amanda shouted. "Now it's got tentacles and beaks and what might be fangs."

"Of course it does," I panted, as I sped up as much as I could. We still weren't gaining on the door. "Just keep running."

"I'd make a snide comment about your being obvious," Maurice said, "only I'm too terrified to be witty."

I lost count of how long we ran—it felt like hours but was probably only fifteen minutes. But just when I was ready to suggest we see if we could get past the spike wall without too much injury and use the convergence point, the door we were trying to catch stopped moving. We all slammed into it.

"Ouch," Amanda said. "I guess this door opens in, not out."

"Of course it does," Maurice muttered. "I hate the Prince, the Depths, and, most of all, our professor."

I pulled the door open to see a dark hollow nothingness that was somehow far creepier than anything we'd experienced so far.

Sniffed deeply. "I get a trace, a faint trace, of the professor." Meaning he'd made it this far.

"I don't want to jump into that," Maurice said. "Because I truly have an aversion to dusting. And pain. I also have an aversion to that."

We all looked behind us. The thing pursuing us was even more horrible than Amanda had described. It was possibly even larger than it had been—there was no way we could get around it unscathed. And it was still coming for us.

"So, we can try to fight the horrifying spike monster thing or we can leap into the blackness that will, presumably, take us deeper into the Depths. Gosh, this is the best class ever."

"You're the one that made us take it," Maurice said. "I just want to mention that again before we all get dusted. The end of my unlife is on your furry head." Claw Face eeped. "And Claw Face's dusting is your fault, too."

"Glad to see, despite your insistence to the contrary, that you're keeping your sense of humor and ability to make wolf jokes intact. And I'm also glad that you've finally found a friend after all these years. We were figuring it would never happen."

"The convergence point is still an option," Amanda said. "It's bigger. I think we can all get through it together." Sure enough, the convergence point had reappeared and was with us once more, between a rock like I'd never imagined and a truly terrifying hard place.

I wanted to leap through the convergence point. But I didn't. "The professor is somewhere in this weirdness, and I have to figure that this field trip isn't going according to his plan. We can't leave him here. And if he didn't get a traveling convergence point, then he went through this. So we're going, too."

With that I shifted into werewolf form, stopped thinking, and leaped into the black.

To discover just about the last thing I'd expected.

I landed back in our classroom. Lovecraft was there, along with something that was about the size of a well-fed housecat, if that housecat had a head that looked like a goat skull with extra eye sockets and was also mostly tentacles with weird, tiny eyes at their ends. The thing was floating in the air next to Lovecraft. I saw no wings but chose not to ask how levitation was being achieved.

"Ah, Victoria, I'm so proud of you for being first." Lovecraft beamed at me. "And my sibling vampires right after. So pleased."

Claw Face eeped, this time happily, pulled out of Maurice's arms, and zipped over to the thing floating next to Lovecraft.

We all shifted into our human forms. "Ah, professor? I know I speak for all three of us when I ask what in a long tail is going on?"

Lovecraft grinned. "A test. You three passed with flying colors."

I looked around. "The convergence point is gone."

"Because it was part of the test," Lovecraft said. "Everyone is always allowed to fail."

"We told the others to wait for us," Amanda said. "Should we signal them?"

"No," the thing with Lovecraft croaked, sounding like something that had spent its entire existence at the bottom of a murky ocean. It smelled as if the murk had been created by a wide variety of rotting dead things. "They will either come through or they will not."

No sooner said than Hansel and Gretel bounded into the room. Gretel was holding another Claw Face, which did what ours had done—pulled out of her paws and floated over to the thing that had just spoken, eeping happily.

"You were gone for too long!" Hansel growled as he came to a skidding stop that just managed to end before he bowled Lovecraft over. "And that was horrible, worse than sitting through the Annual Hellhounds Talent Show."

"Why are you with a tiny Shub-Niggurath?" Gretel asked, sounding ready to pounce. "Did it come through that blackness after you, professor?"

Lovecraft beamed. "Well done! This is Shublet. She's actually on the side of the Gods and Monsters."

We all stared at the creature. I managed not to share that Shublet neither smelled nor sounded female. "Ah, nice to meet you?"

Shublet kind of nodded and bobbed in the air. "The pleasure is mine."

Before more pleasantries could be shared, the rest of the class came through, with everyone else hiding behind Henry, which made sense—golems were slow but hard to hurt. And, now somewhat unsurprisingly, Henry had a Claw Face in his hands. It did what the others had and zipped over to Shublet, who wrapped all three Claw Faces into her tentacles. The three Claw Faces shimmered, then disappeared. Shublet grew larger.

"Was that thing part of you?" Henry asked, sounding a little grossed out. Not that I could blame him. Maurice gagged quietly behind me.

"Yes. They were my avatars," Shublet said. "Your guides. And the defenseless creatures in your path you could either kill, ignore, or save. You all chose to save them, proving your worth as those who will protect and serve."

Lovecraft clapped. "Well done, everyone! This is going to be a fantastic class."

"So, this was all an elaborate setup to see how we'd react to going into the Depths?" Maurice asked.

"Possibly." Lovecraft looked right at me. "What is it that you think I was testing, Victoria?"

I considered all the options before I replied. "Bravery and loyalty. Or stupidity. I'm honestly not sure which, professor." As I said this another idea occurred to me. "Or else it's a form of reverse hazing."

"Oh, call me H.P. We're all friends here. Now."

"Reverse hazing it is, you sadistic being," Maurice said, though he didn't sound upset anymore. Nor did this statement seem to upset Lovecraft, who merely chuckled rather fondly.

As we took our seats, Shublet floated to the chalkboard and started drawing a variety of horrific creatures that appeared to be her relatives. "Next week, I believe you'll be visiting the Original Old One. Try not to let him eat you."

Lovecraft winked at us and I laughed. "This class is going to be great."

The Greatest Leader

By Aidan Doyle

OUR FIRST STOP in Pyongyang was the Victorious Fatherland Liberation War Museum where we learned how the Koreans overthrew the evil Japanese and triumphed over the imperialist Americans. Next it was the Museum of Metro Construction to get instructed on how Kim Il-sung chose the names for each of the metro stations. In the afternoon we visited the Museum of Glorious Victory Against the Great Old Ones and discovered how the founder of North Korea had personally defeated Cthulhu in hand-to-hand combat.

"I'm sick of all this propaganda," Chooka complained. "Everyone knows it was the Japanese who defeated Cthulhu."

"Shhh," I told him. "You don't want Captain Kim to hear you saying that." I glanced behind us. Captain Kim was busy showing Red Dave a diorama depicting Kim Il-sung planting a flag in Cthulhu's smoldering corpse.

Like many Old Ones, Cthulhu had been baffled by modern technology. A team of Japanese superhackers had taken it down using a suite of custom designed anti-eldritch smartphone apps. When I was at school all of my teachers stressed the importance of keeping your anti-eldritch apps up to date. An app a day keeps Cthulhu away.

"Everyone in this country is called Kim or Park," Chooka said.

"You're not exactly qualified to complain about names," I added.

Chooka puffed out his chest. "And what's wrong with my name?"

It wasn't his real name of course, but he'd been called Chooka ever since he was a kid. He was a big, doofy guy whose parents owned a chicken farm.

Captain Kim led us onto the tour bus and we drove to the Gate of Eternal Freedom. A giant statue towered over us, depicting Kim Il-sung booting a cowering Shub-Niggurath through an extra-dimensional gate.

"People who don't understand Korea think our monuments are designed to make our citizens feel insignificant compared to the power of the state," Captain Kim pronounced. "This is false. The scale of our monuments gives us pride in the greatness of our leader. He is the only one standing between us and ineffable cosmic dread."

Captain Kim's English was pretty good, but I was still impressed by his use of ineffable. It was difficult to know how much he believed what he was saying and how much he was spouting scripted party policy.

After posing for photos next to the gate, we drove back to the hotel, a hulking monstrosity of a tower situated on an island in the center of Pyongyang. The hotel had a revolving restaurant on the top floor and the lobby was a mixture of faux glam and revolutionary slogans. A lonely looking octopus traversed the aquarium next to the reception desk.

I had the dubious pleasure of sharing a room with Chooka. We'd been friends since we were kids, but he wasn't the easiest person to get along with. His world view had been shaped by watching too many *Vice* documentaries and his conversations were peppered with references to AIDS monkey islands and suicide forests. He was the kind of person who'd wake you up in the middle of the night to have an earnest conversation about whether or not haddocks were named after the sea captain from *Tintin*.

He had turned on the TV and was watching seemingly endless footage of parading North Koreans.

Chooka and I had both grown up in Dingo Creek, a small outback town in Australia's Northern Territory. We were members of the Dingo Creek Science Fiction Club, a social club run by Red Dave, a retired university professor who had made it his mission to bring socialism and *Star Trek* to the outback. Red Dave had somehow managed to organize the Dingo Creek Science Fiction Club Pyongyang Cultural

Exchange—an international peace mission designed to break down cultural barriers.

"Conan is so much better than Star Trek," Chooka announced. It was his default choice of discussion topic when he'd run out of other things to talk about.

I liked *Star Trek*, but it wasn't as though it was my one of my favorites. Red Dave was the real Trekkie—he had given us a long spiel about how it was our duty as science fiction fans to promote contact between different cultures. I think he secretly fancied himself as the outback equivalent of a Star Fleet captain. Crocodile Kirk venturing where no science fiction fan had gone before.

"No one is preaching the prime directive to Conan," Chooka proclaimed. He looked as pleased with himself as a chess grandmaster who has just punched their opponent in the face.

I had been exposed to more than my daily recommended dosage of nonsense and wasn't in the mood to debate Chooka. I put in my headphones and watched a movie on my phone. *Dial M for Miskatonic* was about the elite squad of Japanese hackers who used their phones to conquer Cthulhu.

Chooka was asleep by the time I finished the movie. I was tired, but I made sure I did my daily training on my aquatic abomination app. *How to Train Your Dagon* teaches important hand-eye coordination and underwater survival skills. I had even jailbroken my phone so I could install a Special Forces version unavailable to the general public. My version came with ninety-nine extra levels, plus bonus Deep One facial recognition technology.

In the morning we assembled in the hotel lobby after breakfast. While we were waiting for everyone to arrive, I admired the posters adorning the walls. Along with the usual exultations to dedicate your life to Korean solidarity, there were photos of the Arirang Mass Games. Red Dave had promoted the games as the highlight of the trip, an unbelievably extravagant spectacle featuring tens of thousands of performers. We were scheduled to go to the stadium tomorrow afternoon.

The hairs on the back of my neck stood up. Something was watching me. Throughout the trip we had been watched by guides and secret police but this felt different. I turned around and saw the octopus in the aquarium staring directly at me, glaring with a malevolent alien intelligence. Not creepy. Not creepy at all.

I wondered if it somehow knew I had been playing *How to Train Your Dagon.*

"Let's go," Captain Kim announced.

I tore my gaze away from the octopus. There were only six of us in the lobby. "Red Dave isn't here yet."

"He's not feeling well," Captain Kim said. "He's resting in his room."

Red Dave had put so much work into organizing the trip that it was a shame for him to miss any of it.

The rest of us clambered aboard the tour bus. I forget the name of the university we visited, but it probably had Kim somewhere in the title. We got to see an English class in progress, which basically consisted of a teacher shouting phrases at meek-looking students who dutifully wrote everything down, but didn't say a word.

When we returned to the hotel I knocked on Red Dave's door, but there was no answer. I figured he was sleeping and tried again an hour later. Still, no answer. I knocked loudly. No answer. Now I was getting worried. What if he was really sick?

Captain Kim was staying on our floor, so I went and knocked on his door.

"Hello, Michael. How can I help?" he asked.

"Red Dave's not answering his door. I'm worried about him."

Captain Kim knocked on Dave's door, but there was no response. "I'll get someone to check on him."

He returned in a few minutes with one of the hotel staff who unlocked the door.

The bed was empty and didn't look as though it had been slept in. There was no sign of Dave or his clothes or luggage.

Captain Kim looked genuinely shocked. "I'll find out what's happened."

I followed Captain Kim down to the lobby, where he disappeared into the staff office. I waited impatiently while the octopus glared at me.

Captain Kim returned a few minutes later. "David's condition worsened and he was taken to a hospital."

"What's wrong with him?"

"There is no need to worry," Captain Kim assured me. "Our doctors are the best in the world."

"Can I see him?"

"That's not possible right now, but I will inform you as soon as his condition improves."

I went back to my room and filled Chooka in on the news.

"He'll be fine," Chooka announced. "He won't want to miss the mass games."

That night I dreamed a huge tsunami had somehow made it all the way to Dingo Creek and the only place I could hide was on the roof of the local sushi restaurant.

In the morning when I went to get some fresh clothes out of my suitcase I discovered a red USB stick drive hidden amongst my T-shirts. "Is this yours?" I asked Chooka.

He shook his head. "Nope."

Bringing religious or human rights material into North Korea could get you into a lot of trouble. I wanted to see what was on the drive.

I had brought only my phone, but Chooka was old school enough that he'd brought an actual laptop. "Can I use Crom?" I asked.

Chooka's battered laptop was almost certainly older than Cthulhu himself.

Chooka grinned. "I knew that one day you would come back to the cult of Windows."

I switched on his laptop and plugged in the USB drive. It contained only a single file called *elder.exe*. I knew the risks of running unknown executables, but I needed to know what the file was.

After I double-clicked the file, the screen went black. Then a picture of a five-pointed star with a burning candle in the center appeared. I waited, but nothing else happened.

Chooka peered at the screen. "That's an elder sign."

"What's that?"

"People used them before the anti-eldritch apps were invented. They're supposed to provide protection against Old Ones."

"How did this get in my suitcase?"

Chooka shrugged. "No idea."

At breakfast, Captain Kim apologized, but said there was no news about Red Dave. "I'm sure he's fine."

Even if he had been in a coma, Red Dave would have dragged himself out of bed for a chance to watch the mass games.

Red Dave had a red suitcase and a red laptop bag. The USB stick was red. What if he'd had another reason for organizing this tour?

I made sure all of my apps were up to date and asked Chooka to bring his laptop and the USB stick with him.

We got on the tour bus and went out to the Revolutionary Martyrs' Walk of Fame, which was lined with red stars representing the Koreans who had died in the Eldritch Wars. In the afternoon we drove to the Rungrado May Day Stadium, the biggest stadium in the world. In contrast to our side of the stadium, which was mostly empty apart from a few groups of Chinese tourists, the other side of the stands was occupied by tens of thousands of North Koreans. When the performance began, they moved with synchronized precision to hold up different colored boards to form images of revolutionary slogans and the North Korean flag.

Thousands of performers ran into the main arena and began their routine. Children performed incredible feats of acrobatics. Soldiers performed incredible feats of acrobatics. People in panda suits performed incredible feats of acrobatics. Apparently the pandas were supposed to represent friendship with China.

The whole thing was an amazing spectacle, a giant production rivaling any Olympic opening ceremony in grandeur, but the longer the show went on, the more uncomfortable I felt. What if the dancing pandas were part of some kind of hideous plot?

The sun set and the stadium lights came on. The stars came out above us. The pandas kept tumbling and waving their swords.

The colored boards on the other side of the stadium formed into the image of an arcane rune—a non-Euclidean shape burning with eldritch energy. A feeling of terror gripped me and I averted my gaze.

The stadium lights flickered and went out. The air in the arena's center shimmered and filled with an unearthly yellow light.

The pandas screamed and fled.

"What's happening?" I demanded of Captain Kim.

"One of the generals must have changed the routine to include a summoning symbol," said Captain Kim. "They are probably working with the Japanese."

A tentacle appeared amidst the glowing yellow light in the center of the arena.

The Koreans on the other side of the stadium dropped their boards and fled in a surging mass of panic. All around us, other tourists fought to get to the stairs and out of the stadium.

Even though the arcane symbol was gone, the yellow light only increased in intensity and more writhing tentacles appeared.

This was the moment I had been waiting for all of my life. I launched my Cthulhu Defender app and pointed my phone at the tentacles. I pressed the banish button.

Nothing happened.

I pressed the button again.

Nothing happened.

I had the latest version of the app. It was guaranteed to deal with 99.8 percent of all known eldritch threats. Cthulhu must have found a way to upgrade itself when it was in sleep mode.

I tried calling the app's support number, but a recorded message informed me that they had detected my phone was jailbroken, so I was no longer eligible for priority customer support. I tried a general eldritch help line, but only got a recording which patronizingly asked if I had tried turning my phone off and on again. If my problems persisted, I was invited to send a *screamshot* to a support email address.

My phone flooded with summoning requests. Cthulhu had somehow got my number.

My phone started ringing, but I blocked the call of Cthulhu.

Red Dave must have known something was going to happen and had planned on stopping it. But someone had got to him first. He had entrusted the elder sign program into my care for a reason. It was up to me to save the world.

I grabbed Captain Kim by the arm. "I need some of kind of projector that can put images onto the stadium."

Captain Kim shook his head. "Our great leader will deal with the situation."

Maybe the North Korean leader was as great at fighting Old Ones as his grandfather was supposed to have been, but I didn't believe the propaganda. Someone needed to step up and deal with the forces of darkness. This called for a Crocodile Kirk kind of response.

"Help us find a projector."

Most of the mass games relied on the agility of the performers rather than special effects but Captain Kim led us to an audio-visual control room. The room had been deserted, the operators probably having fled in terror.

Chooka connected his laptop to the projector and Captain Kim helped us navigate the Korean menu.

An enormous octopus-like tentacled creature now occupied the arena's center. There was no time to spare.

I started the elder sign application and the image of a five-pointed star beamed out onto the arena.

The creature writhed its tentacles in pain. It tried to advance, but it looked as though it was trapped within the confines of the elder sign. We had stopped it!

"Sometimes the old ways are the best," Chooka said.

"How long until we're able to banish it?" I asked.

"We have to keep it trapped in the elder sign until dawn."

It was only eight-thirty. The laptop's battery wasn't going to last that long.

Chooka fumbled in the laptop bag and produced his charger. "This is the last time I listen to you badmouth Windows."

I was never going to say anything bad about Chooka or his antiquated operating system ever again. "You did good, Conan." I slapped him on the back.

I tried using my phone, but the chthonic malware had totally disabled it.

I spotted a network port and connected the laptop. The internet was severely restricted in most of North Korea, but it looked as though the control room had access. I had to leave the elder sign program running on the screen, but I wanted to be ready to send emails to my parents, the Australian prime minister, and the media as soon as Cthulhu was banished.

The three of us turned our attention to the stadium. The writhing tentacles were now barely visible behind the glowing elder sign. The beast was trapped.

The panicking crowds had fled and the stadium was empty, save for the eldritch presence. I could tell Captain Kim was waiting for the great leader to make an appearance but we were left on our own.

We made small talk and asked Captain Kim about his life in the North Korean army while we waited for dawn to come.

When I glanced back at the computer I was horrified to see a popup on the screen.

Windows has installed critical security updates and is now restarting.

I lunged for the keyboard, but it was too late. The popup disappeared and the screen went black. The elder sign disappeared.

Yellow light once again enveloped the arena. Glowing tentacles spread across the arena.

Chooka sighed. "Maybe Windows does have some issues after all."

Hideous protoplasmic creatures appeared alongside Cthulhu. The shapeless slithering masses were covered in thousands of eyes in the form of pustules of green light.

"Now that's what I call an impressive retina display," Chooka said.

"We have to do something!" I shouted.

Chooka glanced at the laptop and sighed. "It's going to take forever for that to restart. I'm out of ideas."

"Captain Kim! There must be something we can do!"

"I'm sorry, but it is too late," he replied.

The tentacles were almost upon us.

The revolutionary poster on the wall behind him depicted a long line of burly workers marching proudly into a steel mill. If only there was enough time to reset my phone to the factory default.

I was a proud member of the Dingo Creek Science Fiction Club. I wasn't going to give up that easily. "You don't understand!" I shouted at Captain Kim. "If we don't do something a terrible being will rule over us. A creature without pity. A creature who will control our thoughts and destroy anyone who opposes it."

Captain Kim nodded. "I understand more than you realize."

The darkness engulfed us.

But Someone's Got To Do It

By Konstantine Paradias

November 6th

Ma,

I started work today at Miskatonic University. Mister Carter was really pleased with me; he told me he didn't need no resume to see that I was a "fine, upstanding young lad." I told him about the work I used to do for the church in Innsmouth and he was very pleased with it. He told me I was gonna be paid a dollar an hour. A whole dollar, Ma, twice the money Barnabas Marsh paid me for cleaning the cages in the harbor! And a lot less chance of losing any fingers to Missus Marsh! Please don't tell him I said that. I think he would be mad, if he knew I had gotten intimate like that with his wife.

Mister Carter showed me around the grounds, too. He showed me the floors of the university and the dormitory and all the labs. He even showed me the ones I wasn't supposed to go to, with the big doors and the bulletproof glass. "No such thing as a closed door for a janitor, eh Roger?" he told me. He showed me the library too and explained to me the Do-ey system. He told me it wasn't worth much, not when the books had opinions. Doctor Armitage was there, he is chief librarian. He grabbed me by the shoulders when Mister Carter wasn't looking and was all funny and his hair was falling out in clumps. "You run, child. You run away and go back home. This is no place for men," he told me. I told him, "I can't see how a woman could ever want to be a janitor, Doctor Armitage." But by then he had run off screaming. I think I knew a couple of the words he was babbling, like the kind Dad would mumble when he landed on the beach and he was moon-mad.

Mister Carter then showed me the basement. It's a big old musty place, all roaches and dust and spiders and rows and rows of drawers, far as the eye can see. "Paperwork Hell," Mister Carter called it. "Best not to stick around too much. We lost the last groundskeeper here. We keep smelling him, but we can't find him." He told me there's a bit of a rat problem. Apparently, the rats have stolen the old accounting books and are threatening to go to the IRS with them if they ever try to call an exterminator. "I don't think we can account the revenue of the last twenty-five years to anonymous donations, haha," he said.

We saw the campus grounds last. They got a nice big garden with lots of flowers and grass and even a forest! They got a whole forest in the university, Ma, with pine trees and bushes and even the wriggle-trees, the kind that cousin Obadiah has in his plot in Dunwich! They stood real still but I could see them. Mister Carter told me I should keep a look-out for trespassers. "Don't go too hard on them, though. Most of them just loiter and will scatter soon as they see you. But just in case they don't go away, you best leave." Then something howled and Mister Carter went pale. I didn't ask him about it. Don't want to be pressuring Mister Carter on my first day on the job. You always said you never get a second chance at a first impression.

Then, Mister Carter showed me my shed! Yes, I have a shed all to myself, Ma! Got a bed to myself and a table and a dresser, too! I miss home a lot, but I never had so much to myself before! I always had to share a bed with Jemima but she grew up way too fast when she changed and when she went to the beach to live with Dad I was too big for the bed. I'm too big for this bed too but I'll manage! Mister Carter told me I could eat from the campus cafeteria, but I didn't have to stick around with the staff if I didn't feel like it. I don't really want to. I think most of them are crazy. Mister Carter seems pretty crazy to me. He wouldn't go in the shed and he jumped when I wished him sweet dreams. "I am afraid this is no longer an option for me," he said and he left, just like that.

I hope everything's well back in Innsmouth and Jeb hasn't gotten himself in trouble with the church again. I know he is a handful, but I think finding him work in the docks like you said would really help him. I will try to get you something nice soon as I've got paid. Kiss Dad for me, will you?

Your son,
Roger Wilkiss

November 21st
Ma,

I just had my very first janitorial challenge. Mister Carter called it that, said it was "one of the less illustrious duties of my profession." He showed me a patch of grass that had been pounded in and there was something pooled inside. Mister Carter told me it was Doctor Armitage. They had found him like this. He asked me very kindly to get rid of it and not to call the police and he gave me ten whole dollars to myself! I don't know why I should call the police. We don't call the police either when someone is found out like that, especially if he's from out of town. I scooped Doctor Armitage into a dozen buckets and I filled the hole as well as I could. Mister Carter had left by then without telling me what to do with the buckets, so I went into the forest and emptied them by the wriggle-trees. They will have made them go away by now.

I didn't tell Mister Carter that Doctor Armitage had been crazy the other day. Perhaps he wouldn't have wanted to listen. He's probably too busy being insane, himself. The other day, I saw him walking the grounds with something in his hand, talking the language of the church.

The good news is I do a lot of other things, except sweep the floors and clean the windows and wash the test-tubes. Just last Monday, I helped Mister Freeborn the anthropologist translate this big hunk of rock that looked just like the rocks that are buried under the church! Only his was dented and chipped and looked like it was a million years old. Some of the letters had faded but I knew some of the words from the hymns we sing on the beach and I told him all about them! "M'boy, you might have just helped me make the biggest breakthrough in the history of anthropology!" he told me and he gave me twenty whole bucks to myself! Twenty bucks, Ma!

And then there was Professor Derleth. She's a very nice lady. Very learned, like you Ma, only she's not half as pretty. She was struggling with a thing she'd found in a box, like the one that Barnabas Marsh had in his shed, all strange corners and blinking lights. She wouldn't know how to make it work, wouldn't you know it? And she's got all these degrees framed behind her desk! So I just grabbed it the way you taught me, from the inside, and I flicked the switch on. Professor Derleth was jumping with joy! I didn't tell her I did it though. She thinks she turned it on by reading a bunch of church-gibberish from an old book. Some women are just not as smart as you, Ma.

I do lots of other stuff in the campus grounds, when I'm not taking out the garbage or scrubbing the urinals or dumping the chemicals in the river (Professor Brightmeer told me this saves the campus a lot of money. I also get thirty bucks every time I do it!). For example, on Mondays, I get to go in the Black Wing, as they call it, where they have all these strange things in ice! There's a buzz-bee from Yuggoth (I've seen one of those before, back when we went to the Dunwich woods with my cousins when we were kids, only it was all shriveled and dead) and there's a frozen big bug and there's a thing that has a face like a sea anemone. There's also some photos of Uncle Bert, only he's all cut up and his guts are showing. I guess that's where he ended up, after he got hit by that fishing boat propeller.

On Tuesdays, I visit the labs and they let me get real close to all the things they have in the glass cases! And oh, the things they have in there, Ma! There's this cube that isn't a cube and there's a shiny big thing that looks like a gun and they have pages from books like the kind we have in the church and they've even got bits of wreckage from some sort of ship! I don't know what it is, but it's all crawling and making my head spin when I try to read the labels on the controls (they think it's a statue, Ma, can you believe that?).

On Wednesdays, I get to feed the books in the library. Get them some meat or blood or pour something yellow that smells really awful from some vial. Used to be, they would get nasty at first. The meat and the other stuff was hardly any good. Until I switched it for the stuff I got from the butcher's and the campus chemistry lab and now they're purring anytime they see me. And they all have such nice things to whisper in my ear.

On Thursdays it's my day off, so I usually stay at home or go to the river. It doesn't smell quite right, but it helps when I'm homesick.

People dump so much gunk into the river, it makes me almost sad to see it. But you get used to it and the other night I thought I saw one of the boys from Innsmouth there! Of course, I couldn't make him out in all that big mess and he probably doesn't remember me anymore, but he turned when I spoke to him in hymn-tongue. I am not so sure, but he sort of looked like Mike Coolidge, my high school bully.

On Fridays, I go with Mister Whateley, the forester, into Miskatonic Wood. He says we go there to shoo off any loiterers but he never goes too deep. He won't even go near the wriggle-trees, can you believe that? A man twice my age and he's afraid they might stomp him. Then again, he did try to burn them once. Why would someone try to burn a wriggle-tree? They usually stay put, if you keep them fed.

On weekends, most professors go home, except for Mister Carter. He likes to go to the basement and scream at the rats or climb up to the rooftop and whip himself bloody. One time, he broke into my shed and stole the bucketfuls of gravel I was going to pave the parkway with and made a shape on the grass then tore off his clothes and ran back into his office. He had made that bad-luck shape the church has told us about, so I made it go away. He didn't say a word about it, but he gave me thirty bucks for my trouble!

It's gonna be payday soon and then I'll buy you something nice, Ma! With all the money I got, I can get you a new set of chiseling tools and a boning knife for Dad! Or would you rather I got you curtains? The living room could use some new curtains. We still have those tattered ones from when the out-of-towner bled all over them.

With love,
Roger

December 5th

Ma,

I met a girl! There's been a ton of other stuff, but I met a girl, Ma! Oh, you're gonna like her, I bet you will! She's like us, but you haven't met her. She lives in the Miskatonic River but she's only here for the Solstice and she's an Initiate of the Mysteries and she swam with me when I jumped in the river. She bled me but she didn't gut me, just like you did with Dad! Oh mom, you should see her, she's so pretty and she's smart and she knows so much stuff. Can you believe it's her first time near land? She wouldn't even come to the bank with me but we stayed all night together and I helped her drag that old drunk that lives under the bridge under the water. She invited me over for Dagon-phtha, would you believe that, Ma? On our first date, even!

But things haven't been really great over here, Ma, I'm afraid. Seems like there's trouble here at the campus and I might lose my job, if things keep going the way they're going. Remember Mister Freeborn? The man with the rock? Turns out he went crazy, Ma. And not good-crazy, like Grandpa Zeb went and we had to chase him all over town and Dad had to cut him apart with Mister Marsh's good knife. I mean bad-crazy, Ma. He locked himself in his room and he was chanting for days and nobody could get inside, no matter how hard they tried. There was a buzzing there that wouldn't stop and something smelled like rotten meat. I wanted to help them get him out, but they're already suspecting I might have done something, because he told everyone I was the one who figured out the stone. Then one day, the smell went away and Mister Freeborn got all quiet-like and the door opened and when we got in, he was everywhere, Ma. He was all over the walls and the floor and in mid-air, too! He looked all tore up and one of the corners was all skewed (like the one we got in the attic), but none of the professors could see it.

Professor Derleth was really suspicious of me; she changed the locks in her laboratory so I couldn't get in. I tried to explain to her that I wasn't doing anything and that I was just the janitor, but she said she'd "file a formal complaint and have me fired." Now I don't know how much harm a file can do, but I need this job, Ma! So I didn't tell her nothing, even though the machine in her lab was already overheating and it needed somewhere to release its p'rlui before everything got all skewed up again, like it happened when Grandma died. But she wouldn't listen, Ma, and she wouldn't let me near it and it went off just as she was about to call the police. I think it was fast, because she didn't have time to scream but I don't think it was painless.

I stayed well away from everyone, didn't need the grief. Only one who'll talk to me is Mister Whateley. Even Mister Carter won't come near me. I saw him the other day in the library and he just gave me this dirty look. He was reading a book that looked a lot like the one that out-of-towner stole from the church, too. I could tell 'cause there was a nipple on the cover. He didn't talk to me, just handed me my paycheck. But Mister Whateley is nice and he's been around, like he says. "This place is just brimming with bad-gunky since the forties. Don't you fret now. They're just mad it's not us schmucks getting killed insteada them," he told me. Then I shooed away a wriggle-tree when it reached down to grab him. It's good to have a friend like Mister Whateley at a time like this.

My hair started coming off in clumps and I'm getting the flakes, Ma. I know you told me this wasn't supposed to happen, but I think I'm changing. I don't wanna change, Ma. I like it the way I am and I like my job and I can make all this work and I met a girl! If I change, I won't remember any of it and I'll forget, just like Dad. Please, Ma, I got to know: how can I stop this? You got to know a way!

Your son,
Roger Wilkiss

P.S.: I got you those curtains, after all. I could not get the knife set you asked for, on account of none of them having any "ceramic cutlery" as they called it. I didn't ask for ceramic; I asked for obsidian, like you said. The store lady told me tricolette is in fashion this year. I think it's going to really bring out the carpet.

December 10th
Ma,

I got the package back from the post office. It said that the address isn't there anymore. I tried calling Mister Marsh and the church and I tried to reach Mister Zahn in the post office, but nobody will respond. Is everything okay? Please write to me as soon as you can. My hair's almost near fallen off and half my face is flaked. I won't be able to hide it much longer. Just write to me before I forget.

Love you, Ma

December 19th
Ma,

I killed Mister Carter. He tried to shoot me when he took me down to the basement, said he needed help moving some stuff and I lost it. I think he found the letters you'd sent me, because they'd gone missing and I found them in his office drawer, after. I took his head off, Ma. I didn't mean to but I was hurting and I lashed out and his head just rolled clean off his body.

The rats told me they'd take care of it, but I couldn't trust a rat. I tried looking for the head, but I couldn't find it. So I took him to the library, on account of Mister Whateley prowling around the woods. I left him there and there were lots of sucking noises. I think he's gone for good now.

I won't go to see that girl on Solstice. I think I'll stay at home. It's quiet at the campus and it's well away from water. I don't think it'll help much, but I don't want to be anywhere near the river tomorrow. I keep dreaming that I'm back home, Ma, but everything's drowned. I see our house and Mister Marsh's house just floating by and there's the church there too, only it's caving in and swallowing everything up. And we're all going down with it; you and Jemima and Dad are there too, but I haven't forgotten, Ma. I see all of us swimming in the halls of the campus and floating past the dead books and the wriggle-trees at the bottom of the ocean. And Mister Carter is there and Mister Freeborn and Professor Derleth and even Mister Whateley and we're all happy, Ma, and we have nothing to hide no more!

My nails dropped clean off, Ma, and I'm having trouble breathing. I don't want to go to the water. I don't want to forget. Please Ma, when you see me, don't let me forget.

Please.

★ ★ ★

December 25th

Ma,

I'm going away now. I went to the water, after all. I had to, when Mister Whateley stormed the campus with all those policemen. But he didn't count on me knowing how to bend my d-kha, Ma. I always knew how to do it, it had just slipped my mind. I got away and I went to the water.

She was there, Ma. She offered me her n'kur and we became one as we slipped into the vur-gal, the inward facing inward. We went into the water, down in the dark and it was warm, way it was when I was in your belly. I don't know how I know that, Ma, but I remember every bit of it. I can't remember what your face looks like, but I know this:

We became p'rlui, she and I, in His presence. He sleeps beneath the rivers, Ma. He dwells in the waters. We drowned for him, Ma, and he bled us. He released our n'gatha and we offered him our fhtagn. It changed us, Ma, it made us perfect and free.

I will be on the beach, but you probably won't know me. I won't know you either, not really. But I'll remember you.

Goodbye.

The Call of Uncopyrighted Intellectual Property

By Amanda Helms

IT'D BE INCORRECT to say that the trouble began when Leyla burst into my office brandishing silky black blindfolds and two pairs of headphones. It had actually started with the arrival of Diabolical Pictures' cease and desist letter two hours prior.

But Leyla's appearance compounded things.

I turned away from the response to Diabolical I'd been preparing— I'd gotten so far as reminding Diabolical that titles aren't copyrightable; therefore anyone could use the title *Booty Call of Cthulhu*—and looked up at Leyla, which she took as invitation to dump the blindfolds and headphones on my desk. "Chastity, would you say you're more auditorily or visually stimulated?"

"If this is some sort of come on—"

"God, no! Do you seriously think I'm stupid enough to hit on an *employee*?"

Rightly speaking, I wasn't Leyla's employee; while she was a producer at Brightdark Productions, I was its on-retainer legal counsel.

If you think it'd be odd for a b-movie horror studio to keep legal counsel on retainer, you'd be right. And if you'd think that the need for said studio to keep legal counsel on retainer would be due to repeated past issues regarding copyright infringement—similar to the sort mentioned in Diabolical's cease and desist—you'd have earned a cookie.

Sadly for you, I'm gluten-intolerant.

Leyla leaned across my desk and snapped her fingers in my face. "Auditory or visual?"

Grimacing, I pulled my printout of Diabolical's cease and desist out from under the headphones and shuffled it off to the side of my desk, where it'd be safer. Past experience with Leyla had taught me the fastest way to get rid of her was to indulge her.

"Visual, I suppose. Why?"

She shoved a blindfold at me. "Put this on." Not waiting for a response, she jammed a flash drive into my laptop.

"Hey!"

"You need to watch this." She paused. "Well, listen to." She pulled up a chair and clamped a pair of headphones to her ears. They were the over-ear sort and so clunky I suspected she'd sweet-talked a helicopter pilot out of them. "I'll watch."

Either her headphones were noise-canceling, or she did an excellent job at pretending to ignore my protests as she minimized my reply to Diabolical. Then she glared at me until I sighed and tied on the blindfold. Too loudly, she said, "You can't see the screen, right?"

Light spilled in around the edges of the blindfold—and I tried not to think too deeply on what previous life the black silk might have lived before I wrapped it around my eyes—but I couldn't make out the screen.

"N—" I started to say, then remembered myself and shook my head.

"All right then," she said, still too loud. "Get ready."

There was some shuffling from Leyla's direction, and then a girlish giggle from my computer's speakers. *"Oh, I didn't know this was going to be a* nude *beach!"*

A bass male voice said, *"It is now."*

I fumbled for my cellphone. "Voice memo: Add to Brightdark's suggestion box: veer away from the 'teen sex equals death' trope to further differentiate ourselves in the market."

Leyla batted my arm, but said nothing; she hadn't heard me.

"Oh, my! How did sand get in my bikini bottom?"

"I'll just clean you up."

Water sloshed and splashed. "So, um," Leyla said. "At this point, the Great Old One is rising from the deep."

That brought me out of my reveries of thinking that at least the male hero hadn't said he'd clean his girlfriend *out*. "What?"

"Entirely unscripted. We didn't have Cthulhu coming up until the um, 'climactic moment,' but word got out and—oh, here's the acolyte, running onto the beach in front of the actors. Also unscripted. See, this is why I don't like shooting on location; you can never close the set entirely."

"All hail Vagalith, Eldritch Bride of Cthulhu!"

Abject fear and desolation clenched my bowels. *"Leyla! I told you, I won't do tentacle stuff—"*

The woman's shout of outraged defiance devolved into a guttural howl similar to a hell-beast sounding warning, or the stomach of someone who had eaten the Taco Supremo Grande at Claude's Authentic Mexican Ristorante.

My body shaking, I slumped in my chair. The acolyte shifted to a gibberish tongue, and nausea roiled in my stomach, as if my very body resisted hearing the words, and screams emitted from the speakers of my computer—

They stopped.

"It's okay," Leyla said, a little quivery. She cleared her throat. "I've paused it. You can take off your blindfold now."

I did, with shaking hands. Leyla's forehead was covered in a sheen of sweat.

"So, we have a problem," she said.

"What the hell was that!"

I made the mistake of looking at the video paused on-screen, and beheld the two mostly naked actors crouched on the beach in the foreground, clapping their hands to their ears and their faces twisted into visages of horror, while behind them rose a monstrosity the likes of which I'd never before witnessed, the head a beaked muzzle with thick, ropy tentacles dangling from the maw, set upon a sinuous snakelike body four times as thick as Our Hero's torso, and all a grayish color that put me in mind of putrescence, and all of which together combined into a hideous form that defied imagination and description, except for the fact that I have indeed described it.

Leyla snapped the laptop shut. "The short of it is, apparently that writer dude—"

"You mean H. P. Lovecraft?" He was in my response to Diabolical as well; while there was argument about just how much of his work and the mythos he inspired was in the public domain, I maintained that our "interpretation" was wholly based on the works of his that *were*, and that any resemblance to Diabolical's own interpretation was coincidental and originating from working with the same source material.

Speaking of, I hadn't yet included that in my response. I started to open the laptop, saw a single tentacle, and slammed it shut again before my intestines could rebel against me once more.

"Sure, Lovecraft, whatever. Anyway, it seems he tapped into something *real*, and so did his various successors. Word got out what we were doing, and so the acolyte—Kristoph, nice enough guy when he's not babbling about the imminent destruction of the world—and this Great Old One interrupted our filming of *Booty Call of Cthulhu*."

"About that title. We can legally use it and all, but considering this cease and desist from Diabolical—I emailed you about it this morning—you might want—"

"We have bigger problems than Diabolical, Chastity! Horace can't edit this footage. Every time he listens to or watches it for long, he starts shuddering and foaming at the mouth and usually goes into some sort of seizure, or he collapses unconscious. One time, he started spouting gibberish. He sounded nearly identical to Kristoph. Now he—I mean Horace, not Kristoph—refuses to look at it anymore; he's worried for his sanity. He threatened to spread word round to other editors that this footage is, um, dangerous." Tears filled her eyes. "We're over budget on *Booty Call* already. I can't scrap this; if I do, the studio will take me off the movie."

I stared at my closed computer. What if I just threw it away and bought a new one? It'd be better than re-subjecting myself to that freeze frame.

All at once it hit me that a Great Old One had risen from the vastness of the deep, and again I felt my insides coil with trembling fear and desire to pay obeisance.

Even when my flu turned into pneumonia two years ago, I still managed to straighten out the fiasco regarding Klogan the Skunk Bear of the Y-Men, which is *not at all the same thing* thank you very much. I had a job to do, and I was going to do it. "You need some guidance on the wording for the warning, then? Similar to how some video games include warnings about flashing lights inducing seizures?"

"*No!* Oh, that'd do wonders for the studio, if we put out a movie that could literally cause people to go *insane!*" Leyla wiped a hand over her face. "No, I need help on getting out of our contract."

I frowned. "Leyla, Brightdark is my client, not you. I can't help you get out of your contract."

"Not *my* contract, *our* contract." She cleared her throat. "With Vagalith." She coughed. "I mean, we were on the spot. You can't just say no to a Great Old One."

Leyla hadn't wanted to bring me the contract directly—"It's written on the desiccated skin of a whale, and let me tell you, those things are heavy"—so she explained the pertinent details on the way.

"Okay, so like I said, word of our filming of *Booty Call of Cthulhu* got out. It reached Kristoph, who, um, felt we weren't treating Cthulhu with the honor and respect an ancient being of terror and madness deserves." She made a sharp left. Her Tesla cut off a Prius and just made the light before it turned red. Ignoring the blaring car horns, she went on: "So Kristoph prayed to Cthulhu, but got Vagalith instead. Just between you and me, I think he was a little disappointed about that, but didn't want to let it show, you know?

"Anyway, once Kristoph explained to Vagalith what we were doing, she surprised us all by indicating that she wanted in on the profits." Leyla glanced at me. "Which, um, is another reason why we can't let this fail." She huffed out a breath. "My crappy insurance doesn't pay for mental health visits. I can't afford to go insane."

"Considering we have Vagalith on film, why not change the title to *Booty Call of Vagalith* instead?"

The light ahead of us turned red. Leyla slammed on the brake and came to a stop well past the white line. "There is a reason why you are a lawyer instead of a creative, Chastity," she said. "No, we cannot change the name to *Booty Call of Vagalith*. Our title is supposed to be tongue-in-cheek and self-referential. Hardly anyone's heard of Vagalith."

Leyla's criticism didn't mean I was going to stop work on my screenplay *Lawyers vs. Aliens vs. Tornadoes*, but no reason to mention that to her. "Why does Vagalith want profits from a b-level flick? Isn't she all pro-destruction of the world?"

"I guess she wants to destroy the world in style." Leyla shrugged. "How are we mere mortals to ever understand the tortuous thoughts of a Great Old One?"

I had little time to ponder the veracity of that statement, because we pulled into the parking lot for Brightdark, where Leyla had had her on-again off-again boyfriend haul the contract in his pickup.

Ten minutes later, I stood before the contract. It let off a sickly pelagic smell, like rotting blubber and seaweed. Well, I didn't know that that was what rotting blubber and seaweed smelled like, but considering what the contract was made of, it seemed a solid guess.

It stretched six feet long and three feet wide. It was a mottled grayish color, and the reddish-brown eldritch characters scrawled upon both its sides were written in a tiny cramped hand.

I feared it was too short to cover all the contingencies.

"Luckily, all we Brightdark folks had to do was sign our names," Leyla said, pointing at the bottom of the contract. "Kristoph supplied the blood for the rest of it."

I knelt beside the contract. "You know I can't read this. I hope someone interpreted it for you before you signed?"

Leyla was too quiet for too long, so I turned and glared at her. She wrung her hands.

"Leyla. Tell me you didn't sign this without knowing what it says."

A blush suffused her cheeks. "We had Kristoph start from your boilerplate contracts for both performer and writer. Figured that'd cover Vagalith's . . . ad-libbing."

I sighed. "I need a computer that has this font installed."

I didn't like to rely on Google Translate for these sorts of things, but you work with what you've got.

All told, the contract wasn't that bad. For the most part, my boilerplate setting out the expectations of the Contributor—in this case, Vagalith—remained untouched, at least as far as I could decipher Google Translate's English rendition of the Great Old Ones' language. There were a few additions, though: Leyla blanched a little that she needed to sacrifice her firstborn on the first moon of the new year, but she managed a small laugh and said, "Joke's on Vagalith; the only time I'm ever taking out my IUD is to have it replaced." Then she paled a little and added, "Um, don't let her know I said that."

Aside from knowing the law and how to manipulate its loopholes, a large part of a lawyer's job is discretion. I was used to keeping my mouth shut.

But the biggest issue with this contract was that I didn't *see* a good loophole. I suppose it comes from having a Great Old One on your side; when they deal with issues of life and souls and sanity and whatnot, they don't leave much wiggle room. Plus, we were dealing with *my* boilerplate.

It's the one time I've ever regretted being good at my job.

I didn't like watching Leyla's expression fall as I told her so, however.

"At least you negotiated her down to twenty percent of the profits," I said.

"I don't expect we'll have any profits, if people go insane when they watch the movie." Leyla shook her head. "Maybe in the days before Twitter and Facebook."

I patted her arm; I knew it hurt her to denigrate social media even in so small a fashion. "I'll keep working at it."

She offered up a small smile, but it didn't bode well; it was the same one she used when Oliver had suggested she test-drive a Kia.

The contract was too large and too smelly to bring home, so I took pictures of it with my phone and kept a copy of the translation close by.

I wasn't yet well-versed in the mythos, only having started to investigate it after receiving Diabolical's cease and desist. Thinking that the more I knew about Vagalith, the better chance I'd have at figuring a way out of the contract, I started my research with her.

Three point five billable hours later, I rang up Leyla and had her contact Kristoph.

Leyla and I stood with Kristoph on the beach where filming for *Booty Call of Cthulhu* had been interrupted just days before. Again I wore a blindfold while Leyla wore the headphones; Kristoph wore neither. We had the contract spread out before us, and I bore my copy of its translation and the historical document that proved Vagalith's violation thereof.

Kristoph protested at what Leyla and I aimed to do, but the law was on our side. Between that and our offer of a fifteen-dollar gift card for Claude's Authentic Mexican Ristorante—it seemed the resultant stomach grumblings *did* provide an avenue to understanding cosmic horrors—we swayed him to our cause, and he agreed to help summon Vagalith.

He prostrated himself on the beach and bowed toward the undulating waves. "O Great Vagalith, O thou of protuberant eyes and sinuous tentacle, O thou Eldritch Bride of Cthulhu, I beg thee, come!" He shifted to the eldritch language, and the syllables grated against my rebellious ears as if a thousand screaming tongues wailed and cried, and at last, long last, the surf surged and wind swept over me; the great Vagalith had risen from the depths and lurched toward shore. I cleared my throat and locked my knees, which trembled with the urge to collapse.

But lawyers never kneel.

"Vagalith! I am Chastity Jones, legal counsel for Brightdark Productions, and I find you in violation of this contract signed on the third of June!"

Hideous consonants and vowels spewed forth from her scabrous lips (which I hadn't seen, but they *sounded* scabrous nonetheless), and my spirit quailed within me, but I threw back my shoulders in solid defiance; Vagalith's inducement to purple prose was no contest to my legalese.

I held up the translated contract. "Clause 23: 'The Contributor hereto warrants and attests that all material and representations provided by her in conjunction with the work *Booty Call of Cthulhu* is in no way a violation of copyright, common law, or trademark right, or privacy rights; furthermore, the Contributor warrants that the work violates no other rights of any third party'—" I shoved the translation under my armpit. "It goes on, but the point, Vagalith, is that you do not own rights to yourself!"

Truth be told, I'd reverted to my original boilerplate wording. Google's translation had read something like, "Contributor options and guarantees, material and statements, do say *Booty Call of Cthulhu* not to connect it in a relationship that any way a violation of intellectual property rights; in addition make sure friends do not infringe the right of the other three." My original was more in keeping with the spirit of intent.

Vagalith spewed out a string of cackles and screeches that I took to be a protest of the legalities; Kristoph wailed "Forgive me!" and then let out an *oof* that I figured meant Leyla had kicked him.

I pulled forth my second sheaf of papers. "Behold, a copy of 'Vagalith, Eldritch Bride of Cthulhu,' a short story authored by Alfonso Montega, and appearing in a little-known, long-defunct pulp magazine entitled *Darkling Tales of Terror!*" The exclamation point belonged to both the magazine title and my own proclamation.

I licked my lips; my throat was starting to go scratchy, but I still had to finish. "Published in 1946, and therefore protected by the copyright laws of the United States of America! Which means," I continued, despite the moaning Vagalith and Kristoph both started up, wailing that shook me to my inner core and near set my thoughts to gibbering, "that your contract with Brightdark Productions is *null and void*, per Clause 31!" So saying, I gestured to Leyla. We'd thought of devising a more elaborate cue, but in the end figured that we might both be too out of our minds to understand much more than general flailing in each other's direction.

Unable to stop myself, I pulled the blindfold free of one eye so that I could see Leyla stumble toward the whale-skin contract. She stabbed a serrated boning knife into it, then sliced it top to bottom. Vagalith emitted a great wail that even Leyla had to hear, for she grimaced. The sound drove Leyla to her knees, and it felt as if my head would burst.

A vortex swept up Vagalith. Even as she continued her unearthly howls, it drove her back into the depths of the sea. Frothing from the mouth and shouting in that eldritch tongue, Kristoph stumbled into the sea after her. As if she rejected him, the surf surged and threw him back to shore, where he collapsed to hands and knees and pounded the sand, weeping.

It was the most dramatic dissolution of a contract I have ever witnessed.

Three days later, I opened my email to find another missive from Diabolical. The subject line read "Second Warning." They must have heard that filming of *Booty Call of Cthulhu* had recommenced. After the termination of Vagalith's contract, Horace had found himself capable of editing the footage to cut Vagalith, although he needed breaks every half-hour to look at cat pictures.

I opened Diabolical's email. The phrase *failure to communicate sufficient evidence of originality* stood out. I snorted. Like Diabolical's own *Booty* was any better.

I drummed my fingers on my desk, then smiled and picked up my phone, and dialed.

"Kristoph? Yeah, yeah, I will rot in the most squamous cell for all eternity. But listen: Have you heard of Diabolical Pictures? . . . No? Well, let me tell you about how *they're* defiling the great name of Cthulhu."

One philosophy that many lawyers won't admit to, but I will:

Turnabout is fair play.

Cthulhu, P.I.

By Laura Resnick

THE DAME who entered my office that dank, rainy evening was the kind of woman that makes mortal men start sacrificing to the wrong gods—which is usually fine by me, but it does involve some unintended consequences.

So did taking this lady's case, but I didn't know that yet.

A green-eyed redhead with long lashes and high cheekbones, she was built like the Mountains of Madness, with just as many deadly curves. Under the short hem of her little black dress, she had legs that went on forever—so I suggested she leave them outside my office, because it's a small place.

"What did you say?" Her voice was smooth and seductive, like the rest of her.

"Mwrph!" Business had been so slow lately that I hadn't spoken in a while. I realized my tentacles had fallen asleep and were blocking my orifice. I gave them a quick slap with one terrible scaly claw and then shook them awake. She flinched. A little slime flies around when I shake my head—but I use a good cleaning service. "Never mind," I said, "I guess your legs fit, after all."

"Pardon me?"

"How can I help you, sister?"

She blinked. "I'm not a nun."

"And I'm not a pardoner."

"Huh?"

"It's a turn of phrase."

"What is?"

"Let's start over," I said. "How can I help you, Miss . . .?"

"Johansen," she said. "Emma Johansen."

"What brings you to my office after dark, Miss Johansen?" I waived to a chair across from my desk, inviting her to take a load off. "And in weather like this?"

She scoffed. "The weather is always foul in Innsmouth. If I were going to wait for a balmy evening before seeking you out, I might just as well wait for the heat death of the universe to solve my problem for me."

"And what is your problem?"

Seated across from me now, she studied me, those lush eyes as full of secrets as the black seas of infinity. "Are you really the Dread Cthulhu?"

"I don't go by that title anymore." Not since the nightmare corpse-city of R'lyeh had been "discovered" by the cruise ship industry and turned into a souvenir paradise for day-trippers. I said morosely, "You really can't go home again."

"Yes, I can," she said with a frown. "If you intend to hold me prisoner here, then I should warn you that I have powerful friends who will—"

"No, I meant, *I* can't go home again."

Her frown cleared. "Oh. Right. Yes, that's what they say about you. Something about a licensing dispute with the corporation that bought up all the rights to your image?"

"I guess it's no secret," I said. "I had a lousy lawyer. So now I'm not allowed to show my face—or any other part of my anatomy—in R'lyeh. Nor am I allowed to generate income, attention, or public notoriety anywhere in the world through the use of my own image, which description includes my actual physical person. These terms are in effect until the corporation's exclusive license to reproduce and profit from my image expires. Or Doomsday. Whichever comes first."

The subject agitated me, which made my tentacles wave around reflexively. She had guts, though. Didn't bat an eyelash.

"You really did have a lousy lawyer," she said. "You should sue him."

"I did better than that. I ate him."

"Effective," she replied without missing a beat. "But not lucrative."

"The only money he had when he died was mine, which I got back." I shrugged. "But I put all that behind me when I came to Innsmouth. Hung up my shingle here and started a new life."

"Why did you go into private investigations? As a former underworld god, you could have—"

"This was a good fit for me. I have a knack for getting people to tell me what I want to know."

"I really, really believe that."

"It's a living," I said philosophically.

"So," she said. "No more being worshipped at dark altars of evil, no more blood sacrifices, and no more ruling great Cyclopean cities of titan blocks and sky-flung monoliths?"

"You've done your homework," I said coldly.

"You don't sound happy about that."

"I like my privacy," I said. "The corporation with deep pockets and good lawyers that owns my image also likes my privacy."

"And I like to know who I'm dealing with."

"I don't encourage mere mortals to poke around in my business," I warned her.

"And I don't usually discuss delicate personal matters with a total stranger," she shot back.

"You're sitting right next to the door." Like I said, the office is small. "You can use it whenever you want, Miss Johansen."

"I'm here because I was told you could be trusted." She lifted her chin. "I'm here because you are the Great Cthulhu."

"Not anymore," I said. "These days, I'm just plain old Cthulhu, private eye."

"But you'll help me?"

"If I can. What seems to be the problem?"

"There's this . . ." She paused and looked me over, her expression doubtful. "I don't mean to sound rude, but . . . well, I thought you'd be bigger."

"And I thought I'd be ruling the solar system by now," I said with a wave of my tentacles. "But it is what it is."

She didn't let it go. "I mean . . . a *lot* bigger."

"Look, if you really want to hire someone the size of a football stadium, maybe you should go—"

"No, I want to hire *you*. That is . . . I just want to make sure I'm dealing with Cthulhu himself, not some gumshoe imitation of the real thing. And, well, descriptions of you—"

"Tend to be exaggerated," I said. "For obvious reasons. After all, how many worshippers of a boundless evil entity from the nether regions really want to know that their bloodthirsty god wears a forty-two long? What high priest is going to tell the masses that their dark deity fits quite comfortably into the passenger seat of a taxi cab?"

"Ah. I see your point." She added, "I suppose that goes for your enemies, too? They get more juice out of making grandiose claims about you when they tell the tale of facing Cthulhu."

"Indeed. By comparison, corporate marketing teams are fumbling amateurs when it comes to building an image in the public's mind." I added bitterly, "In fact, everything those overpaid cretins are saying about me in their advertising these days was stolen straight from the lips of my acolytes."

"What happened to your acolytes after you were, er, obliged to enter private life?" she asked curiously.

I sighed. "Oh, they moved on and started worshipping someone else. You know how it is. Dark gods are like buses—one comes along every fifteen minutes."

"Well, then," she said, leaning forward to display the low cut of her neckline. Or maybe she was just leaning forward to confide in me. "You've convinced me. I'd like you to take my case."

"Then you'd better tell me what's troubling you, Miss Johansen."

She took a deep breath, hesitated, then said one word explosively: "Blackmail."

Emma Johansen told me her fiancé, "the brilliant geologist" William Dyer, was a professor at Miskatonic University. He was currently away ("*far* away") on an expedition in Antarctica. They had become engaged shortly before his trip ("a *very long* trip") and planned to be married after he got back.

In addition to being "a true genius" and a "noble man who would never callously break his word," Dyer was also heir to a substantial fortune, which meant he was funding the expedition himself—and doing so without even dipping into capital.

Quite a catch, was Professor Dyer.

However, Emma was a woman who possessed what corporate marketing mavens might call "a healthy sexual appetite." Her fiancé's absence had imposed on her a longer period of celibacy than was comfortable for her. She struggled for months with the tension created by the conflict between her "sinful impulses" and her promise to Dyer that she "would wait for his return" when they could be "joined together in wedded bliss."

Emma Johansen had apparently read too many Victorian novels.

Well, as any dark god could have predicted, Emma took a little misstep, stumbled into temptation, and dived headlong into sensual abandon. And the architect of her downfall violated her trust by recording their secret trysts.

In other words, Emma dropped her knickers for an opportunist who had a concealed accomplice take photos of their meetings.

"The photographer's good," I noted, looking through the sample pictures Emma had recently received. They'd been slipped under her door in an unmarked envelope, along with a note demanding a large sum of money if she didn't want her fiancé to see the rest of the collection. "Despite the dim lighting, I can see your engagement ring quite clearly in these shots."

"I know," she said between gritted teeth.

I could see a whole lot of other stuff, too. But I'm a professional, and I stuck to business.

"You're wearing a different set of undergarments in every photo," I noted.

Now her face was almost as red as her hair. "Do you have a point?"

"There were multiple meetings."

"Yes."

"How long did the liaison last?"

"Six months."

"Hm. Dyer *has* been gone a long time."

"He's an observant man," she said. "If he saw these pictures, I'd never be able to convince him it was an impulsive one-night stand after too many cocktails."

"I gather that seeing this evidence that, while engaged to him, you had a long affair with another man might be a deal breaker for your intended?"

"There is no 'might' about it."

"So you want me to get possession of all the photos—and any other evidence linking you to this guy?"

"Yes. Name your fee. As long as I continue on my path to becoming Mrs. William Dyer, money is no object."

She said her lover's name was Bryce or Brand or Brock. Something like that. The events which followed made it a minor detail that I don't remember now.

I found him pursuing another conquest in the same yuppy uptown fern bar where Emma told me she had met him.

This being the modern era, where one is exposed to unfamiliar and shocking things on a daily basis, many people take no notice of me in public places. But it's nonetheless not unusual for my appearance to attract some attention. There are always a few people who stare when they see me. If they're drinking alcohol, they often point at me and cheer, convinced I'm wearing an elaborate costume. Occasionally people flinch, scream, weep, drop whatever they're carrying, tremble in fear . . . I hate such reactions, because it makes me yearn for the good old days, when I inspired such terrified awe in everyone I encountered.

But time marches on, and even nostalgia isn't what it used to be.

I recognized Emma's lover easily, thanks to the photos of him I'd seen (and now could not *un*see, no matter how hard I tried). He was flirting with a young woman at the bar, and he seemed on the verge of gaining her consent to the assignation he proposed—when the mere sight of me approaching him made her gasp in horror and then faint.

I liked her.

Bryce (or Brand, or Brock) glanced over his shoulder to see what had frightened the lady—and as he froze with surprise, I grabbed him by the throat, dragged him outside, and threw him against a cold, wet wall in the alley behind the bar.

"I want all the photos of you and Emma, and everything that can connect you to her," I said, ignoring the rain that fell on us both.

"What did you say?" he asked breathlessly.

I realized the exertion had led to some of my tentacles getting into my orifice. I spat them out and spoke again.

"What photos?" he wailed. "I don't know anything about any photos!"

"A man with a camera hid in your bedroom night after night for months, and you never noticed?" I struck him with enough force to send him flying across the alley. "Try again."

He bounced off some garbage cans and landed in a large puddle of dirty water. He groaned and tried to get up. I kicked him and sent him flying into the garbage cans again, where he lay like a limp squid.

"This is the last time I'll ask nicely," I said, hoping he wouldn't lose consciousness before he talked. "Where are the rest of the photos?"

Behind me, I heard the door we had come through open again. I whirled around to snarl at the intruder, claws and tentacles extended.

I found myself facing the barrel of a shotgun.

"Don't touch him again!" barked the young lady who had, only moments ago, convincingly portrayed fear and fainting upon seeing me.

"That was a fast recovery," I noted.

"What did you say?" she asked.

The woman wasn't reckless enough to get near me. She would definitely have time to pull the trigger before I could close distance and seize the weapon. A dark god—even one relegated strictly to private life—could survive being wounded by a shotgun at such close range, but the event would be messy and uncomfortable, and the noise would certainly attract enough attention to cut our meeting short.

The woman looked past me to yell at what's-his-name, "I told you this would happen! Didn't I tell you?"

"Don't say anything," the man ordered in a weak voice. "Stay out of it."

"So *you're* the accomplice," I said to the woman.

"The crumpet fish?" she asked with a frown.

I tried to spit out my tentacles, but the rain complicated things. "Accomplice."

"A compass?" She added, "Don't spit at me."

I impatiently brushed aside my tentacles with one terrible claw.

She fell back a step and pointed the shotgun at my head. "Don't come any closer, octopus face!"

"You're his partner in crime," I said. "You took the photos."

"Oh." She nodded. "Yes."

"May I say, young woman, I am most impressed with your eye."

"I have two eyes."

I made sure to enunciate clearly. "Even in circumstances that were patently difficult for a photographer, you really captured something in those photos."

Her expression changed. "Oh?"

"The visual detail, the composition, the intuitive understanding of your subject matter . . ."

She straightened her posture a little while rain dripped down her face. "Do you really think so?"

"There's a chiaroscuro quality in some of those shots that's reminiscent of a Caravaggio painting. Have you ever studied photography seriously?"

She smiled, "Well, I've taken a few lessons, but I'm mostly self-taught. I do take it very seriously, though. Maybe you'd be interested in seeing some of my other work?" Relaxing now, she lifted one hand away from the shotgun to brush the rain off her face.

That was when I struck! I leaped forward and seized the shotgun before she could regroup and gain control of it. Using it like a baseball bat, I swung it and knocked her straight into her prone collaborator. The two of them lay there, winded, groaning in pain, and looking scared as I pointed the shotgun at them.

She feebly punched the man. "I told you she'd send someone after us. I *told* you it was too dangerous!"

"Now you're going to give me what I want," I said to them. "Does everyone understand me clearly?"

"We don't have what you want," the woman said.

"So I'll shoot one of you," I said, "and I'll kill the other the old-fashioned way—slowly."

"The photos still exist!" she said quickly. "*We* just don't have them."

"What?" her companion said. "What do you mean, *we* don't have them?"

"I sold them."

"You did *what*?"

"I sold them to Zadok Allen! I knew what you were going to do, and it was too dangerous." She gestured toward me. "I knew you'd get us both killed."

"You *sold* them?" he bleated.

"They're gone." She looked at me and repeated, "They're gone. Killing us won't change that."

"Letting you live wouldn't change that, either. So if you have any gods, now is the time to make your peace with . . ." I stopped speaking when I heard the shrill wail of police sirens. A few moments of listening confirmed my initial impression that they were headed for this spot.

I looked at the woman, realizing that in the moments after I entered the alley and before she followed me, she must have summoned the authorities. I was surprised that a blackmailer would do that.

Damn. I couldn't risk becoming a police target.

"I'm going," I said. "But if you put them on to me—"

"We won't," the woman said.

"Not a word," the man promised.

"We were mugged by an average . . . by two or three average guys. That's all we know," she said. "Now or ever."

"It had better be." I looked at her and added, "By the way, I was sincere about my admiration for your photography."

Taking the shotgun with me, to keep those two irresponsible youths from getting their hands on it again, I fled the scene seconds before the police arrived.

The two people who had ensnared Emma Johansen in their blackmail trap were clearly amateurs. But the individual to whom the woman had sold the compromising photos, Zadok Allen . . . he was something else entirely.

I'd never met him, but I was familiar with his reputation as a dangerous criminal whom no one dared cross. He had arrived in Innsmouth a few months ago, and almost immediately his name started being whispered in the shadows. He was as elusive and secretive as he was feared. It was said that if anything profitable, illegal, and deadly was happening in Innsmouth, he was the one pulling the strings, though no one could prove his connection or trace his web of crime.

Blackmailing a reckless woman who was on the verge of marrying into a considerable fortune seemed right in line with the sort of rumors that circulated about his activities.

The girl who'd sold the photos to him had made a smart move, even if Brand/Brock/Bryce didn't appreciate that. In exchange for earning a modest profit on their sordid venture, the couple turned all the real risk in their blackmail scheme over to Zadok Allen. He, in turn, would reap a much bigger profit from taking that risk, if he succeeded.

However, when making that tidy deal, Zadok Allen hadn't counted on one thing: Cthulhu, P.I., was on the job now. And apart from my standard daily pay, no one was going to profit from those photos.

This wasn't personal, it was strictly business.

Or so I thought.

It took me most of the night to track down Allen's lair, since he was good at keeping a low profile. But if an aspiring blackmailer could find him, then so could I—and in the end, I did. Since so many rumors connected him to illicit cargo, I decided to search the old caves down at Smuggler's Cove. By day, it's a public beach that no one ever visits; the sand is full of rocks and the water is stagnant and oily. By night, it's dark, sinister, and forbidding—just my kind of place.

My surmise that it was probably Zadok Allen's kind of place, too, proved to be correct.

But I hadn't counted on the shoggoth.

Damn. I hate shoggoths.

I smelled it even before I heard it lumbering through the eons-old tunnels that twined and intersected inside those seaside cliffs. Shoggoths are not the most hygienic of creatures.

As a dark god, I had no need of a flashlight in those opaquely black caves by night, and I could see the repellant, odorous creature perfectly as it slithered toward me. (Seriously, you'd think the Elder Things, with all their extraordinary insight and exceptional powers, would have thought to give shoggoths a less nauseating stench when they created them.)

This shoggoth was exactly as I remembered them. A massive, shapeless being made of iridescent black slime, animated by protoplasmic bubbling along the surface of its faintly luminous skin. Dozens of glowing eyes—a generous word for those dripping pustules of greenish light—formed, vanished, and reformed on its undulating surface, again and again, as it rolled over and over, tumbling toward me in its clumsy, grotesque, but surprisingly effective manner.

With no innate body shape of their own, shoggoths are able to form temporary limbs and orifices at will. This one did so now, developing long arms that extended huge claws toward me—presumably to seize and feed me to the fang-lined mouth I saw it was also now forming.

"Yes, yes!" screeched a woman from deeper in the cavern, concealed somewhere behind the shoggoth's enormous bulk. "Kill Cthulhu! Kill him . . . it . . . whatever. Kill Cthulhu!"

It had by now dawned on me that this was a trap. I had also just realized who must have set it.

Fortunately, without knowing exactly what to expect, I had come prepared. As a massive, slimy black claw grazed me with its touch, I raised the confiscated shotgun and let the shoggoth have it with both barrels.

This proved to be an effective but *very* messy way of dispatching a shoggoth. It was weeks before I got all the black slime—and the *smell*—out of my tentacles.

The woman screamed—and screamed, and screamed.

This made it easy to find her, despite the black slime that was flying, falling, clinging, and dripping everywhere now.

I took a look at her—screaming and covered in that slippery goo—and saw the shape of her scheme.

"Zadok Allen, I presume?" I said, gazing at Emma Johansen.

"No one told me a shotgun could kill it!" she was wailing. "That wasn't supposed to happen!"

"Why did you lure me here and ambush me?" I asked, feeling baffled. "Does this have something to do with my licensing dispute?"

"How did you do that?" she demanded.

"Do what?"

"Kill the shoggoth," she shouted. "They're supposed to be almost impossible to kill!"

"I don't *use* the title anymore," I said with dignity, "but I still *am* the Great and Dread Cthulhu."

"Not for long, you're not!" She threw herself at me, eyes mad with the lust for violence, and plunged a long knife into my torso.

I looked down at the blade protruding from my body.

"Ow," I said. "That hurts."

"*Good.*"

"This will cost you," I warned her with menace. "Cost you dear."

"Don't call me 'dear,'" she snapped.

I withdrew the blade and tossed it over my shoulder. The

movement made me wince a little. It had been a very long night, and I was starting to feel the burn.

"Noooo!" she screamed.

I thought about just killing her and going home, but I was curious. "Who are you, really? Not Zadok Allen. That's presumably an alias."

She was still weeping with rage and doomed ambition—killing a god is a big challenge to take on.

"Considering tonight's events," I said, "I assume you came to Innsmouth specifically because I was here."

She nodded as she wiped her nose. "I found out about your exile. I thought you'd be vulnerable here."

"There never was any William Dyer of Miskatonic University, was there?"

"Oh, he's real," she said. "But I don't know him. I just figured if I was going to tell you I have a wealthy fiancé, it was safest to name one who's in Antarctica."

She started trying to remove black slime from her hair. It was pretty hopeless.

"And so you enacted a scheme to lure me unsuspecting to these caves in the charmingly naïve belief that a shoggoth could kill me. I gather you've been preparing this plan for a while?"

"Ever since I came here."

No wonder "Zadok Allen" had taken pains to remain such a mysterious, unseen figure. "But why set yourself up as a crime lord?" I wondered. "Why not just live quietly while you studied my habits and routine?"

"I needed power and money," she said bitterly. "Transporting, training, and housing a shoggoth isn't cheap or easy, you know."

"Ah. Of course."

"Why did you bring a shotgun?" she asked, looking at the slime covering her hands now. "Did you suspect me?"

"No, I just happened to have it with me. I got it from your lover."

"From my . . ." She made a dismissive sound as she realized who I meant. "He's not my lover. He's an actor I hired. So is the girl."

I realized that everything in the bar and alley, including the seemingly inadvertent mention of Zadok Allen, had been carefully planned and scripted. "They were very convincing," I said. "But how did you talk them into doing something so dangerous?"

"I offered them a lot of money." She shrugged. "And it's not as if there's much acting work in Innsmouth."

"So all of those photos of you and . . . uh . . ."

"Posed. We were pretending." She gave a watery sigh. "I wanted a plan that would get you here very late at night, a little tired from your exertions, and completely unsuspecting. I thought surely . . ."

"Who's Shirley?"

"But I underestimated you, Cthulhu," she admitted. "I guess you're right—I was naïve to think I could bring you down."

"Which leads to my final question," I said. "*Why?* Who are you?"

"You don't know," she said with certainty. "I saw that when I told you my name at the start of the evening. It really is Emma Johansen."

After a pregnant pause, I prodded, "And?"

"And you destroyed my father!" she hurled at me. "He was a seaman who came across R'lyeh. I don't know exactly what happened, but you pursued his ship, most of his crew died, and he was never the same again."

"I don't know what . . . Oh, wait." It was coming back to me. "Johansen . . . Was that the guy who rammed his whole ship into my head?"

"Yes, that was him!"

"He was a jackass, Emma."

"How dare you!"

"I'm just being honest."

"You're not even going to apologize?"

"Did I mention he rammed his *boat* into my *head*?"

"He said you deserved it!"

I looked around the cave warily. "Please don't tell me the final act of tonight's drama is a reunion between me and your father."

"No." She shook her head. "He's dead."

"So . . . this whole elaborate charade, culminating in an attempt to kill me with a shoggoth . . . is because your father and I had our differences?"

"Yes!"

By rights, I should destroy her. She'd put me to a lot of trouble and made a real nuisance of herself.

But, damn it, I liked her *pluck*.

And Innsmouth was kind of a lonely town. I reflected that maybe now that I had been obliged to enter private life, I should attempt to *have* a private life.

So instead of killing her the old-fashioned way, I said, "Look, Emma . . . can I buy you a drink?"

A Stiff Bargain

By Matt Mikalatos

I WOKE TO THE SOUND of my own name, though it was not yet time to rise. I reached for the comforting feel of my coffin lid and discovered to my dismay that I was lying on a feather mattress, covered by a quilt which must have weighed at least ninety pounds. I had forgotten that I had moved into a boarding house.

"Isaac van Helsing," the voice said again.

I pried my eyes open. Standing at the foot of my bed was my former servant and thrall, Richard. This surprised me, as he was dead.

He thrust out his lower lip, pouting. "You murdered me. Your loyal servant!"

Richard had recently tried to murder me. He had pinned me, sucked my blood to become a vampire and left me to die at the claws of a rather nasty zombie bear. He was a vampire for about thirty seconds before he stupidly walked past a sun lamp I had set up. The last time I had seen him, it had been while emptying out my Dust Buster. I cleared my throat. "You were never particularly loyal."

"Semantics," Richard said. "And now, I've returned as a ghost. For sweet revenge!" With a flourish, he lifted one transparent hand and yanked back the curtains. On reflex, I raised my hand to shield myself from the sunlight, but a weak grey light filtered through the window. It was dusk. Late dusk, at that. Richard cursed.

I lowered my hand and rolled my eyes. "Ah," I said, tonelessly. "The sunlight. It burns."

"Don't mock me! It was daylight when I got here. It's difficult to wake you. You sleep like the dead."

I pulled on my jeans, then my shirt. I padded barefoot toward the kitchen, Richard floating beside me. "This is all your fault," he said. "I don't have a job now. How will I make a living?"

I rolled my eyes. "You're dead. You don't need to make a living." I could hear Mother Holmes, the owner of the old boarding house, clanking pots and humming to herself. She refused to treat me like a vampire, choosing instead a smothering maternal attitude of smug, but loving, superiority.

"Good evening," I said, and Mother Holmes turned, her face wrinkled as an ancient apple. She plopped a bowl of stew on the table in front of me. The smell of garlic wafted from the bowl, burning my eyes and blistering my skin. I pushed it away. "Mother Holmes, as I've told you three nights in a row, I cannot eat human food."

She scowled. "You pay for room and board, and that is precisely what you will get."

She spooned a bit of stew into her mouth and looked at Richard. "It's good to see you again, dear. What are you up to these days? You look much too thin."

Richard gave me a long stare, then turned to Mother Holmes. "I plan to haunt Isaac for a century or two. Maybe murder him if I get a chance. Outside of that, I'm not really sure."

A hearty knock came from the door, and I gladly leapt from my chair to answer. Mayor Rigby stood outside, his hat in his chubby hands and an apologetic smile on his face. "Good evening, Mr. Van Helsing," he said.

He stepped quickly inside and I closed the door behind him. He nodded to Mother Holmes and dropped his hat. His sweaty, nervous manner practically shouted "prey," and I licked my lips without thinking. "Is there a problem, Mr. Mayor?"

"Nothing you can't handle," he said, counting out three hundred dollars in bills and laying them on the table.

Richard floated over. "Is it the squirrels?"

I gave him an irritated scowl. "Be silent, this is business for the living. The dead are best seen but not heard."

Richard mumbled something about how I was undead, and I made a mental note to find a good exorcist. The mayor put his finger on the bills. "This is only the up-front money, of course."

I nodded. This was our current arrangement. I removed supernatural horrors from his community (myself excluded) and he paid me. I then paid Mother Holmes and remained, as always, one of the rare vampires unable to afford a castle or underground grotto. I was never good with money. Still, my current modest room was a considerable upgrade from my previous home: a black, windowless cargo van with a coffin screwed into the floor, currently parked in front of Mother Holmes's house. "Is it," I asked, "the squirrels?"

"No, no," the mayor said, annoyed. "They're a minor inconvenience. Hardly worth the money."

I had no idea what was going on with the squirrels, and must admit to a feeling of relief. I had no desire to chase rodents through the trees, supernatural or not. "What seems to be the problem, Mr. Mayor?"

He looked at his feet and flushed. "It's the leader of our neighboring town. Her name is Katie Lou Riley. Every week Ms. Riley calls and leaves disturbing messages on my voice mail . . . truly disturbing messages. She threatens that she will come and take over our fair town's government. I was hoping you could persuade her to stick to her own town."

I cocked my head and looked at him carefully. "That's all? You're not holding anything back?"

The mayor coughed delicately into his hand. "Well. She does have certain . . . powers."

"Like?"

"Oh, I don't know. Mind control. Things like that."

I shrugged. As a vampire I could hypnotize people, control animals, turn into a wolf or a bat, and live forever, so long as I didn't get a wooden piercing, eat garlic, or wear cross jewelry. Some mayor with mind control powers shouldn't be too much to worry about. "I'll take care of it," I said.

Richard floated through the table. "I'll come with you. To watch your back."

I narrowed my eyes. "Watch my back?"

"In case there's a chance to slip a knife into it."

I couldn't stop him, so he floated alongside me as I drove the cargo van to the next town. As we crossed the town limits I felt a deep shiver go down my spine. I pulled the van to a stop outside of city hall, but it was nearly ten at night. All the offices were closed.

I rolled down the window. A rousing chorus of song came from a nearby church, and lights blared from the windows. Richard and I exchanged glances and we made our way toward the church.

"Something's wrong," I said, as we got closer. A band of people burst from the church, beating spoons against pans and shouting like maniacs.

Richard grinned, showing his ghostly teeth. "They're going to kill you, I just know it."

I snatched a townie out of the dancing, shouting mob and yanked him toward me. "I'm looking for Katie Lou," I said. His eyes lit up and he cheered.

"He's one of us, boys," he shouted, and the crowd let out a huzzah.

I scratched my cheek. That was puzzling. "Where is she?"

"She's sleeping. She's a . . . what's the word?"

Another person in the crowd shouted, "Narcoleptic!"

A third person said, "Well, not exactly. She just sleeps a lot."

I drew myself to my full height, puffed out my chest and bared my canine teeth. "Then let us wake her!"

The crowd, strangely, did not appear terrified. Instead, they let out a terrific cheer, and swept me toward the church. I fought against the dark tide of the crowd, because a vampire cannot enter consecrated ground. I would catch on fire and burn to death, a rather unpleasant way to go. Richard knew this, and it was with obvious pleasure that he began to shout, "Yes, yes, everyone into the church."

I struggled against them, but there were too many, and in my panic I couldn't turn into a bat before they washed me over the threshold. I screamed. But I did not catch fire. I looked down at my cold, pale hands.

Richard squealed and flew around my head shouting, "Call the fire department!" until he realized I was unharmed. He settled glumly beside me. "Never mind."

I sighed. "I expect you to be pleased by my death, Richard, but gloating is beneath you."

He rolled his eyes. "You never really knew me, did you?"

The church looked much like any other church. A small stage near the front with a podium and the black maw of a baptismal font behind it. A neat row of pews lined up like ribs. One thing seemed to be missing. No crosses anywhere. Not over the door posts, not on the stage, not on the hymnals or in the brick work. I hadn't caught on fire because this was not consecrated ground. A tingling sensation traveled across my scalp. The crowd lined into their seats, still beating on pots and pans, blowing trumpets, having loud conversations on their cell phones. I gripped a pew. If Katie Lou could not be on consecrated ground, she was more than just some woman with mind control powers.

A man in a white suit came jogging from the side of the church and onto the stage. "Good evening, everyone!" They all cheered. "Ten years ago I got a woman pregnant and when Katie Lou saw our daughter, well, she decided that this was the sort of baby she would like to eat. Katie Lou said to serve the baby up on her ninth birthday. That's today! Happy birthday." More cheering! He gestured to the side stage and three men brought up a small girl in a white robe, bound tightly with ropes.

My blood started to boil. Well, technically not my blood, but I was the one who had it last, so, finders keepers. No one hurts kids, not when I am around. I became a vampire when I was only eighteen, helping my father in the family vampire-hunting business. And there was no way that an insane town mayor was going to eat a little girl while I watched.

"Never!" I shouted.

Everyone stopped. The man in the white suit looked at his assistants, as if they might know the answer to his questions. "Who is this, now?"

"I'm Isaac van Helsing," I said, my voice trembling with emotion. "And I'm a vampire!" I dropped my jaw and did my best impression of a rattlesnake. I was pleased to hear gasps from the crowd.

The next thing I knew, I was bound to a long wooden plank by heavy metal chains. Richard floated nearby, his head propped on his hand. My head throbbed intensely when I moved it. "What happened?"

Richard grinned. "Someone shot you with a tranquilizer gun."

I frowned. "That works? On vampires?"

"Just kidding. You went into a trance and walked onto the stage and they tied you up. I guess Katie Lou is going to eat you, too." He pointed at White Suit, who was riling up the crowd. "That guy says she likes you."

I shook the chains. I didn't have enough leverage to break them. The little girl was five feet away from me, her face battling between resignation and mild terror. "Don't worry," I said. "I'm going to get you out of here. What's your name, young lady?"

She looked at me uncertainly. Her bangs were cut unevenly, and she looked tiny and helpless in her white robe. "The Sacrifice."

"No, dear, your name."

"That is my name."

I growled. "That is not okay." A growing sense of dread washed over the church. I looked back at the baptismal font. Cold, clammy air came from it. I tasted salt water on my tongue. "If I only knew who Katie Lou is," I said. "Maybe we would have a chance." I turned my attention to White Suit. He was holding a ream of paper over his head with one hand, the other holding a bottle of Elmer's glue.

"Now is the time to wake her from her slumber," he shouted. "Pen and glue!"

The crowd echoed him with fervent delight. A black light came on, and people's clothes started to glow. I could feel a presence, itching at the back of my mind. Richard shimmered, the beginnings of a psychic storm picking at the edges of his existence. "I'm glowin' off Katie Lou Riley!" White Suit shouted.

Wait. Pen and glue. I'm glowin' off Katie Lou Riley. Why did that sound so . . . familiar? It was like hearing someone speak with a heavy accent. I knew I should understand, but I couldn't quite figure it out.

The Sacrifice gave a little scream. "I can feel her coming! If you're gonna do something, it's got to be quick!"

White Suit laughed and held his hands over his head. "We're going to get fat again!"

I swallowed, hard. Those last few words, I thought I knew them. And now they were saying the whole thing, over and over: "Pen and glue! I'm glowin' off Katie Lou Riley! We're going to get fat again."

A horrific nausea gripped me. I knew what they were saying. I screamed for Richard. He looked over at me, unconcerned. "Richard, you have to get us out of here. Untie the girl, get the key and get me out. Right now, Richard, right now, right now!"

Richard looked down at his fingernails. "Why so worried, boss? You can handle anything. Ha ha ha."

I tried not to scream. I could feel her now, rising toward us. My brain started a primal keening, like a monkey alarm clock inside my head. The chanting echoed around the room.

The Sacrifice started rocking back and forth. "She's awake!"

I took a deep breath. "Richard, these idiots aren't pronouncing it correctly. Her name isn't Katie Lou Riley. And stop looking at your fingernails, you're a ghost, we all know you don't have dirt under there."

Richard stuck out his tongue. "Being insufferable is not likely to get you much help. Besides, I can barely move a curtain, I certainly can't break the girl's ropes." He nodded apologetically to the girl. "I would if I could. No one likes to see a young girl eaten, even for a good cause."

I ground my teeth. "I didn't want to tell you this, but it's entirely likely that you can possess human hosts. Lots of ghosts can."

"I can . . . what now?"

"Steal their bodies."

Richard cackled with glee and immediately disappeared. The girl had gone rigid with terror. I reminded myself to take deep breaths. I thought I could see the first tentative bit of Katie Lou pushing its way onto the stage. The White Suit loomed over me, a knife in one hand and a wooden stake in the other. "You were right about the bodies," he said with Richard's voice. "Tell me what's going on and I'll cut the girl free."

"Richard, Katie Lou's sheer psychic backwash could cause you to cease to exist. If you're not going to save me and the girl, save yourself!"

Richard laughed. "You're actually scared." He looked back at the townspeople, chanting and moving into a religious frenzy. "I thought we came here to get rid of a prank caller."

I struggled against my chains. They didn't budge. Richard White Suit dangled a key over me, laughing. I tried to turn into a mist, or a bat, or anything. A rabbit would be fine! But the psychic trauma of Katie Lou's arrival had effectively neutered me. "It's not Katie Lou. Put the pieces together, Richard. I don't want to say her actual name. But she sleeps a lot."

Richard snorted. "Narcoleptic, I know."

"She's really terrifying."

"That doesn't narrow it down much."

"She enjoys blood sacrifice."

Richard shook his head. "I don't get it."

"Imagine the name . . . Katie Lou . . . sound like anything else?"

"Nope. Nothing."

I screamed in frustration. "They're not saying 'Katie Lou Riley' they're saying 'Cthulhu R'lyeh.' They're trying to say Ph'nglui Mglw'nafh Cthulhu R'lyeh wgah'nagl fhtagn."

Richard White Suit's jaw dropped. "Cthulhu? The 'elder god' of terror who will one day rise up and wreak havoc on the universe?"

"So they say."

Richard grabbed the sacrificial knife, his hands trembling, and sliced the ropes off the girl. She jumped up and rubbed her wrists. She didn't hug him or move near him, probably evidence of the troubled relationship between her and her father, who had raised her as an appetizer for the elder god. Richard turned to me, the stake in his hand. "I'll make this quick."

I scowled at him. "Take your time, Richard. Might as well enjoy yourself."

"I'm in a bit of a hurry. I don't want to be here when Cthulhu arrives."

"He's not going to stop until he gets his bloody sacrifice to lull him back to sleep!"

"I thought 'Katie Lou' was a she?"

"It is an ancient alien god who hibernates beneath the ocean. We haven't had a good look at the reproductive organs yet."

Horrific squid-like tentacles burst through the floor, knocking Richard to the side and grabbing me around the chest. The Sacrifice tried to run, but the tentacles grabbed her legs, and then Richard, and dragged us deep below the church building. I fell through darkness and slammed into a wide slate platform hard enough to break the chains on my arms. Richard landed on me next, followed by the girl.

The tentacles recoiled into the black water below us. "Somehow they've moved Cthulhu here beneath their town! What a terrible idea."

"Your phone is ringing," Richard said.

The girl was holding onto my leg, panting. I pulled my phone out and saw a series of horizontal marks with something like letters hanging off of them. "It's Cthulhu." I put one hand on the girl's head and held the phone to my ear.

A feminine, but guttural, voice said, "Cthulhu . . . is bored. And hungry."

"I see. Um. Is there any chance we could entertain you with something other than constant blood-letting?"

There was a long silence. "No."

"Cthulhu, look into my mind and search for something called 'HBO.'"

I felt the dirty water of the elder god's mind wash through my head. "Yes. Bring Cthulhu this . . . HBO. Also. An 'easy chair.'" I felt its attention turn to The Sacrifice. "And bring also . . . marshmallow Peeps. An abundant supply. MAY THE WATERS BENEATH THIS TOWN BE COVERED IN PEEPS!"

"Release us and all of this will be yours."

"Very well."

"Also you have to stop prank calling Mayor Rigby."

"No. He must live with . . . the call . . . of Cthulhu!"

"He's an ordinary man who can't handle your great presence."

Cthulhu laughed, and the horrific psychic backlash caused all three of us to fall to our knees. "He is no ordinary man. Cthulhu must remind him that his refrigerator is running and that he must catch it."

"The thing is, he's paying me six hundred bucks to get your calls to stop."

"Cthulhu has reasons for the suffering inflicted on this Rigby."

Bargaining with an elder god is dangerous business. I didn't want to find myself inside a tentacled maw, but then again I needed that six hundred bucks to pay rent. "Why, O Great Tentacled Monstrosity, must you torture this poor soul?"

"Rigby is his last name. His first name is . . . Zog-Yesseriyal!"

"Soggy cereal?"

"Zog-Yesseriyal! Brother of Cthulhu! The crusher of dreams! The serpent-skirted shouter on the hill! The churner of stomachs!"

I put my hand on my head. "You mean to say that Rigby is one of the elder gods?"

"The horror of lower southeast Burbank! He-who-wakes-me! Devourer of my leftovers! The crosser of the invisible territorial line in the back seat of the family car!"

"I take it you have a grudge against your brother?"

"He-who-makes-tortilla-chips-go-stale!"

"Enough already. I get it."

"There are more names."

I paced the slate platform. Richard and the girl still stood frozen, pushed against the back wall. "There must be some way to get you to stop harassing Mayor Rigby."

There was a long pause, and then Cthulhu inserted a bargain into my mind. She would never call Rigby again if I agreed to it. I considered carefully. Stepping between warring interstellar creatures was dangerous. I reluctantly agreed, and the elder god showed me a narrow stone stairway. I pointed it out to the girl, and she went up first, her legs shaking. I followed, Richard at my back. I was surprised that the elder god had agreed to my bargain without demanding actual blood from anyone.

We walked much of the way in silence. As we neared the top, Richard said, "I saved us by making a mental bargain with Cthulhu."

I narrowed my eyes and turned toward him. "I made a bargain, too."

"What was your bargain?" Richard asked.

"Richard, you shouldn't make deals with creatures like that unless you're extremely careful," I said.

We came up into the church. All of the cult members were lying on the floor, as if they were marionettes without strings. Richard grinned and moved close to me, the stake raised in his hand as he lunged for my heart. "I promised him the blood of all the cult members! And I will give him yours as a bonus!"

Richard knocked me backward and I fell to my back. I could have thrown him off easily, but the girl had fallen beneath me, and I was struggling not to harm her. The stake touched the skin of my chest, the full weight of Richard's body pushing it in. My muscles strained to hold him back. "There won't be any Peeps!" I shouted. "Imagine a Peepless existence!"

Richard's face twisted into a scowl. "At least respect me enough to shout final words that make sense."

I smiled at Richard. "This should make sense to you: the body you're in belongs to one of the cult members you promised to Katie Lou."

Richard's face fell. "And the girl!"

The girl shook her head. "Having grown up as a sacrifice I was never a fan of Katie Lou. I'm Presbyterian."

"Me too!" Richard shouted. "I'm not part of the cult!" The building shook, and tentacles wrapped around Richard's torso, yanking him back toward the abyss. "Noooo! I'll be back, Van Helsing! I will be avenged!"

I snatched The Sacrifice into my arms and sprinted outside. Enormous, unwholesome appendages smashed into the perverse church, eventually drawing the entire building down into the hole. The girl wept, her head against my chest, and I stroked her hair gently. "Don't worry. You're safe now. You're safe."

She put her hand in mine. "Now you're my father," she said.

I didn't know what to say to that. I imagined that Mother Holmes would be glad to have another boarder, and perhaps she would adopt the girl. She didn't have a mother, or any possessions to speak of, but we did go by her house and I wrangled her father's easy chair into the back of the van for a later delivery.

We arrived at Mother Holmes's house almost an hour before sunrise. She made the appropriate clucking sounds and gathered The Sacrifice to her ample bosom. "What's your name, child?"

She cuddled in close and said, "My name is Safe."

Mother Holmes hustled her toward a washroom, a comforting stream of verbiage surrounding them like a cloud. I made sure the blinds in my room were closed tight and lay on my bed, still in my clothes, on top of the quilt, too tired to turn off the light. It had been a long day. After some time I could hear Mother Holmes and the girl in the kitchen, the latter gladly slurping up stew. Mother Holmes said, "You're nothing like your father!"

I felt something strange . . . a small warmth in my chest, the corners of my lips tugging upward. I reached for my cell phone and put the caller ID blocker on before dialing Mayor Rigby. He answered on the third ring.

"Mayor Rigby," I said, muffling my voice. "Your goat is eating everything in my garden."

Rigby, still struggling toward wakefulness, said, "I don't have a goat."

"That's okay," I said. "I don't have a garden." I hung up quickly. Now

I just had to short-sheet Rigby's bed, booby trap his office with Dixie cups full of water and write CTHULHU RULES on his windshield with whipped cream, and my bargain with Katie Lou would be finished. No doubt she would eventually get more followers and send them to harass Rigby another way, but I had earned my six hundred bucks. That was the last prank call. And if Katie Lou tried to back out of our deal I could always cut off her HBO and Peeps.

My phone buzzed. Caller ID made it clear which terrible deity was on the phone. I was tired, and I debated sending it to voice mail, but picked up at the last second. "Hello?"

"Where are Cthulhu's Peeps? Cthulhu has eaten all of her minions and is hungry."

"Tomorrow," I said, yawning. "I'll bring them tomorrow."

A satisfied rumbling came over the phone. "Van Helsing."

"Yes?"

"Is your refrigerator running?"

I sighed. "No. It's standing in the kitchen. Go to sleep." I clicked off the phone, turned it to silent and closed my eyes.

Sometime just before I drifted off, Mother Holmes came and pulled my quilt up to my chin.

Half awake I asked, "The girl?"

"She's clean, with a full stomach and a smile on her face, sleeping in the room down the hall."

"That's a good thing," I said, and slipped Mother Holmes the three hundred dollars for the girl's rent. I felt her warm lips on my forehead. She turned out the light and closed the door behind her, and I slept and dreamed and did not wake, not until night came again.

The Shadow Over My Dorm Room

By Laura Pearlman

"THE SKY IS FALLING," Chicken Little said, but of course I didn't understand him right away. He forgets sometimes that he no longer has lips and teeth and all the other bits you need to produce intelligible speech. I gave him a moment to remember. He isn't stupid—he's better than me at math, and his Ancient Religions project won some kind of award—he just has a hard time facing reality, at least where his affliction is concerned.

He squawked for a minute, the way he does when he's frustrated. Then my phone beeped with a notification: "To: Cam, From: Chicken Little. The sky is falling." I looked up. He was standing by the window, and I finally saw what he was talking about: another meteor shower.

"Good one, Bob," I said. "The sky really is falling." Bob is Chicken Little's real name. Bob Little. He doesn't look like a chicken—or any bird found in nature, really. The back part of his head is oversized, probably to accommodate his mostly-human brain, and of course birds don't have tentacles—but aside from that, he just looks like a guy with a vulture's head and talons.

The nickname was my idea. Bob's appearance can be a little intimidating. The "chicken" in Chicken Little humanizes him. It gets people thinking about wholesome domesticated farm animals instead of vicious carrion-eating scavengers. And every time someone hears or says the name, they're reminded of the children's story, which nudges them into being less afraid—or less willing to admit they're afraid, which is almost the same thing.

His wardrobe was also my idea: button-down shirts in calming pastel colors (T-shirts or polo shirts would have been better, but they don't fit over his head), matching oven mitts over his talons, brightly-colored shorts to draw attention to his normal human legs, and, whenever possible, sandals to expose his feet. He doesn't wear a hat; his head isn't the right shape for it and besides, if you're in a receptive mood, the multi-colored tentacles on the top of his head give him a festive, jaunty look. Small children point and laugh when they see him, but that's better than screaming and crying, which is what they used to do.

They don't teach this stuff in Marketing 101. Or 102, 201, or 202: I know, because I aced them all. Most parents would be proud. Mine never got over the fact that I'd chosen MiskU over Berkeley. They thought the university's culture, traditions and values were straight out of the 1930s.

Things finally came to a head when I told them I was doing my Marketing 301 internship at MegaCorp's Arkham branch. Mom and Dad are throwbacks to the '60s who were, as they so charmingly put it, having grave misgivings about funding the sale of my soul to my eventual corporate overlords. So grave, in fact, they'd decided to cut me off.

There's no way I'd be able to afford MiskU on my own. So I worked out what I hoped would be an acceptable compromise and Skyped my folks. After some awkward small talk about my kid sister's piano recital, I got down to business.

"I think you'll be happy to hear this: it took some doing, but I quit my MegaCorp internship and got one at Arkham Hospital."

"That's great," Mom said. "A much better environment for you. You'll work with doctors and social workers and patients from all—"

Dad cut her off. "You'll still be doing marketing, though, and working mostly with administrators. Right, Chamomile?"

I hated that name, but I had bigger fish to fry. "Marketing covers a lot of things," I said. "We might be doing public service announcements. Encouraging preventive care, recognizing the signs of a stroke, that sort of thing." Anything was possible. At my interview, we'd talked mostly about the new plastic surgery wing. "So, do you think you might reconsider—"

"We've made our decision, Cam," Dad said.

"Do you want me to get kicked out? Because that's what's—"

"That's not the end of the world," Mom said. "That place is a bad influence on you."

Dad nodded. "You can still get a degree. Transfer to a less expensive school, get some loans, work part-time."

"That might be better for you. You'd be exposed to a more diverse—"

"This again?" Mom had been harping on the diversity thing ever since the *Globe* ran that article on MiskU's admissions process. "My roommate is literally a monster! Is that diverse enough for you? And for your information, my marketing skills are the only reason people don't flee in terror at—"

I looked up just in time to see Bob rush out of the room. In the heat of the moment, I'd forgotten he was there.

Bob and I had been roommates since freshman year. He was a nice guy and pretty average-looking until a few months ago. The change had come on gradually. It started the night of a meteor shower. He came in late, after I'd gone to sleep. In the morning, he told me he'd seen a meteorite fall. He said it was the most beautiful thing he'd ever seen, with colors he never even knew existed. He'd picked it up and breathed in its fragrance, and the next thing he knew it was morning and he was in his own bed. It took a while, but eventually he realized it must have been a dream.

His nose seemed a little sharper than usual that morning, but I convinced myself I was imagining things. Each day after that, his nose grew a little longer and pointier, his eyes a little more deep-set, his hair a little thinner. His head began to change shape: his eyes moved farther apart (oddly, this seemed to improve his vision); the rest of his face was pushed upward and forward. His fingers got longer. One day, he tried to trim his fingernails and couldn't cut through them. He began to have trouble eating and speaking. He lost weight. He went to the infirmary; they gave him a referral to a speech therapist, a prescription for Xanax, and a pamphlet on eating disorders.

The speech therapist gave him some vocal exercises to practice: basically just a bunch of nonsense syllables to say at least thirteen times a day. Something like "Fun-glue maw-naff kuh-thoo-loo ruhl-yeh" and some more I can't remember, over and over again. It didn't help, and it was annoying as hell.

Bob was dating a girl called Michelle at the time. She stuck with him until the night her grandmother died. Michelle was heartbroken. Bob tried to wipe away her tears, but by this time his talons had started coming in. Michelle wound up with seven stitches, a prescription for Valium, and a pamphlet on domestic violence.

I apologized to my parents for the outburst, but by the time we hung up, they'd rejected all my attempts at compromise. Bob still hadn't returned. He'd rushed out without his oven mitts, a coat, or even shoes.

I found him by the bushes near the library. His back was to me, and he was crouched down; at first I thought he was sick. He jumped up when he heard me approach, and I saw he'd been bent over something that I believe had recently been a raccoon. Whatever it was, it had been torn apart; there was blood everywhere and chunks of flesh were missing. Bob looked at me, blood dripping from his beak and talons, and I knew instantly what had been going on. He'd been performing CPR on this poor creature. He was the kindest and most hopeful person I'd ever known. How could I have called him a monster?

We had a long talk (well, I talked, he typed) after we got back to the dorm and Bob got cleaned up. He wasn't just upset about what I'd said. That night's meteor shower had put him on edge. His grades were slipping: he couldn't speak up in class, the talons made it difficult for him to type, and lately he'd been having trouble concentrating.

Bob and I both skipped classes the next day. Our first stop was the infirmary, where Bob got a referral to Arkham Hospital's Occupational Therapy department, a prescription for Adderall, and a pamphlet on stress management.

Next was the financial aid office, where I discovered I didn't qualify for any scholarships or grants, and the maximum student loan amount available to me would cover only a small fraction of my tuition.

Then came the Office of Student Disability Services, located in the sub-basement of the Administration Building. Getting there was more difficult than we'd anticipated. We took the stairs all the way down and checked all the offices twice but couldn't find it. When I opened the stairwell door to go back up, there was only a flight leading down.

"Well, that's weird," I said.

Bob nodded.

"You don't happen to remember where—"

Bob shook his head.

"Well, um, the office is probably on this lower level, right? We'll just take care of our business there and ask for directions back."

Bob shrugged.

The first sub-basement had been clean and brightly lit. The second was cold and clammy with dim flickering lights. It smelled like fish that was old enough that your mom would throw it out but that probably wouldn't make you sick if you cooked it thoroughly. Every so often I thought I saw a rat or something darting around in the shadows. After what seemed like forever, we came upon an open door with a Student Disability Services sign.

The office was just as damp and smelly as the hall. A large fish tank on one wall did nothing to brighten up the place; it was full of murky seawater and dull gray fish. There were a few wooden chairs near the fish tank and a reception desk at the opposite wall. The student behind the desk appeared to be doing some kind of math homework. His textbook was open to a page full of unfamiliar symbols and a diagram that looked like an Escher drawing, only more so. It reminded me of the halls we'd just walked through.

"Excuse me," I said. We'd decided that, because of Bob's communication issues, I'd do most of the talking. "This is Chick—uh, Bob Little. Robert Little. We need to arrange for some accommodations for—"

The student—Chad Gilman, according to the name at the top of his homework paper—grabbed a stack of forms and shoved them at me, not bothering to look up. "Here. Fill these out and bring them back. Then call and schedule an interview with Ms. Marsh."

"Can we just fill them out here?"

"Suit yourself," Chad said, not looking up.

We sat in the reception area and filled out the forms. There were a lot of them. Half the questions were about family medical history. We got through those pretty quickly: Bob was adopted, so we just answered "unknown" to all of them. We were almost finished when a woman stepped out of the inner office. I tried not to stare. She had some kind of skin condition, her eyes bulged, and she was extremely pregnant. She stared at Bob.

"Okay," she said. "I can see you now."

I started to get up. She snapped at me. "Just him. Confidentiality."

Bob shrugged, and I handed him the forms. The two of them disappeared into her office. I pulled out my phone, but there was no reception in the sub-basement. No magazines in the waiting area, either. I stared at the fish tank for a minute, but a bunch of gray fish swimming slowly back and forth aren't particularly entertaining.

I walked over to Chad's desk. He'd moved on to another homework assignment. His handwriting was awful, but I could tell it was zoology because he'd drawn a giant squid. The drawing was pretty bad: the proportions were all wrong, and it had way too many tentacles.

"So," I said. "I guess we didn't need that appointment after all."

Chad grunted.

"You would have had us coming here three times, and we're getting it done in one trip."

No response.

"I mean, it was hard enough for us to get here, but this is Student *Disability* Services. Imagine how hard it would be for—"

A student rolled in on a wheelchair. "Just dropping these off," he said, tossing a bulging manila envelope onto the desk. "I'll call later and set up an appointment." He rolled out again and into an elevator directly across the hall from the office.

"Oh," I said.

Bob emerged from Ms. Marsh's office. He seemed happier than he'd been in a long time. When we got back to the dorm, he explained that Ms. Marsh was formulating an accommodation plan for him. She'd have it finalized and in the hands of all his professors within a week.

I was feeling optimistic too: while I'd been waiting, I remembered hearing about MegaCorp's employee tuition reimbursement program. Maybe I could go back to my internship there, convince them to hire me full time, and get them to finance the rest of my degree.

It turns out that quitting an internship at MegaCorp at the end of your first week gets you put on some kind of internal blacklist, so I had to stick with Arkham Hospital. Bob started occupational therapy there the same day I started my marketing internship. It seemed to do him good. He traded his phone for a tablet and ran an app on it that made it easier for him to communicate. He even started gaining back some of the weight he'd lost.

A couple of weeks into my internship, I was returning from a coffee run and got into an elevator without checking the up/down arrows. I pushed "4", but the elevator went down to the basement.

When the doors opened, I was surprised to see Bob coming out of the morgue, wiping something red off his beak. He froze when he saw me, and to my horror it all suddenly made sense: the stuff on his beak, the recent weight gain, his avoidance of the dorm and hospital cafeterias.

I could barely get the words out. "You've—you've been eating. Down here, in the morgue. This whole time, you've been so self-conscious about your beak that you've been bringing your lunch here, where no one can see you."

Bob stared at me for a second and then nodded slowly. His entire posture changed; all the tension melted away right before my eyes. He must have been so relieved to share his secret with someone.

I stepped out of the elevator and hugged him. "Don't worry," I said, "I won't tell anyone. But we should probably find you a support group or something."

By late April, things were going pretty well for Bob. He was using a modified virtual keyboard and voice synthesis app on his tablet. It was slower than normal speech, but much better than the text-based communication we'd been using before. He'd stopped making surreptitious trips to the morgue. He'd even gotten a part-time job. It didn't make full use of his talents, but it was honest work—transporting surgical waste from the hospital to a disposal facility—and he said he found it rewarding. To each his own, I guess.

Ms. Marsh had drafted a disability accommodation plan for Bob, but she'd gone on maternity leave before signing it. This hadn't been much of a problem so far, but midterms were coming up, and that meant timed essays written in longhand. Bob could barely grip a pen, much less write with one. He started talking about getting a full-time job with the medical waste company.

I decided to take matters into my own hands. I wasn't going to be able to continue at the university—all my efforts to secure funding had failed—but at least I could keep Bob from suffering the same fate.

I went to the disability office to confront Chad in person and demand he process Bob's paperwork immediately. At first he insisted there was nothing he could do. After I'd rephrased the question about twenty times, he seemed to have a change of heart. He told me the dean of students could sign the form. Even better, the dean was having a party on his yacht the next night. He'd hired some students to help with the catering; Chad was one of them, and he was willing to let me take his place.

"It's nine o'clock tomorrow night at Innsmouth harbor," Chad said. "I'm not sure exactly where the yacht will be moored, but the locals all know it. Just show up at the docks and ask for the *Dagon Sacrifice*."

The *Dagon Sacrifice* isn't a boat. By the time I figured that out, I had a broken nose and a knife at my throat.

The last bus to Innsmouth arrived at seven o'clock, so I had a couple hours to kill before the party. I browsed the Barnes & Noble for a while, then walked around a residential area near the harbor. The neighborhood was pretty eclectic: lots of new construction, some older homes in obvious disrepair, and the occasional well-maintained grand old house. Eventually I found some shops near the harbor and went into the nearest Starbucks to relax with an iced caramel macchiato until it was time to go find the boat.

I'd never been to Innsmouth before; everyone said the town was creepy and insular. I didn't see any of that in Starbucks at first, just the normal mix of people chatting, reading, or working on laptops. People mostly ignored each other until a couple—two men, one Asian, one black, with a baby—arrived and sat down at a table. Everyone who came in after them stopped to say hi to the men and coo at the baby before placing their order. Everyone, that is, except one pasty-looking foul-tempered man who glared at everyone, including the baby, before stomping up to the counter and demanding a black coffee.

"Tall, grande, or venti?" the barista asked.

"Large," the man said with a snarl.

He glared at everyone again as he took his coffee to go. His eyes were kind of bulging, so it was a particularly unsettling glare.

I left a few minutes later. When I got to the harbor, I didn't see anything resembling a yacht. There were about a dozen people gathered near one of the boats, though.

"Excuse me," I called, as I approached them. "Is this the *Dagon Sacrifice*?"

They all turned and looked at me, but no one answered.

"This boat," I said. "Is it the *Dagon Sacrifice*? I'm supposed to report for work there at nine o'clock. Chad Gilman sent me."

I thought I heard some tittering. A large man with a tattoo of a giant squid on his left arm stepped forward and clapped his hand around my shoulders in what I took to be a friendly gesture. "Oh yes," he said, "This is definitely the Dagon sacrifice." Squid-Tattoo Man walked toward the boat, sweeping me along with him.

More tittering. Now that I was close enough, I could see the name on the boat: the *Unspeakable Horror*. The surly man from Starbucks was part of the crowd. In the moonlight, their faces all looked pale and greenish-gray. No one was dressed for a party. Squid-Tattoo Man smelled like he'd jumped into a bathtub full of halibut a month ago and hadn't showered since. Would the dean really throw a party on a fishing boat? With guests who looked and smelled like this? Where were the other students and caterers? For that matter, where was the dean? Something was very wrong here.

"Oh, good," I said. "I'm not late, am I?" Squid-Tattoo Man relaxed a little; I broke away from his grip and ran. Not fast enough: men swarmed me; there was punching and kicking and dragging. For a moment I was back in third grade getting beat up yet again because Chamomile sounds like a girl's name and I hadn't figured out how to talk my way out of a bad situation yet. Of course, the kids in my grade school typically walked away after administering a beating instead of dragging me onto a boat, producing a dagger with weird tentacle carvings on the hilt, and pressing the blade against my neck.

"Look," I said, forcing myself to remain calm, "I know what this is about: gentrification. The McMansions, the Starbucks and McDonald's all over your town. All these new people moving in, making you feel insecure about your economy. You want to send a message. I can help you craft that message." I was pretty sure they wanted me—or possibly my dead body—to be that message, so this seemed like a reasonable compromise.

"This isn't about 'gentrification.'" I could hear the scare quotes in Squid-Tattoo Man's voice. "You cannot begin to comprehend the mysteries of—"

"Although," said one of the women, "he does have a point."

"Yeah," said another. "My coffee shop went out of business because of Starbucks. And we lost two hardware stores to Home Depot."

Squid-Tattoo Man began to chant something that sounded a lot like those voice exercises Bob did back when he still had a voice.

"Wait. Let's just hear him out," said a voice in the crowd.

"Yeah," said another. "Why rush? We've got almost three hours until midnight." There were murmurs of agreement.

"Fine," Squid-Tattoo Man said, relaxing his grip a little.

"Okay," I said. "What you need is a marketing plan. You need to paint Innsmouth as a quaint all-American town being overrun by chain stores that threaten to destroy your way of life. Have some kind of festival—the kind that's interesting to read about but that people wouldn't actually want to travel to—promoting local traditions. Issue press releases full of words like 'authentic' and 'homespun.'"

I was stalling for time; other towns had tried this and failed. I had to throw in something new. "But don't start with that. Start with something people love to sink their teeth into: bullying. Make something up. Write a tearful blog post about Starbucks telling you you're too ugly to drink coffee in front of their other customers."

"That actually happened to me," said a woman whose appearance I won't attempt to describe.

"That's even better!" I said. "I mean, that's terrible, but it makes a better story."

It took a while, but I managed to convince them to take me on as a consultant. I had to swear my fealty in front of—well, you wouldn't believe me if I tried to describe it, but in exchange they were willing to pay me more than enough to cover my tuition and living expenses. I called an Uber to take me back to campus. I was in pretty bad shape, so I had the driver drop me off at the infirmary. They sent me on my way with a nose splint, a prescription for Vicodin, and a pamphlet on codependency.

Bob dropped out a week later. I ran into him a few more times at the hospital. He seemed happy. He'd ditched the oven mitts—too hard to do his job with them on—but kept wearing the colorful outfits I'd picked out for him. His coworkers joked around with him and called him Chicken Little.

The nickname was an effective bit of branding, and it served Bob well, but he was nothing like the character from the children's story. Bob had never been an alarmist. The real Chicken Littles were my parents, and they couldn't have been more wrong: My overlords were anything but corporate, and they weren't at all interested in my soul.

The Tingling Madness

By Lucy A. Snyder

AS THE INDESCRIBABLE HORROR dragged me down into the black waters of the fathomless quarry, I wondered two things. Had I left the coffee maker plugged in, and would our Siberian kitten Chewie bite through the cord again, resulting in a fire that tragically yet ironically caused my husband to die of smoke inhalation as I drowned? How much frog pee was in the quarry water, and how much of it was I inadvertently swallowing as I struggled against the Horror's slippery arms? And how had I gotten myself into this mess in the first place?

Wait. That was at least three things, wasn't it? They say that your ability to count is one of the first functions to abandon you when madness sets in. "They" being people who probably always had fine arithmetic skills. People who never, ever went crazy from boredom at their day jobs. People who never did questionable things on company time to try to keep their brains engaged.

But I'm not one of those people, and that's how I got into this mess.

I knew I was going to get fired from my content editing job at Skewl about a year before it happened. The signs of my impending unemployment loomed obvious as an Arab sorcerer's curses scrawled in fire upon the conference room walls. Our instructional design group had merged with three other departments, and we'd been moved out of our nice, cheerful offices into a windowless cube farm in the basement. Worse, we kept getting shuffled to new bosses. Half my coworkers quit in frustration because of the supervisor we all called Buzzword Bob, and afterward, upper management had a new reason every week—sunspots! A yeti epidemic in Nepal!—for why they couldn't replace anyone who'd left. Our workload doubled, then tripled, and I was taken off all the art, photography, and literature courses I'd been hired for and put to the task of building the worst online business courses you can imagine.

I know, I know . . . it can't have been that bad, right? I didn't have to gut fish in a chilly room. I didn't have to dig graves in the frozen ground. I didn't have to babysit a kid who wanted to watch nothing but the same episode of *Barney and Friends* over and over and over. But there's a special hell in sitting in a cramped gray cube under a buzzy fluorescent light for nine hours a day arranging blocks of awful, impenetrable text you aren't allowed to change or try to improve. I'm talking about subjects such as "Corporate Governance and Viscerous Control Assessment," "Quantitative & Qualitative Methods for Necropolitan Decision-Making", and "Foundations of Forensic Accountancy for Geriatric Allopathy".

I knew I should keep my head down and be a good hive drone. I knew that they were surely looking for reasons to let people go. I knew that I should not, should *not* give in and read slash fan fiction online during my breaks, and I particularly shouldn't start *writing* slashfic during said breaks, but the relentless boredom and frustration had awoken something terrible inside me and I couldn't stop myself.

So when I went to my supervisor's office for my weekly one-on-one meeting and she smiled and said, "Why don't we go upstairs for this discussion?" I felt a spike of dread and adrenaline but also no small bit of relief: finally it would be over. And then as we walked to the creaky elevator I felt regret: why hadn't I escalated my job search? Why hadn't I just dropped the hammer myself and quit when most everybody else did? Mysteries of the universe.

My supervisor led me to a glass-walled room where the HR manager sat primly at the big conference table with a folder and papers set before her.

"Please sit down." The HR lady gestured at the chairs on the opposite side of the table.

I did as she asked, and my supervisor took the chair beside her.

Grimacing, the HR lady pushed a paper-clipped stack of pages toward me. "Can you explain this?"

I looked at the pages. It was a printout of "Pinkie Pipes Pomp," the most popular story I'd posted on the FrackYeahFanfic site. In just four days, it had racked up over one thousand Loves. I'd used my RhinoScribe69 pseudonym and had erased the tale from my hard drive, but of course I'd uploaded it through Skewl servers.

I paused. This was my opportunity to lie and say I'd just looked at it out of curiosity, but I was too tired to think of a good excuse and just wanted this to be over.

"Yes, that's a story I wrote on my lunch break."

The HR lady looked shocked that I'd admitted it so easily. Clearly, she had expected embarrassed stammering, or pleading, rather than calm. "Is the Don Pomp character supposed to be President Trump?"

"Well, actually, he's more of a mix of Trump and Nixon with some Grover Cleveland style."

Her eyes grew narrower, her voice shriller. "And Pinkie Dinkie is a rhinoceros?"

I blinked at her. "Well, yes. Of course he is. Don't you watch *My Little Rhino*?"

The HR lady and my supervisor both stared at me as if I'd suddenly sprouted a second head that was now rapping tracks from *Free Willy: The Musical*.

My supervisor spoke low and slow, like salty barbecue: "You wrote a story in which the sitting President of the United States is graphically violated and degraded by a talking rhinoceros?"

I shook my head. "Violation implies non-consent. If you re-read page two, you'll see that this is an entirely consensual power exchange—"

"Enough!" The HR lady's voice shook like the walls of Jericho, and her eyes were blue furnaces of judgment. "You have flagrantly violated our computing policies. Your employment here is terminated. Your supervisor will escort you outside, and security will bring your belongings out to the parking lot. Please give me your badge."

I unclipped it from my belt loop and pushed it across the table to her. "Don't forget my Pinkie Dinkie action figure."

The HR lady shuddered.

★ ★ ★

I got home two hours later. My husband Pete rolled his wheelchair down the ramp from the upper level living room. "Darling wife! You're home early?"

I set my cardboard box down on the shoe bench by the front door. "Your darling wife messed up and got fired."

"Oh dear. I'm so sorry. What now?"

"I find a new job. In the meantime, we better mind our money."

That night, we sat down to look at our recurring expenses, and I found out we were spending over two hundred dollars a month on cable television.

"This is insane." I stared at the e-bill on his laptop screen. "I thought this was like sixty dollars a month?"

"That was a twelve-month special for bundling TV, internet, and laundry soap delivery," he replied. "But it expired, and the price went up."

"No kidding. Please call tomorrow to cancel."

My husband looked dismayed. "The internet, too?"

"No, keep the internet . . . we're not *barbarians*. And don't worry about missing out on *CSI: Hoboken*. I'll order an antenna."

The device, which advertised a fifty-mile reception range, arrived two days later. It took less than fifteen minutes to stick the big square antenna to the window and thread the long black coaxial cable behind the bookshelves and our entertainment center to our TV. Pete and I watched in rapt attention as the TV's auto-programmer detected the newly available channels. Five channels . . . ten . . . twenty . . . thirty . . .

"Forty air channels?" Pete exclaimed. "All this time, we could have been watching forty channels for *free*?"

"Don't get too excited," I warned. "We get the major networks, but I have no idea what these others are. Could be most of them are infomercials."

"Can we surf through to see?"

"Sure."

I helped Pete out of his chair onto the couch. Our kitten Chewie settled between us and began to purr and gnaw on the side seam of Pete's jeans. He never chewed on my jeans; I didn't know whether to feel slighted or relieved that my pants weren't constantly wet with kitten drool.

The first channels were what I expected: CBS, Fox, ABC, PBS, NBC. I was pleased to see MyTV, which meant we'd get to watch *Svengoolie* on Saturday nights. Then we found the Comet channel, which showed classic sci-fi movies, and Grit, which appeared to be old war movies and westerns. After that were some religious channels in English, Spanish, and Somali . . . and then a channel that showed hooded figures writhing on the floor of some dimly torch-lit cave somewhere. The picture quality was terrible, grainy black and white, as if we were seeing a feed from a cheap security camera mounted to the ceiling.

"What is this?" Pete asked. "Is it an indie movie? Some 'found footage' *Blair Witch* kind of thing?"

"I have no idea." I pressed the "Info" button on the remote, which indicated that this was the Ia! channel.

"Weird," Pete said.

We sat and watched, waiting for a plot, or commercial, or *something* to make sense of what we were seeing. But there was just more writhing, and guttural moaning, and occasional distant chanting in a language I couldn't place.

"Well, okay, then," Pete said. "Next, please?"

The following channel identified itself as HeWillRise, and so of course I thought it would be a Christian broadcast . . . but it was another monochrome security camera feed. There were no people visible in the frame, just the slow rise and fall of . . . what? There was sound, but all I could hear was a white noise like the constant rush of ocean waves.

"Is . . . is that some kind of big lizard?" Pete asked, squinting at the screen. "Or a crocodile? Or an elephant?"

"It looks a little scaly, and wet, but is that some kind of tentacle?" I definitely saw something like a squid's tentacle slowly curling over the reptilian bulk of whatever body part we were seeing. A flank? A leg? It was impossible to know.

"Maybe? Why are they just showing a little part of it? Is it asleep, or floating and dead, or what?"

"It looks like it's breathing." I was starting to hear something like slow inhalations and exhalations under the sound of the ocean surf. So slow that the creature's lungs had to be bigger than school buses. "It's sleeping. Whatever it is."

"Is this some kind of art film?" Pete sounded annoyed but looked freaked out. "Why won't they pan out so we can see the whole thing?"

"Maybe they can't." I felt a sudden chill. "Maybe it's too big."

Pete turned pale. "This is Weird City. Change it, please."

And I wanted to change it . . . but my hand had gone limp as my job prospects and wouldn't follow my brain's command. I felt . . . strangely compelled . . . to keep . . . watching . . .

Pete snatched the remote from my fingers and clicked to the next channel, which was showing a Squeez-E-Cheez commercial. The logo in the lower right corner of the screen indicated that this was the Tingler channel. Thrillers, maybe? I'd take them over whatever weirdness the previous channel had been projecting into my cerebrum.

"Thank you," I muttered.

"No problem!"

The commercial ended, and suddenly we were watching a man dressed like a gold coin humping a well-built naked man in what looked like a British pub. Their naughty bits were pixilated out. Pete emitted a high-pitched squeal of dismay that scared Chewie off the couch. The kitten fled, leaving a wispy nimbus of shed fur hanging in the air.

"What in the name of hot buttered buns *is* this?" he exclaimed.

"I . . . I don't," I began, then stopped, recognition dawning. "Holy crap. I know this. This is 'Pounded by the Pound: Turned Gay by The Socioeconomic Implications of Britain Leaving the European Union'!"

Pete blinked. "What?"

"Um. It's a short story by Chuck Tingle."

His look of confusion turned profound. "Who?"

"He's an erotica author. He writes about billionaires getting seduced by jet planes and T-rexes and yetis and stuff. His story 'Space Raptor Butt Invasion' got nominated for a Hugo Award. As a joke, but still."

"Do a lot of his stories have 'butt' in the title?"

"Oh, absolutely."

"So his stories are popular?"

"They sell like crazy! But I never thought he'd have his own TV broadcast. This is . . . unexpected."

"Could this be a pirate channel?" he asked.

"Maybe? But I think those are hard to do."

Pete looked pained, but didn't try to switch back to the safety of major network programming. Now, onscreen, the man-coin lovemaking had created some kind of lightning-rimmed portal into the past so that they could change Britain's vote to leave the EU. About half the dialogue was bleeped out.

"Well, this isn't *terrible*," Pete remarked. "But it's certainly more butt-centric than I'm comfortable with."

The movie ended, and a call-in talk show entitled "Voidwatch" began. An actor who called himself Budd Hardmann hosted it. He had apparently worked as a stunt double for Adam Sandler until an accident on-set gave him a near-death vision of a place he called the Void.

"The masters of the Void are always looking for ways into Earth from other timelines and dimensions," Hardmann earnestly told the camera. "And we all have to stay hard to stop them. Good buckaroos always keep their eyes open and their buds close by. Watch for the signs, and if you see something, say something. Caller number one, you're on the air. . . ."

The first caller was Nayad from Madison, Wisconsin, and her voice was tight with fear. "Mr. Hardmann, I'm a long-time viewer and this is my third call to you. The Dreamer is definitely waking up. Anyone can see it. He rolled over just yesterday! I'm so scared about what's going to happen."

"Fear is the fresh-maker, Nayad. And you can use his name."

"I don't want to use his name!"

"That's okay, Nayad." Hardmann rubbed his brow. "You do you. And I know you're a good ladybuck and you can be strong."

"But what do we do?" she pleaded.

"He can't wake up unless his followers all complete their rituals. Watch for the signs; call us for help if you think something is going on near your town. We can send buckaroos to back you up. Call us any time, day or night."

A toll-free number started flashing at the bottom of the screen. I grabbed a pen and bill envelope off the coffee table and jotted it down.

Pete gave me a supercilious side-eye. "You're taking this seriously? Really?"

"I . . . I don't know." I squirmed on the couch, embarrassed but remembering how I'd felt watching the strange security cam channels. "*Something* weird is going on."

"All these bizarro channels are probably part of the same multiplex run by the same broadcast company." He gestured dismissively at the TV screen. "It's just huckster showmanship to get viewers hooked on some imaginary supernatural conspiracy, can't you see that?"

"I guess. . . ."

He sighed in exasperation. "If you do call these people, for God's sake don't give them your real name, or address. *Or* your credit card number."

I felt small and stupid, but I couldn't shake my conviction that I'd seen something real. Something that called me to action. Even if I didn't know what the heck it was. "Okay."

"Good."

He flipped the TV back to CBS, and we watched his shows until he got sleepy.

"I'm not tired yet, honey," I said. "Please go to bed without me."

"All right, but don't stay up too late."

After I'd heard him shut the bedroom door and I saw that he'd turned off his bedside light, I switched back to the Ia! channel. This time, the feed showed figures clad in hooded Hello Kitty bathrobes holding hands around some kind of odd geometric shape painted on a dingy basement floor. It had the look of a rehearsal rather than a real ritual, and that made me feel marginally better.

I spent most of the night flipping between Ia!, HeWillRise, and Tingler, trying to get a better sense of what was going on in this strange new world I'd discovered within our own. I learned a couple of things. First, Ia! switched to a different feed every hour on the hour. And second, Budd Hardmann never seemed to sleep; his live show was on every four hours between commercials for cheese and cheese products and short movies based on Chuck Tingle stories.

I called the talk show number just after midnight, and the operator put me through to Hardmann.

"Hello, caller number three, you're on the air. Can you give us your status, name and location?"

"New viewer, first-time caller, and I prefer to remain anonymous for now." My voice echoed through the TV speakers.

"That's okay; you do you. What's your question or concern?"

"My husband believes that your channel, the Ia! channel, and HeWillRise are all part of the same multiplex. Run by the same people."

"No, ma'am," Hardmann shook his head vehemently. "Ia! and

HeWillRise are a duoplex, and we are independents using the power of love against their devil ways. We are templars to their vampires, Spongebob to their Plankton."

"But why would Ia! and HeWillRise show what they show?" I persisted. "Wouldn't it make way more sense to, you know, be covert about trying to take over the world? Use a slight bit of discretion and not broadcast all your activities?"

"Have you watched HeWillRise?"

I paused, staring at the ceiling. "Yes."

"And didn't you feel compelled to keep watching?"

"Yes. I did."

"That's how they get you. Most humans can't look at Cthulhu for more than a minute or two before they feel the call of the Void. And then, if they can tear themselves away, they flip over to Ia! and think, hey, that looks like fun. I should join in the dance. Boogie down for the Apocalypse. Those channels are traps, like diet soda when you're trying to lose weight."

"But I don't want to join in the dance," I said. "I want to stop the music."

"Stay hard, anonymous ladybuck," Hardmann said. "The forces of love need you. When it's time, you'll know."

I spent the next several nights watching Ia! and Tingler after Pete went to bed. The sleep deprivation was starting to make the world feel unreal, like everything around me was just a painted set, but I couldn't stop myself.

And then, on the fifth night, it happened: I was watching Ia! when the feed switched to figures in hooded rain ponchos cavorting around ritual scrawling on the pebbled beach of a quarry. A local quarry I recognized: Murkstone was an old limestone quarry that had been abandoned when the mining crew broke through into an undetected aquifer back in the 1950s. The whole thing filled up with water in a matter of hours. The rumor was the aquifer went down for miles, and that's why the authorities forbade people from swimming in it. Which of course didn't stop any of the local teens from going skinny-dipping. I'd gone there several times my senior year of high school, allegedly for picnics, but of course we'd all gone in the water. The feed was pretty grainy, but I was *sure* it was Murkstone.

Mostly sure, anyway. There was only one way to be absolutely sure.

So, of course, an hour later I was crouched down in the damp grass behind some leaf-bare bushes staring at wet cultists through the gaps in the brush. There wasn't a set, or a TV crew, just a security cam and laptop sitting on a rock. Yep. I was absolutely, one hundred percent sure.

I eased my phone out of my pocket and dialed the Voidwatch number.

"Someone who knows what they're doing needs to come out here," I told the operator. "I'm at Murkstone Quarry in Central Ohio, and there is definitely a cult ritual going on out here."

"We'll send backup," the young man replied. "Can you give me the address?"

"Yes, it's at the corner of Highway Forty-Two North and French Lick Road."

"Can I get your name?"

I paused, remembering my promise to Pete, and then gave him the first pseudonym that popped into my head. "I'm RhinoScribe69."

"Did you write 'Pinkie Pipes Pomp' for FrackYeahFanfic?" the operator asked.

I blinked, startled. "Um, yes?"

"Oh my stars, I *loved* that story!" he gushed. "Everybody here loved it! What you did to expand Pinkie Dinkie's childhood backstory was nothing short of brilliant! And his domination of Don Pomp was amazing. The sociopolitical metaphor . . . just brilliant!"

I felt my cheeks grow hot in the cool air. "Thank you. You're much too kind. But, you know, the cult is doing their thing, and maybe someone could stop them?"

"Absolutely," he assured me. "I'll send a dispatch ASAP. Stay hard!"

And then rough hands grabbed the back of my windbreaker, and I screamed like a five-year-old. They jerked me to my feet and spun me around. I was facing two scowling cultists in matching scarlet-and-gray Buckeye Football rain ponchos. They were both built like major household appliances and outweighed me by at least seventy-five pounds apiece.

"Looks like we got a spy, Kevin," one growled to the other.

"And you know what happens to spies 'round here."

They gave me meaningful stares, and an awkward silence reigned.

"Actually, I don't know what happens to spies," I offered.

"They get to meet the Indescribable Horror," not-Kevin growled.

"I don't really think that's necessary," I protested as they each grabbed one of my arms and dragged me up the trail and onto the pebbled beach.

They planted me in front of a slender man of medium height. The man wore a fancy silk maroon robe embroidered with curvilinear symbols in gold thread. He was about thirty years old, and had short russet hair styled up into a rain-damp fauxhawk. One of his eyes was hazel, and the other a pale sky blue. They both bulged slightly, and something about his gaze reminded me of a tree frog. His thin, angular face was dusted with freckles, and he had a tattoo of Abe Vigoda on the left side of his neck along with the caption FISH LIFE.

"Who are you?" I asked.

"I," he intoned, "am the Indescribable Horror."

I blinked. Several times.

"I don't mean to be rude," I said, gently as I could, "but you're actually highly describable."

His face darkened with anger. "This mortal shell is but a flesh disguise. Flimsy and disposable. It means nothing! My true self lies within, and none can describe the depth of the blackness of my essence!"

The terrible thing within me that made me write slashfic at work stirred. "How black is it?"

"It is blacker than the night, blacker than pitch, blacker than a starless sky! Blacker than the despair of a man upon the gallows! Blacker than the spawn of Shub-Niggurath! Blacker than the blackest licorice jelly bean!"

"That is very black," I agreed. "But also highly describable."

And that's when he threw me into the quarry.

Like my firing, I'd more or less expected it, and had a half-formed plan to swim for the beach on the opposite shore. But the water was shockingly cold, and so I gasped and floundered as he whipped off his fancy robe and dove in after me.

We struggled. I'm not sure for how long. I've always been a pretty good swimmer, but the Indescribable Horror was nimble as a minnow, and soon he had my arms pinned and was dragging us both down. Questions flitted through my mind, as I said, concerning Chewie and my husband and my ongoing consumption of frog pee . . . but I also wondered if there was an afterlife. Would I become a ghost, my restless spirit eternally bound to this quarry? Would my ghost ever get tired of watching skinny-dippers and couples making out in the bushes? I considered my taste in fanfic and realized: no, it probably wouldn't get tired of it.

Abruptly, Indescribable released me as though some invisible force had snatched him away. As I kicked sputtering to the surface, another pair of hands, gentle as the breath of a unicorn, took hold of the sleeve of my windbreaker and led me back to shore.

It was too dark to see my benefactor there in the quarry, but as I staggered onto the pebbles, coughing up water, I saw two insanely ripped, sopping wet shirtless men putting zip tie cuffs on Indescribable. Other exceptionally buff men in rainbow fatigues were chasing cultists through the trees and erasing the eldritch ritual symbols.

"Thank you," I gasped.

"No, thank *you*," the taller of the shirtless men replied. "We knew the ritual was going down but we didn't have enough intel to identify the location. You provided exactly what we needed."

"You got here super-fast!"

"We always come quickly," his companion replied. "When appropriate."

"Dr. Tingle sends his regards, by the way," said the first. "And suggests that perhaps you should try your pen at writing erotica professionally."

"Really? He doesn't think the market is over-saturated by now?"

"Smut is like Jell-O at Thanksgiving," he said. "There's always room for more!"

"You smell like frogs," Pete complained sleepily as I slipped into bed beside him.

"I'm sure it's just your imagination, dear."

"You went out, didn't you?"

"Why would I go out at this hour?"

"Because of the crazy cult stuff we saw on TV?"

"That seems far-fetched, doesn't it?"

"I don't actually hear you denying any of this," he pointed out.

I fell silent, my cheeks heating in the darkness, waiting for him to tell me what big dummy I was.

He sighed and hugged me close. "I'm just glad you're okay."

"I love you."

"Did love save the day?"

"It always does."

The Girl Who Loved Cthulhu

By Nick Mamatas

WHAT COLLEEN DANZIG, author of Lovecraftian fiction, hated most about the fateful events during and after the fan convention known as the Summer Tentacular was the wildly gleeful looks in the eyes of fans and fellow writers when they asked, "So, how was the mental hospital?" Yuggoth Days, the weird fiction writers' convention where she was the guest of honor, was also turning out to be something to hate, and she hadn't even checked in yet.

The mental hospital hadn't even been that bad. They'd let her write, and in nine days she'd pounded out the first draft of her novel *The Correlated Contents*. It was a unique piece of Lovecraftian fiction, in that normal people who actually wore ironed shirts had read it. It named names, told the real story of what went on behind closed doors at gatherings of Lovecraftians, and was spiced with a soupçon of true crime thanks to the unfortunate real-life murder and mutilation of a minor writer almost nobody cared about. Also uniquely, the novel had even made a few bucks. So Colleen found herself simultaneously feted and despised by the community at large, or at least simultaneously feted and despised by everyone in the lobby of the new Ramada right outside Brattleboro, Vermont.

Well not *quite* everyone. "Colleeeen!" Daria Franklin cried out.

"Helloooo!" Daria was a . . . well, hard to say what she was. Fan, certainly. A creator to a certain extent: she did Lovecraftian needlepoint and knitting. *Ph'nglui mglw'nafh Cthulhu R'lyeh wgah'nagl fhtagn* was framed for display over the mantle, and Cthulhu Toilet Tissue Cozies were her thing. And she was the worst kind of reader—the type who had a lot of questions for authors about their books. She tromped up to Colleen, waving her arms, her curls bouncing, like she had just been ejected from a washing machine a bully had stuffed her into. "It's so amazing! Guest of honor! Did you know that you're the first woman guest of honor Yuggoth Days has ever had?"

"Hey Daria," Colleen said. "Yes, I did know that. Twenty different people tweeted at me that I was the 'first guest of whore-er' when it was announced."

"Do you think they'll pick me one day?" Daria asked. She squinted as she smiled. "For artist guest of honor, I mean."

"Sure . . ." Colleen decided to say. "Anything is possible, right?"

"Wow, that would be so awesome. What's it like, being guest of honor?"

"It's . . . uh, like this," Colleen said, looking around for anyone who might save her.

"Sweet. That reminds me, in *The Correlated Contents*, you know how that dead guy was still the narrator even though he was dead?"

"Yeah . . ." Where was her guest of honor liaison? Shouldn't there be a bellhop in a little red cap rushing over to take her guest of honor luggage up to her guest of honor room?

"My friends and I were arguing about whether that was supposed to be supernatural or not?" Daria started.

"Uh-huh." Colleen looked over Daria's head, waved to someone she thought she knew, but couldn't manage to catch his attention. Maybe it was actually just a lobby fern and she had been feeling too hopeful.

"It just seemed too realistic in a way, I thought, so I wanted to ask . . . have you ever died and come back to life?"

"What?!" Colleen snapped her head down to meet Daria's eyes.

"Have you died!" Daria insisted, her vocals frying. The lights dimmed. Daria's face seemingly filled the room, filled the world. "Have! You! Ever! Been! Dead!"

Colleen staggered, blinked hard, and shook her head. "I . . . I gotta go?" She lurched away from the conversation, toward the elevators, even though she had neither checked in to the hotel nor gotten her con badge yet.

"Oh, and Colleen?" Daria called after her. "How was the mental hospital?"

Thankfully, the bar was on the other side of the elevator bank and Colleen was soon ensconced in a booth, alone, with a drink. The place was crowded with fans in black T-shirts and the occasional feral-looking professional writer in one of the other shadowed corners, just waiting to be nonchalantly discovered. Normally in such a place Colleen would put up her wards: book in one hand, Day-Glo pink earbuds for maximum visibility, phone out in the other hand with her thumb working the screen. But she didn't need to do that here. Colleen was a known commodity in Lovecraft Country; she was given a wide berth and had time to think about her guest of honor speech: "The Girl Who Loved Cthulhu."

Maybe enjoying Lovecraftian fiction is like enjoying The Three Stooges—guy stuff. Not guy stuff like football or being president, but guy stuff like poking dead things with sticks, and bragging about the volume and intensity of one's own farts. She didn't know if she'd get laughs, groans, or walk-outs, but she decided to keep the intro. Let 'em walk out, or groan. She was writing for . . . *The woman who finds something in Lovecraft is a . . .* she composed, mentally. But . . .

Who was Colleen Danzig writing for? As if in answer to the question, Daria Franklin slid into the booth, a copy of *The Correlated Contents* in hand and an official Yuggoth Days tote bag slung over one shoulder. "Colleen!" she said, enthusiastic, all discussion of Colleen's hypothetical death forgotten. "I forgot my copy of the book at home, but I really really wanted a signed copy, so I went to the dealer's room and bought a second copy for you to sign right now. Double royalties, right?"

"Right," Colleen said, quickly doing the math on 7.5 percent of $15.99 and doubling it: two bucks, forty cents. A smile to match Daria's was not forthcoming, but she signed the book and even added a doodle.

"I'm excited about some of the panels," Daria said, as she dug out the program guide. "'Slush Piles—Exploring the True Mountains of Madness.' Did I tell you that I'm working on my first short story,

Colleen? Well, it's turning into a novella, really. Oh, here's another good one—'The Outsiders and Others Othering Others: Identity, Diversity, and the Cthulhu Mythos.'"

"Yeah, I'm on that one." Colleen gestured toward her own breasts.

"Tell it, sister!" Daria said.

"It's me and five white dudes. Should be a drag."

"It's good though, right? It's a chance to show that you're not a man-hater after all."

Colleen raised an eyebrow. "Man-hater," she said, careful not to end the phrase with lilting uptalk. It wasn't a question.

"You know," Daria said, embarrassed. She glanced down at the copy of Colleen's novel she had just bought. "*The Correlated Contents*. I mean, it doesn't exactly make men look good, does it?"

Colleen shrugged. "What Lovecraftian fiction ever made anyone 'look good'? Everyone's either a gibbering cultist or a bookish milquetoast who faints right after he sees the big cosmic scary thing."

"Or a fish person! A fish person happy to be reunited with his long-lost kin under the sea."

"Yes, or a fish person," Colleen said. "Reunited under the sea with the other fish people."

A moment of awkward silence emerged out of the awkward conversation, like something with a dim but cunning intellect out of the primordial ooze. Colleen reached for her phone and said, "Wow, look at the time. I have a meeting with an editor to get to. It's been fun, Daria. I'll see you around. Thanks for buying a second copy of my book. It's fans like you that make it all worthwhile." Colleen had finished her drink in a single gulp by *time*, snaked out of the booth by *around*, and there was no way Daria had heard *worthwhile* because Colleen was back in the lobby by the time that word left her mouth.

The elevators were out of order. The check-in desk was nowhere to be found in the meandering lobby area, and the con registration table was just as occulted. Colleen moved to ask a passer-by where he'd gotten his badge, but he walked past her, eyes straight ahead. Colleen heard Daria's voice wafting over from somewhere. There was nothing to do but hide behind the fern and wait for her to pass.

The girl who loves Cthulhu doesn't take no for an answer, Colleen thought. She'd have to give the speech eventually, right? *Boys are steeped in this squamous, eldritch stuff. Women are the real Lovecraftian protagonists—the ones who discover the occult truth only through whispers and dreams, and then have to plunge deeper into the darkness to truly understand* . . . All right, that was laying it on a bit thick, and from her view from behind the fern the gender breakdown for the con seemed fairly typical—eighty percent dudes, twenty percent women.

"Hey," Colleen heard a male voice from behind her. "How was the mental hospital?"

Colleen smiled in relief. It was Alvin Black, who had formed the basis of one of the characters in *The Correlated Contents*. Unlike a lot of the others, he seemed tickled to be lightly lampooned. Or he was too dim to come away from reading it with a thought other than *Hey, that's me! In a book!*

He laughed. "I bet you've been hearing that a lot," he said with a wink.

"You have no idea," Colleen said.

"How's the fern?"

"Leafy. Green. Out of the way."

"Sooo . . ." Alvin said. "Got a date for R'lyeh Nights?" Yuggoth Days had a "masquerade ball" that mostly involved Utilikilts or funeral suits for the men, and shopping-mall goth poseur outfits from Hot Topic for the women. And nobody dancing, despite the earnest tones of "Head Like a Hole" coming out of someone's laptop in the corner. But Alvin was asking for a "date." Did he really expect a romantic evening of some sort? He couldn't possibly expect con sex, could he? Did he think Colleen had a crush on him? In *The Correlated Contents*, Alvin's alter ego was a gormless weirdo who at least wasn't aggressively awful. The character's only truly obnoxious trait was selling his self-published books out his backpack.

"Oh and my latest in the *Dark Hands* series is out now!" He whipped a copy right out of his backpack in a practiced gunslinger-style move. It was barely one hundred pages long; he put them together himself with an industrial paper cutter and a hot-glue gun. The cover image was a bunch of overlapping dark palm- and fingerprints, as if the book had been handled by an especially greasy child.

"Yeah, out of your bag, you mean," Colleen said. "Listen, I'll definitely be your date tonight. It should be fun. I'll even dress up—"

"I like that you grew out your hair," Alvin interrupted. "Looks more feminine."

"—in my Herbert West cosplay," Colleen finished, coldly. "I just need to find my room. Or anything that actually is to do with the con or even the hotel."

"Yeah, it's a weird place, isn't it?" Alvin said. He wandered off without another word.

It gets dark up north quickly, especially in winter. And the hotel hospitality wasn't what Colleen had been trained to expect from old episodes of *Newhart*. Still no room, still no badge, and some older man walked right into her and didn't even apologize or stop to see if she was all right. Cons!

Everything needed was in her shoulder bag though—if Colleen Danzig couldn't fit everything she needed for a con in a carry-on bag, she'd just stay home—and so she availed herself of the unusually large lobby restroom. The Ramada must have been old mill housing, or part of a boarding school or dumpy little liberal arts college at one point. The suit was a tight fit, but the lab coat fit very well, and Colleen's hair had grown out enough to muss it easily. She was going more for Jeffrey Combs than that *small, slender, spectacled youth with delicate features, yellow hair, pale blue eyes, and a soft voice* of Lovecraft's story, but one of the dirty little secrets of fandom is that people loved films and role-playing games and fuzzy slippers more than the canonical fiction anyway. The cosplay would be a hit, as it always was. She found her syringes. They glowed green, casting a sickly light on Colleen's wide smile. The total effect looked just like the cover of the old VHS tape that had changed Colleen's life as a kid.

One of the most common tropes of the modern Lovecraftian story is to make the real-life Lovecraft a fictional character, and then to transform his fiction into reality. When Lovecraft is real, the Mythos is real too. But what does this mean for a narrative setting with almost no female characters? No one who can "become real" for fifty percent of the population. Do we really want to bring H. P. Lovecraft, the author, back to life, and the world-shattering Elder Gods to boot, just to have a few glorious moments of a boys-only club before the whole universe gets flushed down the toilet . . .

Colleen didn't apply the fake blood on her temple that usually completed the cosplay. Nevertheless, as she left the washroom, she was bleeding slightly from the head.

The thumping bass made finding the ballroom where R'lyeh Nights was being held easy enough. Finally, some part of the con was accessible. Colleen seemed to remember that the masquerade was also the opening ceremonies somehow, and that she might have to give her guest of honor speech right on the dance floor, unless the special Call From Cthulhu Cabaret Revue and Soft Shoe Floor Show went long, which it almost always did. She looked around for Alvin, but instead came face to face, or face to chest, with Daria.

"Hello . . . Dr. West! Fancy meeting you here," Daria said. She was wearing a dark sheet of some sort, with googly eyes of various sizes distributed about it, and wire-hanger appendages. "Said the shoggoth!" Daria added, in case Colleen had just suffered a stroke and didn't understand her obvious costume. Colleen's head *was* throbbing.

"Hey again, Daria. So what's your con been like so far?" Colleen asked.

"It's been great!" Daria opened her arms, like she was hugging the room. The appendages on her costume wobbled. "I've finally found a place where I can be myself."

Colleen smiled. Daria wasn't really so bad. It was her own fault, for being such a snob to these people, people whom she sought to entertain with her writing. Everyone needs a place to just get out of their own heads once in a while. A place to feel important, to escape the workaday world of meaningless toil followed by meaningless leisure. A place to . . .

"Isn't that how you felt in the mental hospital?"

The mental hospital! It all came flooding back to Colleen now. The murder of her friend Panossian at the last Lovecraftian convention she had attended. Her amateur sleuthing, like a mad dog barking at the moon. The crooked police officer controlling events from behind the scenes to make *her* look like the guilty party. The shoot-out in the morgue, the long stay in the mental hospital . . .

The long stay . . . she was still *in* the mental hospital. *The Correlated Contents* hadn't even been correlated yet from the endless yellow legal pads she'd filled, much less submitted and published.

"Hey, Colleen. It'll be fine," a voice told her. "We're not mad at you." It sounded like Alvin, but it wasn't. It was the very large orderly, a Midwestern corn-fed guy the other patients called Frankie behind his back. Short for Frankenstein. "All you need to do is let us bring you back to your room. We weren't happy that you were scuttling around the lobby downstairs all day, but that's my fault. I shouldn't have showed you that book. I like my Kindle, as you know, and *I Am Providence* seemed like it would be your sort of thing."

Colleen grunted at that. "It *is* my thing. I'm the hero of that book! The other guy just lies there, dead."

"Yes, yes Colleen," Frankie said. "You are a hero. A very resourceful one, too. It took us all day and night to get you back up into the ward. Rita here—" he nodded over to the stout nurse who had been trying to talk Colleen down, and now held a menacing looking straightjacket open for Colleen to slip her arms into—"will help you take off the suit of clothes you ah, appropriated, from Dr. Charles in the downstairs washroom." He lumbered closer.

Colleen withdrew the syringes from the lab coat. "Stay back!"

"Put those down!" Rita snapped. "They're not safe!"

"We don't know what's in those . . ." Frankie said, soothingly. "Take it easy. You can hold on to them if you like." The other patients in the day room gawked at the scene. One of them laughed. The furnace clicked off with an echoed *thwump*. No wonder nobody was dancing to it.

"We just want you to feel safe."

"You're bleeding too," Rita said. She glanced up at Colleen's forehead.

"Dr. Charles is fine," Frankie said, edging closer. "Just a little bump where you headbutted him. He's not mad either. Nobody here is mad. We just can't let these . . . delusions continue."

"Did he tell you what's in these syringes?" Colleen asked. "They're . . . green. Like re-animation serum."

"It's nothing to worry about," Frankie said. "But he needs them back."

"Oh, I'm not worried," Colleen said. "I'm in a mental hospital. You're all trained professionals, or harmless people who are just struggling with illnesses for a while. I'm safer in here than I'd be on the streets. People with mental illness are less likely to commit crimes, less likely to be violent."

"Yes," Rita said. She also edged closer, shuffling to the side a bit, trying to get an angle on Colleen.

"Really," Colleen said, "it's how I know I'm sane. A mentally ill person is statistically unlikely to do—"

She lunged and jabbed the syringe right into the side of Rita's neck. Colleen let it go, leaving it hang by the needle, and turned to meet Frankie with the other one. It sunk into his chest as he rushed her. Colleen slammed the plunger, then turned back to Rita as she was staggering away, and depressed the plunger of the syringe in her neck with a slap. Rita and Frankie both wobbled, then fell.

"—this."

Frankie twitched, helplessly. Rita was a rock. "I guess it was *de-*animation serum in those syringes. Eh? Eh?" She shrugged comically.

A few of the patients in the day room applauded. "Well, they say you should always start a speech with a bad joke," Colleen said as she leapt atop a chair, "and that is the lesson of Lovecraftian fiction and the role of women as readers and creators. Women are used to living in a world where nothing is as it seems. Where dark forces are arrayed against them, where they are treated as insignificant, unworthy of sentience. For men, Lovecraftian fiction is frightening. For women, it's the air they breathe, all the time, in real life. We're ready for cosmic horror, because that's life for us. And worse, it's how men see *us*! We're all the Black Goat of the Woods with a Thousand Young. We're the swirling voids Lovecraft feared, yet was so intrigued by. They say that there are no women in Lovecraft's story, but that's not true. All the cosmic horrors, all those inexplicable angles and mysterious desires— they're all women. All the power, all the dread, all the awe. Women. And that, my fellow nightscribes, is why I am a girl who loves Cthulhu. And now, I must collect my novel manuscript and take my leave of this place." She skipped down from the chair, rumbled Frankie, and found his keys and ID card. She returned to her room, grabbed her legal pads, shoved them into a plastic trash bag, then strode toward the day room exit. She had a third syringe in her lab coat for the guard, should he inexplicably decide to look up from his porn-filled laptop screen.

At the door, Colleen paused for a moment. If she needed to steal the key *now* to get out of the day room, how did she escape into the hospital lobby earlier that day? Something else was going on, but there was only one way to find out what it was.

Frankie's keycard worked easily. The door buzzed, Colleen opened it, and . . . met a wall of curved steel.

She took a step back and met another.

"Oh, I get it," Colleen said. "All the Lovecraft stuff is really really real. Everything else is layers of psychodrama thanks to the Mi-Go brain canister I—"

Colleen's eyelids flew open. The enormous winged crustacean squeaked some alien squeak and its limbs fluttered. Colleen reached blindly, found the canister on the shelf, and bashed the Mi-Go's face in.

"—was very nearly trapped in." Colleen undid the small fiber-pipe connecting her temple to the canister and winced when a bit of blood began to flow. She was in a large broom closet crowded with alien technology, lazily tied to a chair. Mi-Go limbs aren't designed for complex rope bondage, she was relieved to discover. The stench of space-lobster ichor filled her nostrils as the Mi-Go at her feet quickly wilted and collapsed into sizzling bubbles. She stepped over it, and opened the door into a cold, dark, and long-abandoned hotel lobby. No electricity, no heat. The snow outside gathered in drifts, licking the bottoms of the windows.

"Yuggoth Days! Figures my first guest of honor gig would be just like this."

There wasn't much left for Colleen to do then except set the entire hotel on fire and drive home to her cat two days early.

He would be very happy to see her.

About the Authors

Esther Friesner is an author of over 40 novels and almost 200 short stories and a Nebula Award winner. She was educated at Vassar College and Yale University, where she received a Ph.D. in Spanish. She is also a poet, a playwright, and the editor of several anthologies. The best known of these is the Chicks in Chainmail series that she created and edits for Baen Books. The sixth book, *Chicks and Balances*, appeared in July 2015. *Deception's Pawn*, the latest title in her popular Princesses of Myth series of young adult novels from Random House, was published in April 2015.

Esther is married, a mother of two, grandmother of one, harbors cats, and lives in Connecticut. She has a fondness for bittersweet chocolate, graphic novels, manga, travel, and jewelry. There is no truth to the rumor that her family motto is "Ooooh, SHINY!"

Her superpower is the ability to winnow her bookshelves without whining about it. Much.

David Vaughan lives in Maryland with his wife, writer M.C. Vaughan, and their three children. He is a proud member of the Baltimore Science Fiction Society Writers Circle and a winner of the BSFS Amateur Writing Contest. David graduated from Georgetown University with degrees in Diplomacy and U.S. National Security Policy, so naturally he now writes comic Lovecraftian horror space operas. "The Captain in Yellow" is his first professional sale. You can follow him on Twitter @DavidVaughanSF

Jody Lynn Nye lists her main career activity as "spoiling cats." She lives near Chicago with her current cat, Jeremy, and her husband, Bill. She has published more than 45 books, including collaborations with Anne McCaffrey and Robert Asprin, and over 150 short stories. Her latest books are *Rhythm of the Imperium* (Baen), *Moon Beam* (with Travis S. Taylor, Baen), and *Myth-Fits* (Ace). She also teaches the annual DragonCon Two-Day Writers Workshop. Visit her pages on Facebook, Twitter, and her website, JodyLynnNye.com.

Kevin Wetmore is an award-winning short story writer whose work has appeared in such anthologies as *Midian Unmade*, *Urban Temples of Cthulhu*, and *Whispers from the Abyss 2* as well as magazines such as *Devolution Z* and *Mothership Zeta*. He is also the author of *Post-9/11 Horror in American Cinema* and *Back from the Dead*. You can read more of his work at www.SomethingWetmoreThisWayComes.com and follow him on Twitter @HauntedKevin.

Mike Resnick is, according to Locus, the all-time leading award winner, living or dead, for short science fiction. He is the winner of 5 Hugos (from a record 37 nominations), plus other major awards in the USA, France, Poland, Croatia, Catalonia, Spain, Japan, and China. Mike is the author of 76 novels, 10 books of non-fiction, and 3 screenplays, plus 284 short stories. He is also the editor of Galaxy's Edge magazine, and was Guest of Honor at the 2012 Worldcon.

Shaenon K. Garrity is a cartoonist best known for the webcomics *Narbonic* and *Skin Horse*. Her prose fiction has appeared in publications including *Strange Horizons, Lightspeed, Escape Pod*, and the *Unidentified Funny Objects* anthologies. She lives in Berkeley with a cat and two men of varying sizes.

Brian Trent's speculative fiction work appears in a diverse array of markets, including *Analog, Fantasy & Science Fiction, Orson Scott Card's Intergalactic Medicine Show, Great Jones Street, Daily Science Fiction, Apex* (winning the 2013 Story of the Year Reader's Poll), *Clarkesworld, Escape Pod, COSMOS, Strange Horizons, Galaxy's Edge, Nature, Pseudopod*, and numerous year's best anthologies, including

Funny Science Fiction and *The Mammoth Book of Dieselpunk*. Trent is also the author of the dark fantasy series *Rahotep*. He lives in New England (not all that far from Lovecraft's hometown), where he is a novelist, screenwriter, and poet. His website is www.briantrent.com.

Alex Shvartsman is a writer, translator and game designer from Brooklyn, NY. Over 100 of his short stories have appeared in *Nature, Galaxy's Edge, Intergalactic Medicine Show*, and many other magazines and anthologies. He won the 2014 WSFA Small Press Award for Short Fiction and was a finalist for the 2015 Canopus Award for Excellence in Interstellar Fiction. He is the editor of the Unidentified Funny Objects annual anthology series of humorous SF/F. His collection, *Explaining Cthulhu to Grandma and Other Stories* and his steampunk humor novella *H. G. Wells, Secret Agent* were both published in 2015. His website is www.alexshvartsman.com.

Ken Liu is an author and translator of speculative fiction, as well as a lawyer and programmer. A winner of the Nebula, Hugo, and World Fantasy awards, he has been published in *The Magazine of Fantasy & Science Fiction, Asimov's, Analog, Clarkesworld, Lightspeed*, and *Strange Horizons*, among other places.

Ken's debut novel, *The Grace of Kings* (2015), is the first volume in a silkpunk epic fantasy series, The Dandelion Dynasty. It won the Locus Best First Novel Award and was a Nebula finalist. He subsequently published the second volume in the series, *The Wall of Storms* (2016) as well as a collection of short stories, *The Paper Menagerie and Other Stories* (2016). He also wrote the Star Wars novel, *The Legends of Luke Skywalker* (2017).

In addition to his original fiction, Ken is also the translator of numerous literary and genre works from Chinese to English. His translation of *The Three-Body Problem*, by Liu Cixin, won the Hugo Award for Best Novel in 2015, the first translated novel ever to receive that honor. He also translated the third volume in Liu Cixin's series, *Death's End* (2016) and edited the first English-language anthology of contemporary Chinese science fiction, *Invisible Planets* (2016).

He lives with his family near Boston, Massachusetts. His website is kenliu.name.

Rachael K. Jones is a science fiction and fantasy writer living in Portland, Oregon. Her work has appeared in dozens of venues, including *Lightspeed, Strange Horizons, Beneath Ceaseless Skies*, and *Shimmer*. She is a SFWA member, an editor, and a secret android. Follow her on Twitter @RachaelKJones.

Yvonne Navarro lives in southern Arizona and is the author of more than 20 published novels and well over a hundred short stories. Her writing has won the HWA's Bram Stoker Award plus a number of other writing awards. She also draws and paints, and is married to author Weston Ochse. They dote on their three Great Danes, Ghoulie, The Grimmy Beast, and I Am Groot, and a talking, people-loving parakeet named BirdZilla. Visit her at www.yvonnenavarro.com or on Facebook.

G. Scott Huggins grew up in the American Midwest and has lived there all his life, except for interludes in the European Midwest (Germany) and the Asian Midwest (Russia). He is currently responsible for securing America's future by teaching its past to high school students, many of whom learn things before going to college. His preferred method of teaching and examination is strategic warfare. He loves to read high fantasy, space opera, and parodies of the same. He wants to be a hybrid of G.K. Chesterton and Terry Pratchett when he counteracts the effects of having grown up. When he is not teaching or writing, he devotes himself to his wife, their three children, and cats. He loves bourbon, bacon, and pie, and will gladly put his writing talents to use reviewing samples of any recipe featuring one or more of them. His ramblings and rants can be followed on Facebook.

Neil Gaiman is the bestselling author of books, short stories, films and graphic novels for adults and children.

Some of his most notable titles include the novels *The Graveyard Book* (the first book to ever win both the Newbery and Carnegie medals), *American Gods,* and the UK's National Book Award 2013 Book of the Year, *The Ocean at the End of the Lane.* His latest collection of short stories, *Trigger Warning*, was an immediate *New York Times* bestseller and was named a *NYT* Editors' Choice.

Born in the UK, he now lives in the US with his wife, the musician and writer, Amanda Palmer.

Gini Koch writes the fast, fresh, and funny Alien/Katherine "Kitty" Katt series for DAW Books, the Martian Alliance Chronicles series, and the Necropolis Enforcement Files series. Her story in this anthology, "H.P. and Me" is set in the Necropolis Enforcement Files universe and is a prequel to Book 1, *The Night Beat*. Book 2, *Night Music*, is forthcoming.

Gini also has a humor collection, *Random Musings from the Funny Girl* and, as G.J. Koch, she writes the Alexander Outland series. She's made the most of multiple personality disorder by writing under a variety of other pen names as well, including Anita Ensal, Jemma Chase, A.E. Stanton, and J.C. Koch. Reach her via: www.ginikoch.com.

Aidan Doyle is an Australian writer and computer programmer. His short stories have been published in places such *as Lightspeed, Strange Horizons,* and *Fireside*. He has visited more than 100 countries and his experiences include teaching English in Japan, interviewing ninjas in Bolivia, and going ten-pin bowling in North Korea. His website is www.aidandoyle.net and his Twitter account is @aidan_doyle.

Konstantine Paradias is a writer by choice. His short stories have been published in the *Dystopia-Utopia* anthology by Flame Tree Press, *The Curious Gallery Magazine,* and the *AE Canadian Science Fiction Review,* among many others. His short story "How You Ruined Everything" has been included in Tangent Online's 2013 recommended SF reading list and his short story "The Grim" has been nominated for a Pushcart Prize. His short story anthology *Nowhere Stories* is published by Mad Paradise Press.

Amanda Helms writes science fiction and fantasy in her home state of Colorado. Her fiction has appeared on the *Cast of Wonders* podcast. She enjoys baking, long walks, and her dog, but does not enjoy identifying the strange things her dog eats on said walks. She sometimes tweets things @amandaghelms and sometimes writes things at amandahelms.com.

Laura Resnick is the author of the popular Esther Diamond urban fantasy series, including books such as *Doppelgangster, Vamparazzi, Abracadaver,* and the upcoming *Goldzilla*. She has also written traditional fantasy novels such as *In Legend Born*, *The Destroyer Goddess*, and *The White Dragon*, which made multiple "Year's Best" lists. The Campbell Award-winning author of many short stories, she is on the web at LauraResnick.com.

Matt Mikalatos has a Master's Degree in Zoology and Culinary Arts from Miskatonic University. His latest book is the young adult superhero novel *Capeville: The Death of the Black Vulture*. You can learn more at www.mikalatos.com.

Laura Pearlman read somewhere that H. P. Lovecraft liked cats; she's pretty sure that's the only thing she has in common with him. Her short fiction has appeared in *Shimmer*, *Daily Science Fiction*, *Unidentified Funny Objects 4*, and other places. Her "LOLcat" captions have appeared on *McSweeney's*. She has a tragically neglected blog called *Unlikely Explanations* and can be found on Twitter at @laurasbadideas.

Lucy A. Snyder is a five-time Bram Stoker Award-winning author. She wrote the novels *Spellbent*, *Shotgun Sorceress*, and *Switchblade Goddess*, the nonfiction book *Shooting Yourself in the Head for Fun and Profit: A Writer's Survival Guide*, the collections *While the Black Stars Burn*, *Soft Apocalypses*, *Orchid Carousals*, *Sparks and Shadows*, *Chimeric Machines*, and the humor book *Installing Linux on a Dead Badger*. Her writing has been translated into French, Russian, Italian, Czech, and Japanese editions and has appeared in publications such as *Apex Magazine*, *Nightmare Magazine*, *Pseudopod*, *Strange Horizons*, *Asimov's*, and *Best Horror of the Year*. She lives in Columbus, Ohio and is faculty in Seton Hill University's MFA program in Writing Popular Fiction. You can learn more about her at www.lucysnyder.com and you can follow her on Twitter at @LucyASnyder.

Nick Mamatas is the author of several novels, including the first Colleen Danzig mystery *I Am Providence*. His other titles include *The Last Weekend*, *The Damned Highway* (co-written with Brian Keene), and *Move Under Ground*. Nick's short fiction has appeared in *Best American Mystery Stories*, *Asimov's Science Fiction*, Tor.com, and *Lovecraft's Monsters*, among many other venues. Also an anthologist, Nick co-edited the Locus Award nominees *The Future Is Japanese* and *Hanzai Japan* with Masumi Washington, the Bram Stoker Award winner *Haunted Legends* with Ellen Datlow, and the cocktail recipe/flash fiction title *Mixed Up* with Molly Tanzer.

ABOUT THE EDITOR

Alex Shvartsman is a writer, translator and game designer from Brooklyn, NY. Over 100 of his short stories have appeared in *Nature, Galaxy's Edge, Intergalactic Medicine Show*, and many other magazines and anthologies. He won the 2014 WSFA Small Press Award for Short Fiction and was a two-time finalist for 2015 and 2017 Canopus Awards for Excellence in Interstellar Fiction. He is the editor of the Unidentified Funny Objects annual anthology series of humorous SF/F. His collection, *Explaining Cthulhu to Grandma and Other Stories* and his steampunk humor novella *H. G. Wells, Secret Agent* were both published in 2015. His second collection, "The Golem of Deneb Seven and Other Stories" is forthcoming in 2018. His website is www.alexshvartsman.com.